DEAD SILENCE

S. A. BARNES

NIGHTFIRE

TOR PUBLISHING GROUP

NEW YORK

DEAD SILENCE

Copyright © 2022 by S. A. Barnes

A Nightfire Book
Published by Tom Doherty Associates/Tor Publishing Group
120 Broadway
New York, NY 10271

tornightfire.com

Nightfire™ is a trademark of Macmillan Publishing Group, LLC.

The Library of Congress has cataloged the hardcover edition as follows:

Names: Barnes, S. A., author.
Title: Dead silence / S. A. Barnes.
Description: First edition. | New York : Nightfire/Tom Doherty Associates, 2022. |
Identifiers: LCCN 2021033054 (print) | LCCN 2021033055 (ebook) |
ISBN 9781250819994 (hardcover) | ISBN 9781250778550 (ebook)
Subjects: LCGFT: Horror fiction.
Classification: LCC PS3611.A29 D43 2022 (print) | LCC PS3611.A29 (ebook) |
DDC 813/.6—dc23
LC record available at https://lccn.loc.gov/2021033054
LC ebook record available at https://lccn.loc.gov/2021033055

ISBN 978-1-250-77854-3 (trade paperback)

Our books may be purchased in bulk for promotional, educational, or business use. Please contact your local bookseller or the Macmillan Corporate and Premium Sales Department at 1-800-221-7945, extension 5442, or by email at MacmillanSpecialMarkets@macmillan.com.

First Nightfire Paperback Edition: 2023

Printed in the United States of America

0 9 8 7 6 5 4 3 2 1

Praise for *Dead Silence*

"This is great, immersive, atmospheric space horror that proves that horror belongs in space."

—*Locus*

"Mixes horror, mystery, and sci-fi into a thrill ride sure to shock you out of your reading rut." —*BookPage* (starred review)

"A compelling haunted-house-in-space frame, excellent world-building, vivid imagery, biting social commentary, sustained tension . . . This SF-horror blend will resonate loudly with readers."

—*Library Journal*

"Truly unputdownable in its purest sense."

—Chloe Gong, #1 *New York Times* bestselling author of *These Violent Delights*

"A stomach-turning, sinister space horror."

—Kendare Blake, #1 *New York Times* bestselling author

"The ultimate haunted house story, in space."

—Alma Katsu, author of *The Fervor*

"Barnes is giving you *Titanic* but make it scary, she's giving you *Event Horizon,* she's giving you *Ghost Ship;* for real, this book will make your skin crawl." —*Book Riot*

"This story slides and slithers from creepy and atmospheric to skin-crawling, edge-of-your-seat terror."

—T. Kingfisher, author of *What Moves the Dead*

"I couldn't stop reading."

—Mur Lafferty, Hugo Award–winning author of *Six Wakes*

"Creepy and satisfying; I'll be checking under my bed tonight."

—Sarah Pinsker, Nebula Award–winning author of *A Song for a New Day*

To my mom and dad,
who let me read whatever I wanted as long as
I didn't wake them up with nightmares.
See? I told you it would pay off.
Also, can you leave the bathroom light on?

DEAD
SILENCE

1

NOW

My head is throbbing again, a white-hot line of pain from the back of my skull down to the right side of my jaw, and a dead man is signaling me from across the common room. His hand waves frantically in a "come here" gesture, his eyes wild with panic.

Resolutely, I turn my gaze away from the hallucination and attempt to refocus my attention on the living visitors across the scarred and battered plastic table from me.

"I'm sorry, what did you say?" My tongue feels thick, unwieldy. That's the drugs. Both too many and not enough.

"I said, you lied to us." Reed Darrow leans forward impatiently. An older, executive-type in a black suit and a vintage watch paces just behind him, supervising our conversation, with a thoughtful—and yet still disapproving—scowl.

"About what?" I'm confused. It's not difficult to do these days, but with Reed, a junior investigator from Verux's QA Department, I'm almost always clear. He's been in here every few days since the *Raleigh* search and rescue team dropped me off into Verux's care three weeks ago.

Max Donovan, my other visitor, clears his throat loudly. "Verux wants to help you. But we need you to help us help you." He nods at me in encouragement, his familiar face wreathed in wrinkles I'm not yet used to. He was just an investigator for my employer the last time I saw him, but now he is apparently the head of the whole QA Department.

"I've told you everything I remember." My skull fracture is, according to the Tower doctors, healed. And during the month-long return trip to Earth, the *Raleigh*'s MedBay staff tested me for every virus, bacteria, and parasite under this sun. Not to mention all the "exploratory" diagnostics and procedures over the last three weeks in the Tower. The results are always the same: the visions, pain, and memory loss are likely psychological, not physical in origin.

Reed ignores me. "You know, some people think you murdered your crew for a larger share of the find before taking that escape pod."

I stiffen, hands clenching against the urge to hit him.

"Then you hitched a ride back here with the *Raleigh* team, gambling that we'd buy this whole amnesia and psychotic break story and you could hide in the Tower." He waves his hand around, as though conjuring an image from thin air.

The Verux Peace and Rehabilitation Tower is a dumping ground for all the broken and damaged. Including me. Verux has more ships, more crews working in space than any other corporation. And sometimes docking clamps don't disengage. Sometimes people can't handle the isolation of years in space. Sometimes a coolant leak contaminates the oxygen, killing off brain cells before it can be corrected. Shit happens. Sometimes even to you. Sometimes even if you can't remember it.

I swallow hard against my dry-as-dust throat. "My crew . . . they're dead, but I didn't kill them."

"You sure you want to stick with that story?" Reed asks with a terse smile. He holds up a folded piece of paper—real paper, which means it came from the highest levels of Verux. "We've been monitoring K147," he says.

Just the sector name makes me flinch. I lost everything there.

"So?" I ask.

"We've got movement, Claire," Max says gently.

Not possible. My lips go numb, and a loud hum starts up in my ears. "The *Aurora*?" I whisper.

Max nods.

"Your ghost ship is on the move, Kovalik," Reed injects with smug satisfaction.

Max leans forward in his chair to meet my eyes. "Maybe it's time you tell us everything again. From the beginning."

2

THEN

I have a loose screw. Somewhere.

Amazing. We've been living on other planets and moons for a hundred years and visiting space for even longer than that, and still, a tiny piece of metal with misaligned grooves can fuck everything up.

"How's it going out there, Kovalik?" Voller's voice pierces the quiet of my helmet, drowning out the soft and soothing rush of oxygen. Somehow he's louder out here than he is in person.

I ignore him.

"Kovalik," he sings out my name. "Hellloooo?"

"It's fine. Better if you'd shut up and let me concentrate." I grab for the screwdriver dangling on a tool tether attached to my suit.

He sighs, the noise right on the edge of a petulant whine. "Lourdes says we've still got a wobble in the signal, TL. And we're going to miss the rendezvous with the hauler if we don't leave soon." As if I'm unaware of those things as team lead. But then again, Voller excels at stating the obvious and being exceptionally annoying while doing so. After twenty-six months in close quarters, I'm ready to murder him for that as much as for the snoring that rumbles through the air vents into my quarters, keeping me awake. Unfortunately, he's a good pilot.

I ignore him and focus on checking the beacon hardware, particularly where we've merged new with old. Software updates can be uploaded via signal from anywhere, but hardware? Hardware is hands-on. And even with years of practice and gloves designed for delicate work, it takes concentration. Snap off a piece or lose too many screws and it's a whole operation to get replacements all the way out here at the edge of the solar system.

Not that there are any replacements, as this is the last beacon. Not just for this tour or this sector, but the *last* last. For us, anyway. The next time the commweb—a network of beacons throughout the solar system designed to boost ship and colony transmissions for virtually instantaneous communication—needs an upgrade, a Verux SmarTech machine will be at the controls.

The machine will probably lose fewer screws.

But no need for commweb maintenance teams means no need for commweb maintenance team leads. No need for me.

This is it. The last time I'll be out here. Not just as TL, but forever. No more peace and quiet of the vast emptiness. No more endless field of tiny stars surrounding me. No more ship with bright lights to beckon me back from the dark.

I shove that thought down. Way down.

Maybe it's the receiver. I slide my hand along the metal support structure, pulling myself along to the other side, trying to avoid getting tangled in the process. My tethers to the beacon and our ship, a commweb sniffer called the L1N4—LINA—keep me from floating away but they're also a pain in the ass.

I tighten up every screw I can find, and eventually, my comm channel crackles. "You got it, TL," Lourdes, my comms specialist, says. Her husky voice is softer in my ear. "Cycling up now. Come back in from the cold."

The gentle tug on the red LINA tether tells me that someone is at the cable controls, ready to reel me in on my signal. Probably Kane, my mech and second-in-command. He doesn't like other people touching the mechanics of LINA, even something as simple as a winch. Anything can break, he says. And repairs are limited out here.

Not that that matters now. I'm fairly sure LINA will be scrapped once we're done anyway. She was already old when I inherited her with this sector assignment. Battered, scratched up, smelling of overheated metal, with shitty airlock seals that are pretty much a full-time job to keep hard-foam-repairing even with Verux swapping them out for equally shitty replacements every time we finish a job.

But LINA is home.

After unhooking the blue tether from the beacon structure, I reattach the far end to the designated loop on my suit. As I do, my gloved fingers brush over the carabiner that connects me to the red tether, to LINA and the future I no longer have.

My whole life I've wanted nothing more than to be out here. Away from everyone. That is the beauty of space. There's nothing out here. Sure, stars, planets, and communication beacons, but no people.

And now . . . that's all over.

For a moment, I consider it, my hand hovering over the latch. It would be so easy: flip the safety catch, unhook myself from the tether, and just . . . push off. Float away. Eventually, I'd have to decide between freezing to death or suffocating as my suit ran out of juice, but it would be *my* choice. My choice out here among the stars, the distant glimmering planets, and the absolute silence of space.

"Kovalik?" Kane asks. "Are you ready?"

No, I'm not. I'm not meant to be dirt-side. Not for long and certainly not forever. Without a ship, you're trapped. Bad things happen when you can't get away. Just the thought of being permanently gravity-bound and surrounded by so many people again makes my breath rush in and out faster.

Guess that means suffocation will probably end up being a problem first.

"Team Lead Kovalik, do you copy?" Kane repeats, his voice taking on urgency.

"Claire?" Lourdes breaks in.

"Come on, Kovalik." Voller sounds irritated. "I have a redhead and a packet of Scotch waiting for me on the *Ginsburg*. Just because you can't handle—"

"Shut up, Voller," Kane says.

My fingers settle on the safety catch.

"Kovalik. Don't move. I'm on my way," he adds.

My vision blurs with tears, smearing the star field into a general haze. Of course Kane wouldn't just let me go. He would make sure they retrieved me, like a rubber duck plucked out of bathwater. He's good that way. Never mind that a duck, rubber or otherwise, has no place outside the water.

It would take him fifteen minutes to get suited up and through the airlock on a secondary tether, and in the meantime, per standard protocol, our ship's log would be recording everything, transmitting back to Verux.

There might be one thing worse than never being up here again, and that would be being locked up in the Verux Peace and Rehabilitation Tower on Earth. In Florida. What's left of it anyway. That's where the company sends all their broken eggs. I've heard that once you're in, you never leave, not even for a look up at the stars.

I take a deep breath and blink to clear my vision. "Negative," I say, forcing my fingers away from my tether. "I copy. Five by five. Momentary . . . glitch."

"Yeah, right," Voller mutters.

I ignore him. "Ready when you are, Behrens."

Kane retracts the tether, slowly pulling me to safety, even though it feels like the exact opposite.

"What was that about?" Kane asks, as soon as I'm out of the airlock and stripping out of my enviro suit. I hang it, along with my helmet, on the peg that's marked with my name above it on a curling piece of magnetic tape. It's hard not to view that bit of flawed tape—and everything else on board—with an overly sentimental fondness, simply because it's about to be gone.

I avoid Kane's gaze as I yank my jumpsuit back on over my T-shirt and compression shorts. Blue eyes that bright are rare these days, outside of old film, and it feels like Kane's see right through me.

"Nothing." I run my fingers through my hair, the sweat-dampened blond strands sticking to my forehead and hanging in my eyes. Now that I'm back inside, my momentary flight of suicidal fantasy seems foolish and pathetic. I could have put my entire crew in jeopardy by forcing them to attempt a rescue. We may not always get along, but keeping them safe is my job. A job that I wanted so badly I'd been contemplating offing myself at the loss of it.

My face hot, I push past Kane and stick my head over the railing for the ramp to the lower deck.

"Nysus," I call.

No response.

"Nysus!" I shout.

A second later, he leans out of his favorite hidey-hole, the "server maintenance bay," which is little more than a nook with a door, near the engine room. "What?" He blinks up at me, spiky black hair rumpled from his hands, gaze dreamy and impatient, still mostly focused on whatever he was doing before I called for him. Probably something on the Forum.

"We set?" I ask.

He nods. "Bank's open."

Ignoring Kane still hovering nearby, I turn and head up the ramp to our primary level, then down the narrow alleyway through the small galley to the bridge. Kane follows me but more slowly because he has to bend slightly to keep from smacking his forehead on the overheads. LINA, like all sniffers, is small. We're a short-term vessel. The haulers bring us out and bring us back, handle resupplies. So, there's just enough room on board for five crew—pilot, comms, tech, mech, and team lead—and the equipment necessary for our work.

The bridge itself is barely bigger than those old-fashioned space capsules, the ones Verux has on display in their company museum. There's enough room for three of us in here at a time. Four, if someone's willing to loom in the doorway. But there are seats only for comms, pilot, and me, the team lead. I end up standing most of the time anyway.

"Status?" I ask Lourdes, who's folded up in her chair at the communications board, one side of her headphones pressed to her ear. Her curly dark hair has grown in again where she shaved it, and she's braided it all to one side, away from her preferred listening side.

She swivels to look at me, her expression cautious. A thin gold necklace gleams against her brown skin, the tiny matching capsule at the center containing a tightly rolled scrap of scripture. Her verse, assigned by her church. "Testing alignment and connection now. Are you sure you're okay?"

"I'm fine," I say, more sharply than I meant to.

Her eyebrows go up in surprise, eyes widening with hurt, and I relent.

"Just got a little . . . light-headed."

Voller, sprawled out in his chair behind the controls, with his safety restraints dangling and dragging the floor, turns to make sure I see him roll his eyes.

Lourdes starts to say something, but then her gaze goes distant and she presses her hand to the headphone against her ear.

"We should talk," Kane says to me, the second he emerges from the corridor, as if Lourdes and Voller were not present. But even if they weren't, this is not a conversation I'm having.

I ignore him and look to Voller. "Are we good to go?"

"As soon as you give the word," he says, cracking his knuckles. It's his tell in poker. I don't play with them, but I've watched enough to know. This is what he does when he has a decent hand. He's impatient, eager.

Kane steps closer. "Kovalik . . ."

"It was nothing," I say, and try to make it sound like the truth. "You do your precheck?"

"Hey, guys," Lourdes says. "I think I've got something."

"Yeah, Kane, it was nothing," Voller says, mocking. "If Kovalik here wants to become a permanent resident of K-fucking-middle-of-nowhere-147, whose business is—"

I glare at him. "That is not what I was—"

"Shut up, Voller," Kane says at the same time. "I'm the designated medical—"

"Who wants to get into her crazy pants?" Voller offers.

In shock, I go still.

"Watch your mouth," Kane says sharply.

"Why are you always defending her?" Voller demands. "We're not a real team. We all just got stuck with a shitty assignment for the last go." He shoots me a disgusted look. Clearly, I am part of said shittiness. "Who the fuck requests permanent assignment out here?"

Voller is not wrong. Under normal circumstances, this is an eighteen-month gig or more, with no breaks, no close-by colonies to visit or the chance to sleep in your own bed. No one ever *wants* to be assigned to the most distant section of the commweb, L52 through K147.

No one, of course, except me.

I asked for this section when I made team lead eight years ago, and Verux couldn't wait to unload it. Which I guess gained me a bit of a reputation. But there's more freedom out here where no one is watching and usually a new team with each go-round, which I prefer. Even with the bonuses, it's rare for people to volunteer for the L–K run.

This time, especially. Because it's the last time, the rotation is even longer than usual. Twenty-six months and counting, as we do final checks and minute tweaks, the final human hands to touch the beacons before the machines take over.

Kane took the assignment only because he needed the extra money. Voller ended up out here by default, all the better sectors taken by pilots who don't have a permanent smirk and possible personality disorder. Lourdes is still green, just out of training, and forced to go wherever the company sends her. And Nysus, well, Nysus is Nysus. He doesn't care what section we're in as long as he has access to the Forum.

"Show some respect," Kane says, pushing past me to stand over Voller's chair. "You're not in charge here."

"Maybe I should be," Voller says defiantly, his gaze moving to me, daring me to say something.

I should interject, shut this down before it gets physical. Kane is right; I am the one in charge, theoretically. At least for a little while longer. But I can't seem to make myself speak up. It's as if leaving that tether in place took the last of my energy and I've got nothing left to give now. Besides, what's the point?

"Hey!" Lourdes shouts, catching all of our attention. "I said, I think I've got something."

After a moment, Kane steps back to stand next to me, but his cheeks are still flushed with anger. When Kane is involved, cooler heads—his—will usually prevail. Usually.

Tensions always run high at the end of a rotation in my experience, but the two of them have been at each other's throats from almost the moment they walked on board at the start of their assignment with me. Kane might be in charge of the engine and the function of LINA, but Voller is the one who controls her. They are perpetually locked in conflict, one in charge of the body, the other in charge of the brain.

"Oh, good," Voller says to Lourdes, smoothing a hand over his wrinkled T-shirt. Today's shirt says FUCK ME with a smiley face sticking its tongue out. I can't tell if it's meant as an invitation or an expletive. Knowing Voller, probably both. "You can do your job. Can we get out of here now?"

Lourdes ignores him. "It's an automated distress signal. I think," she says. "One of those R-5 repeating beacons."

My interest flickers vaguely to life, surprising me. "Out here?" I ask. There's nothing out here. Verux's exploratory vessels should all be well out of range, even with the upgraded network. Unless one of them came back early.

"But it's weird. No ship name, no personalized message, no other data. Just coordinates and the preprogrammed SOS. And it's not transmitting on the emergency channel." Lourdes pauses. "At least not on the emergency channel we use now." Her forehead wrinkled in thought, she swivels in her chair and picks up her tablet, fingers flying across the surface in a query.

"It's just an echo. Old data. The new hardware probably has something to do with it," Voller says, sounding bored.

"Nysus?" I ask the air. "Are you listening?" It only took me a couple days on this tour to realize that my brilliant but introverted tech had wired the internal comm channels on the bridge and common areas to stay open, permanently. He could always hear what was happening, even if he chose not to respond.

"It's . . . possible," Nysus says after a moment. As always, he sounds distant, distracted. Like he's on an entirely different ship than the rest of us and we caught him at a bad time. "The upgrade allows the network to pick up weaker signals. It could be that we have an overlap, fuzz."

"See? Told you. Ghost signal." Voller swivels in his chair, tapping in coordinates, and the engine pulls itself from idle with a rumble that I feel through the decking. "Let's go. Bigger and better things ahead. Even for you, Kane."

Kane, leaning against the bulkhead, flips him the finger.

"Or it could be that we're picking up a signal from a ship at a greater distance than expected. The new hardware is one hundred and twenty percent more efficient," Nysus says.

Voller groans.

Unreasonable hope sparks bright desperation in me. "If it's an emergency, we're obligated to try and render aid," I say, after a moment, trying to sound normal, as if this were not the stay of execution that I'd given up waiting for.

"No, no, you don't." Voller turns in his chair and stabs a finger in my direction. "I know what you're thinking. If we miss the rendezvous with the *Ginsburg,* we're stuck out here another month. With no extra pay. Just because you have nowhere to go, rejected for transport and stuck at a desk job for the rest of your life, some has-been wannabe captain, doesn't mean that's true for the rest of us."

His words ring out shockingly loud in the small space. It's nothing

Kane, Lourdes, and Nysus don't already know, but hearing the facts spoken aloud brings a new level of humiliation.

Shame heats my face, and I can't meet Kane's eyes. If he needed any more proof of what I was contemplating out there, on my last space walk . . .

"I say, if it's not on the emergency channel, it's not an emergency." Voller raises his hand. "Who's with me?"

"Voller," Kane begins, shaking his head in disgust.

"Except this is not a goddamn democracy," I say, startling myself with the fervor in my tone. I'm not one for forcing my authority down anyone's throat. Being team lead was never my aspiration, just a side effect of my desire to stay out here as long as possible.

Kane's head jerks up, his mouth open in surprise.

"Actually," Lourdes speaks up, "about that. I think it *is* an emergency channel."

"But you just said—" Kane begins.

"It's just not the one we use now," Lourdes says. "They're on the old channel." She holds up her tablet. "I looked it up. When Verux did the last big upgrade, after they bought out CitiFutura, they changed the emergency channel designation. Fifteen, maybe twenty years ago. Before our time."

Before *their* time, but not mine. Possibly not Kane's, either. He's only a few years younger than I am, I think, and fifteen years ago, I was eighteen, walking out of a Verux-sponsored group home and on board my first Verux sniffer for a training assignment.

"I remember that," I say. "The merger." That was big news even in the home.

Nysus speaks up. "She's right."

"Why would anyone use an old channel?" Kane asks.

"I'm not sure it's a deliberate decision. I mean, we learned about it in class. Automated distress beacons are . . . automated. They get triggered, they go off as programmed. Old channel, new channel." Lourdes lifts her shoulder in a shrug. "Just means someone's out there pretty far with some seriously old hardware."

That rules out a Verux exploratory vessel. They were all top of the line when they left a few years ago.

"How far?" I ask.

"According to these coordinates? Into the Kuiper Belt, for sure," Lourdes says. "Ninety-some hours from our current location."

"No," Voller says, shaking his head. "No way. That's the opposite direction we need to go to meet the *Ginsburg*, and way the hell outside our assignment."

"That's no one's assignment," I remind him. The last of the commweb beacons stop well before the asteroid belt. It's the end of the road, so to speak. Just a bunch of rocks, ice, and dwarf planets too small to be of interest. Billions of kilometers away from everything else. Which doesn't sound so bad at the moment.

"Exactly," Voller snaps. "It's in the middle of fucking nowhere, and it's dangerous. We'd be off charted and tagged space, and there's all kinds of random shit floating around out there. The company doesn't want a commweb maintenance team messing around with that. If you're so worried about the signal, contact Dispatch and tell them to send somebody else."

"It'll be months before they can get another ship out here, though," Lourdes points out. "If they have to launch a—"

"They're not going to launch anything," Voller says. "I'm telling you, it's a ghost signal."

The sound of them arguing makes the steady ringing in my left ear worse. I have limited hearing on that side. Childhood illness. The only sounds that come through loud and clear are the perpetual buzz and crackle of tinnitus. Verux doctors tried to correct it when I was a kid, but all they succeeded in doing was making the tinnitus louder and clearer. They wanted to try again, but I was done.

Lourdes straightens in her chair, flicking the braided ends of her hair over her shoulder. "So you're the communications expert now, Voller? Is that it?"

"Oh, come on, you're basically a goddamn trainee and—"

"Enough," I say sharply.

The three of them look to me, and I sense the expectant silence on the open channel from Nysus.

"Someone is in trouble. We're obligated to try and render aid. Chapter five, regulation thirty-three." Of course, those same regs also suggest contacting Verux Dispatch first, if at all possible. But that wouldn't be the first regulation that we ignored out here, away from the corporate types who made the rules without ever leaving Earth gravity. We're also supposed to be in Verux uniform and strapped in at all times. As if there's anyone else out here to see us. As if there's anything we might run into. And if our micrograv generator fails, we'll be in more trouble than safety restraints could help.

Besides, if we contact Dispatch, they'll just hold us up to get permission from succeeding layers of management, each passing the buck until they reached someone actually willing to make a decision. If someone's really in trouble, every minute counts.

"Voller, set a course to the coordinates Lourdes gives you," I say.

Voller opens his mouth to protest, and next to me, Kane tenses. But I've got this.

"I might be a has-been, wannabe captain," I say. "But if you want that shiny new job of yours to stay yours, you're going to do what I say until we're back on the *Ginsburg*. You might not care what I think, but I bet your new captain, a *real* captain"—I can pretend that designation doesn't hurt, sure—"will have a different opinion."

With a sullen look, Voller closes his mouth with an audible click, and then swivels in his chair to face forward.

Lourdes shoots me a grin. She's a good kid. With a better future than all of us. And I'm glad to have been part of that on my last rotation, if nothing else.

"Okay, let me know when you're ready," she says to Voller, with exaggerated patience.

I wait for his response, just in case he tries to push her. "Kid, I was born ready," he says, sounding sulky. But his hands fly across the boards without hesitation.

Lourdes rolls her eyes but recites the coordinates.

Turning away, I head for my quarters. It already feels too . . . close in here. Too many people, too many emotions. Not to mention the sensation of having just escaped the guillotine with a close haircut.

Voller was right; I might have just earned myself another month out here. But at the end of that month, there will be no continuance, no mysterious signal to chase.

I'm done. After this, no more ship, no crisp pinpoints of stars on an eternal black background, no more control.

And *people* everywhere.

The thought sends panic scrabbling at my ribs like claws again.

I'll have to find a place to live. Some tiny closet-sized cubicle to call home, where I'll be able to hear my neighbor coughing for the next thirty years as I shuttle back and forth on sweaty, overcrowded pub tran between "home" and my desk with thousands of mind-numbing pages of training manuals to review and revise based on my "years of valuable experience." I'm only thirty-three, almost thirty-four, and it feels like my life is over.

Kane follows me. I sense him behind me, the question before he speaks it. I pause at the threshold of the tiny galley. I can still smell the orange-y scent of Lourdes's tea in the air.

"I said I'm fine," I say. If I turn around now, Kane will be a few paces back, arms folded over his chest, forehead furrowed in concern. In fifteen years, I've worked with eight different crews, thirty-six different team members. Some more skilled than others. Some . . . more challenging. Leave it to the last team, my last rotation, to contain the one person I've encountered with a better bullshit detector than mine and the moral compunction to use it.

"I don't believe you," Kane says quietly. "Talk to me."

Because of his extra training as our medic, Kane knows more about me than anyone else on board. That should make interacting with him so much worse. People who've heard my story usually can't help themselves, staring at me with disgust or a mix of pity and prurient curiosity that feels like a violation. But Kane is different.

I'm caught between the impulse to get angry, to push back and reinforce my long-guarded boundaries, and the desire to face him, to open my mouth and let the words come spilling out. The latter feels like a physical force pushing against my insides. He would listen, I know, his gaze carefully fixed on me.

Just the idea of that makes my chest tight and warm with emotion.

And that cannot happen.

I could blame it on the length of this last assignment or the shitty vulnerability that comes from being booted out of the only job you've ever loved. Maybe I would feel this connection with anyone with a kind face and a sympathetic ear who happened to be nearby at the impending worst moment of my life.

But it's more than that. I've heard Kane and his daughter talking on video chat a few times over the past couple of years. The warmth and affection in his voice set off this powerful and dangerous ache in me.

Kane makes me feel like somebody. He makes me *feel*.

Jesus. Is there anything more powerful, more dangerous than that?

I close my trembling hands into fists, trying to ignore the damp sweat on my palms. "I don't have anything to say, and we've got work to do." Never mind that this is part of Kane's job, checking up on us. Particularly when one of us seems inclined to push off into the nothingness.

Kane sighs. "Claire. You scare the hell out of me sometimes, you know that?"

Startled, I turn to look at him. "Why?"

He eyes me carefully, and I force myself to remain still beneath that gaze. "It's normal to be upset that things are changing, to worry about what the future holds. But you?" He shakes his head. "I've never met anyone so determined to prove that they don't care. It's terrifying."

Kane's words strike a soft spot at my core with swift and painful accuracy, like a driving punch, and I recoil, my teeth landing on the edge of my tongue and sparking surprised tears.

But I straighten my shoulders and lift my chin to face him head-on. "Then I guess it's a good thing you won't have to put up with it for much longer."

"Claire . . ." he begins. "That's not what I meant—"

"And I don't care what you meant," I say. "See? You were right." His jaw snaps shut, and a dark ruddy color floods his cheeks.

"Check with Nysus, make sure he's working with Lourdes to track the signal." A bullshit assignment because rabid dogs and the reincarnation of his personal hero, Berkeley Blue, couldn't keep Nysus away from a mystery signal, but an assignment nonetheless.

I turn away from Kane and quicken my pace, trying to ignore him and the odd mix of pride and hurt welling up inside me. Pride that I've managed to at least partially fool him; hurt because I still somehow expected him to see through the act.

3

"We're here," Voller says over the intercom in my quarters ninety-four hours later. "Coming up on a whole lot of empty space, TL." His announcement holds more than a tinge of glee.

The stab of disappointment in my gut is quick but not unexpected. We'll clear the signal source, tag it as a ghost, and head to our rendezvous point with the *Ginsburg*. We might even yet make it back to catch our ride with them, if they wait for us.

Back to nothing.

The open storage crate at the foot of my bed takes up all the floor space. I climb over the bed to reach the intercom switch on the wall and flick the channel open to respond. "Yeah. On my way."

I'm nearly all packed. No sense waiting until we reach the *Ginsburg* and then having to rush. I finish folding the scrap of blanket—its edges are filthy with red-stained dirt, no matter how many washings, and tattered beyond repair—and tuck it carefully into the open crate. The piece is, admittedly, a little disgusting in its age and condition. But it's one of the few things I still have that's mine, actually mine, given to me by someone who knew and loved me rather than a stranger with good intentions. My name and hab number are stitched in one corner in two perfectly even lines. My mother was a Verux-sponsored doctor—one of the only doctors at Ferris Outpost—and her stitching skills got a lot of practice.

The outpost, not even a fully-fledged colony yet, was a rough place, nothing more than a series of interconnected Verux hab modules and desperate people trying to make a go of it, with little or no help from their corporate sponsor. But if Ferris had survived past the ten-year mark, establishing their residency on Mars and sustainability of their efforts, then Verux would have swooped in and claimed another colony.

"You'll have to be responsible for your own things," she said to me, when we first moved to Ferris. I was five, and my father had died the year before. She'd taken the post—dangerous but highly paid—out of desperation. I didn't handle my father's death well, apparently. Plus, MedBots were already at that point cheaper and considered more reliable than the general practitioners they were replacing on Earth. They made fewer mistakes, according to some vaguely sourced statistics. (Although when they missed, they whiffed it completely, the robotic equivalent of a batter swinging at a ball so hard he spun in a circle when the bat failed to connect. They lacked the imaginative thinking and creative problem-solving skills of those same replaced humans.) "There's not enough space in the hab for everyone to leave their possessions lying around. They have rules here."

She'd tried to warn me, but I was not yet a colony kid, still a spoiled Earther, used to the luxury of breathable air everywhere and having someplace else to go, even if it was just to the crowded sidewalk outside.

My mother saved me, devoted her last living moments to my care. And she tried to save everyone else. Probably would have, if she'd had more time—Verux ended up developing a powerful (and pricey) new antiviral from her recovered research.

But I'd screwed that up for her.

Padding down the corridor barefoot, the grit of soil from the greenhouse still beneath my toes and between my fingers, I pause at the sight of the shiny blue-and-white caution tape across the airlock to the neighboring module flapping gently in the breeze from the air recycler. The word QUARANTINE *ripples like it's alive.*

I shake my head, stuffing that memory down, way down, along with the lid on the storage crate holding the blanket. When search and rescue found me, they scooped me up where I was and took me away—no packing, no suitcases. I was holding on to that blanket, even though, at eleven, I was too old for the comfort it provided.

So I hold on to it still. I'm not sure why when it more often reminds me of my mistakes than my mother.

Before I head to the bridge, I glance back at my quarters. The walls are barren, empty, echoing metal. My bunk holds only a pillow and bedding and enough official Verux jumpsuits to carry me over until we reach the *Ginsburg*. It looks nothing like the home it has been. But it's better to keep harsh reality right in front of me. It felt like a trick to keep pretending that this wasn't going to happen sooner rather than later, that my home was not going away. At least this way—no matter how many days I have left here—I'm choosing to face it rather than clinging to a desperate illusion.

That's how I see it anyway. Others may have a different view.

On my way out the door, I bump into Kane—my shoulder into his chest—as he steps out of his quarters, no doubt summoned by a triumphant Voller or by the feel of the ship slowing as it reached its coordinates.

"After you." Kane steps back, gesturing for me to go ahead, while avoiding meeting my eyes. His curly hair is rumpled, and a fingerprint of grease decorates his left temple. His worn jumpsuit is open to the waist, the sleeves tied around his middle, revealing the cotton T-shirt beneath. It looks worn and soft to the touch, and the imagined sensation of my cheek pressed against his chest, against that fabric, stalls me out for a moment.

But only for a moment.

I move past him without a word. My shoulder, though, still feels warm and electric from the unanticipated contact.

Cut it out, Claire. Don't do this.

Voller barely waits until I clear the threshold of the bridge. "See, I told you." He throws his arm out toward the viewport at the front of the bridge that shows an empty expanse of space. "Nothing."

"Distress signal?" I ask Lourdes.

She spins in her chair toward me. "It's weaker out here. But the coordinates are right." She frowns, her smooth forehead creasing. "I just don't understand—"

"Because the commweb boosted the distress signal," Nysus

breaks in on the intercom. "We're closer to the source now, but that means we're picking up the signal from the beacon directly. We're outside the commweb now, too, so the signal doesn't have the same juice."

Outside the commweb. I've never been this far out. None of us have. Our job is literally the commweb. We live and work on it, like a spider spinning and respinning silk lines, checking and rechecking connection points.

It's hard not to feel a little dizzy when staring out the viewport, like looking down toward the ground from an extreme height. Or into an endless black sea that will simply swallow us whole without remorse or leaving behind any sign of us.

"How's our charge?" I ask Voller. If we get into trouble out this far, the only vessel in range and capable of picking up a distress call would, ironically enough, be *us*. If we were where we were supposed to be. Which we're not.

"Yeah, yeah, we're fine on that," Voller says, waving a hand to dismiss my concern. "But can we get the hell out of here now?" He leans forward to peer upward through the viewport. "We are way outside of known territory and I would prefer not to get smacked by some piece of shit asteroid or whatever."

Voller actually sounds a little uneasy for the first time since I've known him.

"Understood," I say. "As soon as we clear the signal."

He groans.

"So, Nysus, you're saying that whatever we're getting is from the ship itself," I say.

"You got it," Nysus says.

Voller scrubs his hands over his face. "There is no ship!"

Lourdes glares at him. "There's *something*. It doesn't have the echo a ghost signal would. And it should be right here. But I'm not getting any collision alerts. I can't see anything through viewports or on the cameras." Lourdes waves a hand toward the six monitors lined up on the sides of the small panes of thick glass at the front of the bridge.

She sounds frustrated. And understandably so. We have cameras outside to cover almost every conceivable angle of our ship and the surrounding area. But we don't have scanners like the larger transport, military, and exploratory vessels. Short-range sniffers moving from one beacon to another just don't need them. We make short hops in known space, between points that have been mapped, tracked, and visited for years, well outside the traffic lanes used by the big boys, so there's little danger of running into something.

But out here? Everything is a little less certain, a little less defined. More like finding your way through the forest instead of following the well-paved, mag-lev highway.

So . . . now what?

"Turn on the stern-side working lights," Kane says from behind me.

I glance back to find him leaning against the bulkhead, arms folded over his chest.

Voller gives him a scornful look. "Pretty sure I would've noticed if we flew past it, chief."

Kane ignores him and steps up even with me. The open space in the center of the bridge is tight with the two of us. His arm brushes against mine. "And angle our current position to negative twenty-five percent."

Suddenly I see where Kane is going with this. "Do it," I say to Voller. We all have our blind spots. As born-and-raised planet-dwellers, we have one in particular.

Voller shakes his head but does as I ask, muttering under his breath the whole time.

"Put the rear-camera feeds up on all the screens, Lourdes," I say.

The brilliant beams of light that we use to illuminate the beacons so we can work—tightening or replacing all those tiny screws—snap on. The monitors flash the sudden burst of brightness, blotting out the images on-screen in a wash of white until the camera adjusts and then . . .

"Holy shit," Voller breathes.

On the monitor, a ship floats on the perpendicular to us, like a shiny metallic wedge of lemon in the dark tea of space.

"I don't . . . how did you . . ." Lourdes gapes at the images. Admittedly, it does feel more like a magic trick. *Look over there, and ta-da!*

Kane grins at me. "There is no 'down' in space." It's a phrase that's repeated, over and over again, in Verux commweb team training, to the point where it's become a joke among the commweb teams. On a previous tour, one of my team members, Gerta, posted a sign in the head over the toilet—"There may be no 'down' in space, but there sure as hell is one in here. Aim, please."

But the idea that something is just as likely below you as it is above is a hard concept to wrap your brain around for those of us who grew up with dirt beneath our feet and the sky overhead.

The urge to smile back at Kane is too strong to resist, and I give in. Just for a moment.

He holds my gaze for a second too long, and a feeling of connection zips through me, like a pleasant shock of electricity.

"Wait, wait," Lourdes says, drawing our attention back to her. She squints at the monitors and then gets up to look over Voller's shoulder, until he waves her away like a buzzy mosquito. "We're still at least twenty kilometers away. That means . . ."

"It's fucking huge," Voller says flatly, not happy at being proven wrong on such a large scale, no doubt. "What do you expect us to do with this, TL? No way we can transport passengers from a ship that—"

"Why does it look . . . weird?" Lourdes traces the outline of the ship on the screen, the rounded bottom, the pointed ends, the tiny dark buttons of portholes along the one visible side.

Recognition clangs a sudden and discordant note inside me. *No. It can't be.*

"I've never seen a passenger vessel like this," Lourdes says. "Are those smokestacks on top? For what? And the decks are open at either end. That can't be right. That would mean huge glass enclosures. No one does that. It would be too risky."

Chills race along my skin, and my left ear is once more buzzing and crackling. Lourdes is right. No one does that . . . *anymore*. To be fair, as far as I know, they only did it once.

Next to me, Kane goes still. "Does that look to you like—"

"Yeah," I say, but it comes out too close to an awed whisper. I try again. "Yes, it does."

Voller lifts himself partially out of his chair for a closer look. "No. No way." He glances back at us in disbelief.

"What?" Lourdes asks.

Kane clears his throat, but the words come out sounding rough anyway. "They wanted it to evoke nostalgia. To make people feel more comfortable by reminding passengers of something familiar. The design was intended to mimic a leisure vessel, a cruise ship for the ocean on Earth. Back when you could do that." He pauses. "My dad and my uncle . . . they worked for CitiFutura back then, before Verux acquired the company. They did some of the plumbing on this ship. And the other one, the sister vessel, I can't remember what it was called."

"The *Cassiopeia*," I say softly.

Kane nods. "That's it. They decommissioned it . . . after."

"But what—" Lourdes begins.

"It was destroyed. Blown up!" Voller says, arguing with everyone and no one and just the fact of the ship's existence. He jabs a finger toward the screen. "Catastrophic engine failure. CitiFutura was rushing to hit the launch date, and someone fucked up. CF went down for that mistake."

"Chat room rumors, unfounded speculation," Nysus says over the intercom, with the preoccupied air that said he was digging in his downloaded Forum threads for more information. "In the aftermath of the disappearance, search and rescue ships found metal fragments on their projected course that might have been part of the hull. Or not. CitiFutura filed for a total loss, but there was no proof. Everyone had theories back then, and then the lawsuits started."

"What lawsuits?" Lourdes almost shouts. "What are you guys talking about?"

I tear my gaze away from the mystery made reality currently floating on the monitors in front of me and look to Lourdes.

She lifts her hands in exasperation, a mute demand for explanation. It seems impossible that she wouldn't know, but then I realize she was probably a toddler when all of this was going on.

"That"—I point to the screen—"is the *Aurora*. The first—and only—luxury space cruiser. Every possible amenity you can imagine. Gold faucets." That's always the detail that sticks in my head.

"Real wood floors, coffee from actual beans, meat that was once alive," Voller adds, sounding both awed and bitter.

"Twenty years ago, five hundred passengers and a hundred and fifty crew left on a maiden voyage for a tour of the solar system," I say. "It was supposed to take a year. But the *Aurora* disappeared six months in. All souls presumed lost."

"One of the biggest space disasters in human history and high on the list of unsolvable mysteries," Nysus adds, sounding a little too excited. Every nerd has his day.

Lourdes's gaze flicks back and forth between the image of the *Aurora* on the monitor and me. "Until now," she murmurs.

"Yeah. Until now," I say.

"Holy shit," she whispers, consciously or unconsciously echoing Voller. "Where's it been this whole time?" she asks in a more normal voice.

"No idea," I say, folding my arms across my chest as if that would help slow my galloping heart. *The* Aurora. *Here.* "This is hell and gone from where they last checked in. I don't think they were even supposed to be out this far."

"Because no one is," Voller mutters, but not quite as sullenly as before.

Lourdes's fingers fly over her control panels and the images on the monitors shimmer, blurring out of focus for a moment before they return, slightly larger than before.

"Sorry, cameras weren't meant to zoom that far. This is the best I can do," Lourdes says. "But look, definitely no signs of an explosion. At least not from this view."

She's right. The starboard side of the ship appears as shiny and pristine as it did in the departure videos that the news outlets showed over and over again after the departure—and then again after the disappearance.

I watched those videos in the group home, riveted and already plotting my way into those stars. If I'd been a few years older, I would have begged, borrowed, and blackmailed my way onto that ship's crew. For weeks after the departure, I'd dreamed of future cruises, future chances.

"The ship is drifting," Voller says. "No propulsion."

"No comm chatter, either," Lourdes adds reluctantly. "I've been sending a response to their distress call since we first picked it up, but . . . nothing." She hesitates. "Do you think there's anyone still alive or . . . ?"

Six hundred and fifty lives. Six hundred and fifty bodies.

The bridge falls silent. The ship appears cold and still, frost glittering in a light sheen across her hull. Not even a flicker of light from one of the tiny portholes to indicate life.

"Records indicate that the *Aurora* had a water generation system. State of the art at the time," Nysus says over the intercom finally. "But they only had eighteen months of food. I guess they figured that would be enough for someone to reach them if they ran into trouble."

Except, for whatever reason, that was not what had happened.

"Oh my God," Lourdes murmurs, tugging at the scroll capsule on the chain around her neck. "Those poor people. Starving to death out here, all alone and—"

"We don't know that," Kane interjects soothingly. "It's possible they used the escape pods. We can't tell from here." He gives me a sharp look, but I see no point in lying to Lourdes.

Is it possible? Sure. But if so, those escape pods were also never found. And if the passengers ejected out here? They'd have run out of air long before anyone arrived to save them. A different, equally horrible death.

But I keep my mouth shut on that. I've been told I have a "cava-

lier attitude toward mortality." The psychologist Verux brought in
to evaluate me after Ferris Outpost is the one who first tagged me
with that gem, and it's followed me ever since. That evaluation—
from when I was a kid—kept me off the Verux exploratory missions
and I suspect played a role in my being turned down for transport
captain. Apparently being "cavalier" is also interpreted as "reckless."

Which is not true. I'm not reckless with anyone but myself
and I've never lost anyone on my team. But I will say this: once
you've been in a position to watch everyone you've ever known die,
the light go slowly out of their eyes, transforming them from this
magic assemblage of quirks, habits, preferences, and dreams to an
inert pile of spent flesh and bone, you realize not only that life is precious but also that death is absolutely inevitable. No matter what
you do. The people you love will die one day, and sometimes it happens sooner and faster and more horribly than you could imagine.
Sometimes it's even your fault.

I prefer facing that particular unavoidable reality rather than
pretending it doesn't exist. The same way I'd rather limit my attach-
ments. To anyone. Why set myself up for that pain? But apparently
that kind of thinking makes me "detached," "cold," and, as I once
overheard, "sort of creepy."

"We need to get back," Kane says. "Make contact with Dispatch.
They'll send someone. Search and rescue."

I appreciate Kane's optimism, the hope that it springs from. It's
a part that I'm missing.

But there's nothing to rescue. This is just recovery, plain and simple. And if that's the case . . .

I study the *Aurora,* the dark windows, the cold engines, the likely
luxury—and horror—inside. The construction costs alone had to
have been billions. And that was twenty years ago.

An ugly flicker of an idea passes through my mind. Our regs are
based on the old maritime laws. Even for the relatively obscure stuff
that doesn't happen out here as often as it would have in the days of
Spanish galleons and navigating by starlight.

But an unclaimed wreck is an unclaimed wreck.

"What are you waiting for?" Lourdes asks Voller, his hands un-
moving on the boards. "Let's get out of here and report it." She
shudders. "It's like staring at a mass grave."

She's not wrong. And yet . . . a dozen of those rumored gold
faucets—branded with the name *Aurora*—would be more than
enough to start my own transport company. If not in genuine market value, the oddity/souvenir black market would certainly do it.
You don't have to be "hireable" or a "people person" if you're the
boss.

Voller's leg jounces in a nervous rhythm, but his hands remain
still.

Is it possible that, for once, Voller and I are on the same page?

Lourdes glances back at me in uncertainty. "TL?"

"Claire," Kane says, and his voice holds a warning.

At my silence, Voller swivels his chair toward me, head tilted
in consideration. Whatever he sees in my expression must confirm
what he's thinking because a slow smile spreads across his narrow
face.

"Oh, yeah," he says, pointing at me. "Exactly. Now that's the kind
of crazy I'm talking about. Fuck the *Ginsburg*. We're going to be
rich!"

Voller spins around and taps in coordinates, and LINA accel-
erates, sending us toward the *Aurora* rather than away. Our bodies
sway slightly with the abrupt change in direction as the micrograv
generator catches up, recalculating "down" for us. Nausea swirls in
me momentarily, but I'm not sure if it's the sudden motion or the
decision I just made.

"We have no idea what happened," Kane says to me, edging away
slightly so he has the space to turn and face me. "We don't even
know if it's safe to—"

"It doesn't hurt to check it out," I say, folding my arms across
my chest.

"It doesn't hurt?" Kane repeats in disbelief. "Are you kidding?"

"What is happening? What are you doing?" Lourdes asks Voller, the anxious pitch in her voice increasing.

"The Law of Finding, baby," Voller crows.

I grimace. He's correct, but that doesn't mean he needs to be quite so ghoulish about it.

"What does that mean?" Lourdes looks to me and Kane.

But Kane steps back, raising his hands in surrender or frustration, before stalking off the bridge.

"It means we found the *Aurora,* and it's abandoned," I say. Or, at least unoccupied by anyone still breathing and therefore able to claim it. "Which means—"

Voller cuts in. "It's ours."

4

The *Aurora* is discomfortingly large, once we're right up on it. In the LINA, it feels like we're a tick crawling on a sleek silver beast that hasn't yet noticed our presence or been annoyed enough by it to shake us loose.

Our working lights skate over the smooth surface as we fly over. Occasionally they catch the glass behind one of the portholes just right, sending a flash back toward the cameras and making my heart jump.

But no one is signaling us from inside. There have been no signs of life whatsoever. And a few signs of something far worse.

At the stern, a dozen escape pods are gone, their external docks empty and dark like rotten fruit in a cluster of healthy, shiny berries still clinging to the stem.

A few others look like failed launches. They dangle, slightly crooked but still attached, their sides blackened. It looks as though someone started to evacuate and then simply didn't release the pod once they were inside. The engines, designed to be automatic, flared but couldn't pull away without the clamps released.

Panic, maybe. And inexperience. That tells me it was probably passengers trying to get away without a crew member to guide them.

Above the escape pods at the stern, in one of the two large glass enclosures, a swathe of shocking green greets us.

My breath catches. *Grass? If they managed to grow grass, then they're probably growing food, too, and . . .*

But almost as soon as the thought occurs, other details register and reality checks in hard.

The grass is *too* green. And a cheerful red flag still stands at the opposite end, stuck in the simulated ground. Café tables and chairs bolted down around the perimeter give it a country club look.

"A putting green," Nysus says over the intercom. "For golf. Specs say the enclosure on the other side is a pool."

As we move around the outer edge of the glass enclosure, I catch glints of light reflecting back at us. Tiny, twisted golf clubs sail lazily through the space, bumping into each other and the walls. An emergency fire extinguisher, the bottom deformed and bashed in, spins in an endless arc.

"Grav generator is off," I say.

The green itself is shredded and furrowed near the entrance to the interior corridor, as though something has been dragged away. Or someone. And the metal door to the corridor is dented and bowed out, torn partially from its hinges. What happened here?

Lourdes, standing next to me and watching the monitors, edges closer. Her cold fingers find mine and squeeze tight.

I allow it for a moment, before that familiar *too close, too much!* panic starts to rise, and I yank away.

She gives me a wounded look that I have to pretend I don't see.

I don't *want* to hurt her feelings. Being a team lead is, at times, a combination of parent, camp counselor, and stern but well-meaning principal. But with some things, I just . . . can't. People can only need me so much before that button inside me is pushed and I have to walk away. And I'm not allowed to need anyone at all. Except in the strictest sense—I cannot physically run LINA by myself. I would, if I could.

"I'm not seeing any damage here either," Voller says, as we come around the stern to the port side. "Definitely nothing that looks like an explosion. Or catastrophic engine failure." He tosses that out, though that's not really his area of expertise. Just Voller being a provocative asshole again.

Silence holds for a long moment. Then the intercom clicks. "Engine failure doesn't always result in explosion," Kane says with obvious reluctance. And yet, he's clearly watching from another monitor, probably in his quarters. So he's angry with me, but not *that* angry. "It might not even be visible from the outside."

"Right, right." Voller makes a jerking-off motion without looking up from the screens.

The port side is as smooth and undamaged as the starboard. No curling flaps of metal hull that would indicate a forcible depressurization, no hole blasted through from an unexpected collision with a meteoroid. Micrometeoroids are still a possibility, I guess, but the hull shielding should have protected the ship from everything but a mass storm of them, and we'd see signs of that.

But mainly, it looks like a perfectly whole . . . abandoned ship.

"Fuck," Voller says. "Look at that."

As we come up on the bow, the glass enclosure at the front of the ship glows brighter beneath our lights, the normally clear surface frosted white.

Voller angles us closer to the top of the enclosure, where we can see down and inside.

The large rectangular-shaped pool has an infinity edge, likely to create the impression that passengers were swimming in the stars. But the water has floated out and away from the pool, probably when the gravity generator went down, and then it froze in the air and against the glass. Wooden deck chairs, which were apparently not bolted down, stick out of the ice at odd angles like toothpicks.

So environmentals are down, too. No heat, no air, no life support.

"If something went wrong with the environmental systems, then maybe that's the first domino," I say, trying to play the scenario through in my mind. It's never just one factor, one element in play. There are too many fail-safes and planned redundancies. For this many people to be at risk, for a system this complex to falter, it has to be a combination of unexpected events.

Like, a previously unknown virus lying dormant in a soil sample until it's revived by exposure to oxygen, thanks to rushed decontamination procedures. And then that virus spreads, in part, due to a delayed upgrade in the air filtration system—budget cuts. Add to that a lonely eleven-year-old who understands quarantine procedures but—

"TL." Lourdes grabs at my wrist, pulling my thoughts away from Ferris Outpost and the past. "What is that?" She points to a mix of odd shapes beneath the surface of the ice, like shadows in it, with a few swatches of brightly colored fabric.

I squint at the screen until my reluctant brain finally produces a match. That long, slender silhouette with a starfish-looking element at the one end . . . is an arm with an outstretched hand, seemingly in supplication. The arm cuts off abruptly, however, with no shoulder or associated body.

Those are people. There are people trapped in the ice. Maybe a dozen of them. Or . . . pieces of them.

"What the fuck?" Voller whispers.

Involuntarily, I take a step back, and Lourdes frowns at me, then back at the images on the monitor. And this time, she sees it.

Lourdes sucks in a squeaky breath. "Oh my God. Oh my God. They're dead!"

"It's fine," I tell Lourdes. "We're fine. Some fatalities were expected, remember?"

"But not like this!" she protests.

Oddly enough, several of the bodies—the intact ones, anyway—aren't even dressed for swimming. There's a woman in a tight, copper-colored ball gown with ruffles near her bare feet. Mermaid, I think the style is called, ironically enough. One man is in a tux, bow tie still in place, and another wears what looks like a set of pajamas, matching top and bottom in a shiny dark blue fabric. Which means they weren't in the pool when this happened, or they weren't expecting to be in the pool but died close enough to it to be absorbed in the water when the gravity generator gave way. It's hard to say exactly what sequence of events is the right one.

Red encircles the head of Pajama Guy, a bloody halo in the water, now encased permanently in ice.

These people did not die from starvation. Or an environmental systems failure. Whatever happened here was violent and seemingly unexpected.

The little black spots creep across Mama's cheek, like mold spreading over bread. And I try to wash them off, but her skin is so cold . . .

I squeeze my eyes shut for a moment and shake my head to clear the image.

"Mutiny?" Nysus asks.

Voller scoffs. "On a luxury ship? These assholes rebelled because, what, their sheets weren't soft enough? They paid to be here."

"It could have been crew," Nysus points out.

"Right," Voller says. "Sure. 'We don't have equal access to the *swimming pool in space,* so let's grab a fire ax and chop this guy's arm off.'" He shakes his head in disgust. "No, no way, man. It was a cush job. I've seen the videos. Crew quarters were double, triple what we got here. Plus real food."

"If something went wrong in the environmentals, it's possible they were suffering from hypoxia or—" Nysus continues.

"Since when does hypoxia turn you into a fucking homicidal maniac?" Voller demands.

"No one knows what happened," Nysus says, sounding a little frosty at being questioned. "CitiFutura called off the search after a year, and they never announced any kind of official explanation. Here, look."

One of the monitors flashes away from the view of the *Aurora* to a screen of text, a piece from the Forum's treasure trove, undoubtedly:

Aurora Search and Rescue Ends

By Jessie Culbert

May 3, 2130: The Swedish flag is flying at half-mast at the Royal Palace of Stockholm and the royal family's residence of Drottningholm Palace after CitiFutura officials announced today that the yearlong joint search and rescue for its missing vessel, *Aurora,* has been called off. Princess Margaretha Sofia of Sweden—a popular figure worldwide for her philanthropic efforts and her viral pop hit "Just Enough"—is among the 657 persons on board, now presumed dead.

CitiFutura lost contact with its ship, a new luxury spaceliner model on its maiden voyage, six months into its yearlong cruise. No sign of the vessel has been found, and no official cause for the disappearance has been identified.

The Aurora represented a new way of space travel, luxury instead of survival, at an exorbitant price. Amenities on board included premium suites, a spa, casino, shopping, and gourmet meals from a private chef.

The complete passenger manifest for her maiden voyage, still unreleased at this point, is widely rumored to consist of luminaries from all aspects of society.

Houston Seahawks fans have redoubled their petition efforts for Theo Graves, former star quarterback in the Zero Grav League (ZGL), to be inducted into the hall of fame. Graves and his wife, Lilah, are believed to be on board, though the Graves family and ZGL have refused to confirm.

CitiFutura, with their primary competitor, Verux Inc., and supplemental support from the diminished National Aeronautics Space Administration (NASA) and Chinese National Space Administration (CNSA), launched the largest-to-date search and rescue operation shortly after CitiFutura was unable to raise the vessel on comm and emergency channels. No distress or emergency signals have been detected.

"It's a terrible tragedy, of course," a Verux spokesperson said today. "We are a community, not competitors, when it comes to working together to pave the way for humanity to live among the stars. There is no reward without risk, but it is unfortunate to consider those who may have sacrificed their lives for the advancement. We offer our deepest condolences to the families of the Aurora passengers and crew."

Approximately 150 crew members were aboard the Aurora at the time of its disappearance, including the command crew: Captain Linden Gerard, First Officer Cage Wallace, and Pilot James Nguyen.

The comments below the article, archived from the publication date, are about what I would expect: mourning for the loss of a pair of celebrity sisters on board, wild conspiracy theories involving aliens, and commenters fighting among themselves over the validity of said conspiracy theories.

"Those poor families," Lourdes murmurs as she sinks into her seat. She grips the edge of the board in front of her, as though she needs it to keep herself steady. "But can we go now? Set a flag or send a message or whatever we have to do to claim it and then get out of here? Please?"

Silence holds for a long moment. Lourdes doesn't know how the Law of Finding works, but no one is volunteering to give her the information she lacks.

Voller spins around to face me. "Are we leaving?" he asks, challenge biting in every syllable.

The food printer is almost out. Just three packets of protein left. And the water is starting to taste weird. Like metal. Mama says that means the filter is going bad. She says I need to get out of here or I'll be trapped forever, dead like the rest of them, like her . . .

I shove the memories down, hard. This is not the same. Not at all the same. I'm not alone, not this time. And I'm not a scared little kid on a remote outpost. I'm a team lead and the LINA is under my control. I can leave anytime I want.

Including right now, claim or no claim.

But that would mean walking away from the only chance I have left to build a life I want to live—on my own, without Verux. Verux sent my mother—and me—to Ferris Outpost. After everything that happened there, Verux brought me back and kept me in one of their group homes. Until I was old enough to work. And then guess who was the only one willing to hire me with my history?

And now, Verux is done with me, except in a formal, administrative, pat-on-the-head capacity. Whether I agree or not.

Fury and frustration ignite anew within me.

My portion of this find would mean freedom, no more Verux

pulling the strings and no more depending on their generosity to keep me up here, doing what I'm good at.

"No," I say finally. "We're not leaving." There's too much at stake.

Voller lets out a whoop of triumph.

"Nysus, I need a way in," I say.

"On it," Nysus says immediately.

"In?" Lourdes asks. "Why would you want to go in?"

"Kovalik, we need to talk. Now," Kane says, and his end of the intercom clicks off abruptly. He'll be on the bridge any second. That'll be fun.

"Voller, head back portside," Nysus says. "I've got limited data without access to the commweb, but there should be a cargo bay door for loading passenger luggage and supplies. I've got something that will get us in, assuming there weren't any last-minute upgrades to the published specs. Bay should be big enough for you to guide us right in."

"Claire?" Lourdes asks. "What's happening?"

I hesitate. She's so young and . . . unjaded. It would be nice if she could stay that way. On any normal day as a commweb maintenance team member, this wouldn't be an issue. Yes, accidents still happen. Space is dangerous. Lourdes isn't stupid; she knows that. And the daily and occasionally grim reality of working out here will eventually take its toll, but I feel like we're inflicting a dozen years' worth of damage all at once.

"Seriously doubt they've had time to do any upgrading with being dead and all," Voller says to Nysus with a snicker.

Lourdes flinches and turns her attention to the communication boards in front of her. Her hands shake as she runs through a comms system test, even though we're not connected to anything out here. At this point, we can send a message and hope it has enough strength to reach the commweb, just as the *Aurora*'s distress signal reached us. But that's about it. And if it did work, all that would result in is Verux Dispatch telling us to return to known space and wait for further instruction. Which . . . I'm not going to do.

That being said, there is comfort in routine and I'm not one to deny anyone that. She's right to be terrified. That's the normal reaction. Whatever normal means out here.

"Lourdes," I say, and wait for her to look over at me.

Eventually she does, her fingers locked around the scroll at her neck, her eyes shiny with unshed tears.

"It's part of the Law of Finding," I say. "You have to bring a documented artifact back and make a public claim." But I'm not taking any chances. *One* artifact might be ignored. It might even "disappear," depending on how determined the remains of CitiFutura, now owned by Verux, is to hide whatever happened here and their potential culpability.

"But the people . . ." she begins.

"We're not going to disturb them or their things," I say.

"TL, no one else is going to be that particular," Voller protests, spinning around in his chair.

I glare at him.

"All due respect," he amends quickly—and less than sincerely. "But this is our one shot. We should be grabbing everything we can get our hands on, no matter who it belongs to. It's all ours technically anyway. That's what everyone else would do."

Unfortunately, he's right. We'll make the claim but other ships—salvagers, scrappers, traders, just plain old mercenaries—will, as soon as they hear of our find, get out here and take what they can to sell it. Back to the families of the victims or just to interested parties wanting to own a piece of history. A Law of Finding claim is only as good as your protection of it, and since Verux will have to first send out a team to verify our claim, that leaves plenty of time for other interested parties to go nosing around.

"We're not everyone else," I say.

His face flushes with anger. But then he clamps his mouth shut, seemingly with effort, and turns his attention back to piloting.

"It'll be quick," I promise Lourdes. "I just need to grab a few things—one of those faucets maybe—to prove we were here and what we found. Not dangerous at all."

Kane, who's reached the bridge just in time for that last bit, shakes his head, jaw tight.

I ignore him. "And think of it this way. The families of those people on the *Aurora*?" I gesture toward the image of the ship on our monitors. "They've been waiting for answers about their loved ones for twenty years. We'll be helping with that. Helping them find peace."

Lourdes takes a deep breath. "Right. Okay." She straightens her shoulders.

What I don't say is that while the families might want answers, in my experience, they probably won't want the kind of answers that we'll have.

"You have no idea what you're walking into," Kane says, arms folded across his chest, watching as I struggle into my enviro suit outside the airlock. The biohazard plastic bags I nabbed out of the bench that serves as our "med bay" lay in a slippery pile at my feet. Anything I take out will have to be quarantined. Just to be safe.

"I know that if it was environmental failure, I'm protected by the suit," I say. "If it was a hull breach, same thing. And if it's some kind of virus or plague . . ." The thought makes my palms sweaty and the ringing in my ear louder. "The filters on my—"

"That's not what I mean," Kane says, and his gaze is too serious. I have to look away, focusing on flexing my fingers to situate my gloves.

"The conditions over there won't be good," he continues. "Decomp would have stopped when the environmentals went down, but it won't be pretty. Not based on what we've seen so far." His voice is calm, practical even, but warm with concern. For me.

I work to ignore it.

"You don't have to do this," he says, edging closer. "No one would expect you to, after everything you've been through."

As a minor, my name was never released to the public, but Kane, as the primary medic on board, has access to relevant details. Details that couldn't possibly be more relevant than in this moment.

But the point is, no one else knows what to expect from me, because no one knows what happened, no one knows that I was once Child #1. The sole Ferris Outpost survivor.

Sometimes I wonder if that, too, is part of why I continue to feel that pull toward Kane. He knows too much and somehow doesn't blame me when he should.

I take a step back, despite the small but clamoring part of me arguing for the opposite. "If you're going to help me, help," I say to Kane. "If not, then get out. Wait it out in your quarters."

He rocks back, stunned. "Claire, I *am* trying to help."

"No. You're trying to talk me out of it." I tug the cap up from inside the collar of my suit and tuck my hair inside.

Kane pauses, and then gives a bark of laughter.

The noise catches me so off guard, I glance up at him directly for the first time. He's watching me, frustration and admiration warring in his expression. "Has anyone ever managed to talk you out of anything?" he demands.

A reluctant smile pulls at the corners of my mouth. "No."

He steps closer and reaches up to tuck a strand of hair that I missed inside my cap. The edge of his thumb is rough from work and repeated scrubbing with the harsh soap in the engine room, but his touch is gentle and warm. Against the warning voice in my head, I tip my head toward his touch, like a cat seeking the sun.

"You are a good leader, a strong person. You don't have anything to prove," he says, tracing the line of my cheek.

Alarms are ringing in my head. This is dangerous. Letting myself feel. I can't take it back, and it will hurt when it's over. The kind of hurt I've worked hard to avoid for most of my life. "Who says I'm trying to prove anything?" I whisper.

"You. Every damn day. Like you have to show you deserved to survive." He pauses, searching my face with his gaze. "Or like you have to give fate a second chance to take you because it screwed up the first time."

It is a shockingly accurate summary of several ugly interior monologues that I've pushed down so deep that I barely hear the whispering in the background anymore.

The heat of embarrassment scorches my skin. How does he know me so well? What, exactly, does it say in those files? I feel exposed, like I'm standing naked in front of him but not in the mutual, private way that I've barely let myself imagine. No, this is the harsh, evaluative light of a clinical visit.

Stung, I step back from him. "Thanks for the assessment, doc." My heart is beating too hard beneath my suit. I make myself take a deep breath so the alarms on my vitals don't go off before I even leave the ship.

I expect Kane to push, to keep after me about my supposed death wish—why does everyone think that?—but instead he folds his arms across his chest, giving me a knowing look. "It's too risky to go alone. You'd never let anyone else do that."

I shrug, as best as I can in the tight fabric. "Because I'm responsible for the safety of my team."

"Which includes you," he argues. "You'll have to go off tether. We won't be able to pull you back if you get into trouble." He rakes a hand through his hair. "And the inside of that ship is probably one big hazard. You could get caught in debris or tear your suit . . ." He pauses, his expression darkening. "Or worse."

"Worse? Like what?" Suffocating from a microscopic rip in my suit before I could get back out to the LINA sounds bad enough. Not that that's going to happen. I have multiple patches on me at all times when I'm out in a suit—we all do. Kane's just being paranoid.

Or overprotective. I can't decide how I feel about that. The needle seems to be caught between irritation and nostalgic appreciation. No one has cared that much about me in a long time.

Kane starts to speak, but Voller appears in the corridor, clomping toward us.

"TL's not going alone," Voller announces.

Kane hesitates, but then clearly decides any ally is better than none. "See?" he says to me. "Even Voller thinks it's too—"

But then Voller pushes past us, dropping a couple more bio-hazard bags on the floor next to mine, and grabs his suit. "Buddy system, right?"

It takes me an extra second to process what he means, just because I can't believe it, even with the evidence right in front of me. "No," I say flatly. "No way. You're not going."

Kane steps in front of him. "If anyone is going with, it should be someone who's got med training. You're a pilot. What the hell are you going to do over there if there's trouble?"

The needle tips toward irritation. "I can handle myself just fine," I say to Kane. "Trouble or no."

Kane glances back at me in disgust. "You're the TL. You're supposed to be smarter than this. No one goes into a potentially dangerous situation without backup."

"You do remember that I'm in charge, right?" I ask.

"Exactly," Voller says at the same time.

"Hell no," Kane says. "Not you."

But instead of throwing a punch, as I'm half expecting, Voller smiles pleasantly. Which raises my hackles. He's up to something.

"She's team lead and you're second-in-command. You can't both go," Voller points out, far too reasonably. Never mind that any time the issue of command structure has come up in the past, he's always pointed out that the pilot is "technically" also a second. Even though there can't be *two* seconds, even "technically." Otherwise, it's not a chain of command so much as a circle. "Lourdes is freaking out, and Nysus gets all cranky when he has to leave his tech cave."

He's not wrong.

"That leaves me," Voller says. He sits down on a nearby storage crate to begin stuffing himself into the suit.

"I don't need anyone to go with me," I say sharply over Kane's sigh.

"Do you know how to pull the black box?" Voller asks, eyebrows raised with a knowing smirk.

"Black box" is an outdated term, one we've held on to from

the early days of aviation. It's an independent recording system, a backup of the navigational computer, the captain's log, the bridge recordings, environmental readings, etc.

In other words, it's the one thing that will tell Verux what actually happened on the *Aurora*.

Like I promised Lourdes.

Fuck. I rub my forehead, forgetting that my cap is already in place, knocking the whole thing askew. "All right. Fine," I say, shoving my hair back under the cap. The black box would, if nothing else, help prove our Law of Finding claim. "Kane, you're in charge while I'm gone. Voller—"

"Hey, TL?" Nysus speaks up over the intercom. "I think we should pull the distress beacon in and deactivate it before you go on board. It's about three kilometers off the bow."

"I can do it," Voller says immediately, and once more, I'm struck by the sense that he's being a little *too* helpful. Not a comfortable feeling.

"Why?" I ask. "Nysus, that's one hell of a souvenir."

But it's Kane who answers. "Because once you're inside the ship, you're vulnerable if someone else picks up on the signal and checks it out." He holds up his hand to ward off my protest. "However unlikely that might be. There may not be other sniffers out here, but there are salvagers everywhere."

Salvagers who are usually heavily armed and significantly less preoccupied with the right thing to do versus whatever they can get away with. Like gutting the *Aurora* of everything they can carry, taking the LINA so we can't report them, and leaving us for dead. Or, just straight up murdering us to begin with.

Kane's not . . . wrong, much as I would prefer him to be. Because if he's wrong on this, then he could be wrong on everything. Including thinking that this whole expedition is a bad idea.

"Fine," I say with a sigh. "We'll pull the beacon first."

I expect an explosion of further protests or grumblings, but I get silence followed by a variety of affirmatives. Then Kane is rummaging in one of the storage lockers lining the wall for something, while

Voller, for the first time in his existence (probably), gets up without complaint and heads back toward the bridge, his suit halfway up at his waist. The quiet compliance should feel like victory in that at least no one is arguing with me, but it's bitter compromise on my end at best.

"Here," Kane says, holding out a black plastic hard-case toward me.

I frown at it and then him. "The plasma drill?" We use it on rare occasions if we need new holes in a commweb beacon's external framework. "Why?"

"Because it's the closest thing to a weapon we have," he says, his mouth a grim line.

I gape at him. "You think Voller is—"

"No, no." He shakes his head. "Not Voller."

"Well, there's nobody else alive over there." I push the case away, but he refuses to give in.

"You don't know that," he says, popping the lid and tugging loose the strap that's attached to the base of the drill handle so it can be attached to a suit. "Environmentals are down in the areas we can see. Doesn't mean they're down for the whole ship."

"For twenty years?" I give a disbelieving laugh. "The food and water stores wouldn't—"

"For one or two people, careful with rationing?" He hesitates. "And with a sizeable store of protein available, if they're desperate enough?"

Protein. The image of the detached arm, frozen in the former pool, resurfaces in my memory, carrying with it new and horrific implications.

"It's not unheard of," Kane reminds me.

But I know Mars history as well as he does, perhaps even better. Ferris Outpost was hardly its first tragedy. "Daedalus," I say.

Eighty years ago or so, some of the first colonists on Mars, a scientific expedition called Daedalus, were trapped when the early skirmishes of the first Corporate War prevented the production and/or distribution for shuttle parts the already ailing NASA needed to send additional supplies. A series of crop failures in Daedalus's ru-dimentary greenhouse led to starvation conditions, and then NASA lost contact. By the time CitiFutura and Verux, the two victors in the aerospace industry of that round of price-gouging and corrup-tion, finally arrived on-scene in their own vessels a year later . . . it was bad. Old-school Jonestown bad. Most of the colonists had starved to death. The few who survived had resorted to desperate measures to survive, eating whatever they could to stay alive.

Including their former colleagues.

"I doubt that's what's happened here," I say.

But I take the drill, attaching it to my suit. Just in case.

5

NOW

"So you admit that you brought the drill on board," Reed says, leaning forward in his eagerness. "And according to your own report, Kyle Voller died from injuries sustained from that same drill."

I grit my teeth. But playing along is the only way to get the information I need. Still, I direct my answer to Max. "I also said that he killed himself."

Max nods. "So you did."

As if on cue, a male voice cries out in a hoarse scream somewhere deeper in the facility. Reed starts in surprise, then recovers himself.

Reed is probably a decade younger than I am, in his midtwenties, with a precisely fitted suit that borders on fussy. You can tell at a glance that his whole world makes sense to him, and he wouldn't accept any other outcome. Then again, as a junior QA investigator for one of the largest companies on Earth, how would he have personally experienced anything else? His existence has neat edges, sharp lines, with no shadows or uncertainties.

The Tower and its occupants are nothing but shadows and uncertainties.

In the far corner, Vera, the woman who cries at night in the room across the hall from mine, huddles near the wall screen. It's acting as a window with a view on a winter scene. Today it's Central Park in New York, sometime in the last century, based on the fossil-fuel vehicles in view. But she doesn't seem to notice or care. She huffs a breath on the screen, tracing her fingers through the nonexistent fog on the nonexistent glass.

Disgust flits across Reed's face. "You have an answer for everything."

"If you don't like the answers, ask different questions," I say, as the hum in my ears increases. *Someone* is coming. My hands tremble, and I ball them up in fists in my lap. Voller maybe, or God, Lourdes. They seem to take turns, Kane, Voller, and Lourdes, haunting me. Though never Nysus. I don't know why.

The doctors say they're hallucinations, triggered by "severe mental and physical trauma." I don't think so, though. Ghosts, maybe. Vengeful specters come to warn me, Jacob Marley–style, of my sins. To blame me for their deaths. And I deserve it.

I keep my gaze fixed steadily on Reed's suit jacket, and the shiny Verux insignia pinned there. I've worn the same symbol on my shoulder for most of my life, one way or another, though usually with a ship designation and always as a patch made of thread and fabric instead of precious metals.

Reed's pin is a viciously pointed *V* in gold, longer on one side than the other, more like a checkmark than a letter. Three diamonds glitter on the long side, but that just draws more attention to the two as-yet-empty locations on the shorter side. Someone in security wasn't paying attention to let him through the door with a sharp like that. Or, maybe Reed pulled rank to keep it on him. I could see that. He's proud of his corporate family status. Three generations, I think, to get that pin. And that just means he's that much more desperate to prove himself as worthy. I wonder when he decided I was the route for that.

Over Reed's left shoulder, Lourdes flickers into view and the buzzing in my ears vanishes temporarily with her appearance. Her eyelids blink over the red and empty sockets of where her eyes used to be, and her lips move but so slightly that it took me weeks from her first appearance to interpret her words: *I don't understand.*

My legs twitch with the impulse to move, to rush toward her to help.

But she is, like all of us, beyond help now.

"Claire?" Max turns his head to follow my gaze but sees nothing. No one else ever does. And Lourdes vanishes a moment later anyway. She never stays very long. Unlike Kane. Another reason it's so hard not to reach out and try to grab her, to keep her here.

Against my will, my gaze is drawn across the room. Kane is back. He looks as solid and as real as anybody else in here—which isn't saying much—except his torso ends abruptly and alarmingly in the back of the worn gray sofa, and when he speaks, no sound comes out.

It's like a video on a loop. He gestures emphatically, raking his hand through his close-cropped hair, a classic Kane frustration move, and then, as alarm slowly fills his expression, he leans forward to shout and urge me toward him.

As soon as it completes, it starts over. And over and over.

"Hallucinations again? How convenient," Reed says, his lips curving in a mocking smile. "I have to admit, you are rather convincing when you—"

"What's the heading?" I ask. It's hard to stay focused; the drugs are pulling at me, whispering at me to let go.

Reed blinks, taken aback. "The—"

I shift my attention to Max. "The ship. You said she's moving. What's the heading?" I repeat.

Max's mouth tightens into a thin, sad line. "I think it's best if we focus on what *you* know."

Twenty-three years ago, Max Donovan was the lead QA investigator for Verux on the Ferris Outpost incident, and I'm sure Verux sent him today because we have that history. He used to bring me tubes of soda, boxes of real sugar candy, and, once, one of his daughter's discarded dolls—never mind that I was eleven and a colony kid so the idea of playing at childcare was completely foreign to me. Why would I play at what I was expected to do anyway?

But Max's well-intentioned awkwardness has apparently not stopped his ascent at Verux. Perhaps because that awkwardness signals that he's a real person, someone who will understand the ugliness and imperfection of being human. And how that sometimes blows up in your face.

He must be getting close to retirement age, but the lines near his eyes and deep furrows in his forehead are still a surprise every time I look at him. My mental image of him is that of his younger self.

Max was kind to me, back then. The nameless orphan in the news with no family left to retrieve her. He came to visit me several times at the group home after I was out of quarantine to make sure I was settling in. I'm fairly certain he put in a good word for me years ago, when I applied to the Verux commweb training program. And he's trying to help me now, even if it doesn't feel like it.

Max thinks I did it. He thinks I'm responsible. Am I?

I scrub my hands over my face, trying to pull myself out of the mire I've willingly sunk into over the last few months.

Reed eyes me speculatively. "So maybe you didn't kill your whole team. Just left one person behind to hold your claim. And to bolster your story. Millions of dollars are at stake, after all."

His words ignite a flicker of uncertainty. I don't remember leaving the ship. Is it possible someone survived this long?

I shudder but the movement feels slow, underwater. "You better hope that ship is headed out into the dark, never to be heard from again," I say, carefully enunciating each word.

"We can't let it go, Claire. You know that," Max says gently. "We'll be sending a vessel to intercept the ship, based on your recommendation."

"We" being Verux, presumably. I narrow my eyes at him. "That is *not* my recommendation." Staying the hell away from it would be their best bet.

"Well, your sudden and newsworthy arrival has made any alternative solution impossible," Max points out, showing the first hint of irritation.

I shake my head. "You can't let whatever is on board get back here—"

"You're referring to the *presence* you claim you felt on the ship, during explorations you were not authorized to conduct," Reed says, with open skepticism.

I look to Max for help, but he holds his hands up, surrendering the conversation to Reed.

"You understand how convenient this all sounds," Reed says. "You and your team score the biggest and most controversial find in the history of manned space flight, right before you are wiped from the rolls as a team lead." He ticks off the point on his fingers. "Everyone else had employment on other vessels lined up, but your loan application to start your own transport company was denied." Another finger. "You had no money, no future, beyond a pointless desk job, an administrative bone tossed your way. And then, none of your team survives to tell about this big find, but you do." Two more fingers. "Which means it's all yours." He raises that last finger, then lets his hand drop.

Except that my share, one-fifth of ten percent of the salvage worth, would have been more than enough to accomplish my goals. On a practical level, killing my crew to get the whole thing—and blaming it on a mysterious entity—was not only unnecessary, it actually made the situation more difficult, landing me here in the Tower. But that's not the answer Reed Darrow wants to hear, the box he wants to check next to my name.

"Have you ever seen someone commit suicide by plasma drill? Or gouge out their eyes?" I ask. "It's anything but *convenient.*"

"And yet, somehow, you managed to survive. And it's not even the first time 'lone survivor' has been attached to your name. Is it?" Reed asks, though he clearly already knows the answer.

The sense of betrayal—cold and sharp, like a knife at my throat—startles me. I thought I was past all of that. My gaze shoots straight to Max, who looks down at his hands.

"On Ferris Outpost, you broke quarantine protocol, claiming that one of the other colony children summoned you past the caution tape and into the sealed sector," Reed says, reading notes off his comm implant's display.

Becca. I can still see her in my mind. Small and pale in an oversized white nightgown with little blue flowers. She was barefoot, her dark hair still plastered to her forehead with sweat, but her eyes sparkled with mischief as she waved at me from the other side of the tape, urging me to follow her to her family's hab.

I remember being surprised and impressed at how quickly and

quietly my friend slipped through the passageway airlock. It was like she hadn't even opened it.

But Reed is correct: I followed her in. It had been days since I'd seen her at work or our makeshift school. Everyone was worried about her family—and others in the same hab sector—dying. I was just happy to see she was okay. Clearly the danger was over if Becca was out of bed and standing just behind the tape.

"Never mind that the girl was dead, had been dead for more than a day by that point," Reed continues.

I squeeze my eyes shut against the tremor starting up inside me. "I was eleven and spent a month alone in that hab. My memories are—"

"After? Perhaps," Reed says. "Maybe your recollections would be tainted by stress or post-traumatic . . . whatever." He waves his hand, dismissing years of therapy and multiple professional evaluations and treatment plans with a single gesture. "But this was before everyone died. Your mother's explanation of the quarantine break is mentioned in her notes."

I freeze at the mention of my mother. I don't even remember talking to her about Becca. Everything about those last days at Ferris is a blur.

"When search and rescue found you, you told them your mother helped you signal them," Reed continues. "You know why that's impossible."

Because I'd watched her die weeks before. The fluid filling up her lungs until she couldn't breathe.

Except . . . I remember the whisper of her words in my ear. The light caress of her hand against the top of my head. Both long after I'd left her body behind in the MedBay hab.

Jumbled memories and a traumatized kid making up things to comfort herself. That's all it was. Every evaluation I'd ever had backed that up.

Trying to rally, I turn to Max. "Something is on that fucking ship. And if it's coming here, Verux needs to destroy it."

"Along with all the evidence of your malfeasance," Reed argues. "Are you honestly trying to imply that some kind of alien lifeform—"

"Where is the *Aurora* now?" I persist, ignoring him. "Is it following a course or just drifting from an initial engine boost? Have you seen course corrections?" That would imply a thinking human—or nav computer—in charge. If not, the ship might simply be following the heading Voller set. *Before.* "Have you tried communicating with it?"

Max shifts in his chair, the plastic squeaking slightly under his weight. "We need to know the rest of the story first, Claire." He seems tired. Or resigned to some answer that I don't know.

"But I've told you everything that I remember! I didn't kill my team!" I shout. The nurse at the station nearby stands up to head toward us.

But Max shakes his head, dismissing her.

"Here's the thing, Kovalik." Reed leans forward. "How can you be so sure if you don't remember? If this thing that you claim was on board made everyone else lose their minds, how do you know it didn't make you lose yours?"

My mouth works, but no sound comes out.

"You do seem particularly susceptible to . . . shall we say, instability, to begin with," Reed points out.

I have a loose screw. That's what he's saying. A bubble of hysterical and desperate laughter lodges itself in the back of my throat.

And the thing is, I realize with a dawning sense of horror, he might be right. I have no way of proving what I remember is accurate. What if my memories—the few I've retained—are wrong? What if I conjured up whole conversations and scenarios? Whole people? It's happened before. Not just with Becca.

The meds in my system make everything soft and hazy, which means my grip on rational thought slips away that much more easily. It feels like the room is spiraling around me, pulling me down with the force of the motion. A ship plummeting toward an abrupt end on a rocky surface. I draw my knees up to my chest, trying to hold myself together. *I can't breathe. I can't . . .*

My lungs seize up in their struggle, and I hear myself panting, but it doesn't seem to be helping.

"Claire," Max breaks in gently. And then a little more sharply, "Claire!"

I drag my gaze to him.

"Finish your account," Max begins.

I'm already shaking my head, trembling. I just want to go back to my room.

"Finish your account," he continues. "And I'll tell you about the *Aurora*'s course heading and what we know so far."

Reed's mouth pops open in surprise and objection, but Max shoots him a warning look. A muted sound of protest emerges from Reed but that's all.

Even in my panicked state, I dimly recognize that as an interesting interaction. They *know* something. Something that they—or Reed, at least—don't want me to know.

"Max," Reed says carefully, his voice sharp like the crack of the ice on our frozen water stores when it begins to melt. "Are you sure that's a good—"

Max dismisses his concern with an impatient noise and looks to me, waiting for a response.

It takes me a moment to marshal my resources, curiosity slowly creeping in, taking over in place of fear. Maybe I'm crazy, maybe I'm not. Only one way to find out. "All right," I say after a moment, working to catch my breath.

Max leans back in his seat, another fascinated spectator in a tale of woe.

I open my mouth and then close it again, a thought occurring to me as I try to wrest my thoughts back in line. "Communication attempts, too," I add.

Reed looks ready to yank Max off to the side for an angry whispered discussion, just out of my earshot.

But Max shrugs in easy agreement. He is, clearly, the one in charge of this investigation, no matter what Reed said when he first introduced himself. "Yes, I'll share details on our communication attempts with the *Aurora* as well."

Good enough.

6

THEN

"Theoretically, the *Aurora* could receive shipments from resupply vessels while cruising. State of the art for the time," Nysus says, his voice high and reedy with excitement. "So the outer doors could be independently operated if the setting was engaged and you had the override code."

And clearly, he does.

After Voller's successful retrieval of the emergency beacon, which is now taking up most of the limited floor space in our tiny galley, I watch on the monitors outside the airlock as the *Aurora*'s outer doors open with a rush of escaping air and random bits of detritus that indicate the hold was pressurized. The dark and cavernous cargo bay swallows us whole, the cameras outside going black for a moment, and I shiver. It feels like a giant shadow has fallen over us, even though the lighting inside LINA remains steady and bright.

Then our working lights kick on outside, giving us our first look inside the *Aurora*.

It is shockingly normal, other than the field of debris, bits of flotsam and jetsam in the air that came up from the floor when the gravity went. Screws, scrap wood, a folding chair, sheets of protective plastic, rolls of packing tape. A coffee mug, absurdly upright, floats by, as if carried by a caffeine-seeking ghost.

Hundreds of large hard-case storage bins line the walls from the floor to about eight feet up. Most of them are still securely strapped in. A half dozen or so, missing their lids, bob gently around the perimeter, where they've been abandoned. Someone searching for something? Food, maybe.

But then . . .

Above the crates, a four-legged object, glossy with black paint that reflects our lights back at us, drifts aimlessly in the far left corner.

"Shit." I lean closer to the screen, trying to make sense of what I'm seeing. It takes a second for my brain to flip the image over into its more expected position.

It's a baby grand piano, floating upside down.

The top is folded flat and carefully secured with a fuzzy fabric strap to keep from damaging the wood, a useless precaution now. Even from this distance I can see that the edges of the piano are dented and smashed, revealing the paler shade of wood beneath the lacquer, where the piano has crashed into walls or other objects.

It just looks wrong. I shiver.

"They were supposed to have shows on board," Nysus offers. "Entertainment."

In the opposite corner, yellow metal glints between the slats of a giant wooden crate. Some kind of construction equipment, maybe? MIRA is burned crosswise across the front of the crate. Three enormous flat-packs that I recognize as hab extensions lay stacked in front of it, strapped to the deck.

"Nysus, why is there Mira stuff here?" I ask. The *Aurora* is . . . was a CitiFutura ship and Mira is a Verux-sponsored site on Mars. They were competitors, of a sort. Verux, at the time, was more ground-based, habitation and colonization focused. CitiFutura had cornered the market on shipbuilding. Though the *Aurora* might have been seen as a bit of a dig at Verux's specialty, offering luxury in space on a ship rather than a hard, bare-bones existence in a ground-based hab.

"Hang on." He sounds distracted. "Um, okay. Based on some old Forum posts, it looks like CitiFutura agreed to coordinate a supply drop for Verux at Mira on their way back."

It's hard to believe that enough people are that interested in the minutiae of a ship that went missing so long ago to have specific chat threads about it online. But then again, Nysus apparently has the information archived and available offline—or basically memorized. So . . .

"Verux and CitiFutura were getting along okay back then, I guess," he adds.

And they'd be getting along even better a short few years later once the tragedy and scandal of the *Aurora* caused CitiFutura to implode and Verux to swoop in and scoop up the remains.

I roll my eyes. Of course, Verux consumes without hesitation. Companies. Equipment. Lives. Families. Anything and everything to appease their board and shareholders.

Ferris Outpost was wiped out because Verux had delayed sending new air filters, trying to squeeze a few more months from the old ones. And then it took them a month to reach me because they refused to retask the closest ship—a mining vessel heading out for ore—for rescue. It would have cost too much in time and operating expenses—something I found out only after I was employed by them and able to dig a little in the old files in the company archives.

And yet, they didn't hesitate to promote my rescue on all the media sites as a "miracle." The miracle was that I survived that long at all. Sometimes I wonder if Verux was hoping that if they left me alone long enough the problem would solve itself.

Too bad for them.

The lights continue to sweep the area as Voller edges us toward the center of the *Aurora*'s bay.

This time, they catch a familiar low-slung shape, the windshield bright and shiny, the cobalt blue metal curves as pristine as the day it slid off the factory line and onto the mag-lev highway. The car is firmly attached to the metal decking beneath, with no visible straps or restraint mechanism, the magnet still holding its own out here after all this time. Twenty years ago, it would have been one of the first of its kind. Mag-lev vehicles were bigger back then, resembling the fossil-fuel behemoths they were descended from, and manually guided, nothing like the autopilot personal transports of today.

"What the hell?" Kane says, his voice tinged with awe. "That's a Mach Ten. I've only ever seen one in museums online."

"Mach Ten, Special Edition," Nysus corrects. "Yeah, one of the passengers paid extra to bring it on board."

"Why?" Voller scoffs. "It's not like they could drive it anywhere."

Which says a lot about the type of people who bought passage on this first solar system cruise. Then again, it's not like you install pointlessly lavish faucets for people who *aren't* expecting that level of treatment.

"Since when has practicality ever stopped a rich guy from doing anything?" Lourdes asks, dryly, sounding steadier, more like herself.

"How do you know it's a guy?" Voller demands with righteous indignation.

Lourdes snickers.

"Please," I mutter at the same time.

"Right," Voller says. "Blame it all on the men. Like there aren't a hundred real fur coats on this temperature-controlled boat, never mind the fact synthetics are even warmer than—"

"Um, Andrew Davies?" Nysus says. "That's the name on the official documents. Someone leaked verified cargo and passenger manifests to the Forum a few years after the accident."

Kane's sharp intake of breath is audible even over the intercom. "Wait, he's . . . Davies was on here?" Kane asks.

"Who's that?" I ask. The name rings a distant bell, but not enough for me to pin it down. Sometimes my Ferris Outpost education trips me up.

"He's that . . . whatever comes after billionaire, yeah?" Voller asks. "Old guy. Made all his money a long time ago off code that connected prosthetic limbs to a chip in the brain or something like that."

Now doctors could just print a new limb from the patient's DNA—nerves, tissue, and all—and attach the thing. But back in the day, when Davies was apparently a big deal, people were still dealing with mechanical replacements—a direct connection to the brain would have been a huge deal.

"But then he spent most of his fortune investing in mag-lev technology," Kane says, his words coming rapidly in excitement. "He's the reason we have the highways and the high-speed trains in the United States, not to mention the cars. He's like Andrew Carnegie and Henry Ford in one."

And evidently something of a personal hero to Kane.

Kane pauses. "So Davies died on the *Aurora*?"

"It's unclear, but according to the Forum, that's what everyone assumes," Nysus says. "He was listed on the manifest, his luggage and the car made it on board, and no one ever heard from him again. But his wife—the third Mrs. Davies—insisted that he canceled at the last minute for some emergency business meeting in the Philippines. She claimed he'd been kidnapped by a rival or some group trying to extort money. She fought against having him declared dead for years after the *Aurora* disappeared and spent thousands on private investigators to find him. On Earth, that is."

Voller snorts. "Let me guess, chica wanted the cha-ching to keep cha-chinging."

"Is it possible for you to be more offensive?" Lourdes asks.

"Probably," Voller says thoughtfully, after a moment. "But I'd have to put real effort into it."

"Please don't," Lourdes says, disgusted.

"Enough," I say, intervening before Voller feels the need to prove himself.

"Rumor has it that the last Mrs. Davies wouldn't stand to get much unless their marriage made it more than ten years," Nysus admits.

"Which is probably exactly when she gave up her 'fight' to find him, right?" Voller asks.

"Voller," I say with a sigh.

But Nysus remains silent, which is confirmation of Voller's guess in and of itself.

"Told you," Voller mutters. But he navigates the rest of the way in silence, until I feel the familiar thud/pull of LINA's landing gear attaching us to the deck.

"It's not as secure without clamps," Voller says. "But the magnets should hold us long enough."

Another inheritance from Mr. Davies and his love of mag-lev? Possibly. The magnetized landing gear was meant to be a backup option, in case of docking clamp or grav-gen failure on a hauler. Redundancies everywhere. A necessity in space.

"Closing the cargo bay door," Nysus announces. The occasion is marked only by a slight shudder beneath my feet, and the increase of dread in my gut. Rationally, it's the safer move, especially with two of us moving around the ship, untethered. At least this way, we're held within the confines of the ship.

Held. *Trapped.*

I watch the monitor for a moment, the cargo bay detritus swirling around us. It's an odd feeling to know that every person who last touched those items has been dead for twenty years but is probably still here somewhere. At Ferris Outpost, it felt more immediate. Like if I could find the right sequence of actions, I'd be able to rewind time those few hours or days and bring everyone back to life again. This feels more like ancient ruins, abandoned and then rediscovered centuries later. And yet, still somehow ominous and threatening.

"All right," I say. "We've got work to do."

"TL, I know you've got a hang-up about those faucets, but I'd skip them," Nysus says. "Forum says several high-end hotels bought a load of them about the same time as the *Aurora* was being built. It might not be enough for our claim."

And likely not worth enough, I mentally add. The faucets are intrinsically valuable but what would really bump up the price—and solidify our claim—is something that's exclusive to the *Aurora*.

"Who cares?" Voller asks in the corridor, yanking up his suit as he heads toward me. "We're going to have the black box, that'll be more than enough to prove we were here."

"Until Verux claims it as confidential and locks it away in a vault somewhere, threatening to sue us if we say anything. Information isn't enough," I say. "Just like a video of us on board isn't enough. Someone will say it's faked."

"I'll go over the ship's manifests and check my Forum threads for possibilities, see what I can find," Nysus says. "Keep an eye out for something not only easily mobile but also pricey. We might not get anything else out of the claim once Verux is done with us in court."

"Got it," I say.

Kane appears in the passageway from the bridge. He watches me for a moment, long enough to make me squirm, but he doesn't ask me if I'm sure. Doesn't ask me to stay behind.

Which is good because I'm going either way.

"Remember, you've only got a couple hours of air," he says finally.

At the end of every assignment, I'm always scratching the bottom of the barrel for resources for myself and my team. So, low air is nothing new. But Kane's right; it'll be easy to get distracted in this scenario. "I'll keep an eye on it," I say, resisting the urge to add *I promise*. He didn't ask for that promise, and I shouldn't be so inclined to give it.

Once Voller and I are suited up and in the airlock, Kane steps up to cycle the airlock for us. I could do it from this side, but his way is faster. And the space is small enough that Voller and I are forced to stand back-to-back. So yeah, faster is better.

I watch Kane through the visor on my helmet and the small circular window at the top of the door. The concern in his serious expression makes my heart lift slightly.

Be careful, he mouths.

I bob my head, which, in the suit, is a full-body movement. If this works, if we manage to pull off this claim, I'll have my transport company. Kane will have enough money to support his daughter for three lifetimes.

The outer door on the LINA opens, and Voller and I stumble and trip over each other to the threshold.

"Airlock to the corridor entry in the northeast corner," Nysus says in my ear. "Take it toward the center of the ship and that should lead you to the main staircase, and then follow that up toward the bridge for the black box. We've got your helmet feed on-screen, TL, but I also pulled up the ship schematics so I can talk you through it if we lose your visual."

Our helmet cams are too old to be completely reliable. And even when everything is working at peak-for-us condition, Nysus can only have one of our feeds up at a time.

"Got it," I say, flipping on the light at the side of my helmet.

Voller bounds off the lip and into the dim cargo bay, the microgravity field on the LINA releasing him with a suddenness that's always startling to experience or witness. "This way to fame and fortune, bitches," he crows. Then a moment later, "Nothing personal, TL."

"Show a little respect," Lourdes snaps at Voller. "People are dead."

I follow him more cautiously, pushing off from the LINA in the direction we need to go. We're outside the bright, comforting circle of LINA's working lights almost immediately, leaving us just two bright specks in the darkness, which is a little . . . disconcerting.

A memory leaps forcefully to the foreground of my mind. Me, crawling through a darkened outpost corridor, feeling my way through to the generator room. My hand slipping over and then into soft rot, the slippery release of former flesh. The smell of "used to be a person" curling up in my nose until I gag and . . .

I shudder inside my suit, my palms going sweaty inside my gloves. I curl my fingers up away from that remembered sensation. *This is not the same. Not the same at all.*

"Good luck," Lourdes says softly.

I open my mouth to say thanks, but then the outer edge of Voller's helmet light catches something on the wall to his left—a spray of dark red arcing out in a fan pattern.

Blood.

It's impossible to tell how old it is. And Kane's warning about survivors on board is ringing in my head.

Voller moves past it, oblivious, his focus on reaching the airlock door.

"Wait," I say. "We should stick together just in—"

Motion to my right catches my eye, and the words die in my throat as I twist my head awkwardly to look.

My mother, my long-dead mother, floats just above me in her white lab coat, strands of her long dark hair standing out around her head in a cloud and her mouth stretched wide in a scream.

7

My throat convulses but no sound emerges. Instinct overrides years of training and experience, my arms and legs flapping uselessly in zero grav as I attempt to run.

But it does no good—my body continues on the trajectory set by my initial push-off. I cannot get away. I am a fish in a dry bucket, a bird without wings.

"Kovalik, what's wrong?" Kane asks in my ear. "Claire! Talk to me! Did you see something?" Then, presumably to Lourdes, "Zoom in. I want to see what she's seeing."

What she's seeing.

Kane's words make me realize I've squeezed my eyes shut. I'm not seeing anything but the blackness of my own eyelids. Dangerous in this environment.

But opening my eyes and seeing her again would be worse.

"It's not real, it can't be real," I whisper, trying to convince myself to look.

"TL, we didn't copy," Nysus says. "Repeat."

"Your vitals spiked," Kane adds. "Slow your breathing."

I'd laugh if I wasn't so close to screaming.

"I'll come back and grab her," Voller says reluctantly.

"Just stay there until we know what we're dealing with," Kane orders.

"Claire?" Lourdes asks, her voice taut with tension and a little too loud.

I need to get it together. Now.

But it's the light tap on my arm through my suit that finally snaps my lids back. My eyes are watering heavily, blurring my vision. I blink, expecting to find bony fingers plucking at me. Instead, I discover a storage crate, one of those floating freely, the shattered and sharp edge of it rubbing against my upper arm.

Not quite hard enough to create a tear, but a risk nonetheless. I bat it away from me carefully and then turn to look to my right, breath caught painfully in my chest.

A flap of translucent plastic sheeting glows white in my helmet light, and above that, a frayed and shredded safety strap dangles its loose black threads over the plastic.

My breath escapes in a rush and a slightly hysterical laugh. "Holy shit."

"What is it?" Kane demands. "Is someone there?"

I shake my head, even though he won't really be able to see the motion. "No, no. I just saw movement, that plastic sheeting, and freaked myself out." Add to that the low-level dread of being trapped on the *Aurora*, Kane's warnings about possible cannibalistic passengers, and blood on the wall behind Voller's head, and it's a wonder I didn't imagine a whole ship's worth of ghosts.

"Come on, seriously?" Voller complains.

"Shut up," Kane and I both say at the same time.

Though . . . why my mother? And why would I imagine her screaming? She was always very calm, controlled, even at the end.

What about after the end? A tiny voice whispers in my head, and I grit my teeth until they squeak to make that voice shut up.

It was nothing. Just stress and the product of an active imagination in a life-or-death situation. That's what the Verux therapist's official diagnosis was, and it had to be. End of story.

"Next time you're going to have a meltdown over floating garbage, how about a little heads-up?" Voller says to me. But, keeping one hand on the airlock door, he reaches out and grabs my hand to pull me down with him when I drift close enough. And then he nudges me into the airlock ahead of him.

Working together, with our feet braced against the wall, we manage to pull the door shut behind us. Manual cycling to equalize the pressure without any power involves a hand crank, but eventually, the switch flips and the outer door leading to the corridor pops open silently.

"We're in," I say.

For a second, I feel the urge to rub at my eyes to make sure I'm actually awake. I spent so many hours dreaming about being on this ship, being part of the crew—before it disappeared. And after? How many hundreds, if not thousands, of people had dedicated months and years of their lives to a search that would allow them to be the ones standing right here? At the threshold of the most famous missing ship ever, about to discover what happened.

But instead, it's us.

I shiver a little in awe and maybe anticipatory dread.

The interior passageway ahead of us is a dark and narrow crowded tangle of floating furniture, pool towels, serving carts, and safety straps. It's an obstacle course out of a claustrophobe's nightmares.

"You're in crew quarters," Nysus says. "It's going to be tighter down here, but it'll get better as soon as you start to go up."

"No shit," Voller grunts as he works to squeeze past a stack of chairs, braced between floor and ceiling, and blocking most of the hall.

"Looks like they were barricading themselves in," I say, using the doorframes to pull myself along the wall ahead of Voller. The wooden doors themselves, still closed in most cases, are dented, with chunks missing, as though someone took a heavy object to them.

"Fuck. That sounds cheery," Voller says.

"I don't think so," Nysus says suddenly.

"What do you mean?" I ask.

"If they were barricading themselves in, why is all the furniture out here?" Nysus asks.

"To block the hallway," Voller points out.

"Except wouldn't it be easier to just block the door to your room from the inside?" Nysus says. "And look at that one, the door you're passing right now, TL."

I pause. The door is pocked with holes on the outside, like the others, but a black cord runs from the handle on the door to the chaotic stack of furniture jumbled in front of it. Glimpses of the cord appear, wrapped around a chair arm, up a table leg, before it disappears into the mess. It's as if someone on the outside was trying to keep the door from opening. From the inside.

A flicker of panic lights up in me. What happened here?

"Let's just keep moving," I say firmly. I don't like the feel of this place. The sensation of being silently watched—*observed*—from corners and shadows raises goose bumps on my skin even under my suit.

"Fine by me," Voller says, drawing even with me at the doorframe on the other side of the hall. "This place is fucking creepy."

Nysus is right; the next level up is easier. The hallway is slightly larger and not as difficult to navigate. It's the lowest level of passenger rooms, the cheapest of the paid accommodations available on the *Aurora* and generally reserved for assistants, dog sitters, assistant dog sitters, wardrobe and makeup experts, and a camera crew apparently following around the Dunleavy sisters.

"It was a reality show," Nysus is saying. "*Doing It Dunleavy Style.* Or just *Dunleavy Style.* They were supposed to be spokespeople for the cruise line, recording their experiences and sending them back. The first five episodes aired before CitiFutura lost contact with the *Aurora.*"

A click sounds inside my helmet and then audio plays.

"Oh my God, this place is scorching! Did you see the pool?" a high-pitched female voice demands. In the background, I can hear the low murmur of conversation. The other passengers, maybe?

"Calm down, Cattie, don't be such a fundie." Another girl's voice, this one pitched lower and smoother, emerges over the rustle of fabric. "I'm going to the spa. I heard Linx is here."

"But you're supposed to be avoiding him," Cattie says. "The restraining order—"

"Doesn't count in space, duh." The second girl lets out an impatient huff, and the door slams shut.

Then the audio cuts off.

"The rumor is other episodes were shot but never released. Their father worked as a lawyer for the president of the United States at the time and his daughters were always in the spotlight for trouble they were causing or for promoting a new line of . . ." He pauses. "Lip plumper? Is that a . . . what is that?"

"Wait, so Dunleavy Cosmetics? That's who this is . . . was?" Lourdes asks. "That company is still around. My sisters use their stuff." She sounds stunned.

"One and the same," Nysus confirms. "The other siblings took over after they disappeared. The *Aurora*'s passenger list was high profile."

Except down here, where the high-profile guests paid for others to stay, literally beneath them.

Though, on this level, the chaos we saw on the crew deck is completely missing. Voller and I, following the signs for the stairs/elevators, make our way down the hall easily enough. The doors stand like silent soldiers in long, obedient lines down either side of the passageway, awaiting their next orders in perfect form.

Voller reaches out and jiggles one of the door handles as we pass.

"Hey," I protest.

He shrugs. "Just checking, TL. It's locked."

But there are no dents or damage from someone trying to get in—or out. No piles of chairs or carts floating around as potential barricades.

Just the regular detritus you'd expect—random shoes, a suitcase or two, a room service tray still surrounded by a halo of glass and flatware.

The only unusual object is a long, shiny strand, floating in mid-air, which, when we get closer, turns out to be a loose dog leash. The diamonds on the leather are catching the light from our helmets.

Voller pauses long enough to snatch the leash out of the air and stuff it into one of the biohazard bags.

"Stop," I say.

"What?" he asks. "It's not like anyone else is using it."

I shake my head. "Put it back."

"Why?" Voller demands. "If you think we might not get our percentage, then why not take a little something extra for ourselves? Just to be sure."

"Because it's grave-robbing, asshole," Lourdes hisses over the comm channel.

I grit my teeth. I knew this was going to be an issue. "Voller—" But my words curl up and die as we pass one of the last rooms.

Words are scrawled across the door and onto the wall, in sloppy, unsteady handwriting from a dying marker. The loops and lines of the letters cut in and out, like a transmission interrupted by static.

i see you
leave me alone

"Jesus," Voller mutters.

The words are eerie enough. But the bloody handprint smeared beneath the words, like punctuation at the end of the statement, raises goose bumps over my skin even with the heat of my suit.

The message is old. Not for us. With the environmentals off, blood would freeze far too quickly now for anyone to write a message in it.

And yet . . .

Voller shakes the leash loose out of the bag.

"Hurry up and get back to the LINA," Kane says, tension threading through his voice.

We locate the central stairway at the end of the hall.

"Okay, take these stairs to the Diamond Level Atrium," Nysus says. "That'll put you on the entertainment concourse and then you can take the main staircase up to the Platinum Level suites and beyond. I think we'll have a good shot at finding something up there for our claim. The bridge is up that way, too."

"Two different staircases?" I ask.

"Uh. Yeah. The Forum thinks that it was intended to subtly distance first class from the other classes."

I snort. Pretty sure the money did that all on its own, but okay.

Voller and I begin pulling ourselves up the stairs via the railing. We're getting deeper and deeper into this ship and it feels like we're marching farther into the gullet of something that has yet to decide whether it will digest us or spit us back out.

We ascend several flights—each one more spacious and increasing in luxury. On the Sapphire Level, most of the space appears to be taken up by a theater. Double doors—made of gleaming, polished real wood—stand open at the entrance, and a quick look inside reveals a sea of empty red-cushioned seats, with matching plush curtains on either side of an honest-to-God stage.

Thanks to the lack of gravity, though, the curtains now stretch out over the stage horizontally, like invisible arms in swooping velvet sleeves grasping for something just out of reach.

On the Gold Level, we find a closed dining room—La Fantaisie—one of several on the ship, Nysus tell us.

"This one was for the Platinum Level guests who elected not to dine with private service in their suites," Nysus says.

"Obviously. Private service, such a pain in the ass," Voller mutters.

It's a small, but elegant room with an imposing maître d' lectern just inside the threshold. Bolted-down tables and curved sofa seating in subtle but expensive-looking hues of purple, blue, and silver dominate the space. Cream-and-silver-striped wallpaper reflects our lights back at us, from between artwork in gilded frames. Fluted columns that don't appear to support anything—they don't even reach the ceiling—further add to the exclusive air; they mark the boundaries of each table, giving the illusion of a separate dining area. The Platinums didn't have to share even in shared space. It looks like a slightly larger version of a rich person's dining room, or so I would guess, never having seen one in real life.

Except, of course, for the black metal gate pulled down from the ceiling and latched to the floor. The gate is scraped and bowed inward, to the point of pressing against the maître d' stand, as if someone—or something—large tried to break in.

I reach down to confirm that the plasma drill is still tethered to my suit.

"Let's keep moving," I say.

Finally, after one last flight of stairs, we reach an open level at the top.

"Wow," Voller says.

And I have to agree. The Diamond Level Atrium is an expansive, multilevel space, covered by a domed ceiling that disappears into darkness. The floor is pale-veined marble. Expensive-looking couches and chairs, bolted into place and made out of what appears to be real leather, lounge together in conversational groups. Frozen plants, trapped forever in a moment of decay, wave their green-and-brown-splotched strands from built-in planters all around us, in what once must have been a gardenesque setting. When the ship was fully functional, there must have been a light setting for imitation sun.

Even in its current condition, it's more luxurious than any place I've ever set foot in. Setting aside the expensive and hard-to-find materials, like leather and the marble, it's more that everything is so *clean*. And nothing darker than a pale shade of gray or a dark cream. Colors that would never withstand heavy use. Unless, of course, you have a full-time staff to clean up after everyone.

In one of my last group homes, the chipped tile floor still had the sticky black residue from the glue where the indoor-outdoor carpeting had been glued down and then torn out years before.

Shops and other establishments circle the outer perimeter, along with directional signs for the Crystalline Ballroom, Star-Swimming, and The Green. The latter two are surely the infinity pool and the putting green.

The Peaceful Reverie Spa offers massages and an aesthetician consultation, NO APPOINTMENT NECESSARY, according to the script on the windows out front. But its glass doors are firmly closed and a metal security bar blocking the entrance is visible. Small, brightly colored bottles, tubes, and jars drift through the space behind the closed doors, endlessly tumbling.

A casino lies silent at the far end—a CLOSED sign attached haphazardly to the craps table closest to the front. Not one but three different jewelry stores stand proud behind their gated security enclosures, their glittering wares drifting through sealed glass displays. A smoking room promising real—and illegal—tobacco products holds court on the other side of the casino. A Parisian-style café still has umbrellas up at its tables, each tilted at a jaunty angle, the metal framing inside the fabric holding the shape in place.

But the bake case out front has been ravaged. Glass sparkles in the air around the case, and one of the café chairs is sticking out of the spiderwebbed and cracked remains of the enclosure, wedged in by the force of the attack.

And from what I can see, the case is empty. Food is gone.

"So something happened at night," I say. "They weren't open. Shops closed like normal and never got a chance to reopen."

Or, the empty bake case might have happened days after the initial event, when survivors became desperate. One of the perks of working and traveling on the *Aurora* was to have been real food from trained chefs. But there should have been standard food printers on board in case of an emergency. And by the time those ran out, the bakery items would have been long gone to dust or mold.

None of this makes any sense.

"Mutiny, like Nysus said?" Kane asks. "Or maybe riots?"

Next to me, Voller shifts, changing his grip on the wall at the threshold to the atrium, where we're hovering. "Maybe," Voller says. "But where the fuck is everybody? Even if all the escape pods that got out of here left with a full load, we're still looking at, what, a couple hundred bodies here somewhere?"

I wince, but he has a point, much as I'm loath to admit it. In the lower levels, it was easy to assume that the passengers had taken cover (and subsequently died) in their rooms. But up here? The atrium has doors, it could be sealed off, but it wasn't. What are the odds that no one was here when whatever happened happened?

Looking more closely now, it's easier to see smaller signs of disorder and disruption. The marble floor is chipped and pitted in several places as though someone took a heavy object to it. One of the pale leather couches is adorned with a dark smear that might be another bloody handprint or just blood in general. An electrical cord knotted into a noose floats by, followed by the shattered remains of a wooden chair and one of the putters from the green, broken in half with the metal end sticking out like a shiv.

"We're not here to figure out what happened," I say, reminding myself as much as the others. It's hard not to wonder, not to speculate, when you're standing in the middle of one of the greatest unsolved mysteries of the century and it's not getting any more solved, despite your proximity. "That'll be up to Verux when they take it back."

"Bullshit," Voller mutters. "It's ours."

I ignore him. "Come on. Let's go."

"Wait, TL. Stop," Nysus says excitedly. "Look to your left. The stairway."

I do as directed and notice, for the first time, a set of steps in roughly the center of the atrium. The stairway is a perfect gold-and-white spiral, arcing upward to levels above. It looks like it's floating in midair, an optical illusion, obviously, but even more impressive in zero grav.

"Okay," I begin. "What am I—"

"The Tratorelli sculptures," Nysus says.

"The what now?" Voller asks.

Nysus sighs. "Tratorelli, the sculptor? CitiFutura commissioned him to make two sculptures for the *Aurora* specifically. Both of them based on the emblem for the ship." He pauses. "It looks kind of like an angel in flight."

His description rings a vague bell in my memory, maybe something I saw in the news stories at the time.

"You'll find it everywhere, on the walls, in the flatware design," Nysus continues, "but the sculptures are one of a kind. They're a matched set. *Grace* and *Speed*."

That sounds exactly like what we need for our claim. "Great job, Ny," I say.

"And Tratorelli died shortly afterward, which ups their value even more," Nysus adds.

"Even better," Voller says.

"So where are they?" I ask.

"Well," Nysus says. "That's the tricky part. Did you by any chance bring a saw?"

"No," I say, drawing the word out. "I don't think we even—" I stop. "Why?"

"The sculptures, they're, uh, kind of attached to the main staircase. One at the top and one at the bottom. On these tall post things."

The stairway base is angled away from us, but over the lowest curve of the stairway, I can just make out what might be the tips of angel wings, peeking out over the top. Tall is right.

Shit.

Voller laughs. Because he's an asshole.

"Great," I say. Cutting anything without gravity—never mind a saw—is almost impossible. No leverage, no weight.

"Plasma drill," Kane speaks up, reminding me.

"Yeah, okay," I say to him. "Let's see what we can do, Voller."

Voller and I make our way carefully into the atrium, gently pushing off and leapfrogging from furniture cluster to furniture cluster or planter.

The Tratorelli sculpture is exactly where Nysus said it would be and looks to be in good condition. It's a delicate female figure, raised up onto her toes, her head and back arched backward, wings pulled back to a point, mid-flight. Fabric is loosely draped around her otherwise nude body, like an artfully arranged toga, though still revealing one breast. Because, of course.

Nysus lets out a breath and a shaky laugh. "She's even more beautiful in person."

I can't argue with him. She, *Grace and Speed*—or perhaps one sculpture is *Grace* and the other is *Speed*—is incredibly, almost eerily, lifelike. This close, I can see the curve of her high cheek-bones, the individual tendrils of her hair blowing backward. But the arch of her back, the pull of her wings in the metaphorical air, looks painful and the details of her expression include a tight smile that seems more like a grimace and a tiny furrow in her otherwise smooth forehead.

If she must be one or the other, I'm guessing this one is *Speed*.

The sculpture is attached to a wooden base at the top of the newel post. The tips of her wings reach probably three feet above my head. And my feet aren't even on the floor.

I fumble for my screwdriver with my gloved hands. If I can find where they attached the base, the drill might not be necessary. I really don't want to take the risk of damaging the sculpture in try-ing to remove it.

It takes me a minute to find the cleverly concealed screw holes and then another few minutes to chip away at the wood putty covering them. And it requires both hands, leaving me no way to hang on.

I push a little too hard at one point, and when the screwdriver slips, I start to slide past the post from the force of my effort.

With one hand on the newel post, Voller grabs the back loop on my suit to haul me back.

"Thanks."

He grunts in acknowledgment.

"Everything okay?" Kane asks.

"Don't worry, chief," Voller says. "*I'm* fine."

"Got it," I say as the final screw loosens, releasing the sculpture and her base. *Speed* floats free, and Voller helps me open a biohaz-ard bag and guide her inside.

"One down, one to go," I say as Voller seals the bag.

I take it back from him, and attach it to me by bunching the plas-tic into a neck and knotting one of my empty tool tethers around it. It's too loose, not a perfect solution, but it'll do for now.

Ascending the staircase by clinging to the outside of it and hold-ing the railing is easier than trying to navigate the narrow curves, so we pull ourselves up, hand over hand.

At the top, though . . .

"Shit," I say.

The post—or pillar, as it seems would be more appropriate—holding *Grace* is *much* taller than the one at the bottom. The base is about six feet off the ground. And there's nothing else to hold on to up there.

If my hands slip, like before, I might end up floating across the open atrium with no way of stopping myself. If I hit the opposite wall, I'm lucky. If not, I might end up out in the middle of open air, under the dome, with no easy way down, while I run out of air.

"One is more than enough, Claire," Kane says in warning. "Just forget it."

"The sculptures are more valuable as a set," Nysus says. "But it's not worth the risk."

"Just come back," Lourdes says. "I don't like this. At all."

Voller jabs my shoulder to get my attention. "The bridge is that way," he says, pointing to a discreet sign on the Platinum Level wall ahead of us. "We can just go and grab the black box."

Since when is Voller so concerned about my well-being?

"That's going to be worth more to them anyway," he argues.

Ah. There we go.

"But it's safer, too," he says.

"We're not going to blackmail them for the black box," I say.

"Why the fuck not?" he demands. "We're the ones taking the risk. This whole ship should be ours."

"Just . . . shut up for a second," I say, returning my attention to the statue. "I can get this." But none of my tethers are long enough to attach to the start of the railing on the staircase.

So I'll just have to be careful.

Grace is a different woman in a similar position. Her hair is in tight curls close to her skull. Her arms are up in the air and her wings are pitched perfectly perpendicular to her body, with only a slight arch to her middle, like someone preparing to dive. She, too, is dressed in precariously arranged folds of fabric but fully covered.

I pull myself up to the base of the statue and search for screw holes.

Voller makes an impatient noise. "Forget this." He pushes off the post, his hand accidentally colliding with my feet and making me grab at the base of the statue for my balance. My heart thrums with panic at the near miss.

"Voller!" I shout.

He doesn't respond, and when I manage to get myself straightened up enough to glance back at him, I see the back of his suit heading down the hallway to the bridge. Son of a bitch.

"I'm coming," Kane says immediately.

"No, you're not," I say. "You're staying with the LINA and that's an order. I'm going to finish this and then I'm going to kick Voller's ass."

"Sorry, TL," Nysus murmurs. "It was my idea."

"Not your fault." I take a deep breath. "Now just let me concentrate."

The first two screws come out easily, the third sticks a bit, and the fourth is impossible. I'm reaching for the plasma drill when a low-level rumble starts up, all around me. I can feel the tremor of it in *Grace*'s base.

"Kane?" My voice is unsteady. "Did you copy that?"

"We hear it too," Kane says. "Get back here, now."

The noise grows louder before I can respond. Except it's more than just a noise—this is the sound and sensation of movement, a giant shaking itself awake.

Fear dries my mouth, but I force the words out. "Voller, do you copy?" I ask, scaling down from the pillar, leaving *Grace* dangling by that last remaining screw. "Answer me, goddamnit."

No reply.

We haven't seen anyone else, and conditions in the areas we've searched so far would seem to make life here improbable, if not impossible. But worry clutches at me all the same. If someone survived out here for this long, they would not likely be sane.

"Nysus, switch over to Voller's feed," I say.

"I'm trying, TL, but it's not—"

Then without warning, a warm buttery glow pours down from above. I automatically throw my arms up to protect my eyes. It's like going from midnight to midday in a blink.

I lower my arm slowly as my eyes adjust. And it takes me a second to process what's going on. "The lights are on," I say in wonder.

"TL, that noise, I'm pretty sure that was the engines rebooting," Nysus says, restrained panic in his voice. "Someone flipped the switch."

"But how is that—" I start to ask, but stop when a shadow drifts over me, blocking the light temporarily. Followed by another, and then another. Almost like fan blades passing through a patch of sunlight, only more irregular.

The helmets on our suits make it almost impossible to look directly up, so I have to grab hold of the post and tilt myself backward until I can see.

My lungs lock up tight, and I can't move, can't breathe, for a moment. I blink, trying to will the image away or turn it back into its component pieces, as it did when I thought I saw my mother in the cargo bay.

But this . . . this is no hallucination.

"Oh my God," Kane whispers. "You found them."

At the spot where the enormous dome joins the hull and all the way into the dome's slightly rounded peak where the light shines down, dozens, maybe as many as a hundred, bodies hover above me, in a graceless ballet.

The ones closest to me, their eyes are open, their mouths contorted and frozen in a rictus of terror. They're dressed in all manner of clothing—evening gowns, tuxedos, bathrobes, lacy lingerie, pajamas, swim trunks, and the dark blue *Aurora* crew uniforms—and their skin is covered by a thin layer of frost and tinted bluish-purple, especially around their mouths. They were clearly alive when the environmentals went out.

One woman drifts over, her long lavender-dyed hair floating around her close enough to be within easy reach when I was at the top of the pillar, working to release *Grace*. She's one of those in an *Aurora*-branded bathrobe, the ship's name embroidered in a discreet but swirly font across the left side, the dirty white fabric knotted tightly at her waist.

It is only luck—and timing—that her hair didn't brush over me as she passed.

But on closer inspection, she is slightly different from the others.

Her lavender hair has turned a deep burgundy near her temple, a trickle of blood frozen in an aborted drip down her cheek. One red-painted palm is up by her head, as if she was applying pressure when the gravity betrayed her.

But in her other hand? A six-inch butcher's knife, one that must be from the *Aurora*'s kitchens. The shiny blade projects out, away from her lax hand, but the wooden handle is bound to her wrist, in layers upon layers of duct tape that scream desperation.

The knife itself isn't a big surprise. Depending on what went down and how, it's easy to imagine some passengers feeling the need to defend themselves. But that tape, turning a temporary weapon into a semipermanent accessory, that says something else entirely.

8

Silence holds over the channel in my helmet for a long moment, my harsh, uneven breathing filling all the empty space, drowning out even the noise that might be the engines.

Then an explosion of voices, talking over one another.

"—out of there right now," Kane says.

"—dead. What happened to them? What happened to them?" Lourdes demands, her voice breaking.

"I think that's Opal Dunleavy." Nysus's soft astonishment and very near gleeful delight comes through quite clearly. "She looks *exactly* the same as she did on the show. Minus the knife, I mean. And the head wound."

Being dead and frozen does tend to be a rather effective preserving agent.

I tear my gaze away from the dead woman floating above me in an endless orbit and try to regulate my breathing.

Okay, okay. Get it together, Claire. This isn't Ferris. But my brain isn't buying it, flashing me memories of dark hab rooms lit only by a battery-operated portable work light I'd pried off the wall in one of the labs in desperation. Dark forms slumped over furniture, collapsed on the floor. The acrid scent of vomit and the coppery smell of blood. They'd coughed up the lining of their lungs. That's what I'd overheard some of the Verux scientists saying later. The emergency generator had kept the air and heat on just long enough for me to be rescued.

I exhale deliberately, counting to myself, until the panic recedes slightly. *It's not the same. You're not the same.*

"They've been dead awhile, it looks like," I say when I can manage it. "Definitely not recent." My voice has a faint tremor in it, despite my best efforts. "None of them look like they were starving or scrambling for survival out here. Must have happened pretty close to when the ship disappeared." Or, perhaps this event, whatever it was, is what caused the ship to disappear. It does seem to be too large of a coincidence, otherwise.

"There's no way to know that for sure. Stay where you are. I'm already through the airlock," Kane says. He must have been standing by, suited up and ready just in case.

"Negative," I say sharply. "We have no idea what we're dealing with, and I won't risk anyone else. I need someone to be able to get the LINA home."

"We're not leaving you behind," Kane says in disbelief.

"I wasn't suggesting that you should," I say as close to steady as I can manage. *Not yet, anyway.* But if there's even a chance that whatever happened here could spread . . .

Somehow, I always knew it was going to come back to this. Me. Alone with the dead.

A mocking whisper rises up at the back of my brain, like a pointed nudge in my shoulder blade. *Got you.*

"Uh, TL? I'm replaying your footage," Nysus says. "I'm not seeing anything that looks like natural causes on those bodies. A lot of wounds. Stabbing, blunt force trauma, strangulation. That security guy's got a belt wrapped around his neck. Another passenger's still got the other end in his hand."

I flinch at the memory of the electrical cord noose that we'd seen floating by. Nysus could be right. I hadn't been looking for those details in my first glimpse of what remained of the *Aurora* passengers.

"Definitely hypothermia and oxygen deprivation from when the environmentals went down . . ." Nysus continues.

I ignore the shiver skittering down my sweaty skin, fighting the urge to look up again. I'm half-afraid the woman above me will still be there, only closer. Face-to-face, her filmy eyes unblinking but somehow still staring directly at me. Then her mouth will open, with the sound of ice cracking, and . . .

Awkwardly, I turn away from the post, deliberately putting my back to the atrium. "Voller, do you copy? Repeat, Voller, can you hear me?" I can't leave—I *won't* leave—without him.

"His vitals spiked a few minutes ago," Nysus says in my ear. "But he's still alive. I'm trying to switch to his feed."

I'm half expecting only more silence, so Voller's reply, after a moment, startles me.

Voller clears his throat. "I copy, TL." He sounds shaken, which is alarming in and of itself.

I angle myself to face the direction he went, looking for his return. "What the fuck just happened? Where are you? Did you see anyone?" He'd taken off for the bridge, so if anyone was alive and cycling up the engines, he'd surely have seen something.

"Captain and first officer." Voller coughs, and the noise makes my nerves twang.

I open my mouth to ask, but he beats me to it.

"Dead. Outside the bridge. A lot of blood. It looks like they attacked each other," he says, sounding a little more like himself, but with a thin wire of tension underlying his words. "The first officer, he . . . I don't know. There's a hole in the side of his head that you could put your fist through."

I wince.

"He's, uh, still holding the gun. Suicide, I guess." He pauses. "But you need to see this, TL. On the bridge. I went to pull the black box . . . you just need to see it."

I tense. "Voller, we have to get out of here and—"

"Hell no," he says flatly. "You need to see it because I'm not taking heat later for tampering with evidence or making this up when someone decides not to believe me."

"I'm almost to the atrium," Kane says.

Son of a bitch. I turn and moments later, across the room on the level below me, I see movement at the door. Kane, in his suit with his name emblazoned in bright orange lettering across his chest, emerges from the darkened hallway. His helmet light is a bright pinprick of familiarity in this sunny and expensive corpse-filled courtyard.

At the sight of him, relief blooms in my chest with such intensity, I'm ashamed of it and myself. I shouldn't *need* him that much. Not for this, not anything.

"I told you to stay with the LINA," I snap, louder and meaner than I intended.

"Write me up later," Kane says, ascending the staircase along the outside of its curves, just as Voller and I had done. But he's moving even faster. "Voller, you need to shut the diagnostic off."

"Diagnostic?" I ask. "What diagnostic?" Once Kane reaches my level, he moves past me without hesitating. At the top of the stairs, the corridor branches into two options, one on either side of the nonfunctioning elevator.

"The corridor on your left," Nysus says helpfully, and Kane follows the suggestion, pulling himself along the wall through an open bulkhead doorway. I trail behind him, working to keep up. The lights aren't on in here. But at least this portion of hallway is also uncluttered, unlike the ones Voller and I encountered on the lowest levels.

Actually, this section appears untouched. The Platinum Level suites are all gleaming wooden doors, lush carpeting, even a side table—bolted down—with a vase of wilted and frozen but still beautiful fresh-cut flowers. Orchids. In space. I can't imagine how much that one line item must have cost. I bet every single one of these rooms was the recipient of those gold faucets. Forget the dog walkers and assistants to assistants. *These* are the people who need fresh flowers and water delivered via precious metal. Of course, *their* section would be untouched.

But then, as we pass, I catch a glimpse of smeary bloody letters, written on the wall near the floor. The words are too muddled to decipher without stopping.

"Voller!" Kane says again.

"No fucking way," Voller shouts, and my uneasiness increases.

He's always been a bit volatile, but not like this. "That's what shows—"

"I know what it shows," Kane says. "Turn it off before it gets to the gravity generator and the heat."

As if the ship is reacting to Kane's words, I feel the disorienting pull and release of a gravity generator, like a hand tugging you gently beneath the water and then letting go. It's a warning sequence, three blips—minor, temporary increases in gravity—usually accompanied by a countdown over a ship's PA system.

I have no idea what diagnostic they're talking about or why Voller thinks it's important, but I can now see the more immediate problem Kane is worried about.

"Voller!" I shout, then I make an effort to temper my voice. Shouting at him hasn't worked so far. "We have frozen bodies in the atrium. They were above us. Just floating out there in the dome. A hundred or more. And those are just the ones we found. If the gravity kicks on in full, they're all going to come crashing down." I hesitate. "There will be . . . pieces everywhere. And we have no idea what kind of damage sudden gravity could do." Anything not strapped down would fall at full force. Not to mention the strain on the ship itself, out here in the cold of space decades longer than she was supposed to be.

And if the heat and oxygen came on, it wouldn't take long before decay became an issue. There wouldn't be anything left for the families of the *Aurora* passengers to find. The same warmth that had kept me alive on Ferris for a month had turned the dead into . . . puddles of barely recognizable biological material.

Voller doesn't respond, and the grav generator gives another warning tug.

Ahead of me, Kane pulls himself along faster. Where exactly is this fucking bridge?

We round the corner at the end of the corridor and find ourselves in a wider but more utilitarian space. The carpet here is an industrial blue, and the walls are metal rather than wood over metal. Emergency lights are on, casting harsh shadows on everything. A tiny, shiny red bead clicks against my helmet faceplate once, and then twice, before floating away to join hundreds just like it in the air around us.

I catch my breath. Blood.

To our left, about twenty feet away, a metal door stands open slightly. It's marked BRIDGE and marred with blood spatter and clumps that look like gray matter, hair, and bone splinters, now frozen to its surface.

My stomach roils.

Near the door, two bodies in *Aurora* uniforms float in and out of the shadows, locked together, their arms linked in eternal struggle. The stitched *Aurora* patches on their left sleeves are a simple but elegant arrangement of two triangles with a circle rising above, in what might look like an alien moon rising above mountains. But given what I know now, I suspect it's meant to be another representation of *Grace* and/or *Speed*. The silver pips on the uniform collars and the embroidered stripes at the shoulders—respectively four and three—identify them as the captain and first officer, but I don't need that to recognize them.

Captain Linden Gerard looks just as she did in the launch coverage I watched so obsessively all those years ago. Only now her eyes are closed, her expression almost peaceful beneath the blueish sheen of frost. Her blond hair is coming loose from its tight braid, standing around her head in a fuzzy crown. If not for the small, ragged hole in her uniform, just above her left breast, and the wide circle of blood around it, she might be sleeping.

First Officer Cage Wallace, by contrast, is missing a good portion of his left temple in a gaping exit wound, his expression—what's left of it—pained.

"Fuck!" Voller snarls. "Shutting it down," he says through clenched teeth, right as the third gravity tug starts.

The pull at my body vanishes immediately, and the emergency lights shut off, leaving me blinking to adjust to the dimness of just our helmet lights. A moment later, the hum of the engines grows quieter and then stops.

Kane and I make our way to the bridge door, and I carefully avoid looking toward Gerard and Wallace, lest they be doing something that should be impossible for the dead to do. ,

Inside the bridge, wide windows looking out onto a black field with faint pinpricks of stars offer a little more illumination. The arc-shaped space is larger than I expected, and it's not the site of utter chaos that I imagined. Darkened banks of control panels toward the front of the bridge and along the back walls reflect our helmet lights back at us in their smooth, unbroken sheen. Empty chairs—captain, first officer, navigator-pilot, and communications—wait in readiness for their occupants to return. Polished woodgrain deco-rates the base of the heavy cushioned seats and along the housing for the control panel banks. Lush carpeting adds a hint of elegance to soften the obvious work space. Hints of the luxury seen in pro-fusion elsewhere in the ship.

However, unlike what we've encountered in the rest of the *Au-rora*, I see no signs of violence or anything even out of place. No scorch marks from damaged control panels, no equipment or tools left out after an attempt at a frantic repair, no nooses floating through the air, or bloody handprints on the carpeting or walls.

Everything is . . . pristine.

One control panel is lit up along the back wall, and Voller is a pale shadow in front of it, motionless in his suit.

"Voller," I say as Kane and I pull ourselves toward him. "We're here."

Voller doesn't respond, and Kane gives me a warning look as we move to either side of him.

"Kyle?" I try again, his first name awkward in my mouth. I know it, of course, but that doesn't mean he's ever been anything but Vol-ler to me.

And that seems to move him. His head shakes back and forth, the movement almost entirely lost in his helmet. "Please, TL," he says in disgust.

The knot of tension in my gut eases a little, leaving behind an-ger. "Then what the hell is wrong with you?"

He gestures to the panel in front of him. "I went to pull the black box," he says, his voice still sounding fainter than usual. "And it . . . the central computer woke up and asked me if I wanted to run another diagnostic."

I look to Kane because I don't get it.

"It's an automatic query, as long as there's enough reserve power," Kane says. "When you bring a ship back online, even one as small as the LINA, safety regulations require a diagnostic to ensure everything's in working order before you cycle up the engines, reengage the environmentals. Otherwise, you can cause further damage."

"Okay," I say slowly.

But Kane's attention is focused on Voller and the screen. "It also requires one when you voluntarily shut down." Kane's voice holds an odd note, one of both disbelief and uncertainty.

Voller turns toward Kane suddenly, his hand gripping the darkened control board in front of him. "Exactly! You see it?" He gestures to the screen, which is still flashing abbreviations and notations, seemingly random numbers and letters, none of which I can make heads or tails of. Another way in which I'm not a "real" captain, I realize with chagrin. My Verux team lead training never extended far beyond the bare minimum for daily and emergency operations—managing others, not taking over for them. There were contingencies and cross-training in place, in the event of the loss of a team member, but nothing to the level of detail that would let me understand what they're talking about now.

Kane nods slowly at Voller. "Affirmative."

I bite back my impatience and embarrassment at my own ignorance to speak up. "Sorry. You're going to have to explain it to me."

Voller lifts his hands in an exasperated gesture. "There was no accident! No explosion, no catastrophic engine failure, no nothing!"

Once again, I shift my gaze to Kane. "The last diagnostic," he says, his gaze still focused on the symbols in front of him on the panel. He points to the first column. "The one the computer is using for comparison was run twenty-one years ago. Shortly after

CitiFutura lost contact with the *Aurora*." Now, he looks at me, his expression taut with unhappiness.

"I don't—" I begin.

Voller makes a frustrated noise. "Someone brought the *Aurora* out here, way the fuck off course, and then they shut down the engines and the environmentals, everything. This wasn't an accident or an emergency—there's no time for an automatic diagnostic when something's blowing up."

I blink at him, trying to wrap my head around what he's saying.

"Claire," Kane says finally. "It was intentional. Someone beached the *Aurora*, effectively murdering everyone on board."

9

NOW

"Bullshit," Reed says, jerking me back to the present.

It takes me a moment to adjust, to find myself back at the table with Reed and Max in the common room at the Tower. Instead of on that darkened bridge with Kane's face, pale and strained behind the faceplate of his helmet. I blink rapidly, the pain of loss striking hard and anew, as if I was just there in that moment. As if I might be able to reach out and still touch Kane.

"Those were highly respected senior officers on that bridge crew, with years of loyal service," Reed continues. "You can't seriously expect us to believe any of this, especially on *your* say-so."

The word of an obsolete, out-of-work—and obviously unstable—commweb maintenance team leader. He doesn't say that.

He doesn't have to.

"It doesn't matter if you believe it," I say tightly. "That doesn't change the truth."

"Before, you said you didn't know how the *Aurora* ended up off course. Just that that was where you found it," Reed says. "So, are you lying now or were you lying—"

"I knew you wouldn't believe me," I say, my grip on my temper slipping. "You'd have questions that I don't have the answers to. There wasn't any point in bringing it up." My goal, back then, when I first entered the Tower, was simply to be left alone. But things are different now.

Max clears his throat, looking uncomfortable. "It's a very serious accusation, Claire."

Mutiny, he means. But it was murder, too.

"None of them were in their right minds," I point out. "Whatever affected us, I think it affected them, too."

Stunned silence hangs for a moment, then Reed laughs in disbelief, shaking his head. "This is just a last-ditch attempt to bolster
your fictional account by dragging others into it. If some mysterious
event happened to the *Aurora* officers first, then clearly you can't be
at fault for what happened to your crew—"

"What exactly do you think happened on the *Aurora*?" I demand,
sitting forward. "How do you think all those people ended up
dead and floating around the atrium with the environmentals shut
off? Even if someone else, a random passenger, killed Gerard and
Wallace, how would that person have had access to essential ship
systems? To the helm?"

Reed's mouth works for a second before any sound comes out.
"Well, that's not . . . we don't have enough information—" he
blusters.

"You don't have shit," I say, patience evaporating. "Twenty-plus
years of nothing on the *Aurora*. You guys couldn't find it, we did.
And that's why I'm trying to tell you what happened. Something
is wrong on that ship, and it was wrong *before* we got there." I jab a
finger in Reed's direction for emphasis with the last of my energy.

I sit back in my chair, feeling so very tired and ancient, like my
bones might turn to dust at any point in the next few minutes. "You
need to make up your mind whether you think I'm crazy or a liar,"
I say to Reed. "Either way, it doesn't matter to me. Just tell me the
ship's course heading and if you've heard from anyone on board."

A silent exchange passes between Max and Reed. "You should
continue, Claire," Max says, after a moment. "We're listening."

"Max," Reed objects.

The older man glares at him. "We're *listening*," he says, this time
more to Reed than me. "No more interruptions."

Behind Max, Voller appears, a shimmering spot against the wall
before he takes full form. His T-shirt, one of his favorites, reads
SUSPICIOUS PACKAGE in big letters, with an arrow pointing down
to his crotch. Voller smirks at me, giving me a mock salute. Then
I see the drill in his other hand, and I look away swiftly before he

lifts it to his temple. Again. It's always the same with Voller. I don't know why.

The spatter of blood sounds like rain. Not the light, even rhythm, programmed for exact distribution and soil absorption, that I remember from my childhood at Ferris Outpost. This is something wilder.

I let the silence hang, trying not to stare at the spreading pool of blood on the floor. It's creeping slowly toward Max's worn leather shoes.

"Fine," I say finally. I don't know how to tell them so they'll believe me, but it only gets worse from here.

10

THEN

The tiny galley area on the LINA was never meant as a gathering place. It's just a slightly wider area of corridor with a sink and a food rehydrator and a suggestion of a table in a hinged flat surface that unlatches from the back wall. On poker nights, the four of them would gather and wedge themselves in around the table, even Nysus drawn out by the prospect of entertainment or, more likely, the chance to improve his card-counting skills.

The three of us—Lourdes, Kane, and I—standing at the threshold of the galley is about two too many in this space, especially with the emergency beacon on the floor taking up valuable real estate, but I'm not complaining. The door is closed, the airlock is sealed, and while we're still technically on board the *Aurora*, it feels a lot safer in here than out there. And once Voller is dressed and ready, we'll be gone.

The focus of our attention, *Speed* and *Grace*, still in their sealed biohazard bags, sit back-to-back on the table, their wings touching in what would have been a messy midair collision. Kane pulled *Grace* free as we hurried out.

Without the black box. On my order, over Voller's vehement objection.

Not that the sculptures or black box will matter. Not now.

"So," Lourdes says, her voice softer and slurred from the sedative Kane had given her. "Someone lost their nuggets"—her mouth ticks up briefly in a pleased-with-herself smile—"and started heading off course, and the passengers rebelled."

"By killing each other?" Nysus asks, over the intercom. "That doesn't make sense."

Kane glances to me over Lourdes's head, his gaze taking in my damp hair and fresh jumpsuit. His hair is still wet, too. We don't exactly have decontamination protocols on the LINA. We aren't that kind of ship. Our suits are stuffed in biohazard bags inside the airlock, and Kane, Voller, and I used up more than a week's worth of water rations in extended showers. A line item I would have to justify somehow on our return. And I'm still not sure what, if anything, I'm going to say about all of this.

Okay? Kane mouths.

I don't know how to answer that. So, I look away, returning my attention to the sculptures.

"I think it's far more likely something like mass hysteria or mass psychogenic illness," Nysus says, continuing his conversation with Lourdes and anyone else listening. "The passengers were isolated and trapped on the ship, for months. They weren't used to that kind of life. Emotions get heightened. It's easy to lose perspective. Maybe there was an issue with the food or something, people panicked. This kind of thing dates back centuries." As always, Nysus sounds happiest—and most distracted—when he's digging into some kind of research. "The Salem witch trials. Dancing frenzies in the Middle Ages. Mass poisonings in the midtwentieth that turned out not to be poisonings at all but people collectively panicking over the idea of being poisoned."

"That doesn't explain the crew," Kane points out. "There's no way CitiFutura sent out a high-profile ship like the *Aurora* with inexperienced hands at the helm."

"They didn't," I say. "Captain Linden Gerard. First Officer Cage Wallace. Pilot was James Nguyen." I knew the names from all the reports at the time. I'd dreamed of reporting to the *Aurora*, after all. And who is more famous than the crew who disappeared with the most expensive ship ever created?

"But they were outnumbered by a bunch of spoiled civilians who had no training or preparation but a bunch of money and an overdeveloped sense of entitlement," I continue. "And because of that they all paid with their lives—rich people, maids, dog walkers, crew. Just so CitiFutura could make a few bucks. Sending people who had no business being out here." The words burst out of me in a bitter torrent that I couldn't have stopped if my life depended on it. Inwardly, I cringe.

Kane cocks his head sideways, giving me that insightful look that feels like it turns me see-through, lighting up the mess of me and scars of past trauma that I work to keep hidden. I want to shout at him to shut up, even though he hasn't said anything. *Yet.*

"I'm not sure it's that simple," he says eventually. "CitiFutura never received a distress call, or a request for help." He hesitates. "Claire. It's not the same as Ferris—"

"I know that," I snap. And I do—Ferris was obvious negligence and this appears to be simply an unanticipated and terrible outcome to a new venture—but it *feels* similar. Careless. Reckless with human life. Arrogant.

"Someone did try," Lourdes points out.

We both look at her.

"The automated distress beacon," she says, enunciating each word carefully. "Remember? If the ship wasn't in distress, someone had to trigger its release. Right?"

"She's right," Nysus says after a moment, sounding stunned. "If the ship was shut down deliberately, then the ship itself wouldn't have met conditions to trigger the distress beacon. Someone must have set it off."

"But that would have to be someone with access, and that means bridge crew," Kane says. "The captain. First officer. Pilot. Maybe the security chief." He frowns. "But why wouldn't they have tried to keep the ship on course and powered up instead?" He shakes his head. "None of this makes sense."

"And it never will," Voller says flatly, from behind us.

Lourdes jumps, startled.

"Enough," Kane says, turning to face Voller.

Voller gives a harsh laugh. "Of course you're still defending her."

"I don't need any defending," I say sharply, turning toward Voller. "I'm the—"

"Yeah, yeah, you're the TL. The one in charge. But have you

considered that maybe you shouldn't be? I mean, even the saint here"—he jerks his hand in a wild gesture that comes dangerously close to Kane's face—"isn't sure walking away is the right move."

I stiffen, gaze shooting automatically to Kane.

He looks away, unable to meet my eyes.

Hurt sears like a fresh burn from touching a still-hot engine, but I shove the pain down, forcing myself to focus on the issue at hand.

"I'm trying to keep us safe." I inch closer to Voller, crowding him in the already crowded galley. "Let me ask you something. Do you think that cushy job of yours is still going to be there when you bring back proof that someone on the CitiFutura crew killed everyone on board? Verux *bought* CitiFutura. They're one and the same now. Do you think Verux is going to pat you on the back and give you a fat bonus for bringing back that news and all the trouble that will come with it?" Especially with Zenit, their latest competitor, breathing down Verux's collective necks. First it was Verux on CitiFutura. Now it's Zenit on Verux. It's always someone, a company-eat-company-eat-company world.

"We don't know that's what happened. We don't *know* anything," Voller says pointedly. "Maybe shut down was the safest option. Someone set off that beacon, trying to get help. Maybe that was the only choice for whoever was in charge at the time."

Taking a step back from him, I roll my eyes. Right.

"I mean, clearly, the captain lost her shit," he continues. "And the first officer had to—"

"You don't know that," I say, oddly defensive of Linden Gerard.

Kane sighs, rubbing a hand over his face. "Claire is right," he says finally. "As much as I'd like to turn this over to Verux so the families of the passengers and crew will have some closure, I don't think we have that option. With something this big, even money says Verux will try to cover it up."

Lourdes gasps. "They wouldn't do that."

A harsh laugh bubbles up from my throat. "They would. They have." Never in any of the Ferris Outpost post-tragedy analysis was there a mention of the air filters and Verux's decision to hold off on sending more. The focus of those news stories was my rescue and the valiant work "the medical team" had done to try to save everyone before the virus took over.

And as for the colony itself, all the habs were burned in a planned detonation. For "safety." That included all of the dead. My mother never came home from Mars. She has no grave for me to visit. No place for me to see her name or leave flowers. My father, whom I barely remember, rests in a cemetery alone on Earth, with a blank headstone connected to his, where my mother is supposed to be.

Kane nods. "Verux won't want the financial hit that this story will bring. Not to mention the bad optics. They're not exactly Citi-Futura, but with that merger, they're close enough," he continues. "And if we try to speak up anyway, Verux can just fire us and claim we're disgruntled ex-employees, lying about finding the *Aurora* to cause trouble." He hesitates, conflict flickering in his expression, and I know he's thinking about his daughter. "I can't afford that."

"But we have proof!" Voller points to *Speed* and *Grace*. "And we would have had more if *Claire* hadn't—"

"It won't matter," I say. "That's what I'm trying to tell you. Who's going to listen to us over the sound of a hundred Verux lawyers?" My emotions are complicated on that subject. The same web of corporate secrecy and complicated legal maneuvers that had protected Verux for decades had also protected my name and identity. People were interested in me, the survivor, but they would have been even more interested in learning the cause of the Ferris Outpost disaster. The old air filters, yes. But also the Ferris resident who broke quarantine and inadvertently caused the deaths of seventy-three men, women, and children.

So, yes, Verux kept me safe, fed me, housed me, along with any other children who had been left parentless by their various operations/decisions. But those other children were innocent, and I was not.

I am Verux's very own dirty little secret. Perhaps not the only one.

"Wait, does this mean that we're just going to leave these people out here?" Lourdes asks, from behind us, where she's still staring at the sculptures. She sounds wobbly and close to tears again. "We're not going to tell their people that they've been found?"

Shit.

"And if you think Verux will try to hide what happened, then they'll never go home. They'll just float through space forever," Lourdes says, her voice growing louder. "Their families will never know what happened, and they'll never find peace and—"

"I don't know that that's what's going to happen," Kane says gently, taking her by the shoulders and bringing her around to stand with the rest of us. "It was just a guess, Lourdes."

I hesitate. "We could mention that we picked up the beacon's signal, but didn't have time to check into it."

"Good idea, TL," Voller says. "And I'm sure no one will put that together with why we're over two hundred hours off schedule."

The last of my patience evaporates. "And you'd rather, what, march right up to the fucking corporate office and hand over everything they need to—"

"Hell, yes! So what if they fire us? It'll just add credence to our story. They're dumping your ass anyway, so I'm not sure why you care," he adds.

I struggle to keep from reacting to the deliberate barb.

"If they don't honor our Finding claim, so what? With the sculptures and anything else we take now"—Voller gives me a reproachful look, as if my command not to steal from the dead is a ridiculously stilted and antiquated notion, like shaking hands or reading on paper—"we could sell it all to collectors. Shit, some of Nysus's Forum buddies would probably pay big money for anything *Aurora*-related."

He's not . . . wrong. I'd considered it before when it was about removing a faucet or two. But the thought of taking and selling *personal* possessions—a favorite dress, a watch, even a diamond-studded dog leash—makes my stomach roil. Those things belonged to someone; they meant something to someone. Detaching them from the person, literally or figuratively, to sell as objects of interest for collectors obsessed with the tragedy feels . . . obscene.

Items from Ferris Outpost pop up every once in a while, in private auctions, in raids on collectors of other less-than-legal things. I read about them in the newsfeeds. Most of the "relics" are fakes. Or supplies created for Ferris—more jumpsuits with the colony name patch already sewn on and names embroidered just below—that didn't reach us in time.

But some are not. My rescue team apparently stopped for souvenirs when they were supposed to be searching for me. Mostly small things, but they go for big money. A still-folded pair of worn socks with the Ferris name stitched in the cuffs. A plastic bowl from the mess hall hab with "the remains of a final meal still inside." A pair of eyeglasses that I recognized as belonging to one of my mother's colleagues, Dr. Thoreau, who'd always refused to risk her eyesight to corrective surgery or implants. A gold locket that haunted me for years because I have vague memories of a similar necklace around my mother's neck. I never was able to determine whether it was hers. The only photos I have of her—and my father, before he died—show the delicate chain against her neck or the hint of a curved locket beneath the fabric of her shirt, but there's no clear shot of the necklace itself.

Various Verux personnel in white biohazard suits had tried to take my blanket—the one my mother had stitched my name and hab number on—for decontamination once I was away from Ferris. I refused and carried it with me through my decon sessions. Sometimes I wonder if I'd let them take it, if it would have ended up on one of those newsfeeds. In someone's collection.

"No," I say flatly to Voller.

"You're disgusting," Lourdes chokes out.

"No, sweetheart, I'm a pragmatist," Voller says with a tight smile and an obnoxious wink. "And a survivor."

"Like a cockroach," Kane mutters.

"And fucking proud of it," Voller says. "Look, you want to run and hide, that's fine, but—"

"We're not talking about hiding," I say through gritted teeth. "But there's a time to be smart about—"

"Smart means scared. And in this case, poor," Voller says.

It's too hot in here, all of us jammed in together, and I can feel my grip on my temper slipping. "Goddamnit, Voller, if you could just use your brain for once instead of—"

"Everyone, just take a breath," Kane says, holding up his hands. Voller and I both glare at him.

"Actually, there might be another option," Nysus says, his quiet voice breaking through in the moment. He pauses. "According to the Forum, there's something called the Versailles Contingency."

"What the fuck is that?" Voller asks, for once taking the words right out of my mouth.

"It was top secret at the time, not acknowledged in the marketing materials or the released schematics, but some of the high-profile guests were told about it before the launch, as a reassurance of their safety while on board. Like the safe room fads of the late twentieth / early twenty-first century?"

Kane and I stare at each other blankly. Voller shakes his head in annoyance.

Nysus makes an impatient noise at our ignorance. "Never mind. Not important. What's important is that the forward section of the Platinum Level is equipped with bulkhead doors. It can be sealed off—with the bridge—from the rest of the ship. Like a self-sustaining lifeboat inside the ship itself. Its own independent air filtration, grav generator, food supply, water, all of it. It requires the main engines, of course, but—"

"Why would they want that?" I ask. It was a waste of resources to duplicate whole systems like that.

"Versailles," Kane says suddenly. His expression goes grim. "The French Revolution. Eat the rich."

"Exactly," Nysus says.

"You're going to have to give me a little more than that," I say in exasperation. Earth history is not my strong suit.

"It's a reference to a war, four or five centuries ago. The haves versus the have-nots," Kane says. "This contingency Nysus is talking about was meant as extra protection for the wealthy in case something went wrong."

I stare at him in disbelief. "So, in other words, if the main air filtration system goes bad, it's 'good luck, everybody who's not a multibillionaire, we're sealing ourselves up tight with our own air'?"

"Specifically, it was more in case the less fortunate on board decided to take advantage of the isolation and rise up," Nysus clarifies. "A year is a long time. Social order can shift quickly in such seclusion. But yes. You've got it."

"That's repulsive," I say.

But Voller laughs. "That's fucking brilliant. Housekeeping gets tired of cleaning up dog shit and decides to strike, what can anyone do to them? The brig, if there even is one, isn't big enough for everyone. Can't kick them off the ship or send them home. Not for a whole year. They can live like kings and queens, and there's way more of them than the Platinum Level eggs." He sounds delighted.

"Why the hell didn't they actually use this Versailles thing instead of taking the ship off course?" I demand.

Voller shifts his attention to me, striking a mock thoughtful pose, his fingers on his chin. "It's interesting that you should ask that. Because we just don't know. Hmmm. Why is that again? Why don't we know fucking anything? Because somebody—"

I launch myself at Voller, shoving him back against the wall until his head hits with a muted thunk. "Will you shut the hell up about that black box?" I say through clenched teeth.

"Claire." Kane intervenes, looping an arm around my waist and pulling me back. The urge to fight free rises up, but I manage to quell it in time, embarrassment taking its place.

"I'm fine," I say after a moment, twisting away from him.

"We don't have the codes to open it anyway," Nysus points out. "Only CitiFutura—or Verux now—does."

Voller rubs the back of his head with an exaggerated wince. I know it's exaggerated but that doesn't stop the flood of shame from pouring over me, until I feel stripped bare. I lost control. I don't ever lose control, not like that. Then again, I also saw my dead mother today for the first time in more than twenty years. Or, thought I had.

Not command material. Those three words stamped in conclusion on my record, on me.

Maybe they were right, after all.

"Can you get to the point, Nysus, before TL kills me?" Voller asks, grinning at me, pleased to have triggered a reaction. Because he's an asshole. Though he may be an asshole who has a point. I don't know anymore.

I squeeze my eyes shut, rubbing at the stress headache forming in the center of my forehead.

"I think we could do it," Nysus says, his words speeding together in his excitement. "Clear the Platinum Level and the bridge of . . . any former occupants. Run a diagnostic on the lifeboat systems. Check for known contaminants throughout the ship, just to be sure. Air and water. Though I didn't see any evidence of anything like that, vomiting, illness, et cetera." He seems to be talking to himself now as much as us. "And of course, we'll need to make sure that the main engines still have enough charge to—"

"Nysus," Kane says, even his tone beginning to sound strained. "What are you talking about?"

"Oh," Nysus says, sounding startled. "I mean, we could seal ourselves in. Use the Versailles Contingency and bring the *Aurora* back ourselves."

11

Silence has a different quality to it when you're the only one left alive. It's thicker. Heavier somehow. When I woke up in the Med-Bay hab at Ferris, that last morning that I expected everything to be normal, still covered in the dampness of a fever breaking and dizzy with the ringing in my ear that would become my new constant companion, I noticed the change immediately. The sound of my mother's labored breathing was gone. No voices or footsteps in the corridor. No jagged bouts of coughing—nearby or in the distance—as there had been constantly for weeks.

Just a weighty, unnatural silence that refused to break, even with the sound of my sobs, my footsteps staggering down the passageways, my voice calling for someone, anyone.

Until days later, when little noises resumed. In the dark, the sound of a single step, from rooms and passageways where there were only bodies. The shift of fabric over skin in movement. The susurration of whispers nearly lost in the uneven roar of the air filtration system. My name called over and over again. *Claire. Claire. Claire.* Becca's giggle inviting me to come play.

My mother telling me what I needed to do to survive, even as her body lay still and empty, slowly decaying on the floor of the MedBay.

I was alone, and somehow not.

According to my file, the official diagnosis upon my rescue was that of a particularly severe case of post-traumatic stress disorder, complete with auditory and visual hallucinations.

And yet, I know that wasn't true. Isn't true. I was there. I know what I saw, what I heard.

So, the thought of voluntarily submitting to a similar experience locks my voice in my throat and raises goose bumps along my arms and at the back of my neck, despite the heat of the four of us in the galley.

"That would take months," Voller protests.

"I don't want to leave them behind, but I don't want to lock myself up in a tomb with them, either," Lourdes says shakily.

"I don't see how it's any different than being in LINA outside the ship. Or even as we are now," Nysus says. "We would be sealed in."

Next to me, Lourdes gives a shudder. And she's right to. Doors didn't matter on Ferris. I can't imagine that sealed bulkheads would be any different.

"No," Kane says flatly, his mouth a thin line. "This is not a viable option. We're still not sure what happened to them, and months alone, locked up inside—"

My throat closes off my air abruptly, and I cough, turning away from them as I try to catch my breath.

"Claire?" Kane asks. His hand catches my shoulder, and I'm caught between the urge to lean into the comfort and the desire to pull away to prove I don't need it. In the end, I do neither, staying still beneath his touch. "Are you okay?" he asks. "I'm sorry, I wasn't thinking," he adds in a quieter voice, sounding chagrined.

I shake my head, waving away his words. ". . . okay."

"Why are you apologizing to her?" Voller demands. "It's our lives you're ruining."

Kane's hand leaves my shoulder as he turns away, and I feel the loss as if he's taken something vital from me.

"That's being a little dramatic, don't you think?" Kane asks Voller. "Even for you."

"Dramatic?" Voller scoffs. "Me? I'm not the one who was planning to off herself by floating off into—"

"Just stop!" Lourdes shouts, holding her hands over her ears. "I can't stand this!"

Beneath their bickering, I can hear Nysus saying something over the intercom, but his words are lost in the noise. My temper flares to life, and I spin to face them. "Everyone, shut up!" I shout.

A moment of stunned silence follows, but I know it won't last.

"What was that, Nysus?" I ask.

"Oh, uh, I said, what if it wasn't months? What if it was just a few days?"

My goose bumps return, prickling my skin.

"Not possible," Voller says immediately. "We're already ninety-some hours away from where we were in K147 and that's hell and gone from Earth. What good would that do us?"

His words trigger a connection in my brain. "The commweb," I say slowly.

"Exactly," Nysus says with satisfaction.

"What are you talking about?" Voller asks in exasperation.

"We don't have to get all the way to Earth," I say, piecing it together. "All we need to do is get the *Aurora* back to known space. Back to the commweb. We send a message, a live feed from the *Aurora* bridge, something that couldn't possibly be faked, tagged with her signature—"

"Upload to the Forum, the newsfeeds," Nysus adds, excited.

"We'll be sitting in the middle of our proof," I say. "Proof that everyone will be able to see and hear. They can even come see her for themselves, if they want to come out that far. Mystery solved. The *Aurora* has been found. No opportunity for secrecy."

"And what fool is going to punish the heroes who found and returned the *Aurora* to safety?" Voller asks, a grin sliding across his pointed face, making him look even slyer, though his delight is clearly genuine. "Sure, go on, give them a reward. Give them their percentage for the Finding claim. They brought back the whole damn ship." He gives a whoop and slaps the wall behind him for emphasis.

"They'll finally get to go home," Lourdes adds, with a relieved nod, finally releasing her death grip on the scripture capsule around her neck.

That alone brings a small smile to my face. Because the other part of this plan, the part where we spend days alone inside the *Aurora* . . . my heart lurches in my chest, like it's trying to break free of my rib cage.

Kane clears his throat. "Can I speak to you about this? Privately?"

No. Because I know exactly what he's going to say.

I look to Lourdes. "Will it be a problem connecting the *Aurora* to the upgraded commweb?" We'd be dealing with old tech. The commweb was much smaller and less sophisticated, in its infancy, when the *Aurora* launched.

"I . . . I don't think so," she says. Then she nods, growing more confident. "I can do it."

I turn to Voller. "Do you know how to fly it?"

"I can fly anything with wings, baby," he boasts.

I sigh. "Do I really need to remind you that it doesn't have wings?"

"It's a saying, boss. I got it. No worries."

It's hard not to roll my eyes. Suddenly I'm the "boss" once we're doing what Voller wants.

"I can work with him," Nysus pipes in. "The basic controls should be the same. The operating system is an older and slightly more complicated version of our own Shenandoah 15.7. I'm sure I have the specs for it in here somewhere . . ." He trails off as he, presumably, begins digging for the stored information.

"Great," I say in a clipped voice. All business, professional. That's the only thing that's going to get me through this: focusing on the job. "Also, I don't think we should eat or drink anything on board, just in case. It's possible the water may have been—"

"It's too risky," Kane interjects, moving around Lourdes to stand in front of me. But what his gaze tells me is that he thinks it's too risky for *me*. Maybe he's right. He's seen my file.

Claire. Claire. Claire. Those voices calling to me.

Sometimes I still wake up in the night, hearing them, hearing Becca's laugh, and it always takes me a minute to realize it's a nightmare. It has to be a nightmare.

But none of that's going to change my mind.

"Listen up." I focus my attention on Voller and Lourdes because I can't quite look at Kane. "I'm not going to order anyone to do this. Did you hear me, Nysus?"

"Affirmative," he says in a distracted tone.

"If we have to, we split between the LINA and the *Aurora*. Kane and Lourdes, you can take LINA and follow us."

"But you're going on the *Aurora*," Kane says.

"Yes," I confirm. "I am."

"You know I'm in," Voller says, quite unnecessarily.

"Nysus?" I ask.

Voller snorts.

"Are you kidding? This is the chance of a lifetime," Nysus says. "To be inside the *Aurora*, frozen in time, exactly as they left it when . . . whatever happened, happened?"

"I'll go," Lourdes says in a small voice. "I don't want to be here by myself." She shoots Kane an apologetic look. "Sorry, Behrens."

He shrugs tightly.

I make myself meet Kane's eyes, asking the silent question.

Kane exhales in a sigh, and I know I've won. If boarding and staying on a ship of the damned can be considered winning.

"So, it's settled," I say crisply. "Lourdes, work with Nysus on what you'll need to get connected to the commweb. We may need to borrow parts from LINA," I say.

She bobs her head in agreement and then squeezes past Voller to the corridor, heading for Nysus.

"Voller, get ready to head back over. If the diagnostics show anything out of the ordinary, we're done. Kane and I will help with . . . other prep." While also making sure that Voller's enthusiasm doesn't cause him to "miss" anything.

Voller salutes and saunters off toward his quarters, leaving just Kane and me.

The air immediately thickens with tension, and I wish I could run. But I keep my boots firmly planted in place and straighten my shoulders. If he wants to do this, we're going to do it.

Kane studies me, gaze boring into me. "They don't know. They can't understand." Jaw tight, he shakes his head in disbelief. "But I do know and I still can't figure out what you're thinking. Why are you doing this?" He throws his hands up in exasperation. "I don't think it's possible to dream up a worse scenario for you, one that could possibly include more triggers." He edges closer to me. "A month. You were trapped, alone in the dark for a month, with nothing but the dead and your hallucin—"

"I know," I say tightly. "I was there. Remember?"

"Do *you*?" he shoots back. He pauses, his eyes widening slightly. "Wait. Is this about what happened? Are you trying to punish yourself for—"

"No!" Not exactly. How do I explain that I always knew the consequences would one day come back around? That there's a difference between me punishing myself and punishment being exacted?

"Then what are you thinking?" he demands.

"I'm thinking I don't have a choice. I want a future that doesn't exist for me right now. One I choose, out here." I jab my hand in the general direction of space. "I want my transport company, something I own and control for the first time in my life, even though it scares me. I want Voller to blow his share on expensive Scotch and redheads. I want Lourdes to donate it to her church for that new building she's always talking about."

His eyebrows arc upward in surprise. I *do* listen, even if I don't interact.

"And I want Nysus to be able to buy . . ." I pause. "Whatever it is he'd want to buy."

Kane's mouth quirks in a reluctant smile.

"And I want you to have time with your daughter, to see her more than once every eighteen months for a couple of weeks." My voice cracks, and I avoid his eyes, then, afraid mine will reveal too much. "And if I have to go through hell to get all of that, then fine." I've been expecting hell, via the other shoe dropping, for years anyway.

"Claire," he says softly.

"And yeah, maybe some of it is about righting a wrong." I fold my arms across my chest in defense, keeping my attention focused on a deep scratch on the floor. "My mother has no grave on Earth because Verux destroyed the habs at Ferris. There's no place to visit her or leave flowers."

Or beg for her forgiveness.

"CitiFutura is responsible for those people, whether they died through an accident or a deliberate act," I continue heatedly. "Their families deserve answers, they deserve to have their people back. Not just the wealthy news-getters but the crew who served, too. They don't get left behind because it's more convenient for Verux these days, their names just carved into another shitty monument in marble with no truth behind it." The Ferris memorial is in what's left of Grant Park, in Chicago. I've seen pictures. The *Aurora* monument is actually on the Verux campus in California, a tribute to "pioneering souls lost," erected on the ten-year anniversary of the day CitiFutura lost contact.

As soon as I stop talking, silence crowds back in, and the creeping horror of having revealed too much, of having peeled back layers of defenses that took years to construct, crawls over me.

My face goes hot, eyes stinging, and I turn away to stare up at the light panel overhead, willing the moisture in my eyes to evaporate. I can't look at Kane and risk seeing pity.

"Besides, it's three days," I add, working to make my voice sound less choked. "It won't be that bad."

At this point, I'm not sure who I'm trying to convince. Damnit, I should have just kept my mouth shut.

His hand on my shoulder gently tugs me back to face him.

"You are either the bravest woman I have ever met or the craziest," he says, before pulling me closer, his arms encircling me.

I *know* I should shove away, but in that moment, my weakness is stronger than my resolve. My arms seem to rise of their own accord, locking around him, my fist wrapping tight in the back of his T-shirt. To hold and be held for the first time in a long time doesn't feel as scary as I expected, like tiptoeing to the edge of a dark abyss and staring down.

Instead, it feels like a relief, a weight lifted.

"Why can't it be both? It's probably both," I say, my voice shaky and muffled against his collarbone. He smells of warm cotton, the comfortingly familiar faint metallic tang of LINA's water, and soap.

"It probably is," he agrees with a laugh.

Kane steps back without letting go, his hand tipping up my chin, and he frowns at the tear tracks on my face before he wipes them gently away.

My gaze catches on his mouth and before I can stop myself, before I can even think, I push myself up and press my lips against his.

He makes a soft noise in surprise, and then pulls back. Just an inch or two, but enough. "Claire," he begins in that gentle voice.

Shock at my behavior roils me, followed almost immediately by the scorching heat of utter and complete humiliation. What the fuck was I thinking? What am I *doing*?

I yank away from Kane, scrambling for words, something, anything to make this moment end. "I . . . um, glad that's settled and we're on the same page. Let me know if you and Voller have any questions about prep."

"Claire, wait," he says, his forehead furrowed with concern.

"I'll see you later." I push past him to the corridor and blessed escape, the flush in my cheeks pulsing in time with my heartbeat. *What the hell is wrong with me?*

Definitely not the first occasion I've had to ask myself that question. Probably won't be the last, either.

12

The second trip through the *Aurora*, however disturbing, should have been less alarming, simply for its familiarity. The mobile of the dead floats on in the atrium. The smeary message in blood is unchanged—I expect the one on the Platinum Level remains unreadable—and no new ones have appeared that I can see.

The only difference—a sign of our presence—is simply dust from the wood putty and splinters from where we pulled the statues free. It floats like a cloud of tiny confetti at the top and bottom of the stairs.

And yet, the weighted feeling of dread has not abated in the least. If anything, it's worse. What was once an uncomfortable tightness in my chest is now a booted foot standing on my breastbone, heavy heel digging in. The silence around us feels expectant, as if we're performers in front of an unseen—but curious and impatient— audience. My skin crawls with the sensation of being watched, and my head feels tight, like my skull is being squeezed in a vise.

It's in your mind, Claire. Stress and bad memories. That's all. Get over it.

It doesn't help, of course, that Kane is right behind me and Voller, bringing up the rear. Kane hasn't said anything yet, but I can *feel* him wanting to.

Once we reach the spiral staircase in the atrium, Voller bounds ahead, up the side, just as we did before.

"Remember, check the air quality and engine function for the main diag, and see if you can find the ship's log," I say to Voller over the open comm channel in my helmet. If the air is contaminated in here or the engines aren't capable of propulsion, then game over. The log, if we can find it, may contain helpful information on what happened. "Then the lifeboat systems, and tell me before you start on those." I have work to do before the separate gravity generator and environmentals system associated with the Versailles Contingency can be tested.

"Yeah, I got it, TL."

"And if you can get the lights on, all the better."

Voller raises a gloved hand in acknowledgment or dismissal as he pulls himself along the wall before disappearing around the corner on the Platinum Level.

"Behrens, you go, too," I say, beginning my ascent. "I want your take on the engines before we commit to anything." I sound calm, efficient, just a team leader giving direction. Nothing to see here. Avoiding Kane entirely would have been easier, but it's not an option right now.

And it really won't be an option if we seal ourselves into this ship. Then we'll be out of routine, out of our familiar roles. I won't technically even be the team leader anymore, and the thought of operating without that familiar and comforting cloak of authority, the boundary that can't be crossed, the necessary distance between the others and me, makes me feel exposed and shaky.

"I can still hear you, you know that, right?" Voller asks. "I don't need help with the engines."

"Negative, TL," Kane says after a moment. "This is too much for one person."

I freeze, my grip tightening on the stairway railing. "Too much for one person or too much for *me*?" The words roll out cold and hard before I can stop them. *Poor Claire, Child #1, a survivor and brave, but pitiable.* "I can handle it," I say through clenched teeth, which sounds oh so convincing.

A beat of silence holds on the open comm channel.

"This is fun. I'm uncomfortable," Voller announces.

"Shut up, Voller," Lourdes whispers from back on the LINA where she and Nysus are still working.

"The search will be faster and more thorough if we're both on it," Kane says evenly, as if he completely missed the byplay between

Voller and Lourdes. "We can start at one end, work our way up port-side and down the starboard, so we don't miss anything. Then I can check on the engines, make sure we're good to go."

I don't need a babysitter. It's on the tip of my tongue, but I stop myself. Because I don't want to raise more questions than this conversation already has. Voller, Lourdes, and Nysus don't know about my past, and I'd prefer to keep it that way.

"Fine." I pull myself up the rest of the way on the stairwell without waiting for a response. At the top of the stairs, I push off toward the corridor on the left.

The first suite is just inside, and I catch myself on the doorframe.

"Twenty-four suites in the forward section on the Platinum Level. Each with a sitting area and a private bath," Nysus says helpfully in my ear. "Twelve on portside, where you are. Twelve on starboard. Once the bulkheads are sealed, going past the bridge will be the only way from one side to the other. Oh, and there's an emergency crew bunk room across from the bridge."

I try to picture what he's talking about. I hadn't noticed another door near the bridge. But I'd been distracted by Linden Gerard and Cage Wallace at the time.

"Records of who booked what suite were—and still are—confidential. So I don't know what you're going to find," Nysus adds grimly.

He means *who.* Maybe these suites will be empty, the occupants already down in the atrium. Or on a lower level somewhere. But maybe not. And we can't implement the Versailles Contingency without being sure. No matter what killed them, trapping decomposing bodies in here will put us at more risk of disease—not to mention creating a thoroughly unpleasant and horrifying environment for the trip.

A thorough search—and relocation of anyone we find—is necessary.

"Engines cycling up in diagnostic," Voller announces, and the low hum-rumble begins again and grows louder.

I can feel the vibration of the engines through my gloves, and after a moment, the atrium glows brightly once more. Some of the light reaches into the corridor but not enough.

Kane joins me, catching himself on the opposite side of the doorframe. Then he reaches down and tests the old-fashioned brass lever handle. It moves under the pressure, but only a little.

"Locked. You have the key?" he asks.

"Yes." I fumble for the utility pocket in the right leg of my suit.

"Are you sure about this?" I ask Nysus, pulling it free and holding it up.

"It's a Platinum Level master key," Nysus insists. "Housekeeping had them. Should open any and all of the suites." Nysus had it printed according to the *Aurora* specs on the Forum.

"But it's . . . weird." Granted, it was printed in the bright green recyclable plastic we use to print new toothbrushes and coffee mugs when needed. But it's more than that. It is huge—probably five inches long—and oddly shaped. A long, skinny barrel with two downward-pointing projections near the end.

I've never seen a key like it before. Even the concept of a physical key is antiquated, though I've seen a few. Mostly in online museums.

"It's based on something called a skeleton key," Nysus says. "Old, wealthy house tradition. Each suite has its own individual lock and key, which would have been replaced between cruises. No digital locks means the doors are completely unhackable. Another security measure. Only housekeeping and crew would have the master skeleton key."

Kane grunts. "Sounds kind of expensive." He looks at me, seeking more than agreement.

"Impractical, a dumb idea," I add firmly, avoiding his gaze and focusing on getting the key in the lock.

"If you watch some of the earlier *Dunleavy* episodes, the keys were status symbols," Nysus says. "Something to wear on display. Platinum Level passengers had special jewelry made at the jeweler on board, long necklaces and belts in precious metals, to display the keys. Cattie and Opal were arguing about what to get, and then

Opal accused Cattie of copying her idea. It's how they ended the second episode."

"Entering suite 124," I say, turning the key carefully. I don't want it to break off in the lock. That'll only delay us further. The other end of the key meets resistance. I hesitate and then twist a little harder. Something inside the mechanism gives then, and the click of the lock releasing is louder than I expected, clearly audible even through my helmet and over the sound of my breathing.

"Voller, any luck with the lights back here?" Kane asks.

"I checked. Lights for this section of the Platinum Level are part of the lifeboat systems," Voller says. "They'll have to wait. Air and engines first, then lifeboat. That's what TL said." He manages to sound both irritated at the question and delighted to be able to tell Kane no.

"Right," Kane says.

Which means we're doing this in the dark, other than our helmet lights.

Keeping one hand on the doorframe, I push down on the handle and shove inward. The door swings open soundlessly. The wide, darkened space beyond is impenetrable, outside the narrow path of our lights. They illuminate a set of chairs and a sofa in that same cream-colored leather as in the atrium, a glossy wood credenza on the far left side, adjacent to floor-to-ceiling windows, which reflect two bright points back at us, along with our own vague outlines. A half wall to the right divides the sitting area from, presumably, the bedroom. Random items float in and out of view, each moving in its own orbit. Pillows. A hairbrush. Tiny cosmetic jars and bottles and palettes. A scarf. Shoes tumbling together in mismatched clumps.

A bundle of glossy fur . . .

I suck in a breath sharply. There's at least one dog on board, we know that. I saw the leash.

Kane's helmet light tracks the bundle as he pushes into the room. He catches himself on the top of the bolted-down chair, and after a moment, a startled laugh escapes him. "It's a wig, Claire." He touches the edge of it, and it shifts in response, revealing the netting underneath.

I follow him in, catching myself on the half wall, relief pouring over me. The passengers chose to be here; the dog was simply brought along, no decision in the matter.

"Good dog," I mutter, hoping he or she managed to escape to a slightly less horrible fate, though I'm not entirely sure what that would be.

Kane turns to face me, a grin flashing at me beneath the faceplate of his helmet. And for a moment, the hard knot of tension in my stomach eases a little.

But then, that smile melts away, his gaze fixed on something behind me, deeper in the room.

"Kane. Kane? What is it?" I crane my head to see what he's staring at, but my helmet is blocking my view. I twist my whole body around until I'm facing the correct direction.

The sight sends an electric jolt down my spine.

"Oh my God," Nysus says in my ear.

Beyond the half wall, in the bedroom area, a young woman—a girl, really—drifts silently in the darkness, above the king-sized bed.

Her slim legs and vulnerable-looking bare feet peek out from beneath the gently undulating hem of her white dress. Frenzied slashes and cuts mar the tight torso of the dress and the girl's arms and chest, reducing both skin and fabric to ribbons, but strangely, there's little blood.

The nails on her toes have gone blue. Her thin blond hair hovers in a cloud around her head, and her bulging eyes are open and unseeing, filmy with death and frosted over in tiny crystals. Her hand is locked at her throat, fingers looped inside . . . something.

Gold buried deep in her frozen skin winks in the light, and I trace the line of it. A necklace, more of a chain, is around her neck and looped over the brass light fixture on the wall above the bed, holding her in place. She's hanging, or would be if there was gravity. A key—heavy, metallic, and a now-familiar shape—bobs at the far end of the chain, near the fixture. Her fingertips remain caught inside the chain, as if she changed her mind at the last minute, or as if she wanted to be sure it would hold.

Fuck.

I squeeze my eyes shut for a moment, but the image hangs behind my darkened eyelids. Her mouth moves, trying to speak, her fingers wiggling at her throat in an attempt to gain air.

No. None of that. I open my eyes immediately, focusing instead on the carpet, a diamond pattern in cream and brown.

"That's Cattie Dunleavy," Nysus says quietly. "Her sister, Opal, is out in the atrium."

Opal with the knife taped to her hand?

"What . . ." Kane rasps. Then he clears his throat and tries again. "What happened?"

"I don't know," Nysus says, his voice trembling. "I . . ."

"She was already dead," I say slowly, putting the pieces together and glancing up at her to confirm my theory. "That's why there's no blood. Someone stabbed her after she died." After she hung herself or someone else hung her. I suppose it's impossible to know for sure.

But going after someone with a knife like that, when they're already dead? That's rage, both excessive and personal.

Did her sister hate her that much?

I look up to Cattie's face, not even sure what I'm searching for. This time, though, I notice red parallel lines etched into her face, above her eyebrows and just below her lower lids.

"Nysus, do you see that?" I ask, squinting. Maybe it's burst blood vessels or the start of decay. Depending on how long the heat and air were on after this happened, that could be. But the lines are so precise . . .

"What, exactly?" he asks, uncomfortable. "The video feed from your helmet cam isn't exactly high-res and I, uh . . . kind of . . ."

He doesn't want to study her that closely. I don't blame him. But in spite of everything we know—or suppose—I'm still on the hunt for answers as to what went down and how.

I push off the half wall to move closer for a better look. Unfortunately, I miss my grab for the edge of the bed, and I collide with her legs, which are disturbingly solid in a way that human flesh should not be.

Her frozen body dangles and shifts on the chain from the collision, and an involuntary shudder racks me within my suit. But I manage to catch myself on the nightstand, bringing me nearly face-to-face with Cattie.

Up close, the damage to her neck is even more horrifying. The necklace looks like a wire cutting through clay.

Her face, though . . . The lines on her skin are actually thin bloody gouges *in* her skin. Her eyes are open, so it's not possible to tell for sure, but I'm guessing the wounds are continuous from above her eyebrows, across her eyelids, and down. "I think someone tried to claw at her eyes." Jesus, her sister again?

"Claire," Kane says behind me. "Her hand."

Automatically, I look to the fingers wrapped in the chain at her neck, but then I see what Kane has noticed: on her other hand, the one floating gently at her side, her manicured nails are broken and ragged and her fingertips are bloodied.

"You think she did this?" I ask in disbelief. "Why would she claw at her own eyes?" Especially if she was already planning on hanging herself.

"I don't know," Kane says, tension in his voice.

"Oh, Cattie," Nysus says mournfully. "She was always the nicer one."

His sadness makes me feel slightly less gruesome about the next portion of our task. At least someone here knows her—sort of—and cares about her specific fate beyond a general mourning for the loss of life.

Trying not to look too closely at Cattie herself, I examine the loops of chain over the brass fixture. Getting her untangled from that will be next to impossible. It must have taken extreme determination to succeed. Or extreme desperation.

Taking the fixture off the wall is going to be the easiest way.

Carefully, I locate the screws and work them loose with my

screwdriver until the entire fixture comes loose. After disconnecting it from the wires behind, I grab for it before it can float away, my gloved fingers locking around one of the brass arms with an old-fashioned bulb at the end. It surely isn't a real incandescent but made to look like one, which was, once, made to look like flame. A reproduction of an expensive, wasteful technology, simply for that exclusive ambience that certain passengers were willing to pay for it. To show that they *could* pay for it.

Taking a deep breath, with my hand tight on the fixture, I push off the nightstand toward the door. Cattie floats along behind me, like an obscene balloon on a string.

When I have to catch myself at the door to make sure we will both fit through, her body collides with mine, that solid, impenetrable mass smashing right up against me. Only my tightened grip on the wooden doorframe keeps me from flying out into the corridor, all tangled up with Cattie and the chain around her neck.

"Mark the door," I say to Kane through clenched teeth because it's taking more effort than I thought it would to keep from screaming.

Then I lead Cattie out and down to the atrium. At least she'll be with her sister out here, outside the bulkhead doors. Though, it seems perhaps neither of them would be happy about that.

When I return, Kane has two *X*s on the door in the red tape we use to flag potential trouble areas on a beacon.

I look to him in question. He's waiting with the key outside the next suite. "Why two?"

"So we'll know if we've searched it and if it was . . . occupied," he says with a grimace.

That suite and the one after it are both empty. Kane and I search them carefully, just in case. Checking the shower and the closets.

In the third, however, no search is necessary. An older man with a graying beard and a much younger woman, her glossy dark hair drifting around her face, rest on the bed together, so peaceful looking that it's almost possible to ignore the fact that they're floating several inches above the mattress. And that their wrists are bound to handles on the nightstands on either side of the bed and to each other in the middle. Ties, belts, shoelaces, all strung together to keep them in place.

The room is tidy, spotless, except for the two of them, and a water glass spinning through the air along with several small white packets. I pull one from the air as it drifts past me.

"Sleeping pills," I say. "From the *Aurora*'s MedBay, it looks like."

But Kane isn't listening, his attention fixed on the couple on the bed, more specifically the man. "I think this is Andrew Davies," Kane says flatly. "He looks . . . like the images I remember."

"And presumably not his wife," I say.

"Presumably."

He doesn't say anything else for a long moment. Not every day you come across someone you admired frozen (in this case, literally) in their last moments.

"I'm sorry," I say.

He shakes his head. "Why did they tie themselves down?"

"The gravity," I begin.

"No, look." He points to their wrists, which are scraped raw and bloodied. "At some point, they were trying to get free."

It is, unfortunately, yet another scenario that doesn't make sense and likely won't without more information.

"Any luck on the ship's log or remnants of it?" I ask Voller.

"Negative," he responds. "It's gone. That has to be deliberate."

"Ny?" I ask.

He makes a humming-thinking noise. "Usually if there was corruption in a file, we'd see evidence of that." In the background, I hear Lourdes murmuring to him as they work. "But it may be part of a larger data loss. I'll have to check once I'm on board."

In the next suite's bathroom, a woman is frozen in a chunk of water near the ceiling that was once a bath in the tub. It's hard to know if she drowned when the gravity generator shut off or if she was already dead by that point. Her expression, though, one of permanent surprise, leads me to believe it was the former.

"That's Princess Margaretha of Sweden," Nysus says quietly.

The gold faucet on the sink across from her catches my attention, and a pang of ingrained longing hits hard. It's both smaller and more dramatic in reality. The gold gleams in our helmet lights, the name *Aurora* carved in dark swirling letters on both sides. It sets off a strange sense of dislocation in my brain. Like it can't be real. Or I'm not.

But maybe that's just because of the dead princess floating in the corner.

Still, the temptation to unscrew the attaching hardware and take the faucet with me is hard to resist. But I manage.

A couple doors down, two men in pajamas seem to have beaten each other to death with anything that wasn't bolted down—including what appears to be some of the Dunleavy camera equipment—dying just inches apart in the suite, likely from blood loss. Nysus makes me grab the video equipment and any device that looks like it could have footage on it and pull it all into the hall.

Strangely, neither of the men have anything to do with the show, given that one is a former professional basketball player and the other an aging movie star.

I don't recognize the basketball player—Anthony Lightfoot, according to Kane.

"Lightfoot may or may not have been involved with one of the Dunleavys," Nysus pipes up. "Like secret sex vid involved."

I wince. "Yeah, got it, Ny."

"But it's never been confirmed," Nysus adds. The collected video equipment in what is, presumably, Lightfoot's room seems to indicate some kind of connection, though.

But the actor is Jasen Wyman, most familiar to me for playing the doting grandfather in the kids' fantasy adventure movie *Castle Roarke*. But he was famous for his heartthrob blue eyes and lust-inducing smile about three decades before that.

It's surreal to see him here, what's left of his famous face staring sightlessly across the room.

In the next suite, a skinny guy in a crew uniform hides in a closet, probably under the pile of furs that now float around him and surrounded by a small hoard of food. His arms and legs are huddled around his body, as if that would help with the cold.

We come across another famous actress, two more world-renowned athletes (soccer and golf) and their wives, a model that I recognized from a perfume commercial, and several more royals from various countries, per Nysus.

In all, fewer than half of the suites are . . . were occupied. But the deaths are all the same: suicide, murder, death from exposure. Over and over again.

The emergency crew bunk room across from the bridge is empty and mostly undisturbed. The sheets are pushed back—and floating—on one of the four mattresses, but the other bunks are still made tightly. Similarly, one of the metal lockers at the foot of each bunk is open an inch or two. When Kane opens it to look inside, it's a random assortment of personal items. A change of underclothes, a comb, shaving kit, etc.

A locked door on the far wall reveals emergency rations and water stored neatly on shelves, seemingly untouched.

All of which supports my theory that whatever happened, happened fast. And, based on the deaths we've seen, violently.

Which may help explain why we miss the last passenger. At first.

We're midway down the port side again, on our final cursory glance-through of the cleared rooms, when Kane stops me in one of them. "Wait. Do you see that?"

He gestures toward the bed in front of us.

At first I don't see anything different than before. Pillows and a rumpled white comforter hovering above the bed. But then I glance down.

"Are those . . ." he begins.

"Yeah," I say flatly.

Fingers just barely poking out from beneath the shelter of the bed. Attached, presumably, to a hand and a possibly whole person. Damn.

I push to the edge of the bed, catching hold to balance myself, and take a breath. Whoever it is is long dead. They can't hurt me.

I bend down to shine the light underneath the bed, to see what we're dealing with.

And she's staring right at me. Or, she would be, if she still had eyes. The place where they should be is a smooth white strip. Like someone simply erased them.

I jerk back.

"Claire?" Kane grabs at me to keep my momentum from carrying me backward.

"You okay, TL?" Nysus asks. "Your vitals—"

"Fine," I gasp. "I'm fine. Just . . . surprised me." Nothing like looking under the bed and getting a face full of nightmares.

"She's . . . something's wrong," I say, panting.

"Watch your oxygen," Nysus says.

I nod, but I can't seem to slow my breathing down. My heart is thundering, blood roaring in my ears.

"Here, let me," Kane says.

He works his way around me to the bed and then gently tugs at those stiffened fingers.

It's hard not to squeeze my eyes shut. But I need to see, to understand.

In a moment, she comes free, sliding smoothly out from under the bed.

This woman, whoever she was, is naked and beaten to hell. Her cheeks are purple, puffy and swollen with bruises and cuts . . . beneath the ragged blindfold she wears.

I exhale. "A blindfold."

A narrow band of white cloth is wrapped so tightly around her head that the skin rolls over it at the edges. That's what gave me the impression that her eyes were gone.

"Whoa," Nysus breathes.

"She was hiding," Kane says.

"Probably from whoever hurt her." My breathing is slowly returning to normal. "But why didn't she take the blindfold off?"

"Claire." Kane points. "Look at her ears." He sounds grim.

Beneath the blunt cut of her dark hair, white threads and ragged strands are poking out. Scraps of that same white fabric, stuffed into her ears. Makeshift earplugs of some kind.

If someone else had covered her eyes and ears, why hadn't she removed that stuff before getting under the bed, to give herself a better chance of seeing or hearing her attackers coming?

Unless she did it to herself. I shudder.

"Let's get her downstairs with the others," Kane says.

We carry her, just like the others, carefully to the sunny atrium. I drag the comforter along with us.

"Someone has a lot of explaining to do," Kane mutters after gently letting go of her near the others we've found. "This is going to be big news."

"Yeah," I say. But as I'm attempting to drape the comforter over her—exceedingly difficult without gravity—my gaze is caught by First Officer Wallace, who is lying . . . floating nearby. We'd moved him, along with Captain Gerard, a while ago. But down here, in the light, at this angle . . .

Voller is right; the left side of his head is mostly gone, a gruesome mess of an exit wound. But his ear is still intact and just inside of it, an unexpected burst of color. Bright orange. Not blood, clearly, or bone or brain matter.

I squint at his remains, trying to figure out what I'm seeing. "Kane, do you—"

But his hand grasps tight on my arm, too tight, and his breath catches audibly over the mic in his helmet.

"What's wrong?" I look toward him. His gaze is fixed on a darkened hallway across the atrium. Not the one we came in; another leading to more lower-level guest rooms. But I don't see anything alarming. Or, at least, more alarming than what's been here the whole time.

"I thought I saw . . ." He shakes his head, releasing my arm. "Never mind."

But the adrenaline once awakened in me again is not likely to go back to sleep so easily. "No," I say firmly. "Tell me."

"It's nothing."

But I wait, and eventually he continues. "I thought I saw some-one at the edge of the corridor, watching us."

Alertness topples into a clear, pure spike of panic. "Voller, do you have a read on another ship out there?" With the LINA in the cargo bay, we're blind and trapped. If a salvage team has boarded another way—by cutting a hole through the hull somewhere—we're in big trouble.

No response.

"Voller?" I repeat, raising my voice.

"Never mind, Voller," Kane says. At the same time, Voller finally answers with a distracted, "Yeah, what?"

I stare at Kane in astonishment.

"Make up your minds," Voller says. "Some of us are trying to work here."

"It's not necessary," Kane says to me, and even through the face-plate I can see his chagrin.

"You can't know that," I argue. "And before we—"

"I can," he says, clearly trying to keep a lid on his frustration. "Because it wasn't someone in an enviro suit. Just something vaguely person-shaped. Which is impossible." He shakes his head, the movement minimal with the restriction of his suit and helmet. "I guess I'm just more affected by this than I thought."

Which is more than understandable. And he sounds annoyed at himself but certain.

Still, I can't shake the nagging sense that he's holding something back.

"Is everything all right?" Lourdes asks cautiously.

"Yes," Kane answers before I can say anything. "We're good."

"I think Nysus and I have what we need for the upgrade," Lourdes says.

"And I'm already packed up," Nysus adds, eagerness clear in his voice.

I look around me at the passengers we've brought to the atrium, bobbing gently at various heights above the ground. They look like seeds on a breeze just before they land and bear gruesome fruit.

"I think we're as ready as we're going to be. Voller, what's your status?"

I expect to have to prompt him again, but his reply comes immediately in the form of a sigh.

"Air came back clean, no known contaminants," Voller says. "That means dick when it comes to *unknown* contaminants, but as far as the ship is able to tell, it's safe for us to breathe in here once we get the lifeboat environmentals up and running."

"But?" I prompt because I can feel it coming. And because he's said nothing about the engines.

"But we have another problem," Voller confirms grimly. "You and Behrens should come to the bridge."

13

"Primary navigational PCB is fried. Secondary, too. The whole rig is bad. Probably exposure or electrical activity from two decades of solar flares. Maybe both," Kane says, his head still stuck inside the open panel of the navigation control bank.

Nysus pipes in, advising Kane from the LINA. "Do you see the bubbling damage?"

"Yeah, I got it," Kane says. "Hang on." He removes himself carefully, the maneuver further complicated by his helmet and his suit. He's used to crawling around inside the LINA without either.

"What does that mean?" I ask Kane.

"It means we've got engines fired up and nowhere to go," Voller says, sounding distinctly sulky.

I look to Kane. To my surprise, he nods.

"Without the nav rig, we have no helm control," he says.

"Steering wheel's disconnected, TL, and there's no autopilot because the ship can't tell where it is in space," Voller adds in an overly patient tone.

Embarrassing as it is, that makes more sense to me than the technical explanation.

"Okay, so what now?" I ask.

"They might have spare parts somewhere on board," Kane says. "But there's no guarantee that they're in any better shape."

"If we can even find them," I add.

"Exactly."

"We can pull from the LINA and splice to fit," Nysus says. "It's a workaround, but we can make it do what we need it to."

Kane pulls himself upright, keeping a hand on the corner of the control bank to manage his movement. The sooner we can get the gravity on, the better. But we can't boot up the lifeboat gravity generator and environmental systems without closing the bulkhead doors, and I don't want to do that until I'm sure we're not sealing ourselves into a dead ship.

"The problem is," Kane begins.

"If we pull from the LINA, we're rendering her nonfunctional in the same way," I say.

He nods. "Exactly. And if we make adjustments to the rig for the *Aurora*—"

"It won't fit back into the LINA," I say.

"Not easily," he agrees.

Which means, if everything goes to shit, we won't have a way out. Worry gnaws at me. Redundancies. That's what's been drilled into my head, over and over. Redundancies in space save lives.

"Technically, we would be stuck once the bulkhead doors were closed anyway," Nysus offers. "Unless we pressurize the whole ship, those doors won't open. And there's no airlock. No one is meant to leave once the Versailles Contingency is enacted, until outside help arrives."

So, really, LINA's (functional) presence in the cargo bay is nothing more than a comforting thought, anyway.

But I *like* that comforting thought.

"All right," I say with a sigh. "Let's do it."

"I can pull what we need," Nysus says. "Just a minute, and I'm on my way."

"Voller, start running the lifeboat systems diagnostics," I say. "No point in doing all of this if those aren't up to snuff."

I head to the stairway to wait for Nysus. It takes him longer than I expected, but I suspect that's because he's stopping to examine everything along the way with an unseemly amount of glee.

"Did you know that every room, even crew quarters, was stocked with genuine cotton sheets? An obscene thread count. CitiFutura wanted everyone to brag about the experience when they got home. It was meant to prove that the future of space living didn't have to mean roughing it in a hab on a dusty planet somewhere," he says.

From the top of the stairs on the Platinum Level, I watch as he makes his way across the atrium, a small form in a white enviro suit with a black pack strapped to his back.

"Look at this," he says in delight, catching himself on one of the planters. "Genetic copies of rare plant species for that extra-special exclusive feel. CitiFutura even had a botanist on board to care for them."

From what I've seen, I doubt anyone had had the time or inclination to appreciate that level of detail. Even before they started killing each other or themselves.

Then he looks up. "Where did you see Opal again?"

"Nysus," I say with a sigh.

"Right, right." He bobs toward the stairs, hesitating only briefly at the sight of the passengers Kane and I brought down. At the top, he grins at me, his eyes crinkling at the edges. At least someone is happy.

Without gravity, he's floating even with me, though if we were on the ground, he'd be at least six inches shorter. His glossy dark hair is chopped short and ragged, his own handiwork. And he's paler than the rest of us, almost as pale as me, because he doesn't bother with the required time underneath our sun lamps.

"Good to see you, Ny," I say, a smile tugging at my mouth in spite of the circumstances.

Even though we've lived and worked together in the tiny LINA for more than two years, it's still strange to see Nysus in person, out of the server room. He's not, as far as I can tell, antisocial exactly. He just prefers to spend his time alone, connected to us by technology rather than physical proximity.

"You, too, TL," he says. But his focus is already on the corridor of suites behind me. "'Ethically harvested hardwood,'" he murmurs, seemingly quoting from the *Aurora*'s specs or marketing materials. "They grew it especially for the *Aurora*." He moves past me, through the open bulkhead doors, to touch the still-shiny panels. "I loaded my Forum downloads onto a portable drive, so we'll still have access to the blueprints and any other information the Forum has collected over the years."

Great. The solar system's largest collection of facts and fantasy about the *Aurora,* still at our fingertips. Though I can't complain, because the information Nysus has provided so far has been accurate.

Once Nysus is in place on the bridge with Kane, I tell Voller to head back to the LINA to gather whatever he needs for the trip.

"I'm almost done, and it's only three days," he protests, his hands hovering over the board, reluctant to leave as the lifeboat diagnostics run, as if his absence might change the outcome. "I can get by."

"Try again," Kane says, from where he and Nysus are working. "There's no way Verux is going to let us wander through the ship and back into LINA once they get a team out here. We're going to be escorted off, at the very least." *In restraints,* is what he's not saying but likely thinking.

And I can't argue. With sending out a message to everyone on the commweb instead of Verux directly, the court of public opinion will eventually save us—the heroes who brought the *Aurora* home, as Voller said—but it's probably not wise to count on that right away. Verux will be pissed.

For the first time, a squiggle of doubt worms through me. Verux has provided me a home and employment for the better part of my life. Perhaps it was only out of selfish concern and fear of legal reprisals, but still. How much do I owe them for that?

Enough to let them discard you when they're done with you?

No. Definitely not.

I shove my fears down as Voller pushes himself away from the diagnostics with a disgruntled sound. "Don't touch anything," he mutters. To me or Kane, it's impossible to tell, but equally insulting either way. And exactly what I'd expect.

"You should go, too," I say to Kane.

I expect an argument, another moment of heated debate about leaving me here, essentially on my own. Nysus is here, but in another world, utterly transfixed by whatever he's looking at behind the panel Kane removed.

But instead, Kane nods. "Roger, TL."

He doesn't even linger, simply pushes off the captain's chair toward the door. He's no longer even trying to talk to me alone, to explain. And while I'd have rather thrown myself out of an open airlock than have that conversation, it still feels like a loss somehow.

Fuck. I've really messed up.

Or maybe not. Maybe this is just the way it should be. It's hard not to fidget or punch out at something in frustration, both bad ideas in zero grav.

Voller returns in record time, with a bag that I suspect contains mostly alcohol and maybe a change of underwear and a fresh T-shirt, if we are lucky.

Kane returns not long after with his own bag, but even through his faceplate, I can see his expression tight with tension.

"Everything okay?" I ask.

"Fine," he says, avoiding my gaze and tying his bag down to the arm of the first officer's chair.

"Kane," I begin.

"You need to get your stuff," he says to me, meeting my eyes briefly before pulling himself over to Nysus. Kane looks exhausted, pinched lines of worry more prominent on his forehead. "It won't be long now."

Okay. If that's how he wants to play it.

"Lourdes, I'm on my way," I say, my tone sharper than it needs to be. "You can start heading out."

But when I reach the LINA, she's still waiting inside, near the airlock. Her enviro suit is on, but her helmet is still on the storage bench.

I wrest my own helmet free, my hands clumsy and heavy in the renewed gravity.

"I thought I'd wait for you," she says. "In case you want to create a message, too."

"Message?" I ask.

She cocks her head to the side. "Kane didn't tell you?"

"Tell me what?"

"Never mind." She steps back, gesturing to the crate next to her. "I packed the food supplies and added in as much water as we can carry. Just in case."

"Lourdes," I ask, an anticipatory feeling of dread growing in my stomach. "What message?"

"He recorded a message for his daughter. I made one for my mom. We can't transmit anymore, not with what we took for the *Aurora*, but it's attached to the ship's log. It'll play whenever that's pulled, even if we're not on board." She hesitates. "I guess he's worried that even if everything goes right, Verux might not let us go right away?"

Guilt strikes hard and true in my gut. "It's possible," I admit. It's also possible that I am a complete asshole. I've been preoccupied only with my own feelings—what they should or should not be—instead of thinking about the potential risks and penalties that Kane—and all of the others—were undertaking.

They're risking so much on my word, my plan. The thought makes me feel queasy. I am not worth that.

"Shit," I mumble.

Lourdes raises her eyebrows.

"Sorry, no. No message," I say. *Unless I can send one to my dumbass self.* "No one left on Earth who would care." I grimace at how self-pitying that sounds, even if it happens to be the truth. A couple of supervisors at the group home, instructors in the Verux commweb team training program, which, now that I think about it, likely no longer exists.

"Oh," Lourdes says, her expression melting with sadness.

"It's fine," I say, forcing a wry grin. "I never liked Earth much anyway either."

She nods after a beat. "Okay . . ."

I wait.

"Can I wait for you?" she asks. "I don't know if I want to go through that"—she gestures toward the airlock and the *Aurora* beyond—"by myself." Shifting from foot to foot with anxious energy and dark circles under her eyes.

"Yeah. Just give me a minute."

It doesn't take me long to grab from the already-packed crate in my quarters and stuff a few changes of clothes and personal toiletries into a duffel.

My fingertips brush over the soft cloth of my childhood blanket. I hesitate for a moment. It is my only remaining possession with a connection to my mother, but it's also connected to the disaster that was Ferris Outpost. Bringing it with me feels almost like asking for trouble, waving a red flag in front of fate and daring it to strike again.

I shake my head. Ridiculous.

I tuck the blanket inside before zipping the bag shut.

Once Lourdes and I are suited back up, I follow Voller's instructions to shut down LINA's primary systems (including the requisite diagnostic). Behind me, I can feel the pull of LINA, whispering at me to look back, reminding me that this might be the last time I see my home of the last eight years.

But I make myself push on, keeping my gaze focused ahead. There's nothing to be gained from looking back.

It takes us longer to get to the atrium, pushing the crate along between us. Lourdes doesn't have much experience in zero grav, and she's having trouble pulling herself along.

Eventually, it's easier to simply tether her to me.

"TL . . . Claire," she says softly as we reach the threshold of the atrium. "Is it okay if I close my eyes?"

Making her fully dependent on me to get her there safely. Frustration flares in me. I didn't want this. I *don't* want this. My suit feels too tight, too warm suddenly.

Except, isn't that what I'm already doing? Making decisions for people who are depending on me to get it right?

"Sure," I say, and I try not to let the tension seep into my words. In the end, it's probably the better choice for all of us, including Lourdes, that she not have the up-close view of the deceased passengers.

Kane, thankfully, is waiting at the top of the stairs and helps without a word, reaching out to pull the crate up and shove it toward the suites. Then he tugs Lourdes up, releasing her tether from me, and guides her to the corridor, past the bulkhead.

I follow. Voller finally has the lights on and things appear almost normal. Except for the bloody message on the wall, which I still haven't deciphered.

"It's safe," Kane says to her in that same gentle tone I've heard him use with his daughter. It makes me ache with envy and burn with self-loathing at the same time. "You can open your eyes."

I hear her gasp. "It's so pretty! Look at the walls!"

Another real-wood enthusiast. I shake my head.

"The bridge is at the end of the corridor and around the corner," he says to Lourdes. "Just pull yourself along by the doorways. If you lose your grip or miss a handhold, don't panic. I'll be right along behind you in a minute."

"Okay," she says, sounding more certain than before. He has a gift for reassurance.

Kane returns to me and the crate floating on its side nearby.

I owe him an apology. More than one. I open my mouth, but words won't come out.

"You all right?" he asks, keeping his attention focused, deliberately, it seems, on the crate.

Why wouldn't I be? The sarcastic response immediately pops to the tip of my tongue, but I swallow it a second before it escapes.

"Hoping I didn't kill us all by deciding to do this," I admit, surprising myself.

"You didn't force anyone," he reminds me.

"Are you sure about that?" I ask lightly. Even after that kiss, he would feel compelled to look after me. It's just who he is.

"As much as I'm sure we *all* love this heartwarming chat on the common comm channel," Voller drawls in my ear, turning my face hot with embarrassment. "We're ready up here."

Kane flips him the finger, but his voice is calm and even. "Roger that. On our way."

When he catches me looking at him, he shrugs. "Makes me feel better even if he can't see it."

A surprised laugh escapes me. "That is one stress relief measure I had not considered."

"Can't see what?" Voller demands.

"Not important," I say, and it feels, for the moment, like everything is back to normal. Like everything is going to be okay.

We bring the crate of food and water with us to the bridge. Voller, Kane, and Nysus go over the lifeboat data one more time and the engine diagnostics, confirming that everything is optimal. Or as optimal as it can be.

And then there's nothing left to check.

Nysus looks to me, and I give him the nod, feeling my heart in my throat.

"Activating Versailles Contingency," Nysus says.

I hear the hiss of air as the environmentals kick on in high gear, rushing to fill and warm the void.

"Sealing bulkhead doors, port and starboard," Voller adds.

It makes the most logical sense to wait here, to watch as the stars shift and move around us as we get underway.

But instead, I find myself bobbing down the portside hallway, as the gravity generator gives its activation warning, to watch the heavy bulkhead door slowly slide into place.

My hands are tingling and sweaty, and it feels harder and harder to breathe with every inch the door descends.

Get out, get out now! a voice in the back of my mind screams, over and over again. Until the space between the bottom of the door and the floor is too small to squeeze through. Then that voice falls ominously silent.

Lourdes joins me at the door, and then Kane.

The doors connect with their fittings—on this side and the starboard—with twin thuds that shake the ship and us within it.

A moment later, gravity locks on and pulls us to the ground, after the three warning bobs.

"Doors are secure," Nysus says, sounding giddy. "The Versailles Contingency is a success! Oxygen at eighteen percent and climbing. Temperature is rising, too. Negative twenty Celsius."

"I guess that's it then," Kane says, as the three of us stand there, staring at the solid metal wall blocking us from death. Blocking us in, though, too.

A loud pop sounds behind me, and I jump, bracing myself out of habit with a hand along the wooden corridor panels, but the gravity is on.

When I turn to look for the source, my stomach is tight with dread and I half expect to see that rivets are bursting free and we're venting atmosphere.

Instead I find Voller, his helmet off in utter defiance of protocol, holding a green glass bottle that's foaming over the top.

"Is that champagne?" Kane asks in disbelief.

"Where did you get that?" I demand at the same time.

"In one of the rooms. Don't worry, boss," he cuts me off before I can speak. "It was sealed. Who's joining me?" He squints at the wet label. "For a thirty-year-old drink?" He lifts the bottle in a mock toast. "To the start of our high life!"

He puts the bottle to his lips and tilts his head back for a large swallow but comes up sputtering and coughing a second later. "That's rank," he manages, wiping his mouth with the back of his hand. But he's grinning.

To my surprise, Lourdes moves past me and reaches for the bottle. She struggles to remove her helmet one-handed until Voller helps her. She takes a tentative sip, followed by a grimace. "Disgusting."

But she extends the bottle to me and Kane with an expectant look.

Kane holds his hand up. "No thanks, I prefer my stomach lining intact."

It feels, though, less like a shared drink and more like a pact, a promise that we are all in this together. Oh, what the hell.

I remove my helmet, taking a first tentative breath on board the *Aurora*. The air is still icy cold and vaguely metallic-smelling. I grab the bottle from Lourdes, who beams at me.

"To fame and fortune, bitches," I say with a sigh, lifting the bottle as Voller crows in delight.

"And getting everyone home safely," Lourdes adds.

"That, too." She means the *Aurora* dead, I know, but when I lift that bottle, I'm making my promise to the living.

14

"Hey, who took the last fish-and-chips packet?" Voller demands from behind me, rummaging through the crates of supplies from the LINA, near the entrance to the bridge.

I swivel to face him in the captain's ultra-comfortable chair. It's a lushly padded and gorgeously appointed leather creation, one I'm still uneasy about claiming, especially given the proximity of Captain Gerard's remains. "Can we focus, please?"

"But I'm hungry," he says.

I roll my eyes and face forward again.

After all the work and stress of getting over here and getting underway, the actual start of the journey on the *Aurora* has been smooth. Effortless. Mind-numbingly uninteresting.

So effortless, in fact, that I catch Lourdes yawning in her seat on the bridge, her chin propped in her hand on the as-yet-useless communications board.

Kane is occupying himself by going over the *Aurora*'s specs and systems, with some input from Nysus. Who is busy watching the finished but unaired episodes of *Doing It Dunleavy Style* that he managed to recover from one of the newly charged-up tablets, giggling to himself in delight.

Space travel is boring. As a commweb maintenance team, we're used to it. A boring day is a good day. Boring is what we strive for. When things are exciting, someone is usually about to die in some new and horrible way.

But there's such a thing as being a little too relaxed. I think, particularly in this circumstance, there's value in being just that extra bit cautious. A little more vigilant.

"Look, TL, if we didn't blow up in the first hour, statistically speaking, we're probably not going to," Voller says, coming back around to his seat, packet in hand. He drops into his chair and tears into the packet with his teeth.

"That cannot possibly be true," I say, thinking of all the twenty-year-old systems being worked to their maximum after a deep freeze of decades.

"Back me up, chief," Voller says, turning toward Kane.

Kane looks up from the panel where he's working. "It is *less* likely," he allows reluctantly.

"See? Hard part's over," Voller says through a mouthful. "It's time to celebrate."

I wince inwardly. I'm not a particularly superstitious team leader, not like some who refuse to fly without their various good luck charms—my first TL actually rattled with all the various tokens he wore on a chain around his neck—but still.

Kane's gaze meets mine for a brief second in what, under other circumstances, might have been a moment of mutual exasperation with Voller, but then he drops his eyes back to his work, as if I'm not there.

In spite of our earlier moment, where it seemed like everything had returned to normal, he's back to that cool, slightly-more-than-professional distance. And I hate it.

I can't blame him, but this time, blame it on restlessness or not-quite-spent adrenaline, I can't ignore it any longer. I have to try to fix this. "Kane, may I speak to you for a moment? Alone?"

Voller groans.

I'm aware of Lourdes watching with interest, as Kane pushes to his feet.

"Sure," he says evenly.

Folding my arms across my chest, I turn and hurry off the bridge, down the starboard corridor. He follows at a slightly slower pace.

When I reach a distance at which it seems reasonable that everyone on the bridge can't hear us, I stop and face him.

He watches me warily as he approaches, and the heated, cringey feeling in my chest makes me want to avoid his gaze. But I make myself keep my head up.

"I'm sorry, I fucked up," I say, my hands clenching into fists. "I shouldn't have . . . kissed you. That was wrong, especially as your TL." Just the reminder of that—in my mind, we're equals, but in all other ways, including legally and officially, I'm his boss—makes me long to find the nearest dark hole and reside there. *I thought I was a better person than this.* Apparently not.

He's watching me, his head cocked to the side. "Claire," he begins. "What are you—"

"You should file a complaint as soon as we're done here." Once, you know, we're done essentially blackmailing our employer. *Good, Claire. Fantastic.* "And I know it's wrong to ask this of you, but right now, I can't have you taking double shifts to avoid me. I need you to be on my side." My voice is trembling, and I despise myself all over again. For the sign of weakness, for what I'm asking of him after what I did.

He has every right to walk away without another word, or shout at me.

Kane huffs out an exasperated breath, shaking his head. "You know, I tried to get you to talk to me," he points out.

My face flushes. I don't know what to do with that response.

"If you'd have let me explain," he says, moving closer, "I would have told you that you just surprised me."

That's not exactly a good thing, is it?

"And I'm not avoiding you. I was trying to give you the space you seemed to want," he says. He gives me a knowing look. "You're not exactly easy to figure out sometimes, Claire Kovalik."

No surprise there, though Kane always seems to have a better feel for what I'm thinking than anyone else, including me at times.

I shift uneasily. I'm still not sure where this is headed. "I don't want you to pity me, either."

He tugs gently at a strand of hair that's come free from my scraped-together ponytail, tucking it behind my ear. "If you think this is pity, then we probably do need to have a larger conversation right now." His mouth quirks upward as he leans closer.

My heart is beating way too fast. Is this happening?

His mouth hovers above mine, those bright blue eyes tired but filled with warmth. His nose nudges my cheek, and I tilt my chin instinctively. My hands fly up to clutch at his shoulders as if for balance, the softness of his T-shirt molding around my grasping fingers.

But before his lips can touch mine, a sharp intake of breath sounds behind us. "Oh, sorry!" Lourdes's voice comes out loud, too loud.

Flinching, I step back from Kane immediately as Lourdes backpedals, turning away from us. He's slower to let me go, his hands lingering in midair, as if I might return to him, before falling to his sides.

I clear my throat. "What's up, Lourdes?"

She turns around cautiously, her gaze bouncing between Kane and me. I can feel her wanting to talk about it, sense the anxious fluttering cartoon hearts hovering over her head like a speech bubble.

I beam as much *don't even think about it* as I can in my return look.

"Um, Nysus found something he wants you to see," she says, grinning at us. It's taking everything she has not to say something.

"All right. We'll be right there," I say.

She nods and turns to head back.

But it's clear there's absolutely no chance of me and Kane continuing our conversation—or anything else—by the way she keeps looking over her shoulder at us on her slow-walk to the bridge.

I sigh.

"Maybe there's a secret third Dunleavy sister," Kane murmurs as we start to follow, in a warm, amused voice that makes me want to wrap my fist in his shirt and haul him into one of the cabins with me.

"Shocking season finale twist," I add, trying to keep my voice steady. Like this is all normal, so normal. And not everything I've ever wanted but barely let myself consider.

Kane wanted to kiss me. He would have kissed me. Adrenaline rockets through my bloodstream.

As soon as I see Ny's face, though, lined with tension and pale, my giddiness dissipates like air from a popped balloon. Whatever he's found, it's nothing simple. Or pleasant.

He motions Kane and me over, watching to make sure Lourdes returns to her station. That is . . . not good.

"It looks like the cameras were set to automatically upload any new footage," Nysus says in a quiet voice. "When I got to the end of the finished episodes, there were these other random files and the last couple . . ." He hesitates. "Here. You should just watch." He pushes the tablet into my hands, along with the headphones he's been using.

Dread building in my gut, I press one side of the headphones to my ear and start the footage. Kane watches over my shoulder.

It's hard to tell what I'm seeing at first. The camera is jostling around so much, revealing bright flashes of color and brief glimpses of carpeting and polished wood-panel walls.

Someone is running down the hall on the Platinum Level.

"Are you recording?" a breathless male voice asks, close by but not on camera.

"That's the producer, I think," Nysus says. "Ty Rubin."

"Of course I'm fucking recording. I don't need you to tell me how to do my job," another male voice responds sharply. He sounds slightly closer. The camera operator, probably.

"Shhh," the other man says, the noise more like a hiss. "Just shut up. We need to get this."

Whoa. Just a little tension there.

The camera steadies as they slow down, coming up on a slightly open door to one of the suites. Female voices are raised in argument, one plaintive and loud, the other attempting placation through what sounds like clenched teeth.

"You ruin everything!" the first one shouts.

"Opal, honey, you're not listening," the trying-to-soothe woman says.

The camera nudges through the open door, revealing Opal

Dunleavy, her arms folded across her chest, glaring at an older woman with an obvious familial resemblance, minus the purple hair.

I look to Nysus.

"Vi Dunleavy," he says. "Dunleavy matriarch."

Is that what they called her on the show? I want to roll my eyes, but the sight of Opal standing there, furious in her pristine white bathrobe, the same white bathrobe she's still wearing now, only sans knife, makes my skin crawl. This must be close to the end, close to . . . whatever happened.

Opal looks exhausted, brittle, with purplish circles under her eyes that aren't quite concealed with makeup, and absolutely rigid with anger. Her mother, too, looks as though she's not quite well. Her hair is ruffled into short spikes, and her eye makeup is smeared in streaks on the side closest to the camera, as if she was woken from a nap and didn't have time to repair it. It makes her look off-balance, both physically and mentally.

Neither woman seems to notice the camera, but perhaps that's deliberate, for the show.

"If you break a restraining order, darling, then you'll lose any sympathy from your audience," her mother continues.

"You don't know anything," Opal sneers. "This is on brand for me. And I am the brand."

Vi Dunleavy smiles tightly, wrinkles appearing for the first time on either side of her mouth. "Sweetheart, I think you're underestimating the appeal of the whole family. Your sister and I—"

"Shut up, shut up, shut up!" Opal lifts her hands to press them against her ears. "You just keep talking, so much noise, buzzing in my head!" She sways slightly, her eyes squeezed shut, her mouth still open from shouting.

The other woman moves so fast I barely catch the movement before her hand is cracking across Opal's face. "Listen to me, you little whore," she snarls, spittle flying from her perfectly lined lips. "You are not going to ruin everything I've worked so hard for."

Opal steps back, panting with shock, one hand pressed against her cheek where her mother struck her.

"I take it this is not normal for them," I say to Nysus. It's uncomfortable to watch, but not especially alarming.

Nysus jerks his chin toward the images playing out. "No. Not at all. But it gets . . ." He swallows. "It gets worse."

The camera guy seems to realize that this fight is not staged for the audience's titillation and starts to pull back into the hall.

"No, no," the producer urges in a gleeful whisper. "Keep rolling." An antiquated phrase, but the meaning is still clear.

And the camera operator does, just long enough for him—and for us—to watch Opal straighten her shoulders and then slide her hand in the deep pocket of her bathrobe. She pulls out a large knife, blade gleaming, and holds it up, like a magician's finishing flourish.

Vi Dunleavy gasps, a sharp, choked sound.

My stomach lurches in anticipation of what we'll see next, but the screen goes dark.

"Did we find the mother during our search?" Kane asks me in an undertone.

I shake my head. "No." Which means she's somewhere else on the ship. Or maybe she was one of the "lucky" ones to reach the temporary safety of an escape pod.

The tablet flashes to life again, the next file starting up.

More jostling, more running, heavy breathing. Only this time, I can't tell where we are in the ship. The screaming, though, that is unmistakable. Multiple voices raised in outrage, pain, and fear.

The running stops abruptly, and the camera focuses on the floor first. A familiar pale marble. The atrium.

Then the camera sweeps up and it's too much to take in at once. It's the atrium in mass chaos. A woman in a midnight blue gown sits on the floor, huddled in a ball, surrounded by her full skirt, rocking back and forth and sobbing. Two men in crew uniforms are splayed out on the ground nearby, bloodied. Dead. Stabbed, if the handle of the golf club sticking out of one's chest is any indicator.

Across from them, in the distance, a *pile* of people—I don't have another word to describe this undulating mob of humanity— scramble on top of one another, throwing elbows and crashing fists into faces to get at something or someone I can't see.

The camera jerks up, and there, at the railing by the staircase to the Platinum Level, a man in what looks like chef's whites calmly wraps a cord around his neck and then steps over the edge. The cord snaps with his weight, though, and he plunges to the ground below.

I squeeze my eyes shut to avoid seeing him land.

When I open them again, passengers are fleeing from something, running in front of the camera, in singles or small groups.

"Don't you see it? I saw . . . I thought I saw . . ."

"Come back here! I know it was you!"

"Allara, I'm sorry, I'm so sorry." That last is from a woman wear- ing a shimmery bikini beneath a translucent sea-foam green cover-up and dragging her obviously broken left ankle as she limps on.

"What the fuck?" Kane breathes.

I shake my head—I have no words.

The camera shifts abruptly, zeroing in on a section of the atrium, in front of one of the planters. "Leslie?" the cameraman asks, sound- ing dazed. "What are you doing here?"

The camera operator sets the camera on the ground and walks in front of it, the worn heels of his shoes appearing before us as he moves away. "Leslie. You're supposed to be at home. I don't—"

The rest of his words are lost as the camera bobbles and shakes, someone grabbing it up from the floor.

"Mine, mine, mine." The lens is tipped upward toward the per- son clutching it to their . . . his chest. Anthony Lightfoot.

He rushes through the atrium, his rough movement jostling the camera into providing glimpses of his surroundings. The chef sprawled on the ground with his neck at an awkward angle in a growing pool of blood. A man in a pale lavender tuxedo, streaked with dirt and gore, has his hands wrapped tightly around the slender neck of a woman in a matching dress.

Shit. My hand tenses on the tablet, as if I could reach back in time and stop him.

Anthony makes his way up to the top of the spiral staircase, the motion dizzying to watch. He's heading for his suite. Probably.

And he almost makes it.

"Hey! Hey, are you spying on me?" I recognize the gruff voice even with the edge of antagonism. Jasen Wyman.

I can't see him, but I can hear him quite clearly, and so, evidently, can Anthony.

He spins swiftly in a motion that blurs the Platinum Level hallway into a swirl of polished wood.

"I see that camera, you can't hide from me!" Wyman shouts, approaching Anthony. He's in pajamas, his suite door standing open behind him. His silvery hair is rumpled and his craggy face appears further wrinkled by sleep lines, but his eyes are narrowed and bright with hate.

"Mine," Anthony says, holding the camera up, over his head. "Fuck off, old man."

The view is now mostly of the hall, but a tiny corner of that elegant silvering hair is visible in the lower corner.

The hair vanishes abruptly, and Anthony gives a grunt and the camera tumbles to the floor.

If I'm not mistaken, a septuagenarian just rushed a professional athlete for . . . spying on him?

Wyman grabs for the camera, providing a close-up, his *last* close-up, of one of those famous blue eyes, and then he lifts the camera up.

Quickly I reach out and turn off the playback. I don't need to see this. We know how it ends—in Anthony's suite, with the two of them beaten to a pulp.

I shove the tablet back toward Nysus. The footage hasn't revealed anything we hadn't already guessed at from the evidence, the bodies, we found. Murder, suicide, confusion, and chaos without an explanation or any reason.

Seeing it, though . . . I shudder.

"What is this?" I ask Nysus.

He lifts his shoulders helplessly. "I don't know."

"It's not mutiny," Kane says. "Not like that."

"Hey," Voller calls. "What's all the whispering about?"

"What did you find?" Lourdes asks.

I take a deep breath. People are relying on me to know what to do. Because I brought them here.

Everyone you care about dies. Because of you.

The thought sets off a white-hot spurt of shame as I face them. Lourdes is leaning forward in her chair, and Voller is watching us through narrowed eyes, slouching in his seat, his body angled away from his console and toward us.

"Nothing more than what we thought," Kane says, turning toward them. "But watching it happen . . ." He shakes his head grimly.

Why does it feel like he's lying? He's not.

"Did you see anything about why it happened?" Lourdes asks, her fingers wrapped tight around the scroll on her necklace.

"No," Nysus says, sounding haunted.

I clear my throat. "All right, here's what we're going to do. We're fine, and we're going to stay that way. Only our food and drink, no more celebratory anything, even if it's sealed."

I half expect Voller to protest, but he jerks his shoulders in a shrug. "Tasted like shit anyway."

"And we've all been awake for too long. We can't afford to be distracted," I add. Sleep deprivation is not something I want to add into this mix. "Two teams. Shifts of six hours on, six off. Starting now. Voller and I will take the first."

"TL," Voller protests.

"Claire," Kane says at the same time.

"It's fine," I say to Kane quietly. "I won't be able to sleep. Not now." Plus, there's a part of me that's convinced that I need to be awake to keep . . . whatever from happening.

"*I* could sleep now," Voller mutters loudly.

"I'll take the first shift," Lourdes says. "Keep TL company."

"Sold," Voller says, pushing up from his chair.

I could argue, put my foot down, but I'd rather save the fight for a moment when it really counts.

"And no one goes anywhere alone," I say, stopping Voller in his tracks.

"What?" he asks.

"I mean it," I say. "I don't care how the three of you work it out. All crash in the same suite or in the crew quarters, whatever. But no one is alone. Period."

"Gonna hold my hand when I take a piss, too?" Voller asks.

Kane draws a breath to respond, but I'm ready. "If that's what it takes for you to be a big boy, absolutely," I say.

Lourdes hiccups a laugh before clamping a hand over her mouth.

Voller shoots me the finger but waits at the door.

"You sure?" Kane asks me, his voice softer than usual. His gaze moves over my face and for a second, it feels like we're alone in the corridor again and he might lean in closer.

I nod. "Yeah." My voice is breathier than it should be, and I hate it.

"Okay," he says.

I love that he trusts me. More than I trust myself.

No, not love. I flinch inwardly. No love-related thoughts. Not now. Not ever. *Get it together, Kovalik.*

"Come on, Ny," Kane says, over his shoulder. "Leave all that here."

I glance back to find Nysus gathering up every bit of equipment we found for him.

"But—" Nysus starts.

"Sleep, Nysus. You need to rest. It'll all be here when you get back," I say.

He opens his mouth to argue, but the grayish pallor to his skin makes me hold firm. There might be more information on those recordings, something we missed, but I'm not willing to risk his health for whatever small clue he might turn up.

"Do you need me to make it an order?" I ask.

His shoulders slump. "No . . ."

"We need you in top shape," I say. "See you in six."

Nysus gives one last longing glance toward the video equipment, then heads toward the bridge doorway to join Voller.

Kane looks at me and tips his head toward the corridor.

I walk with him, assuming that there's something he wants to discuss further. "We can change up the shifts," I say. "It doesn't have to stay this way the whole time."

But Voller and Nysus, seeing Kane coming, start down the hall, and as soon as we've stepped just out of sight of Lourdes, Kane tugs me around the corner, across from the crew bunk room.

"Wha—" I begin.

His mouth closes over mine, warm and soft. His hands slide around my waist, pulling me tighter against him.

The heat of him surprises me, freezes me in place with my hands in the air for a second. Just a second. Then it's like being lit on fire from within. The whoosh of thrusters catching more fuel.

I grab at the back of his soft T-shirt, trying to lever myself closer to him. If that were even possible. My actions ruck his shirt up, and the smoothness of his skin beneath my grasping hands nearly undoes me. I want to breathe him in, climb him, pull him inside of me.

That's when he steps back, his breathing ragged, his blue eyes bright with affection and something darker. "Didn't want to wait six more hours to do that," he says, tracing a gentle exploratory fingertip across my cheekbone.

I stand there, head swirling and buzzy with too many thoughts and not a single coherent one among them, except: *This is a bad idea.*

His mouth—so recently on mine—quirks in a smile, as he seems to read my mind. He leans forward to press a kiss on my forehead before walking away.

"It's going to be fine," he says to me over his shoulder. "We're all going to be fine."

Even as dazed as I am, I'm still with it enough to wince. I wish he hadn't said that quite so loudly or confidently. It feels too much like tempting fate.

15

I inventory our food and water supplies. Twice.

I make a list of to-dos for Nysus, including asking him to look for some hacker-y method to access the coded captain's log.

Lourdes finds her way into the transmission record for all outgoing communications. We can't view the messages that were sent—they're long gone. But she can see who was attempting to communicate with Earth and how often. I set her to making a list of the names that crop up most frequently. Maybe there's a pattern.

Six hours isn't a lot of time to rest. But it's way too much time not to overthink. And I have so much to overthink about.

This place. What happened here. Whether we're safe (enough) for the next sixty-some hours.

Kane.

That last makes my stomach bubble with both anticipation and dread, like I've stolen something I desperately want and now I'm just waiting to get caught. Waiting for the proverbial "other shoe" to descend from above and smash me into the ground.

Or, like when I applied for the transport captain job, knowing I wouldn't get it, that I shouldn't have it, but wanting that future— any future besides the desk-bound future Verux offered—badly enough to try.

It hurts to want things.

To keep my mind occupied and off the lingering sensation of Kane's hands gripped tight on me, I make myself review the footage from the tablet again, even the finished *Dunleavy* episodes. Looking for something, anything that stands out as a hint or foreshadowing of what's to come.

But there's nothing. It's as if a switch flipped. One minute everything is normal—as normal as it can be on a reality show about spoiled, wealthy people on a ship full of spoiled, wealthy people; I mean, there's an argument about vegan pâté—and the next, it's a murderous hellscape with fancy leather couches and marble floors.

Setting the tablet carefully on the floor, I lean back in my chair and rub my eyes. I don't understand it. I have to be missing something.

Maybe if I go over it one more time, paying more attention to the people and events in the background.

I'm reaching for the tablet when I hear the distinct *clunk-click* of a door shutting down the corridor. I heard it enough times when we were going in and out of the suites earlier.

I check the time. Someone's up early.

Kane.

The bubbling in my stomach intensifies, but I ignore it, giving my full attention to the tablet instead of my nerves that can't seem to make up their mind about how they feel.

I end up getting sucked in, people-watching with the volume off. The server in that fancy dining room whose polite mask strains slightly at the edges when Opal sends her sparkling water back the second time. An elegant older woman in a fancy hat—it looks more like a green fabric-and-feathers sculpture—passes by their table, giving the camera a disdainful glare. A duchess of some kind, if I remember Nysus correctly. From Liechtenstein, maybe? In any case, if she looked down her nose any further, she would cut off her own air supply. Not that I blame her.

After a few minutes, though, I realize no one has come onto the bridge. Not Kane. Not anyone.

I get up to check the corridor in both directions, make sure everything is okay. But it's all as empty and silent as ever.

Lourdes looks up from scrolling. "What's wrong?" She sounds drowsy.

I shrug, forcing the careless movement. "Nothing. Thought I heard them up and moving."

She snorts. "You know Voller won't be rolling in here until ten seconds before."

She's not wrong.

I return to my chair and resume watching the footage. But I'm only half paying attention, a tiny and yet inexplicable knot of tension growing between my shoulders.

The second time, that *clunk-click* is louder. Or closer.

I stand again. "You didn't hear that?" I ask Lourdes.

She swivels her chair to face me. "Hear what?"

Fuck. *Fuck.*

Okay, deep breath.

I sit back down. "Never mind. I think the chair squeaks when I move."

She doesn't seem fully convinced, but she nods. "Kane probably has something in one of the tool kits we brought over that would fix that. I can check if you—"

"No, no, it's fine."

Lourdes watches me for another second, uncertain, and then goes back to her work.

Clunk-click.

This time, I keep my head down, staring sightlessly at the tablet. Lourdes says nothing. She really doesn't hear anything.

Clunk-click. Clunk-click. Clunk-click.

It's getting faster now and more frequent. One right after the other. Like it's dinnertime and all the guests are emerging from their suites to visit La Fantaisie or the creepy theater on the level below for a show.

Sweat pools under my arms and I have to tighten my grip on the tablet to keep it from slipping away from my now-slick hands.

A recurrence of my post-traumatic symptoms due to stress. That's what the doctors would say. Just hallucinations.

Cattie and Opal move soundlessly on-screen, laughing or shouting at each other, I can't really tell. I can't seem to focus anymore, my breath lodged in my throat like a stone.

Then, just as suddenly as it started, the doors fall silent.

But in the quiet, I hear something new. The soft *shush-shush* of footsteps on the carpeting. Getting closer.

I squeeze my hands tighter on the tablet, until the edges dig into my palms.

A hand lands heavy on my shoulder, and a muted scream burbles out of me, a pathetic, shrill sound, as I throw myself forward and turn to see who—or what—is behind me.

"Hey! Whoa." Eyes wide, Kane holds his hands up in apology. "Sorry, I didn't mean to scare you. I thought you heard me coming."

"It's okay," I say, panting. I bend in half, trying to catch my breath and hide the humiliation currently burning up my face and neck. "You just startled me." *Lie.*

"Voller was snoring so I couldn't sleep. I thought I'd come back a little early." He steps closer. "Are you sure you're okay?"

"Fine," I say automatically. *Another lie.*

"Claire," Kane says, reaching out for me.

But I can't do this. I can't have him being soft right now, not if I'm going to keep it together, and I can already feel tears stinging my eyes.

Blinking them back, I straighten up. "I'm good." I tip my head slightly toward Lourdes, who is spun around in her chair and watching avidly.

After a second, he seems to understand. "Okay," he says reluctantly. "But you should get some rest. You can go now."

I shake my head. "No one alone," I say.

But even as I'm speaking, Nysus enters the bridge, with Voller trailing after him, feet dragging.

"We still have fifteen minutes left," Voller protests.

"No, *you* have fifteen minutes left. Kane and I have been awake for an hour because you sound like a human foghorn," Nysus says. He nods at me as he walks past me. "TL." He looks better. Not great but better.

"We'll switch it up next time," I say to Nysus. "Voller can take a shift with us."

"A double? Come on, TL." Voller drops into his seat. "I already have a headache."

"Lourdes, are you ready?" I ask, avoiding Kane's gaze.

She pops up from her chair. "More than."

I hand the old tablet off to Kane. "I made a list for Ny, inventoried the food, and I watched all the Dunleavy footage again. I didn't see anything but—"

"See you in six, Kovalik. We've got it," Kane says gently.

It's too dangerous. I *am too dangerous.*

That's what I should say to him. But I don't. Because maybe sleep will help. Maybe it'll all go away with a few hours' rest.

Right.

I haven't shared a room since the Verux group home and, before that, in the hab with my mother. When I left the group home, I swore I'd never live like that again, even temporarily while on assignment. But it's a small sacrifice to make to keep us all safe and alive.

Lourdes trails a step or two behind me as I pass marked doors, picking the suite that's closest to the bridge without a double *X* on the door. Even though we'd removed the dead, there was something fundamentally creepy about sleeping where you *knew* someone had ended their life. Or, had it ended for them. So only the rooms we'd found uninhabited were up for grabs.

The door opens easily—Kane and I left the single-*X* ones unlocked after our search with the master key—and as soon as I step inside, the lights clicking on automatically, I remember which room this one is.

"Oooh," Lourdes breathes, looking over my shoulder as we walk in.

"Yeah, she was an actress," I say. "Anna something." Before the gravity was shut off, the room must have been a tasteful mess of beautiful fabrics, in all shades and hues, with embedded crystal, real leather plackets, or feathers that couldn't possibly come from a creature in nature. Gorgeous creations that deserved more than the word "dress" to describe them, tossed artfully over the back of the sofa, hanging on the back of closet doors, on the dressmaker's dummy that's currently lying on its side on the floor in the space between the sofa and the credenza.

Now it's just untidy heaps of bright color and textures, like tiny glittery mountain ranges on the cream carpeting.

Out of habit, I half expect Nysus to speak up with Anna's full name and vital info, listening in as he always did on the LINA. But he doesn't, and it makes me feel the tiniest bit more lonely and isolated.

Lourdes squeals with delight, then moves deeper into the room, carefully avoiding stepping on the fabric. "Look at this one," she breathes as she plucks a fluffy cloud of a garment from the floor. It's long-sleeved and completely sheer, a pale pink with crystals embedded in the fine netting. She lays it reverently over the arm of the sofa, her touch careful and caressing at the same time. "Isn't it beautiful?"

"Uh-huh," I say, smiling. I don't know much about fashion, having lived in Verux-provided jumpsuits and gear for the majority of my life, but her happiness is contagious. "I'm guessing that has to be just part of a larger outfit, right?" A layer over the top of something else, maybe. "Or the formal dinners here must have been very interesting." I raise my eyebrows.

Lourdes tuts at me in mock affront. "You have no taste."

I hold my hands up. "No disagreement here."

Lourdes cocks her head to the side. "Except when it comes to men, maybe," she says slyly.

"Okay, we're done," I say, rolling my eyes.

I head toward the back of the suite, where the bed is. On the way, I pause to flip on the light in the bathroom, feeling foolish but unable to stop myself.

When I step in the bathroom to take a quick look, the same pristine white walls shine back at me, the old-fashioned soaking tub as empty and unoccupied as when Kane and I searched in here the first time. The same array of grooming supplies—makeup, hair products, and styling devices, several of which I don't even recognize—lie scattered on the floor, where they fell when the gravity came back on.

I hadn't expected anything different. Not exactly.

I make a face at myself, my reflection in the mirror over the gold-fauceted sink mimicking in reverse simultaneously. Which makes me feel better somehow. Like the rules of the universe are still in operation.

Also? I look like shit. Dark circles under my eyes, strands of dark blond hair stuck to my forehead and standing up in spikes from my hastily constructed and reconstructed slightly-too-short ponytail.

And yet, Kane didn't seem to mind.

I jerk my head in a reflexive "no," heat rising in my cheeks.

I run a lingering finger over the faucet and matching handles. Even if everything were normal with me—which it obviously isn't—there's too much at stake to take that chance. This is freedom. The chance to make my own choices. The chance for everyone else on my team to have that as well.

Besides, Kane has a child and a life on Earth that he'd probably like to have once the money comes in from our "find." That will never be an option for me.

I start to turn away from the mirror when I hear Lourdes laugh. "I can't hear you, TL," she calls from the front of the suite. "What did you say?"

Frowning, I stop for a second, then I step out from the bathroom, to find her coming toward me, a lavish, ruffled creation in purple draped around her and dragging the floor at her feet, her boots just peeking out. The hanger is still in place at the back of her neck.

"I couldn't hear you," she says, beaming at me. She's a little kid playing in her mother's closet.

Her dead *mother's closet.*

Instantly my mind flashes back to the hab module that my mother and I shared at Ferris, her white coats hanging ghostlike in the small storage enclosure, like discarded, empty shells.

Exasperation with myself and that lingering discomfort rises up in me, making my tone a little sharper. "I didn't say anything," I tell Lourdes.

Uncertainty flashes across her face, her smile faltering slightly, as if she thinks I'm teasing her but isn't quite sure why. "Yes, you did. I heard you whispering. You said to be careful, then I couldn't make out the rest of it."

Was I talking out loud? I automatically glance back toward the mirror, as if that would provide answers. But my position now is such that my reflection is gone, and it wouldn't tell me anything anyway.

I'm fairly sure I wasn't talking to myself. It's a habit I broke myself of years ago, living in such close quarters with others who might not appreciate the constant muttered commentary. But anything is possible.

Except why wouldn't I remember it? I was staring at myself in the mirror, and I have no memory of seeing my mouth move, my lips forming any words, let alone telling Lourdes or even myself to "be careful."

Unless, once again, I'm not completely in touch with reality. Or, at least, not the same reality as everyone else.

Again.

An icy spike of fear pierces my stomach, and it's hard not to gasp at the punch of it.

Lourdes is now staring at me, and I fumble for a reassuring smile. "You gotta check out this bathroom. Look at the size of it," I say to Lourdes.

Obligingly, she glances past me, to the sink and the tub. "Wow," she says, her eyebrows going up, a measure of her previous enthusiasm returning. "This is bigger than my room at my parents'."

"Told you," I say, trying to match her tone. I mean, it's possible that I was talking to myself and I just wasn't paying enough attention. Overtired, maxed out on stress. That is the most likely scenario.

Sixty-three hours and some change to go. I can do this. I have to do this.

"As much as I would love for you to continue working this fashion show"—I gesture to the oversized gown hanging off her shoulders, and Lourdes laughs, seemingly relieved of her concern—"we need sleep."

The king-sized bed is made in a flawless, snowy comforter several inches thick and tucked in on all sides. Though the surface is also partially covered with more clothing that must have been circulating in the space above it at one point.

Lourdes and I work to clear it, me handing off to her. Silky scarves, a heavy fur coat, an assemblage of interconnected rubber straps and small fabric rectangles that might have been a torture device, a sex play aid, or, possibly, a bathing suit. I really don't know fashion.

Lourdes takes everything to the sitting area, handling each item as if it were made of frost-thin glass.

Exercising great care as she thought I had instructed her to.

Once the bed is empty, the precise folds on the sheets overlapping the top of the comforter are revealed. It's a simple matter to find and retrieve the pillows from their respective positions on the floor, where they'd fallen.

But I hesitate before drawing back the covers. It's one thing sleeping on a bed that belonged to someone else; another sleeping *in* it. And yet, even with the environmentals pumping at full force, it's plenty cool in here. Maybe it wasn't such a mock-worthy idea, as Voller had thought, to have a fur coat on board.

"Hang on," I say. I head back to the closet up front and on the top shelf find a spare soft, fuzzy blanket marked with CitiFutura's logo, next to—of all things—an emergency oxygen tank and mask. CitiFutura had definitely tried to make sure these people, at least, would survive.

"Here." I toss Lourdes the blanket, and she catches it.

"Thanks, TL," she says with a grateful smile. Then the smile fades slightly. "But what about you?"

I shrug. "I'll be fine."

Before she can protest and try to give me the blanket, I move around to the far side of the bed and sit down. The mattress and bedding are soft enough that I sink in several inches.

"Whoa," I say softly, unable to stop myself as I stretch out.

"Oh, wow," Lourdes says, wriggling into place on the other side. "It's like . . . I don't even know! I don't think I've ever felt anything this soft."

"Nothing but the best," I say, thinking of the oxygen in the closet, the Versailles Contingency backup systems, the ridiculous ornamentation, the one-of-a-kind plants or whatever. "At least for the Platinum people."

Lourdes is quiet for a few seconds. "Which is us now, right?" She turns her head toward me and gives a grin that holds more than a degree of astonishment.

"I guess so," I say. If something like the *Aurora* still existed, we would all certainly be able to afford the highest level of luxury passage once this endeavor is complete.

She hums in agreement or further expression of comfort and then falls silent.

After a moment or two, her breathing evens out and grows quieter. She's asleep already.

But, despite weariness that is pulling at me, making my joints ache and my eyes burn, the buzzing in my damaged ear is loud and annoying and I can't seem to make my brain shut off.

Instead, I'm replaying every moment of the last thirty-some hours in my head, looking for mistakes I made, the things I missed but should have caught. Some of that is simply the result of being in charge; some of it is unhealthy, obsessive anxiety. Another of my diagnoses? Compulsive need to control. Not others, necessarily. But myself and the situation around me.

Well, duh. Experiencing a scenario—or multiple scenarios—where your actions have dictated the fate of other people tends to make one a little edgy.

Normal for someone like me, but not necessarily helpful. Especially when I rerun the conversation with Lourdes in the bathroom—I wasn't talking aloud, was I?—over and over again, not finding anything new except increased levels of paranoia and self-doubt.

And what about those doors opening and closing? What was that? Hallucinations? That would be the simplest explanation, which is certainly telling. It wouldn't even be surprising, given our current circumstances and what happened on Ferris.

Restless, I turn from my back to my side. Something hard digs into my hip, and I reach into the pocket of my jumpsuit to pull out the green plastic master key and set it on the nightstand. I kept it with me after we changed out of our enviro suits, just in case.

Lourdes slumbers on peacefully next to me.

Eventually, I'm stuck replaying that moment with Kane in the corridor. Only this time, in my mental revision of reality, I pull away from the kiss, tell him I'm sorry but it's just not a good idea. He accepts without argument, and we go our separate ways. Disappointing but safer. Much safer.

That, of all things, is what finally allows me to fall asleep.

After some time—long enough that I can vaguely feel the stiffness has settled into my muscles from being still for an extended period—my brain dimly registers the sensation of the covers gripping my right ankle too tightly where it's dangling off the side of the bed and a harsh and uneven hissing sound, as though something is caught in an air vent nearby.

If the effects of Voller's shitty housekeeping in his quarters have made their way into our vents, I'm going to be pissed.

I kick out until the pressure around my ankle vanishes, turn over onto my side, and make a mental note to ask Kane about cleaning LINA's air vents. It can't be that hard, I could help, because that noise *has* to go away . . .

Then I remember: I'm not on the LINA. And I'm not under the covers.

My eyes snap open as adrenaline pours through me. I simultaneously jerk my feet up toward my body and scramble to sit up, panting.

What the fuck was that?

Lourdes's side of the bed is empty, her blanket bunched up between us where she'd evidently tossed it aside. Nowhere near my ankles. The comforter beneath me is now bunched and rumpled from my panicked movement, half hanging onto the floor.

A dream? It has to have been. A subconscious manifestation of all my anxieties and past traumas.

But as I sit there, crouched at the head of the bed, mouth dry and head throbbing, I realize I can still hear it. The uneven hissing sound. Only it's not coming from the ventilation system.

It's closer than that. And—*oh, Jesus*—underneath me?

Underneath the bed. Worse, now that I'm focused on it, the noise sounds familiar. I *know* that sound. Not the continuous wheeze of a trashed-up vent, but the rasp of an inhale, followed by a pause, and then a labored exhale. It's someone struggling to breathe. I listened to that noise for weeks on Ferris, while my mother tried to save the colonists. And then after, when I was alone and there was no one left to save, but somehow, I could still hear them.

Fuck, fuck, fuck. It can't be.

I squeeze my eyes shut for a second, waiting for the click, the recognition that this is a dream. But I can feel the ridged wallpaper pressing into my back through my jumpsuit. The glossy finish of the headboard is slick beneath my sweaty palms clutching at it for balance.

We searched these rooms. We checked under every bed.

Did we? Or did we miss one?

Nothing is alive on this ship. Nothing could have survived. It's not possible. So, it shouldn't matter.

Except it seems to.

I draw in a breath, hold it for a count of four, and then let it out—a Verux-child-therapist-endorsed measure to stave off panic attacks. Though instead of helping this time, it only heightens my awareness of the similarity of the sounds beneath the bed.

It's just some system on the ship. Something I don't recognize. It's just . . . I don't know what it could be. But it's not that . . . it's not a person.

It cannot be.

Cautiously, I release the headboard and inch toward the foot of the bed, across the inordinately soft mattress that makes my balance wobbly.

The noise doesn't change as I move, not even when I yank the edge of the comforter away from the floor where it hides the start of the shadowed gap beneath the bed. That newly revealed space shows nothing but another patch of cream-colored carpeting.

Of course there's nothing.

Feeling stupid, I bend over the edge of the bed slowly, compelled to tip my head down to check the gap between the floor and the bed. I can't help it, even though I know I'll find only a larger stretch of empty carpet or perhaps some kind of additional in-room heater or air ionizer or humidifier. Some fancy "necessity" that the Platinum people might have needed or been expected to need.

So, when my eyes first meet hers—the blank space where hers should be, where that strip of torn white sheet covers them instead—I freeze for that extra second, my brain trying to make sense of what I'm seeing with what I expected to see.

My lungs lock up, holding me hostage.

Her face is an ugly shade of gray, her lips a dark purple and moving as she gasps for air in the shadowed recess beneath the bed. Her head turns from side to side as she struggles, revealing the frayed white edges sticking out from her ears.

I can't move, can't speak, a scream caught tight in my throat, like an interminable lump that I cannot swallow or expel.

But then she seems to sense my presence, her head stilling, focusing. She reaches toward me blindly, her hand shooting out faster than I expected, clawing toward my face. Her nails are ragged, dark, lined with thick, unknown substances.

I hurl myself backward, away from the edge of the bed and up to my feet to bolt.

Or, I try. But the softness of the mattress colludes with the tangle of the now-jumbled comforter, making it impossible to run. My balance is off, and a loop of bedding catches around my foot, and I fall. Off the bed, over the side.

16

My head hits first, a glancing blow against the sharp edge of the far corner of the nightstand, and pain is a lightning bolt, quick and razor-sharp, through my skull.

My shoulders and back slam into the ground next, knocking the air out of my lungs. I arch up off the carpeting instinctively, struggling for breath. But it will not come. It's as if the front and back sides of my lungs have been squeezed together and are now stuck, unable to inflate.

I scrabble my fingers frantically against the carpet, searching for I don't know what. My vision begins to darken, unconsciousness threatening. And right as I'm convinced that I'm going to pass out or suffocate, unable to move with that . . . woman just inches away and likely clawing her way toward me, something unlocks in my chest and I gasp. Air floods in, sweet and light.

Pushing against the bed with my legs, I scoot myself away. Not far, not nearly far enough. But it's all I can do.

I roll onto my side, white spots dancing in my vision. I want to see her coming, at least.

Except.

She's not there.

I blink rapidly, trying to clear my vision of the spots. They gradually recede, but she's still not there.

There's no one underneath the bed. Just the expanse of empty carpeting I expected in the first place.

I push myself up on one wobbly arm—it takes two attempts before I can hold myself up—to look for her. She's not at the foot of the bed. Or anywhere that I can see.

With one hand pressed to the growing and suspiciously damp lump at the back of my head, I struggle to my knees for a better view of the room.

It's empty. She's gone.

Or—more likely—she was never here in the first place.

I sag back to the floor, tears spilling down my face. Pulling my fingers away from my head, I find blood. Not a lot, but enough.

Shit.

It was her, I'm fairly sure, the woman Kane and I found under the bed in one of the other suites. The one with her eyes and ears covered, whose discovery had so bothered me. The one whose body we had removed and placed on the other side of the *sealed* bulkhead doors.

What the fuck is happening to me?

Except I already know. Revisited trauma, hallucinations, leading up to a psychotic break. It has to be. Starting with seeing my mother. My own brain was trying to warn me, and I didn't listen.

But this time, this time is different. When I was eleven and alone, I could feel myself slipping away, could feel my grip on reality loosening. And being a terrified kid, I welcomed anything that made me feel less isolated and scared.

But now? I don't feel that same disconnect. Reality feels as tethered to me as always. And I'm not alone. I have people depending on me. I can't afford to lose my mind.

And yet, here we are.

Carefully, I push myself to my feet, gritting my teeth against the throbbing in my head, and stagger toward the bathroom.

A few moments of rummaging in the detritus on the floor produces what appears to be a clean washcloth, which I press against the back of my head with one hand.

Refusing to look at my reflection in the mirror, I run cold water over my other hand, rinsing away the blood. Then I freeze, realizing what I've done. Contaminated myself with their water, if there are contaminants within to be found.

Fuck. I need to report this—all of this—to Kane. Tell him to take over, and, I don't know, knock me out. Stick me in a room somewhere and lock me up until we get back to sector K147.

My face burns with humiliation and frustration. I was right. I'm too damaged. Too dangerous.

But the thought of ceding control, even to Kane, feels even more dangerous. Like I'm the only one standing between us and disaster, which is a special bit of arrogance. As if I've ever been able to stand between anyone and disaster without flinging the door wide open.

I shake my head and wince.

For the safety of my crew, I need to tell Kane what happened. Let him decide what to do. If I keep it to myself and truly lose my shit, they may not realize it fast enough to save themselves. Someone needs to be on the lookout for aberrant behavior. Rather, *more* aberrant behavior.

I wait until the bleeding has mostly stopped, then I clean myself up, wiping the blood out of my hair and the tears off my face with cool water from the faucet. In for a penny, in for a million more, apparently.

Maybe I would be more convincing to Kane if I showed up tearstained and bloody, but I don't have it in me to go that far. Dignity may be cold comfort in this situation, but I'm going to hold on to whatever I can salvage.

Once I'm as pulled together as I can be, I head out of the suite and slowly toward the bridge, running my hand along the wall to keep my balance steady against the pulse in my head.

When I reach the bridge, though, I find Nysus and Kane huddled over something on one of the screens at the comm station, and Voller at navigation, scowling at the readout projected on the stars through the window in front of him. It provides speed, coordinates of our current location, our projected path, and time to destination.

According to that readout, I was asleep two hours more than my designated six. Lourdes should have woken me up. Not that that matters now.

Except . . .

"Where *is* Lourdes?" I ask.

Only Kane seems to register the question. He looks up and around, distracted, before focusing on me. "She's not with you?" Then he seems to take in my appearance and straightens up, turning fully toward me. "Are you okay?" he asks, his forehead creased in concern.

"I—" I begin.

"You have to see this, TL," Nysus calls to me excitedly.

"Can you guys shut up?" Voller swivels around in his chair. "My head is fucking killing me."

Kane rolls his eyes. "Old champagne seems less than a good idea now, right?"

"Whatever," Voller mutters. "It's not that." He rubs at his temples. "I didn't drink that much, and it was hours ago. Besides, I've had a hangover before. This is different. It's like my teeth are vibrating in my head."

"Uh-huh," Kane says, folding his arms across his chest. He glances to me, and I realize he's waiting for me to make the decision.

"You can take your six in the bunk room, but leave the door open so we can hear you," I say to Voller reluctantly. That should be a decision Kane is making now. But Voller vaults from his chair and leaves the bridge before I can say anything more. I turn my attention back to Kane. "But I still need a minute to—"

"No, Ny is right. You definitely need to see this," Kane says, his mouth set in a grim line.

My eyebrows go up. Kane is not one to exaggerate or overrespond. "Okay," I say slowly.

Kane frowns at me as I approach. "Is that blood on your collar?"

"I hit my head," I say, each word clipped. Telling Kane and taking myself off active duty is the right thing to do, but that doesn't make it any easier.

Which conversely makes it easier to put it off for a little while longer. "I'll tell you about it in a minute," I say. "Part of what I need to talk to you about."

"Are you okay?" he asks, reaching out to tilt my head toward the light. I want to lean into his warm touch, but he spots the lump almost instantly, reaching to probe it with gentle fingertips.

I suck in a breath, and he pulls back immediately.

"That's a hell of a hit," he says. "Did you fall out of bed or what?"

"Something like that," I say flatly.

"Okay, okay," Ny says, shifting his weight from foot to foot, eager to get on with his show. "Can I just tell you now? We found a couple things and—"

"Start with the diagnostics," Kane suggests.

"Fine," Nysus says, his fingers flying across the boards, and numbers and abbreviations dance across the screen above. "Okay, so you know the ship runs a diagnostic every time—"

I wave my hand. "Yeah, yeah, I got that earlier."

"So, I decided to just review the data from the initial diagnostic at the start of their trip until the end. Just to see what I could see. For fun."

That *would* be his version of a good time. "Knock yourself out," I say. At least my sense of humor is intact.

Nysus looks up at me, startled.

Or not. "Nothing. Never mind." I shake my head, forgetting for a moment, and wince as pain reminds me of the injury. "Just . . . what did you find?"

"There are some anomalies I can't explain. Everything is operating within normal parameters until a few days before the last recorded data." He pauses, doing something until the numbers and figures change into a recognizable bar graph. "Look, here, this is the energy draw on the engines. You see some minor fluctuations in the first six months of travel, no big deal, depending on who's running what on the ship. How many people are awake with the lights on, whatever."

The thick yellow lines move up and down in slight increments.

"But if you look at this point, toward the end, that last week . . ." He gestures toward the screen, and I bend forward for a closer look.

The yellow bar jerks up and stays up.

"It's a spike," I say.

"Exactly," Nysus says with satisfaction. "Something was drawing down on their power. Elevating their usage stats by at least ten percent, higher always than their previous high. And consistently, until the last diagnostic."

"What would cause that?" I ask.

"I have no idea!" Nysus sounds thrilled to have a mystery to solve. Oh, to have the mental capacity to enjoy finding one of life's unsolvables—like why my brain is broken and seeing dead people all the time—instead of being defeated by it.

I shove that thought down. "What else?"

"The noise dampeners," Kane puts in.

"Right, right," Nysus says. He slides his hand across the screen, wiping away the yellow bar graph and substituting a similar one, this one in a serene blue.

"So if you look, the noise dampeners are operating at near the high end of their capacity for the first six months of the voyage," Nysus says. "Not great, but fine. Minor fluctuations only when the speed increases or decreases."

"At the time, the engines were larger than anything else previously built, and CitiFutura was trying a new alloy for the outer hull," Kane adds. "They probably didn't know how the engine noise would interact with the alloy. I suspect it was louder than they anticipated. Upgraded dampeners would have helped reduce some of the ambient clutter for the passengers, but even without the upgrade, the passengers shouldn't have been experiencing anything too intrusive. If anything, only the crew and the folks on the lower level might have noticed louder vibrations."

"The cheap seats," I say. "So not a priority, I'm guessing."

Kane nods. "Exactly."

"But then at the same time as the additional energy draw, we have this," Nysus jumps back in. He swipes his hand across the screen, and the serene blue becomes a bright sea of red.

"The dampeners are redlining," I say.

"Maxed out, well beyond manufacturer specs," Nysus says. "But, and here's the interesting thing, *Aurora*'s speed hadn't changed. There's no reason for the dampeners' usage to jump like that."

"Could the dampeners be responsible for that ten percent increase?" I ask.

Nysus chokes on a laugh. "Dampeners? Taking ten percent from *these* engines?" He shakes his head. "Half of that, less, would have fried them completely. No way."

"So what am I looking at here, then?" I ask, trying to swallow my frustration.

"We don't know, I haven't figured it out yet," Nysus says, again sounding delighted.

"All we can say for sure is that something changed right before the end of their journey," Kane puts in.

"Okay, great, good job," I say, not sure what else to add. And I need to stop putting off what I came here to do. "Kane—"

Nysus and Kane exchange a look.

"What?" I ask, that creeping sense of dread returning. Increasing, rather, as it never left.

"There's one more thing," Kane says. "But it's a little . . . disturbing."

More or less disturbing than the ghost of a dead woman under my bed, grabbing at my fucking ankle? Because I think that might have to be my new benchmark.

A hysterical laugh bubbles out of me before I can stop it, and they both stare at me. "Sorry. It's just this whole thing"—I wave my hand to indicate our surroundings and the ship at large—"is kind of disturbing. Don't you think?" I'm not going to drop my experience on both of them like this. I need to talk to Kane privately, let him decide if he wants to communicate my . . . being indisposed.

"Right," Kane says after a moment. "It's the captain's personal log."

I straighten up immediately. "You got in?"

"Not exactly," Nysus says. "It looks like the ship's log and her personal log have been wiped, and really well. By the captain herself or someone using her code."

"Even in the black box?" I ask.

"We don't have the codes to open that, let alone access the data," Nysus reminds me.

"Okay, so . . ." I raise my eyebrows.

"We got lucky," Kane says. "The captain seems to have sent a partial excerpt from her log as a personal message. Or she tried. But they were, at that point, already well outside what would have been an early and rudimentary version of the commweb we have today."

"The message got caught in the buffer," Nysus says. "It's degraded, but I was able to loop it and filter out the noise, but that, of course, meant I also had to—"

"Nysus," Kane says, a verbal nudge.

"Right. Okay, here." He taps across the boards. "On the main screen."

I turn to see a close-up of Linden Gerard. The image is distorted and fuzzy, but I can make out her features and enough of the background to determine that she's in the command chair, just feet from where I'm standing. Her expression is one of forced calm, stress showing itself in the lines in her forehead and the tension in her mouth.

". . . wrong. I don't know . . . Officer Wallace seems to think . . . overreacting. But we've had a spate of suicides and . . . passenger-on-passenger violence is . . . people are reporting seeing things, impossible things . . ."

She pauses, glancing over her shoulder at the doors to the bridge behind her. Reflexively, I mimic her action. The doorway here is empty, as it is in her recording.

"I saw Maria." Linden swallows convulsively. "From the corner of my eye at first, and then at the end of a corridor . . . foot of my bed." Her determined calm breaks. "Mia, if you see this, I know you tried to tell me about omens and warnings." A sob escapes her, and she covers her face. "I'm sorry I didn't take you—"

A moment later, the recording jumps and she's looking straight ahead at the camera again, her face shiny with tears and taut with resolution. "And I want you to know that, no matter what happens, I lo—"

The message breaks off abruptly with a loud crackle of static, and I jump.

"Maria is—" Kane begins.

"Her wife," Ny and I finish.

"I remember," I say, my mouth dry.

"She was at the time, and still is, on Earth," Nysus continues. "She stayed behind to care for their three children. She was not on the *Aurora*, not ever."

"So Gerard was seeing things," I say, feeling faint. How is that possible? My history makes me a prime candidate for another mental break, but Linden Gerard was an esteemed captain, with no known mental flaws or incapacities. CitiFutura would never have assigned her the *Aurora* mission otherwise.

"And it seems she wasn't alone," Kane adds. "She mentions the other passengers reporting . . . oddities." He hesitates for a moment. "And I'm wondering . . . I have to think that maybe I—"

A scream tears through the thick cocoon of quiet, and the sound is so startling, so out of place, we all freeze for a moment.

Kane recovers first, bolting for the corridor, heading toward the sound, down the starboard corridor of suites.

"It's Lourdes," I call after him, trying and failing to keep up with him, the throbbing in my head sending agony with every step.

I follow as quickly as I can. The smell reaches me first—rotting meat and the metallic scent of old blood—and I gag before I can stop myself. I know that smell. Not just death, but death and decay. And that is no hallucination.

17

Instinctively I lift my arm to my nose, using my sleeve to block the odor.

What the fuck?

But as soon as I see Kane, stopped in front of one of the suite doors, I can guess what's happened, though I don't understand why.

The smell gets stronger as I approach him, that particular room. Kane taped the edges on that door heavily, attempting to seal any gaps, because we knew as soon as the heat and oxygen kicked on it would be impossible to stop the decomposition of the blood and bodily matter and fluids soaked in the carpeting. We'd removed the frozen bodies—Anthony and Jasen—but we couldn't do more than that.

But the tape on the door is now broken and peeled back. Kane is pulling a trembling Lourdes from the room, her breathing on the edge of hyperventilation. Why would she do that? Why would she go in there? She knows why we tried to seal the edges, what the double *X* signifies.

I reach out to pat her shoulder in an awkward attempt at comfort, but she jerks away, burying herself tighter against Kane's shoulder. "Why?" she asks, her voice muffled against him. "Why would you do that to me?"

I stare at her and then look to Kane, who gives a helpless shrug. "I don't . . . What are you talking about?" I ask.

"Why would you send me in there?" she cries.

My mouth falls open. "I didn't. Lourdes, I would never—"

"You did! I saw you! You waved at me to follow you, and we're not supposed to go anywhere alone."

"Lourdes," Kane says. "Claire has been on the bridge with us for the last twenty minutes at least."

Lourdes pauses and then shakes her head. "No, I woke up when she left the suite. I followed her. She said she had something special to show me."

Kane glances at me.

"She was already gone when I got up," I say. "I expected to find her on the bridge with the rest of you." My words sound thin to my ears, even though they're the truth.

"What happened after that?" Kane asks Lourdes.

"I . . . I followed her, but I kept losing her. In and out of rooms."

I glance back toward the bridge and stiffen at the sight. Several doors now stand open.

Niggling uncertainty begins to eat at me.

"The door should have been locked," I say. All the ones with double Xs should be. I automatically pat the pocket of my jumpsuit for the master key. But there's nothing. I'm not sure if that makes me feel better or worse.

The last time I saw the key was when I put it on the nightstand, hours ago. It's the only key we have.

"I was trying to figure out what she was doing." Lourdes pauses, her breath hitching. "The corridors seemed so much longer, though, and I . . ." She stops. "But I saw her go in this room, I know I did. She waved at me to follow her."

Could it be possible? Could I have gotten up and brought Lourdes down here without realizing what I was doing? Was the woman under the bed and my reaction to that a complete mental fabrication? Something I dreamed up while wandering down the corridor and leading Lourdes to follow me? I don't think so, but . . . I can't be sure.

Self-loathing churns in me, and I jerk my head in disgust with myself.

My head throbs in response to the sudden movement, reminding me. The bump on the back of my head from hitting the nightstand. That, at least, suggests a portion of my encounter with the woman under the bed existed in reality, and I couldn't be in two places at once.

But I also have a hard time imagining Lourdes reaching over me to take the key and leaving the room on her own. And where was she while I was on the bridge? In one of the rooms looking for "me"?

"Did Claire unlock the door?" Kane asks.

Lourdes's forehead creases, but she seems calmer now that she's in the hall and not alone. "I . . . don't remember. I just . . . I pushed the door and it opened." She frowns. "It was harder to open than I expected."

"Okay," Kane says. "Let's get you to the bunk room so you can rest and—"

Lourdes shakes her head fiercely. "No, not by myself." She avoids my gaze.

And not with me, clearly.

Even though I've done nothing wrong—as far as I know, which I suppose is the kicker—I feel the burn of shame.

"Voller is in the bunk room already. Or, Nysus is on the bridge," Kane says. "How about that?"

She nods, and he walks her down toward the bridge.

I edge closer to the suite for another look.

The red tape on the door edges is curled back and broken by force. The tape gave way when the door was opened. The lights are on inside, and the dried blackish-red lake of blood on the floor looks so much worse than it did when Kane and I were here in the dimness with only our helmet lights to illuminate the scene.

But what's caught my attention is the key in the door. Bright green plastic. One of a kind. And no longer in my possession, obviously.

Kane returns after a moment, without Lourdes. He studies the door, the key, and then me.

I clear my throat. "I was coming to find you because when I woke up, I saw something. The woman we pulled from under one of the beds? The one with the blindfold?"

"Yeah," he says, his face inscrutable.

I brace myself for his reaction and then tell him everything. How she tried to grab me. How she was trying to breathe.

He starts to speak, but I cut him off. "She was gone when I looked again. It was . . . it wasn't real. A hallucination." I hate admitting it, my own brokenness. "I don't think I did anything to Lourdes. The timing is . . . I don't know. But I can't, obviously, guarantee—" I cut myself off and get to the point. "I think you need to relieve me of duty." I force the words out. "For the safety of everyone else."

"That's why you were coming to the bridge," Kane says slowly. "To tell me to relieve you of duty."

"Yes." It is a relief to admit it aloud.

"But you didn't see Lourdes in the corridor." Clearly he's working up to something else, though I don't know what.

"No." I hesitate, then add, "Not that I remember."

"So, you think that you somehow sleepwalked out here and led Lourdes down a hall of horrors, opening doors for her? And she somehow kept losing track of you in a space of, what, two hundred feet?"

"I don't have any other explanation, so—"

"Bullshit."

That sparks my temper. "It's not bullshit," I snap at him. "Do you know what happened on Ferris, Kane?"

"It's in your file, Claire," he says tiredly. "Of course I—"

"No, you have the official diagnosis, all the post-game analysis. But you have no idea what really happened. I killed those people. I knew what quarantine meant." I can still see the tape in my mind. The big block letters in white on the blue background, strung across the hab door. "I broke protocols, crossing into the contaminated zone. Because I was selfish and I wanted to see my friend."

He flinches but shakes his head. "You were a child."

"My friend who'd been dead for two days by that point," I add, daring him to challenge that.

His mouth opens, but nothing comes out and I feel a gritty sense of satisfaction.

I can picture it in my head. Becca still in her nightgown, maybe a little quieter and more distracted than usual. I was just happy to have my friend back. And to not have to cover her shifts in the greenhouse for much longer.

Me chattering away in that too-silent hab.

"I didn't know she was dead, didn't realize anything was even wrong, not until people were rushing me out of there into Med-Bay and decontamination." I give him a tight smile. "I was seeing things before I was trapped on the outpost with the dead. It's not PTSD or a mental break due to stress. I am fucked up." I pause. "Remember when I panicked, getting off the LINA into the shuttle bay here?" I don't wait for his answer. "It's because I saw my mother. My long-dead mother screaming at me."

His eyes go wide.

Yeah, exactly.

I sink to the floor in exhaustion. "When I was seventeen, almost out of the group home and waiting to find out if I'd be accepted into the Verux training program, I caused a ten-car pileup on Highway 5. A man in the middle of the road was calling for help. I went and by the time I got there . . . he was just gone. I didn't even see the cars until after. They swerved to avoid me, collided with each other." The safety mechanisms on mag-lev vehicles are programmed to preserve pedestrian life. So they did, at great cost.

The smell of burning metal and rubber singes the inside of my nose, startling me into alertness. Shiny metal suddenly all around me, tipped over and smashed, like a war zone that I'd been dropped into without warning. A woman is sobbing, and somewhere, in one of those wrecks, a moan of pain, followed by nothing but silence.

"Thousands of dollars in damage and people were badly injured." I smile tightly. "Verux kept it quiet."

"Claire," Kane begins, but with hesitance in his voice. I can't look at him. I might see the fear growing on his face, and that might kill me.

"She never said, but I think my mom took the Ferris job in the first place because I kept seeing my father everywhere after he died." I take a deep breath. "I scared her. So, we moved to a whole other planet. And poof, no more Daddy." I wave my hands, like a magician finishing a trick.

"Stress and trauma seem to make this worse, whatever *this* is. And the more people are around, the more . . . stuff I see. That's why I took this job, out here, away from everyone. Why I wanted this sector that no one else wants." I shake my head. "It doesn't happen much anymore, not when everything's normal. But right now? I can't tell what's real and what's not. Which means I am a danger. And I cannot take the risk of hurting anyone again. You *need* to remove me from the equation until we're back."

I'm breathing hard from the exertion of speaking words I've never said aloud to anyone and with such conviction behind them.

But when he speaks, it's not the resigned acknowledgment or angry accusation I'm expecting.

"I saw Isabelle," he says.

I blink up at him, not processing his words.

"When we were in the atrium," he reminds me.

A wave of affection for him fills me to bursting, though it's also mixed with pain. He's trying to make me feel better, make me feel less crazy. But that can't happen, no matter how hard he tries. "No, you *thought* you saw something, which is completely normal in that situation. But it was just your brain filling in details that—"

"I know what I saw," he says through clenched teeth. "I know my daughter."

I want to argue with him. Wishful thinking is not at all the same as a full-on delusion, and I, of all people, should know.

"Her hair was in braids, with the little yellow butterfly bands at the top. Her favorites," he says slowly, but his gaze is focused somewhere past me.

A chill skates over my skin. His distant stare likely means he's pulling the image up from his memory. But it's hard not to turn and check for myself. Would I see a little girl standing behind me? I shiver.

"In times of stress, we see what we want to see," I say, folding my arms across my chest. "Captain Gerard, in that message, it was probably the same thing. Everything was going to shit, and she wanted to see her wife one more time."

He shakes his head slowly in disbelief. "You are so determined to blame yourself."

I gape at him. "Excuse me? How in the hell is this not—"

"Has it occurred to you yet that that's evidence of four people— you, me, Lourdes, Captain Gerard—seeing things that aren't there?" he demands.

It hadn't, no. "But that's assuming that Lourdes—"

"Yes, that's assuming that you didn't willingly torture Lourdes— someone you've gone to great lengths to protect even at the expense of your own comfort—in some bizarre game of cat and mouse without remembering it." He pauses. "Look at it from my perspective: What's more likely in this scenario? You doing that or Lourdes seeing something that's not there when we have documented evidence that hallucinations have occurred here before?"

I close my mouth.

"Claire, I don't know what's going on here. I don't know what you . . ."

Are. That's the word he wants to say.

". . . what you can do or see or whatever. But I know you." He drops to his haunches, forcing me to look at him. "You wouldn't hurt someone, not on purpose."

The gentle but firm confidence in his voice, in me, makes my vision blur with tears. "But I have. It wasn't intentional, but the results were the same."

Kane makes a frustrated noise. "What happened on Ferris, on that highway, those were accidents. Period. So, yeah, I can lock you up and take charge." He rakes a hand through his hair. "But I'd rather you stop trying to distance yourself because you're afraid and help me figure out what the hell is happening to us instead. *Your* team, your people." He rests his hands lightly on my knees, squeezing. "I need your help."

He waits for me to respond, but I can't. The thought of voluntarily putting them at risk, putting him at risk, feels like a leaden blanket, holding me in place.

His expression shifts, hardens, like concrete setting before my eyes. "Fine." He stands and strides off toward the bridge.

People died the last time I didn't distance myself! The words come to me but he's already gone.

Frustration and guilt war in my chest. If he's wrong and I'm right, that's more pain and suffering laid at my feet, more that I *own*. I've worked hard to avoid that, to avoid getting close to others in general, just in case.

But . . . if Kane's right and something else is going on here? My refusal to get involved might come at a high cost. I, at least, have some experience in dealing with the not-real-that-seems-real.

Which might make me the best person to help. Or, the worst.

Fuck.

I rub my shaking hands along the legs of my jumpsuit, the worn fabric comforting in its familiarity. They're my team, my responsibility. And I'm terrified to endanger them . . . with me. But if something happens to them, when I might have helped?

I can't live with that, either. And in the end, I suppose that's what it comes down to. What you can live with or what you're willing to die for.

Pushing myself to my feet, I head after Kane.

18

"I've ruled out simultaneous psychotic break, because the odds of that seem so low as to be incalculable," Nysus is saying when I walk onto the bridge. "But the fact is we now have record of three people seeing the impossible. Captain Gerard, Lourdes, and Kane."

"Four," I say reluctantly.

Heads whip around to face me. Kane gives me a brief nod, as if he expected nothing less of me. Voller groans. Someone, probably Kane, dragged him from his rest to join us. Lourdes, wrapped in a blanket and seated at the comm station, eyes me warily.

"I saw . . . one of the passengers," I say.

"One of the *dead* passengers?" Nysus asks.

"Uh, yeah." I shift my weight uneasily. "She was under the bed, grabbed my ankle. But then she vanished."

"Oh my God," Lourdes whispers, her hand pressed to her mouth.

"It wasn't real, obviously," I add. "Though it felt real at the time."

"Did she look dead?" Nysus asks.

"Come on," Voller moans at the same time, where he's sitting with his head in his hands in the command chair. He looks pale and sweaty, with that undertone of green still holding steady in his skin. "You pulled me off rest for this bullshit?" He looks over at Kane. "You gotta give me something more for this headache, chief. I'm dying."

Kane ignores him. "Productive conversation at this point would be most useful, Ny."

"I'm trying to gather data," Nysus says, before looking to me for the answer.

"Yes," I say. "She did." Her skin was that horrible shade of gray that just doesn't exist on living humans.

I shudder.

"Interesting." Nysus taps his fingers against his lips as he paces the front of the bridge. "That's definitely what one would traditionally call a ghost. Someone who is confirmed as deceased."

"You're not fucking suggesting that the ship is haunted, are you?" Voller demands, his voice muffled by his head resting in his hands.

"It's a theory," Nysus argues, sounding a little frayed at the edges. He squeezes his eyes shut, as if in an attempt to resurrect the privacy he so valued back on LINA. "Humans have documented supernatural experiences in locations that have seen violent death for centuries. Battlefields are particularly—"

"Except not everyone is seeing dead passengers," I say. "Just me." For now. Forever.

"True, and that's our problem," Nysus says, opening his hands in a wide gesture. "We don't have enough data. Every theory is equally valid right now."

"Not ghosts," Voller mutters. "Ghosts don't exist."

"No?" Nysus asks. "I'm assuming that none of you are seeing my father pacing in that corner over there." He points a trembling finger to the far side of the room, and all of us look.

The space is empty.

An icy chill runs down my back, like an unfamiliar fingertip brushing the length of my spine.

"How do you explain that?" Nysus asks Voller. "I can see him and you can't."

"But what I saw was real," Lourdes says immediately. "I was there. I saw *her*." She can't look at me as she's saying it.

"Here's what we know. TL, you're the aberration here. You're the only one so far seeing the confirmed dead," Nysus says.

I clear my throat. "And that's happened before. To me, I mean."

Lourdes and Voller both turn to stare. My face flushes.

Nysus's eyebrows shoot up. "I definitely want to hear more about that. But for now we have to discard you from the data set. One of these things is not like the others. It could be something in your brain chemistry, a preexisting condition. But we just don't know."

He pauses, rubbing at his ears with a pained expression. "They keep ringing," he mutters.

Kane straightens. "Any dizziness or headache?"

"Yes!" Voller lifts his hand up. "And this weird popping sound? Or tapping?" He scrubs at his ear. "No one else can hear that?"

"You've already had the maximum dose of painkiller," Kane says. "I can't give you any more right now."

"Yeah, well, it's not doing shit," Voller mumbles.

"No," Nysus says. "No pain, no headache. Not yet." He shakes his head, refocusing. "So, we look at the commonalities. We have four people—Kane, Lourdes, Captain Gerard, and me—experiencing hallucinations of people to whom we're emotionally tied."

"That's not—" Lourdes objects.

"People who are, as far as we know, alive," Nysus continues as if she hadn't spoken.

Kane flinches.

"Another commonality. None of this started until we were on board the *Aurora*. Now correlation is not causation, obviously, but given what we know of the events involving the passengers and crew on the *Aurora* prior to our arrival—"

"Something here is causing it," Kane says flatly.

"We're going to end up like them?" Lourdes whispers.

"No," I say quickly, because I can see Nysus getting ready to nod, or, almost worse, shrug. But to be fair to him, that chaotic scene in the atrium we found in the Dunleavy footage is making a whole lot more horrific sense now.

"We've run every test we know to run. Everything came back within normal parameters, with the exception of the noise dampeners and that anomalous energy expenditure," Nysus says. "No contaminants. No exhaust leakage. No unidentified bacteria at mass levels. Nothing that would cause these symptoms."

"So what are you saying?" I ask.

"I don't know why this is happening," Nysus says. "I don't know how to stop it. I need more information."

"We could just leave," Lourdes says. "Just open the doors and—"

"We gutted navigation on the LINA for parts, remember? Plus, the doors don't work like that," Kane says. "They weren't meant to be opened from the inside. No airlock. Our suits would help somewhat, but we could end up with decompression sickness or worse. Unless we attempt to pressurize the whole ship, and that could take almost as long as—"

"I'm not fucking leaving," Voller snaps. "Not when we're this close."

Automatically, I glance toward the countdown on the main screen. Fifty-three hours and counting.

"We also don't know that leaving would solve the problem," Nysus points out. "If we've been affected, infected . . . possessed . . . we might well carry it with us."

"I think we should search the rooms," I say.

"Uh, you did that already, TL." Nysus sounds slightly worried.

Humiliation zings through me, a live spark zipping along my nerves. This is why I never tell anyone about what I've seen. What I see. They don't look at me the same way after. "I know," I say, working for patience. "I remember. But we were looking for bodies. Not for information about what happened." What is apparently *still* happening.

I hesitate, then add, "Also, they had spare oxygen masks and tanks in the suites on this level."

Voller snorts, then squeezes his hand against his forehead in pain. "Fuck. You don't seriously think someone has survived out here for—"

"No, but we didn't search the whole ship," I point out. "We have no idea what the conditions are like. And we left for several hours before sealing ourselves in. Plenty of time for someone to do . . . something. We should at least rule it out." Again, assuming I'm not responsible for what Lourdes experienced. Though Nysus has laid a pretty convincing case that this is not simply a result of my "condition" or a second breakdown.

"Okay, okay," Nysus says, wheels turning in his mind. "Highly unlikely, but maybe you can find something. I think we should also consider the possibility that this ship has been out here for two decades and we have no idea what else might have found it first."

Kane shakes his head.

"Ghosts *and* aliens?" Voller groans. "Are you fucking kidding me?"

"In the absence of additional evidence, all theories are valid," Nysus repeats. "Is it so impossible?"

"That intelligent beings would finally show up and their main game is to hang out on an abandoned ship and start torturing anyone who happens by?" Voller asks. "Fuck yes."

"You're ascribing human motivations and intentions to something nonhuman," Nysus says. "We have no idea what their goal is. We don't even know for certain that they are intelligent. Or, that this is deliberate. Perhaps their mere presence causes our brains to misfire and hallucinate. We don't know. But *something* is happening." He takes a breath, sweat beading on his forehead. "My grandfather has joined my father," he says, turning his head away. "My grandfather is dead, TL."

So it's not just me anymore. Maybe I'm just more sensitive to it, whatever *it* is. Maybe we'll all start seeing the dead eventually. Oh goody.

"If it's ghosts or aliens or some shit, how are you going to prove that?" Voller points out.

"If no other logical answer remains, then we have to assume that it's something previously classified as illogical."

"Great," Voller snarls. "I love this plan."

"I do have one other idea," Nysus says. "But it's risky and likely to make conditions more . . . erratic, especially during a search."

Because *more* erratic is certainly what we need.

"What's the idea?" Kane asks, folding his arms across his chest.

"I think I can push the engines a little harder. Get us through maybe ten hours faster," Nysus says, scrubbing his hands over his eyes, pushing in too hard, as if that will erase whatever he's seeing. "It's risky with as old as the engines are and with this level of charge. But the bigger problem is, with diverting more power to the engines, we may experience instability in some subsystems."

"Meaning?" I prompt.

"The lights," he admits. "Maybe even the temperature. It won't drop to fatal levels, but it may not be . . . comfortable."

So, dark and cold, as well as seeing people that aren't there.

"We need some ground rules," I say. "Like before, nobody goes anywhere alone. No exceptions. If you see someone or something that doesn't belong, you tell your partner. If your partner is the one behaving strangely, then report back to the others."

This is going to quickly spiral into chaos if none of us can be sure what we're experiencing is real.

"Voller, you can crash on the bridge with Lourdes," I say.

"Why are we listening to you?" Voller asks, raising his head. His eyes are bloodshot and narrowed. "How do we know it's not you? That you're not responsible somehow? You're crazy already. Everybody knows that."

Stung, I step back. Voller and I haven't always gotten along well, but the genuine hate beaming from his eyes right now is disconcerting. Lourdes, too, is giving me a less-than-friendly look. And that hurts. More than I expected it to.

"That's not how—" I begin.

"Impossible," Nysus says. "Your theory doesn't fit the data. It can't explain Gerard."

Voller mumbles something unintelligible but doesn't push it.

Nysus turns to me. "I need to stay here to monitor the engines at the increased levels, make sure we're not headed toward a blowout."

So that leaves Kane and me for the search again.

I make myself glance at him, fearing for a moment that I'll see that same hate or fear from him, but he simply nods.

"All right," I say. "Let's go."

"You did the right thing, you know," Kane says as we leave the bridge.

"Yeah, we'll see about that. Voller doesn't seem to think so." We're starting at the far end of the starboard corridor this time.

"Voller is an idiot," he says.

Maybe so, but Lourdes isn't.

Kane reaches out and squeezes my hand. I let myself hold on for a few seconds before letting go. That's progress, isn't it?

The increased ship speed is noticeable almost immediately in the more intense vibrations through the corridor decking beneath my feet. If it's like this up here, I can't imagine what it must have been like on the lower decks.

Where people hid in their rooms . . . or were locked away by others. The engine noise alone might have played a role in the chaos. They must have all been terrified, none of them understanding what was happening. People lashing out at one another, accusing each other of what they thought they saw. Frightened by hallucinations and other impossibilities. The one small advantage we have is that we know something happened on the *Aurora*, and that recent events are likely related.

The passengers and crew must have thought they were losing their minds.

Which, incidentally, is still a possibility for us as well, but at least we know it's not just us.

We make it through the first few rooms without incident. Everything is exactly as I remember it. No sign of anyone or anything unusual. Of course, how can any of us know that for sure now when we can't trust what we're experiencing?

I shake my head.

"What?" Kane asks. He's locking the door of one suite before we move to the next.

"Just thinking about the—"

The lights flicker overhead in an irregular rhythm, creating shadows where there were none a moment ago and the sensation of movement within them. A flash of pale fabric. White with little blue flowers.

I freeze.

"I see it, too," Kane says quickly. "The lights are going on and off, like Nysus said."

Claire. Claiiiiire.

Becca. I haven't seen her in years. Not since Ferris. How is she here now?

I squeeze my eyes shut for a moment, take a deep breath, and then open them. "Okay, I'm okay."

I focus on the spots of light, trying to ignore the writhing shadows, and force my feet forward. Just hallucinations. Or . . . something. I am the aberration, as Nysus said. What's happening to me isn't necessarily happening to everyone else.

Next to me, Kane jerks suddenly, turning to look behind us.

"What's wro—"

But even as I ask the question, I hear it. Footsteps. Somewhere nearby.

Heart racing, I turn, but there's nothing.

Until . . . cool, invisible fingertips brush my cheek. Gritting my teeth, I force myself not to step back.

Claire. Come play with me.

"Do you see anything?" I ask Kane, even as he flinches, swiftly looking down toward the floor.

"It's hard to . . . I keep catching glimpses. A hand. Long hair. Bleeding. I think it's my ex. But she's not . . ." His breath is uneven and harsh.

Shit. It's getting worse. We're getting worse.

"This is me," I warn him as I reach out and take his hand. I squeeze his palm hard, enough for our bones to pinch together uncomfortably.

His gaze jerks up sharply to meet mine, surprise warring with pain.

"If you can, focus on what you know is real," I tell him. "It's hard because you can't trust your senses, but if you can find one thing, that'll help." Just out of the corner of my eye, Cattie Dunleavy waits, her fingers tugging at the chain around her neck, her mouth moving in words I can't hear. Yet.

Kane blinks at me, his blue eyes wide, the pupils dilated in the irregular illumination. "You did this. By yourself for a month."

They aren't questions, but I nod anyway. "I focused on my stomach growling, how dry my mouth was. Things I knew were real."

But I also listened to my mother telling me what I needed to do to survive. The Verux-provided psychiatrists insisted that I must have known what to do and simply "imagined" my mother speaking to me. For some of that, perhaps. But never, in the six years in the colony, had I ever been entrusted anywhere near the communications room. How would I have known what to do, how to signal the rescue team, if my mother hadn't told me? My mother who would have known what to do, as part of her training. She and several others were considered "first responders" in any kind of emergency.

"All right," Kane says, taking a slow breath.

"We can do this," I say, as much for myself as for him. "It's not real. None of it is real." Except I'm not really so sure about that.

We finish out the starboard side in just under an hour and find nothing. The emergency oxygen tanks and masks are still in place. There is no convenient handwritten journal for us to peruse. We find more old-fashioned tablets and ear-comm devices, but the charge is long gone in them. I take a couple of them anyway, in case we ever reach a point where we can spare the energy to keep the lights on *and* charge them.

In the crew bunk room, though, I'm rummaging through the personal products in the one unlocked trunk when something familiar catches my eye. Several sets of bright orange foam earplugs in sealed plastic packets.

I pick up one of the packets. "I've seen ones like these before. I think the first officer was—"

"I didn't! Isabelle, I would never!"

I look up to find Kane pleading with an empty bunk, his gaze at eye level with . . . nothing.

"Kane," I say. "Kane!"

He looks up, tears running down his face, but he doesn't seem to see me.

I drop the earplugs and run toward him. I'm reaching for his shoulder to shake him when someone screams, the sound piercing even through the partially closed door.

I go still, uncertain. I don't know whether it's real or . . .

Kane shifts. "Did you hear that?"

"The scream?" I ask, just to clarify. But he seems more focused now.

"Yes."

"I did," I confirm. Which means there's a slightly better chance that it actually—

Another scream comes, followed by shouting. "Stop, stop! Voller! Help me!"

"That's Nysus," I say, bolting for the door. The bridge is directly across from us.

"I'll be right back, sweetie," Kane says, presumably to the hallucination of his daughter.

Fuck. Fuck. I keep going, not waiting to see if he's behind me.

But once I'm in the corridor, I stop. The commotion—Lourdes sobbing, I think, and Nysus arguing with . . . Voller?—is not coming from the bridge. It's farther away.

When I round the corner to the portside corridor suites, I find them and the sight stops me dead for a moment.

Nysus and Lourdes are yanking at Voller, who is struggling to get away from them, back to the bulkhead doors. The plasma drill— *our* plasma drill—is raised in his right hand. A half dozen blackened spots—one or two still glowing red at their center—show his efforts against the metal.

"If we just let them in, they'll stop knocking," Voller says, sounding remarkably calm. "It'll all stop."

"You can't open the doors, you'll kill us!" Nysus shouts.

Voller throws an elbow toward Nysus, connecting with his temple hard, and Nysus just drops, like someone cut his strings. He doesn't move to get back up. Doesn't move at all.

Lourdes maintains her grip on Voller's T-shirt, trying to haul him back. But he's too strong for her, reaching up to apply the drill once more. I'm terrified he's going to get annoyed with her and simply reach back and aim that drill at her instead.

I sprint down the hallway, trying to focus on the scene in front of me through the off-on-off pattern of the lights. With that added element, everyone seems to be moving in hyper-speed except me.

When I finally reach them, I shove into Voller from the side, knocking him partially into Lourdes and then all of us to the floor.

Breathless from the impact, I struggle to sit up and reach for the drill, which was thrown loose from Voller's hand and is now lying near the base of the door, the bright blue plasma melting the carpet and creating another black spot on the metal.

But I'm a second too late. Voller shoves past me and reaches it before I do. He grabs it and swings up, forcing me to scramble backward.

Lourdes curls herself into a ball in the corner, away from us.

"What the hell," I say as I get to my feet, breathless from panic and my race to reach them in time. "What are you doing?"

Standing, he scowls, but his eyes are not quite focusing on me. "Can't you hear it? They just want to come in."

Who? But I know better than to ask that. There's no answer to that question in this situation that will make anything better, more understandable. "I don't hear anything, Voller," I say. "Just engine noise." And staggering footsteps approaching that may or may not be Kane.

Claire. My name ripples on a wave of whispers behind me, including one I recognize, one that my mind says is my mother, though I haven't heard her voice in twenty years.

Claire. No.

Those chill fingers brush over my cheek again, and goose bumps rise over my skin.

"You're confused, but I can help you," I say to Voller, edging closer. "Take my hand." I have no idea if the pain trick that I used on Kane will work on Voller the same way with as far gone as he seems to be, but I have to try.

"No, no, no," he says, shaking his head. "You just want me to stop. You don't want to let them in. You're afraid."

"Voller, there's no one out there to save," Kane says from behind me. "It's just us, and we die if you break the seal on that door." He sounds steady, unshakable, but I don't know how long that will last.

Uncertainty flickers on Voller's expression for the first time. "My head just hurts," he says. "And all the noise is making it worse." He looks toward the door. "Cut it out!" he screams.

Lourdes emits a small whimper.

I take advantage of the moment and close the distance, reaching for his free hand. "Voller—"

But he turns just as I'm close enough and swings the butt end of the drill directly at my head even as I duck to try to avoid it.

I hear the crack, feel the impact of the hit connecting on the back right side of my skull, snapping my head up and to the left. Hard. But it doesn't hurt. Not at first.

Stars dance and shine in my vision, a rapidly narrowing tunnel, as I fall.

Voller stares down at me, over the sounds of distant shouting. Kane? My mother? I can no longer tell.

His expression is inscrutable as he lifts the drill up, and I'm expecting him to crouch over me at any second and lay that plasma bit against my flesh and bone. I need to get up, to run, but my legs aren't responding.

Instead, Voller grins at me, a crooked and tired version of his normal bluster, tips me a salute, and then, moving so fast it seems almost a blur, he presses the tip of the drill against his head.

I try to move, and pain from my head comes roaring into my consciousness. I think I scream as everything goes dark.

The last thing I register is the drip, drip, spatter of the blood hitting the floor, a warm tapping against my skin.

19

It's my fault. Voller is dead and it's my fault. I shouldn't have, I knew I shouldn't have . . .

"Just stay still, Claire," Kane says, strain in his voice. "Don't move, don't try to talk."

Did I say something out loud? I can't tell. The agony in my head is such that I'm afraid to ask, to move my lips, to draw a deeper breath.

I detect the flickering of the lights, in the alternating patches of soothing darkness and painful brightness behind my eyelids. Beneath me, a hard surface. My left arm is trapped underneath something heavy. Someone heavy. Voller's body.

"I know, I know," Kane says under his breath. "I'm doing the best I can." He pauses for a moment. "No, she won't. I won't let her."

He is talking to someone who isn't there.

"Kane?" Lourdes asks through her sniffles. "Is she going to be okay?"

"I don't know," he says. "I need . . ." He trails off seemingly mid-thought. "I need . . ."

"Well, are you sure this is even the right Claire?" Lourdes asks. "She's over there, too." A whisper of fabric against fabric traces her movement as she stands. "Claire. Wait, come back!"

We are all going to die.

<◇>

The ground is softer beneath me when I resurface from the black-ness again, and my head feels different, thicker.

Bandages. My mother's voice again. A cool brush of a touch against my cheek.

Tears leak from my eyes and trail down my cheeks. *Mama. I'm sorry.*

It's dark now, dim behind my eyelids. No more flashing lights. The grinding pain in my head is less at the moment, but I can feel it looming, waiting to crash down on me again. My left arm is now free, but a tightness grips near my elbow, faint pressure against my skin. I manage to shift that arm slightly, hear the crinkle of plastic, the painful tug of something attached to my skin beneath the surface.

An IV maybe.

Where is Kane? Lourdes? Oh God, I hope Ny isn't . . . that was a hard hit to his temple. Skulls are so fragile there.

With an effort, I open my eyes to a squint. It takes me a moment to recognize my surroundings in the dimness, lit only by the control boards. I'm on the floor of the bridge, near the door, the carpet rough against my back.

After a few more seconds, I realize what I'm not hearing or feeling. The engines. We're stopped or slowed to the point where I can't feel it anymore.

Voices whisper close by, but I can't tell who is speaking.

Then, next to me, there's movement in the dimness. Someone sitting up. "Claire?" Lourdes asks, sounding confused.

It hurts to look her way, but I have to see, have to make sure she's okay.

My breath catches in my throat. I'm seeing double. Two versions of Lourdes. One of them is frowning down at me as she pushes herself to her feet. "I don't understand . . ." she says.

And I don't either. Because the other version of Lourdes is stretched out next to me, her eyes bandaged but not hiding the clawed mess of her cheeks and the great gouts of dried blood down her neck and on her jumpsuit. She's too still.

Then the standing Lourdes stares down at herself and then me. "I don't understand," she says again, as she raises her hands to her eyes, her fingers digging in.

I squeeze my eyes shut reflexively, and the whispers grow louder, spinning over themselves until it sounds more like the wind blowing than voices speaking.

Ignoring the pull of the tubing at my arm, I brace myself against the floor with one hand and slowly push myself up into a sitting position. Dizziness swirls through my head, making me sway and nearly collapse.

When I dare to open my eyes again, blackness oozes at the edge of my vision, but there's only one Lourdes. The one on the floor next to me.

Silent. Empty. Dead.

No! I reach out for her, but that movement is too much. The blackness rises up, like dark water swelling around me. I can't fight it, I can feel myself slipping under its pull, losing my grasp on my surroundings.

And then . . . I'm gone.

20
NOW

"That's the last thing I remember," I say, an involuntary shudder racking my body against the back of the plastic chair at the common room table.

It takes Reed and Max a moment to react to what I've said, both of them caught in the web of my words.

Reed sits forward. "That's it?" he asks in disbelief. "But that doesn't account for how you got out of the—"

I glare at him. "I told you. I don't remember. Things get . . . fragmented at the end."

In truth, that moment with Lourdes (alive? dead? both?) is the last thing I remember that I'm fairly sure *happened*. A version of it anyway. An important qualifier. That snippet feels grounded in a way that many of the other flashes do not. Those are . . . flotsam. Jetsam. Random pieces from a jumbled puzzle that may or may not form a coherent picture, even assuming that I could gather them all. I can no longer tell—if I ever could—which of those images and bits of speech are actual memories and what might be products of my damaged mind (before and after injury) and whatever was on the *Aurora*.

None of that is worth mentioning to Reed Darrow and Max. I've told them what they needed to hear, as much of it as I can.

My mouth is dry from speaking and the drugs and remembered terror. I feel as though, by telling this story, I've expelled a darkness into the room with my air and my words. An entity hovering, watching and waiting. For now.

I squeeze my trembling hands together in my lap, the knuckle bones digging into each other with a painful but reassuring bite. The simple movement takes more concentration than it should, but my head does not feel quite as thick as before. The medications are wearing off. The thought sends a spike of fear through me. I don't know if I want to be that aware, not anymore.

But I've fulfilled my end of the bargain, and I will not allow myself to leave—mentally or physically—until I get what I was promised. I *need* to know. Is someone still alive on the *Aurora*?

Reed smirks at me. "You certainly seemed to remember enough to add ghosts and the possibility of aliens."

"You asked for the whole story," I say to Max through gritted teeth. He's watching me, his head cocked to the side in evaluation, turning a pen—a relic with ink inside and a metal tip, surely as forbidden in here as Reed's pin—over and over in his fingers. "I gave it to you, even the things I left out the first time because I knew they sounded—"

"Conveniently unstable?" Reed asks. "Nothing you've said in any way contradicts the far more likely scenario that you are responsible for the death of your crew."

"I've never suggested otherwise," I say, hands curling into fists. "It was my idea to board the *Aurora*. I'm . . ." I swallow hard. "I *was* TL. And I failed them."

Reed slaps the table in dramatic effect, his face a mix of disgust and triumph. The loud, unexpected noise makes me and the other patients in the common room jump. Loud, unexpected noises in here are not a good idea. Heads turn in our direction. Vera, at the "window," begins to weep softly.

"All that means is that your team would have listened to you, right up until the moment you turned on them," Reed says. "Until you betrayed their trust."

I stiffen. Because he's right, just not in the way he means. If I hadn't led the way, they would all still be alive. My own selfish concerns are what got them killed and landed me in here.

"You're not seriously suggesting that I fractured the back of my own skull," I say, trying to keep a hold on my temper.

"No, I think they tried to stop you, and you killed them. Your history and documented disregard for life made it easy for you,"

Reed says, watching me expectantly, as if those words would trigger a lever inside of me, releasing a long-awaited confession. "A viable option."

A viable option? I could show him a viable option. Two moves, no, three. Sit forward, snatch pen from Max's relaxed fingers, push off the floor and jab that pen right in the side of Reed Darrow's neck, right above that prissy, perfect white collar of his.

Chaos would ensue, screaming from the other patients. It would be precious minutes before the staff could drag him out of here, bleeding the whole way . . .

I squeeze my eyes shut for a moment. "Four against one?" I ask, opening my eyes. "You have severely overinflated ideas about my abilities. I wouldn't underestimate my crew like that."

A sly grin flickers at the edges of his mouth, as if I've admitted something important. "No. I'm sure you wouldn't."

My gaze cuts to the pen, as it stills in Max's hand.

"I think, in fact," Reed continues, "you plann—"

Max sits forward. "Thank you, Claire. I know reliving that must have been difficult for you," he says, cutting Reed off abruptly.

In another situation, Reed's hanging-open mouth might have been comical, like a child caught too shocked to tantrum over his candy being taken unexpectedly from his sticky hand. As it is, it's still difficult not to smile.

"Course heading," I remind Max. "Communication attempts."

"Claire, you did not mention the death of Mr. Behrens or Mr. Yasuda, the one you call Nysus," Max says.

"Which one do you want to hear about?" I ask with a sigh.

"Which person?" he asks. "I want—"

"No," I say. "Which death?" I shake my head. "I don't remember what happened, I told you. But in my head, whether it's real or not, I've seen them die in all kinds of ways." My voice breaks despite my effort to remain calm. "Killing each other. Killing themselves. Dying from lack of oxygen or hypothermia." There's even a version where I killed them, lashing out at what I thought wasn't real. I have them all because I've spent weeks trying to piece what happened together. How I ended up on that escape pod alone.

"I would never have left them," I say. *Are you sure about that? Old habits die hard, too.* I shove that thought down hard. "So the only explanation for me to be here without them is that they must be dead." Otherwise they would have come with me, wouldn't they? Or taken another escape pod or fixed the LINA? "I just don't know how it happened."

Reed makes a disgruntled sound, but Max simply nods. Then his head jerks up, focusing on a signal only he can hear. Someone is calling. "Will you excuse me?" he says to me, a polite fiction that I have the choice, that I have any choice in this, as he taps the comm implant at the base of his ear and stands. "This is Donovan."

Max moves a few steps away from the table, and I watch him, convinced that this may be a ploy to get out of giving me the information I was promised. Fake an emergency, leave the facility and me behind.

"It's a fairy tale," Reed says, leaning across the table.

I glance at him against my will.

"This story that you're spinning with the ghosts and the possessed ship or whatever," he continues. "And I get it."

Max is shaking his head. ". . . seems to be working. I don't think that's a good—"

"You were in an impossible situation," Reed says. "The company was done with you, replacing you. You had no viable career options left with your history. The world was changing without you."

"Shut up," I say, trying to focus on Max's words.

". . . unstable, and might further regress . . ."

"I don't think you set out to hurt anyone. You just needed options," Reed says. "Right? And then maybe things got just a little out of hand. Because once you start down that path, it's hard to stop. You can't put the peel back on an orange." He sounds so pleased with his analogy. As if anyone who'd spent the majority of her life on an outpost and then a corporate-sponsored group home, and finally an isolated and tiny sniffer would have more than a passing familiarity with the luxury of citrus, grown in greenhouses now at great expense. But I'm guessing that isn't an issue for the Darrow family.

"I do think that's a possibility, yes sir," Max says, turning to glance back at me. He gives me a reassuring nod that does nothing to reassure.

"Just tell me what I need to know and this can be over with," Reed says soothingly. "You can go back to your room, and we'll leave you alone."

Until the lawsuits filed by the passengers' families reach court, and I'm hauled out as a witness for each and every one.

And . . . maybe I don't want to be left alone. Not with the *Aurora* currently limping its way back here. Beneath the doubt and guilt and shame, a tiny spark of hope still exists in me. Not that anyone left alive would want to see me, after I left them. So, it seems I'm stuck with two equally undesirable possibilities—either I got everyone killed or I left someone to die.

Either way, what I had is lost, but if one of my crew, my de facto family, is still alive . . . Kane or Nysus. I can barely breathe for the possibility of it.

"Come on, Claire," Reed says. "It's a burden you don't want to carry. Just tell me what happened." But his overt ambition shows behind the thin veneer of civility and compassion he's constructed in the last five minutes. Like a shark trying to hide its teeth. Does he really expect me to fall for this?

His panic is genuine, though. I can feel it pushing at me from across the table. Reed Darrow is aware of some timetable that I am not.

When he glances back at Max, still on his call, it's a microfraction of a moment, so quick it barely exists, but it snags my attention, pulling like fingernails dragging across my skin. Reed Darrow sees his window closing, and it has to do with whoever Max is talking to.

"Clear your conscience, Claire. Get it off your chest," Reed urges, but his façade is cracking and the pleas come out sounding more like commands. "Stop with the aliens and ghosts bullshit, and tell the truth."

"Yes, sir," Max says. "I understand, sir. It shouldn't be a problem." His conversation is wrapping up.

I lean forward a little toward Reed. He immediately mimics the movement, expecting a confession.

"The tall man behind you, over your right shoulder. Gray hair, thinning on top. Black suit, vintage watch. Verux pin, just here." I tap my chest just above my heart. An old first-gen pin, I'm guessing, based on the simplicity of the design—a shield-shaped bit of shiny metal with an engraved *V* in a curving, flowy font. Nothing like Reed's expensive piece of pressed gold and diamonds.

Reed sits back, his face flushing, but his eyes wider than before.

My heart thunders in my chest—I *never* talk about what I see— but I press on. "He's very disappointed to learn that you think he's bullshit," I say.

In reality, he is no such thing as disappointed. Or much of anything. He's a fragment, a barely there shadow tagging after Reed. He doesn't seem to speak or gesture, beyond the pacing. I don't even know if he's with Reed all the time or he's simply drawn to Reed whenever Reed shows up here. It's impossible to say for certain. All I know is I see him only when Reed comes to visit.

"Do you feel him there?" I ask Reed, leaning forward, imitating his "you can tell me" confidant posture. "When you're alone? Always at your shoulder, looking down on you in disapproval?"

"Shut up," Reed snarls, spittle spraying across the table. His skin has gone pale. Interesting. He believes me for some reason on this, but not on anything else.

I cock my head to the side, watching him. I wonder if Reed *recognizes* who I'm describing. The thought raises a chill across my skin. That would definitely put a different spin on what I'm seeing. Maybe this older man in the suit isn't just the result of my malfunctioning brain. Maybe none of them are.

"What's this?" Max returns to the table, eyeing both of us.

But I'm distracted for a moment. On the other side of the room, motion catches my eye.

"She's—" Reed starts in an accusing tone, then cuts himself off.

"Claire?" Max asks.

I ignore him. Kane is back. He's fully visible this time, rather than impeded by the couch. Blood is smeared across the front of his white shirt, but not enough to be fatal. His blood? Someone else's? It takes me a moment to recognize the five uneven lines outside the main blotch as fingers. It's a handprint. Kane's expression is grim determination. He leans down toward something I can't see. I sit up straighter automatically, for a better look, and my perspective suddenly tilts wildly.

I'm on the floor, my head throbbing so hard I can feel it in my teeth. The carpeting beneath me is rough, and I reach up for him . . .

Just as abruptly, the moment breaks, and I'm in my chair in the common room. Kane is gone. And the floor is the same dull gray tile.

"Are you all right?" Max asks.

Another fragment. A new one.

"I'm fine," I say, gripping the edges of the plastic chair beneath me, fingers tight on the safety-molded edges, just hard enough to pinch a little. "I want the course heading."

Max holds up his hand as he retakes his seat at the table. "In a moment."

"Max," I say in warning.

He tuts at me. "Just hear me out. I told you we're sending a ship to intercept the *Aurora*." He looks at me until I nod in acknowledgment.

And it's still a terrible idea.

"It will primarily be a recovery mission," Max continues. "Our team will bring back as many of the remains as we can, along with any survivors."

But I'm already shaking my head. "If you send more people onto that ship, they will die." I don't know how else to be clearer on that point. "Max, we were on the *Aurora* for less than three days and it *destroyed* us." My eyes water at the idea of anyone on that ship ever again, at the memory of our stupid optimism. "Whatever is on there"—I pause to glare at Reed—"ghosts, aliens, some undetectable virus or bacteria, it doesn't matter. It's real and it is deadly. Verux can't negotiate its way out of this."

"We recognize the risk," Max says evenly. "But we can't just destroy a ship with human remains on board."

What he means is they can't destroy a ship with human remains belonging to the world's wealthiest families with everyone watching. Not if Verux has any hope of surviving any of the innumerable pending lawsuits.

"Our team will be going in with a full complement of Verux private security," Max says. "The best of the—"

"Which will do exactly nothing," I argue, heated panic and frustration rising in me, like bright colors breaking through a previously muted landscape.

"And an expert to guide us," Max finishes.

"An expert," I repeat dumbly.

"No," Reed says to Max. "Absolutely not. That would be insane. They can't—"

Max cuts him off. "The only person who's been there, who somehow survived," he says, focused on me.

The connection finally clicks. He wants me to go back to the *Aurora*, and lead them.

A violent chill spreads over me, and the air in my lungs vanishes. I shove my chair away from the table, the legs squawking against the tile in protest. "No." My midsection gives way, as if my spine has simply dissolved, and I end up huddled over my own legs, desperately trying to suck in oxygen. "No fucking way."

"You are the best chance our people have at surviving—"

"Cancel it. That's their best chance," I say, panting. The gray fabric of my patient pajamas covering my legs smells of bleach and antiseptic, a scent that grows stronger with the dampness of my breath against the material.

"We can't," Max says with a sigh. "Your return took that option away from us."

My rescue from a twenty-year-old escape pod that had vanished with the world's first and only luxury spaceliner had made headlines on all the newsfeeds. Even before I'd regained some semblance of coherence—trauma and a head injury combined with days of limited water and food on the escape pod had apparently left me in a dramatically weakened state—and told my story to the crew of the *Raleigh*. Word had spread across the commweb like fire in an oxygen purifier.

I sit up slowly, hands wrapping tight in the excess fabric of my pant legs. "So it's my fault no matter what?" Either they go without me and die while attempting a rescue triggered by my escape and demanded by the public and powerful families. Or I go with them, and we all die together. Somehow I suspect that "third time's a charm" does not apply to narrow escapes from death.

Max doesn't say anything, but he doesn't have to. He's right.

I can't change the past. I could, though, choose not to make the same fucking mistake. I shake my head. "I am not leading innocent people to their deaths." *Again.*

"You survived so you must—"

"But I don't remember how!" I shout. "I don't know what happened. One minute, I was on the bridge with the dead body of one of my crew and a hallucination of her . . . or her fucking ghost, I don't know! And the next I'm on the *Raleigh* in their MedBay."

Max eyes me for a long moment. "I think you know more than you realize."

I glare at him. "What the hell is that supposed to mean?"

"The course heading that you've been asking about?" Max prompts.

I nod tightly.

"Earth," Max says. "The ship is heading here."

Goose bumps rise all over my skin, little pinpricks of sensation.

"According to your story, the destination was the far edge of the commweb in—"

"Sector K147." My lips feel numb.

"Which means somewhere along the way, someone changed course," Max says, confirming what I've already pieced together.

I shake my head. "It doesn't mean anything. I told you, I think I remember the engines being stopped or slowed down when I was . . . when I saw Lourdes that last time. Kane could have changed course then. Before I left, before . . ."

Before he and Nysus died. Or, before I killed them, depending on what version of events is true. I feel sick.

"And then there's this." Max nods at Reed, who reluctantly produces a small flat plastic circle from his pocket and then taps at his visible-only-to-him keyboard.

Sound emerges from the disk; it's a speaker. Nothing at first beyond the rough rasp of static. Then words emerge, like shapes out of heavy fog.

". . . help. Mayday . . . vessel, the *Aurora* . . . rescue requested . . . under attack . . . souls on board."

Even with the interference, I recognize that voice.

Kane.

21

I left him. Oh my God, I left him. Maybe Nysus, too.

Vomit scorches up my throat and out of my mouth onto the floor before I can stop it.

Reed jerks his chair back in disgust, and Max stands. "Excuse me? We need some help over here." He sounds calm, unsurprised.

Two attendants, one male and one female, rush over with such alacrity it feels as though they must have been hovering nearby, expecting to be called or to eavesdrop. Or both. The man addresses the floor with a bottled solution; the woman wipes a towel roughly over my face and bare feet, pulling the towel away from my hands when I try to take it to do it myself. What kind of harm could I do to myself or anyone else with that?

"It's a repeating message on an old emergency channel from the *Aurora* herself," Max says. "Very similar to the one on the automated beacon you described hearing in the first place."

The distress beacon that someone on the *Aurora* had had enough wherewithal to deliberately set off, despite the insanity around them. Despite taking the ship off course and beaching it without so much as a call for help. Which in the sea of illogical and outright insane things surrounding the *Aurora* still stands out as odd.

"We've attempted communication, of course. No response," Max says.

"There might not be," I say after a moment, still dizzy with the revelation. "Lourdes must not have had time to finish the upgrade. How . . . how long ago was this message received?"

"Ten days ago," Max says. "It's likely been cycling for longer than that, but no one thought to check the old emergency channel at first."

Until someone, somewhere, believed at least that part of my story.

Ten days. "You think he's alive," I say. *I left them. Oh God, I left them.* The words just keep beating into my brain, over and over again.

But if they were alive, why would I have left them? *How* could I have left them? And if I left them alive, why am I seeing Kane, like Lourdes and Voller? Granted, my visions of him shift and change, unlike Lourdes and Voller who show me the same thing each time. I've never seen Ny at all. But that had made sense to me, in that he would be as reluctant to show himself in death as he had been in life.

"It's possible," Max hedges.

"Or," Reed interjects, "Mr. Behrens recorded the message before you left, before you decided to eliminate any loose ends."

The urge to launch myself at him, to knock him out of his chair and pound my fist against his face, is overwhelming. I clench my hands, feeling the imaginary sting of split skin on my knuckles. Living in the Verux group home for so many years had been good for a few things, primarily absorbing—sometimes painfully—the life principle of do no harm but take no shit.

This time, though, a bubble of fear stops me. Not fear of Reed. Or even of the attendants and their syringes. No, it's the idea that Max could change his mind. I don't want to return to the *Aurora.* Just the idea—let alone the eventual reality of it—makes me feel like I'm falling endlessly through space, whipping around in nauseating circles, losing track of any handhold or chance to stop my descent.

But the thought of Max retracting his request, of being left behind while strangers search for survivors, for *my* crew.

"I'll go," I say, the syllables sounding nonsensical, just noise escaping my throat.

"Good." Max sounds satisfied, but oddly more than that, almost proud of me, in a paternal sort of way. "You're doing the right thing."

That's the second time someone has said that to me in recent memory. Maybe this time it'll turn out to be true.

"And you won't be alone. Reed and I will be there to supervise and maintain safe conditions to the best of our ability," Max adds.

"We'll be watching," Reed says, clearly meant more as warning than reassurance.

Their words barely register with me.

I shake my head. "But I would never have left Kane. Or Nysus or any of them. Not by choice."

Max reaches over and pats my shoulder. "I think it's impossible for any of us to know what we would or would not do after experiencing what you've been through. On the *Aurora*." He lowers his voice. "And on Ferris. Surviving is nothing to be ashamed of, Claire." He gives me a smile touched with gentle pity.

Except it clearly is. Oh God, it is. The captain goes down with her ship. Leave no one behind. By surviving, I've violated every implicit code of leadership. Of family. And I don't even fucking remember it.

Maybe that's why you don't remember it. You don't want to.

"I'll be in touch with more details soon," Max says with one last pat on my shoulder before he stands. His worn shoes squeak with the movement.

Reed follows his lead, packing away the tiny speaker and swiping through the air above the table to turn off his keyboard.

They start to leave.

"Max," I call after him.

He turns back, eyebrows raised in question.

"If I'm going to do this, I need . . ." I lick my dry lips, all too aware of the remaining taste of acidic vomit in my mouth. "I need you to tell them to pull back on the drugs." I tilt my head toward the attendants, who are standing nearby. The cushion of medication, blunting my emotions, hazing my thoughts, it's been the only thing getting me through each day. But the parade of pills—and occasional injection—have made me a slower, duller, more manageable version of me, even as they have eased the pain of living.

"I need to be . . . myself again." The idea offers distant horror, like a smoking wreck on the horizon. But if this gambit is to have the slightest chance at success, I can't take the risk of being even a little bit removed from reality. Look what happened the last time, when I was in possession of all my faculties. Or, the majority of them, anyway.

Max eyes me for a long moment. "I understand," he says finally. "I do. But I think you can understand why we are grateful for your help and yet . . . not inclined to take that risk."

It's a slap, but one I feel only minimally. Thanks to the drugs he is refusing to lift.

"You need to maintain your equilibrium," Max says. "The treatment plan is helping you do that. This will be a difficult situation as it is. We don't need to make it more . . . challenging for you."

Reed shoots me a triumphant look over his shoulder, and then they leave.

The attendants are on me immediately, shuffling me to my room to change out of my sweat-soaked and vomit-spattered pajamas.

Their hands are not unkind but swift, impersonal. I'm so used to it now, I barely notice.

Perhaps Max is right. Maybe the pills are helping, keeping me level. Maybe if I didn't have them, I wouldn't be able to stop screaming.

Or maybe it's simply easier for Max—and everyone—if I'm more manageable. Maybe it's safer. For them.

I don't know.

Either way, when the male attendant presses the small cup in my hand, full to rattling—like one of those extinct snakes on Earth—of medications, I take it. After what I said to Max, he's watching for resistance. But I know better than to show it. I tip the cup against my lip, letting the pills land against my tongue, the bitterness immediately triggering a wash of saliva and the desire to choke them down to end the sensation.

But in a moment that I fear that I'll second-guess later, I manipulate the pills under my tongue and along the side of my gums, and fake a pained dry-swallow.

"You need water?" the attendant asks.

I shake my head. And then I open my mouth, per routine, to show that I've been obedient and done as required.

Satisfied that I'm not demonstrating any form of resistance, he—also per routine—barely glances at me.

The female attendant shuffles me toward the bed, and when they both have their attention on pulling back the sheet and prepping the night restraints, I spit the dissolving pills into my palm, clenching my fist to keep them hidden.

My heart is pounding as they help me into bed and wrap the fabric around my wrists. Not from the fear of getting caught, I realize, but from what will happen, during a long night of nothing but me and my unmedicated mind. What will I see? What will I remember?

I'm not sure which is worse.

The pills are still stuck against my skin inside my fist and for a moment, I'm tempted to confess. Tempted to bend my head toward my hand as close as I can to try to get them to my mouth and for a deepening of the blissful oblivion they offer.

Instead, I wait until the attendants leave and then I tuck my hand beneath the sheet and shake the pills loose onto the bed. They fall, rolling across the mattress to settle near my leg or bounce the other way, captured between the layers of bottom sheet and top sheet. This ploy will not last more than a day, once they change the bedding. I hope that will be enough time for Max to get me out of here. But mainly, I hope it's not too much time—I don't know how long I can hold it together without those pills. Too many hours of unmedicated madness and no one's going to let me go anywhere.

It turns out, the ward is not an easy place to sleep when you're not drugged into oblivion, even if everyone else is.

Vera whimpers across the hall. Someone, somewhere, is shouting. Then a rush of footsteps head in that direction. No one bothers to check on me as they pass. There are rounds through the night, though, probably. I would think so, though I have no memory of anything like that. Once again, my mind is failing me. But at least this time, I understand the cause of it.

I shiver at the idea of such vulnerability, bound to the bed and completely out of it, while someone stares down at me.

Sweat coats my skin as withdrawal begins. I squeeze my eyes shut. It would be better if I could sleep through most of this.

But my eyelids refuse to stay closed, even though there's nothing to look at. The room isn't dark with dim light from the hall seeping in through the partially open door.

My gaze bounces around my small room, from the plastic visitor's chair across from the bed, the three-drawer bureau on the wall at the foot of the bed, to the Tower-owned-and-installed art panel above the bureau. The normally serene lake scene, with the weeping willow branches swaying gently in the breeze, looks ominous, threatening.

A low moan comes from nearby, and I jerk my attention away from the lake to the visitor's chair.

The man, dressed in gray pajamas like mine, is seated and bleeding from his wrists, the wounds horrible gashes. His fingers loosen and drop a twisted and sharpened bit of metal, perhaps a bracket from the bureau drawers. It hits the tile floor with a soft clink.

My breath catches, and then I realize that I've been waiting. For him. For *them*.

He looks at me, through me, and then vanishes.

A moment later, a woman walks by outside my door, calling for someone. "Tallie? Are you here?"

I can't see her, but when no one rushes to respond to a resident up and out of bed in the middle of the night, I am left with the conclusion that she, also, is not really there. A former resident, like the suicide in my chair?

When I lived on-planet last, in the Verux group home, on overcrowded and under-resourced Earth, it was difficult. So many people, and with them, the others who no one else could see. But I learned to ignore it . . . and to run when I couldn't.

But here, at the Tower of Peace and Harmony—what bullshit wishful thinking—there is nowhere to run.

I pull hard against the restraints, but they have no give. Not that I have anywhere to go, to get away, even if they did.

An old man shuffles into my room, passing through the wall on my left. His hospital gown is white, bearing a large Verux logo on the left side of his chest. Not like any of the clothing I've seen distributed here.

He pauses, seeming to see me, and a chill ricochets through my body.

"Marja?" he asks, then continues without waiting for an answer. "I'm sorry. I didn't have a choice. You know that. Don't you? I didn't know the engines were overheating."

I can't respond. I don't know what to say.

But it doesn't seem to matter. He turns away from me, heading for the opposite wall, and I see the back of his head and shoulders, all blistered, blackened, and burned.

He passes through the wall and vanishes. He's not impeded by the constructs of the physical world, so I can still hear him giving his speech, to whoever is next door, whoever he thinks is Marja. Hallucinations, spirits, whatever you want to call them, their noise isn't stopped by walls, doors, or burying your head under a pillow. Even earplugs are useless. The sounds are *inside* your head, which has nothing to do with actual vibrations hitting your eardrum. Getting out of range is the only solution.

Earplugs. Something about that niggles at me, a familiarity that I can't quite seem to latch on to.

"Marja!" He sounds closer now. In the hall maybe? He must do this every night. Or maybe even throughout the day.

I shudder against the sweat-dampened and sticky sheets, imagining him approaching me while I'm awake but completely unaware.

My chest feels tight, the sensation of the walls closing in on me. So many of them, invisible but still here, crowding in on the living. That's why the LINA had never bothered me. Yes, it was small, but that limited *all* the occupants. The fewer people around, the fewer sightings I'd have.

A flash of motion in the upper right corner of the room catches my attention, and I crane my head in time to see Voller saluting me, raising that drill. The spatter of the blood sounds so much louder in the quiet dimness of my room.

Before he's vanished completely, Lourdes appears, her sightless eyes trying to track, her head cocked as she searches. *I don't understand.*

A whimper rises in my throat. I don't know if I can survive this without the pills.

My fingers scrabble against the sheets, searching for them. But they've scattered out of reach.

The visitations, from familiar faces and not, continue. Some of them touch me, cool hands brushing against my skin when I cannot escape, cannot move away from their grasping fingers.

Others simply walk through me as though I'm not there, which is sometimes worse. The shudder and soul-deep coldness that comes with the reminder that the solid sanctity of your body is an illusion.

The whispers in my ear, the shouts of despair, the weeping reaches a cacophonous level, drowning out even the loud buzzing in my bad ear that has returned.

A scream bubbles to my lips; only the barest restraint keeps it back. Hot tears trickle down my face, and I can't reach them to wipe them away.

My mother's hand brushes my cheek. *Be careful, love.* I hear her in my head. A hallucination, a ghost? I can't tell anymore, if I ever could.

Kane appears at the foot of the bed, hands on his hips, his shirt bloodied beneath his open jumpsuit, but the sight of him is a relief. He is brighter, in bolder colors than the Tower ghosts. They seem to fade around him.

He smiles at me, that warm but worried expression I'm well familiar with from him, and suddenly, I'm no longer strapped in a bed but standing next to him, in a dimly lit suite on the *Aurora,* after everything went to hell. Literally, perhaps.

Recognition clanks in me, like an off-key note. This is . . . this is a *memory.* I remember this.

In a moment, he's going to reach out and touch my chin. And instead of the caress of cool phantom fingertips, I feel the rough, calloused warmth of his hand. *"Are you sure?"*

Then the old man ghost reappears, walking right through Kane. "Marja?"

Kane vanishes and in a dizzying moment of reorientation, I'm back in my bed again, strapped in. Sure about what? What was Kane talking about?

The man in my visitor chair moans and drops his makeshift knife, and once more, I hear the spatter of Voller's blood hitting the floor. Another memory or something else?

Memories, visions, hallucinations all jumbled up in my head until I can no longer tell the difference? How will I know what's real? And this is here, in the Tower, not on the *Aurora,* where it will surely be worse.

I can feel myself spiraling, my breath racing in and out. *Keep it together, Claire. Keep it—*

"I don't understand," Lourdes says, right near my ear. The whisper of her exhale feels cool against my skin. Memory or visitation? I can't tell. I can't fucking tell. Will the rest of my life be like this, either locked up and drugged to the gills or seeing things that may or may not be real?

Panic bursts in me, then, like a river overflowing a dam.

And I scream.

22

"You look like shit," Reed Darrow says loudly, disgust curling the words.

His voice penetrates the haze, and I peel my sticky eyelids open to see him next to my bed, in another of his precise suits, staring down at me with irritation.

It takes me a moment to re-collect myself. I shift, trying to sit up. The restraints are gone and Reed is here; it must be morning. But early. Because I'm not dressed yet, and the injection site on my left arm is still sore. That small pain helps clear some of the fog. Screaming last night brought attendants running with a sedative.

I made it. I survived the night.

Warily, I look around and immediately spot the wrist-slasher in the visitor chair. The sharpened bracket tumbles to the floor as he moans. "Tallie?" the woman calls out over the noise of the residents and the soothing murmurs of attendants in the hallway.

Fuck. I jerk my gaze away from the man—the ghost?—in the chair, as a familiar throat-clearing sound comes from the doorway. Max.

"It sounds like you had a rough night," he says. "You sure you're up for this?"

For a moment, I'm torn. It would be easier to stay away and hide behind the thick fog of artificial and medically induced sanity. But I need to know what happened, how I ended up here, whether Kane and Nysus are still alive. And the sooner I'm out of here and off-planet, the better. I hope.

What if whatever happened on the *Aurora* broke me for good? What if I just keep seeing these people everywhere, the same way I see Kane, Lourdes, and Voller?

My breathing picks up as panic seeps in beneath the remains of the sedative.

"Marja!" the old man shouts from somewhere nearby.

"I'm ready," I say as clearly as I can with a dry mouth and thick tongue. I have to try. And if it's just as bad out there as it is down here on Earth, in the Tower, well, then it'll be a lot easier to end myself in space than locked down in a facility designed to prevent that. The thought brings a surprising amount of calm with it. Just to have a plan.

If I'd had the courage to do it on my last space walk, then none of this would have even happened.

Except Kane would never have left me out there, and he and the others might have died attempting to save me.

So instead, he dies seeing things that aren't there and calling for his daughter? Voller puts a drill to his head and Lourdes removes her eyes because they can't take it? Much better, Kovalik.

I wince inwardly but manage to hold Max's gaze until he nods.

"Good. Glad to hear it," Max says. He jerks his head at Reed, who tosses a pile of fabric onto the bed. I recognize the blue instantly. Verux jumpsuit. Probably with the requisite Verux-branded undergarments. Of course.

Reed leaves, turning sideways past Max. "This is a bad idea," he mutters.

But Max ignores him. "She's ready," he says to someone out in the hall, and two female attendants bustle in. Max steps back into the hall as they start to pull the sheets down to help me out of bed.

"I can stand and dress myself," I say with more confidence than I feel. "Can I have some privacy, please?" When he doesn't respond, I press. "Unless you're planning on dressing me while we're en route."

The two attendants glance back at the doorway and at a signal I can't see, they leave.

I push myself out of bed, putting my feet gingerly on the floor, highly aware of Max and likely Reed in the corridor, waiting for me to fall. To fail.

I'm slow, arms and legs trembling, but I manage to get my patient pajamas off and the new garments on. Though the jumpsuit is crisp and new, instead of worn and soft like one of mine, I instantly feel more like myself when it's on.

I have a harder time with socks and boots. Fine motor skills are . . . rough. Still, I get it done. And I take an extra second for what I hope looks like an attempt at making the bed and sweep up all the pills I can find, dropping them into a tiny zippered pocket on my jumpsuit.

"Okay," I say to Max, who peers back in.

"Excellent." He reenters the room with a wheelchair.

I stare at him. "You've got to be kidding."

He pats the padded back of the chair. "Policy, I'm afraid." He hesitates. "No one will see you, if that's what you're concerned about. This has all been classified at the highest levels."

Yeah, because what I look like is my biggest concern here.

I'd argue with Max, but I can feel my energy flagging already. Quick bursts are all I seem to be capable of at the moment. With reluctance, I move to the foot of the bed and sit in the wheelchair, carefully avoiding the puddle of blood from the suicidal man in my visitor's chair.

Max pulls the wheelchair carefully out of the room into the hall and stops.

"Oh, and we can't forget." He holds out a pill cup over my shoulder.

I take the cup from him, hoping he'll be too distracted with pushing me down the hall to notice that I don't put them in my mouth. It would be easier to take the pills, to stop questioning everything I see, but I need to have a clear head if I want to figure out what happened on the *Aurora*.

But Max waits, his hands on the handles behind me. "Bottoms up," he says after a moment, handing me a packet of water, exactly the kind I'm used to from the LINA. Soft metallic sides on the pouch reflect heat and light, enhancing its shelf life, and it has a wide-mouthed straw opening. Max must have brought it in himself, because Tower staff would never have given a patient something like this. For the exact reason I'm about to demonstrate.

It's a matter of some work, drinking some of the water and shoving the pills down into the packet with my tongue. It takes longer than it should if I were just swallowing the pills.

Vera appears at the end of the corridor, watching me with a perplexed expression before turning back toward the common room. Walking *through* the wall instead of using the doorway.

Water and air collide at the back of my throat, and I have to work not to cough and spray pills everywhere. She's one of them.

My eyes water, but I keep going.

Max says nothing, until I pull the packet away from my lips and show off the lack of pills in my mouth. The metallic sides keep the pills from being visible and the sealed opening with the straw means someone would have to cut into the packet to find them.

"Good girl," he says heartily, patting me on the shoulder.

The words and gesture grate. I'm not an eleven-year-old child anymore. But I manage a tight smile, if only to avoid generating suspicion.

As Max pushes me down the corridor, I fold and tuck the remains of the water packet into the gap between the padded seat of the wheelchair and its side, where it hopefully will not be discovered for a while. I glance behind me and catch Reed watching me with narrowed eyes.

I wait, heart hammering, for him to call me out, to shout for Max to stop. But he says nothing, just meets my gaze with a smirk, and follows us onto the elevator.

He knows exactly what I'm up to. And he's going to let me run with it for now. Because he wants this to fail, he wants me to fail. Or perhaps it's more complicated than that and he wants Max to fail. The tension between them—Reed making suggestions and comments, with Max ignoring him—is impossible to miss. For somebody as ambitious as Reed Darrow, that must be a crushing blow. And an infuriating one.

Fine. I suppose we'll see. One of us—Reed or I—will be right.

In the lobby, lights flash and shadows swarm against the frosted glass main doors as soon as we approach.

I steel myself against reacting. *So many . . .*

Max sighs. "Damnit. Someone leaked to the media."

Then I realize that some or all of the people-shaped forms are alive. Reporters, it seems.

"Transpo is right outside," Reed points out.

"Keep your head down and say nothing," Max says to me with reluctance. "It'll just be a minute."

Why wouldn't they have arranged a more private pickup? This is the front of the Peace and Harmony Tower. *Anyone* leaving here is going to be a story, but my role in the *Aurora* discovery and the ensuing headlines guarantees more-than-average attention. Surely there's a back entrance somewhere.

But Max pushes the wheelchair through the automatic doors, and it's an explosion of light and sound.

"—have a comment on the lawsuit from the families?"

"Did you kill them, Claire?" a man shouts.

"—suggest that the amount of wealth on board is substantially more than reported at the time. Can you confirm—"

"—tell us about the condition of the passengers. Will the families be able to identify—"

"How were you able to survive?"

That last question—quiet in comparison to the others—draws my attention up, but I can't tell who said it. The portable lights for the cameras are dazzlingly bright.

I lift my hand to shield my eyes, but I still can't see enough to make out faces. Except Lourdes's.

I don't understand. She trails her bloodied fingers down her cheeks.

I look away.

Max hustles me out of the wheelchair and into the third car in the mag-lev transport. It's a solo compartment, and for a moment, I'm alone. For the first time in weeks. The relief is instantaneous, like cool water on a burn.

But then the reporters surround the compartment, pressing against the glass with their words and their cameras on both sides.

Eventually, our transportation—a chain of at least six cars—pulls away from the Tower. I avoid the windows as we leave the reporters behind. But there are more of them waiting as we approach the Verux headquarters, shouting as our vehicles approach the electronic gates.

Someone, somewhere, must have told them not just that I was leaving the Tower but where we were going.

As far as I know, the only people who are aware of the plan are Verux personnel. Why would any of them want to leak the information? I suspect my release, however temporary, is bound to elicit strong and likely negative feelings from a portion of the general population, something that's not exactly going to help Verux clean up this PR mess. Granted, it's a mess they inherited when they bought out CitiFutura, but still.

My suspicion is confirmed by the group of thirty or so protestors at the gates, their faces red with cold, their brightly colored signs flashing in the gray morning light. It's easy to track the various branches of the story and the protestors' particular allegiances to said branches by their signs.

Welcome to Earth, Aliens
Aurora Families for the Truth
Bring Them HOME!
Verux Lies
Greed is Death
Thou Shalt Not Kill!

Though, with the last two, I'm not sure whether they're referring to me or to Verux/CitiFutura and the whole space-industrial complex.

If I had to do this over again—*none* of this would be happening—I would have at least kept my mouth shut on board the *Raleigh,* rather than spilling my broken, confusing tale as soon as I was conscious and semi-coherent. Not that I'd been in a good headspace for making any kind of decisions at that point, dehydrated with a skull fracture and missing chunks of memory.

I woke up in the *Raleigh*'s MedBay under isolation protocols, cold, desperate for water, with no recollection of how I got there. They had found me in the escape pod, while searching for us in the LINA. The *Ginsburg* had apparently sounded the alarm when we missed our ride and they couldn't reach us on comms.

Fueled by an urgency I didn't even entirely understand at the time, I told the doctor and the *Raleigh*'s captain everything I knew, everything I did remember, which was both too much and not enough.

My story had reached Earth before I did, triggering hundreds of conspiracy theories and one poorly made docudrama before Verux shut it down.

As our cars squeeze through the barely open electronic gates, I catch a glimpse of a little girl who looks familiar. She's holding hands with a woman shouting in protest. The girl's dark hair is braided in pigtails with a flash of yellow at the top on each side. Butterflies.

Isabelle? I crane my neck for another look, but she and the woman are gone, the crowd pushing forward around them. If they were ever there in the first place.

I squeeze my eyes shut. If nothing else, I have to do this for Kane's family. For all of their families. They deserve answers, and I don't trust Verux to do more than clean up and come up with a pat story that provides little to no actual information beyond their own blamelessness.

The enormous white shuttle hangars rise up in the distance ahead, and an overwhelming sense of déjà vu sweeps over me. I trained here. I took my first shuttle here, from this launch area to my first hauler and my first sniffer assignment, P3T4. PETA. It seems appropriate I should take my last one from here.

Max is waiting at my door almost as soon as our transport stops outside shuttle hangar 4, as if he fears I'm going to make a break for it. Reed waits a dozen or so feet away, both impatient and sulky at the same time, checking his watch.

Max opens my door. "Come on, this way." He gestures for me to climb out, but he doesn't move until I get out. Then he's a step behind me, escorting me toward the open hangar doors.

This is a different side of Max than I've seen before. Brisk, businesslike. It's a little disconcerting, the difference between his victim bedside manner and this take-charge problem-solver persona he has going on right now.

Makes me feel like I perhaps don't know him as well as I think I do.

Three squads of Verux private security personnel, twenty-one men and women in black uniforms and protective gear, stand at attention, waiting in the excruciatingly bright hangar bay in front of the transfer shuttle we will take up to a larger vessel, probably something in the Striker class. More than a few watch our approach, eyeing me with what feels like pretty open suspicion. They're all heavily armed, with weapons I don't even recognize slung over their shoulders, along with their bags. Crates marked with the Verux logo, a fire symbol, and the words AUTHORIZED USE ONLY stand off to the side.

All of which would be alarming enough, but they're surrounded by death.

My breath catches in my throat.

People are weeping and bloodied, hovering nearby or collapsed on the floor at the feet of the security personnel. Victims? Perpetrators? Impossible to know, but definitely not living, based on the lack of reaction from the security teams and Max, next to me.

Others are dressed in similar Verux security uniforms, presumably teammates that have been lost. A few of them are shouting at or pleading with their still-breathing teammates.

I have to look away.

This is going to go badly. On the *Aurora,* that many weapons, combined with what they're bound to see or think they see? It'll be a bloodbath. One that will jeopardize all of us, including anyone who might still be alive on board.

"Max," I hiss as he charges past me, heading toward the squads like a man who has finally seen a clear solution to his most vexing problem. "Max!"

He pauses and turns back toward me, irritation clear on his face before it smooths out to his normal concerned expression.

"You can't shoot at whatever it is. It's not some minor warlord in a country that Verux is tired of doing business with," I say.

Max gives me a disapproving look. As if I don't know who I'm working for.

"It doesn't work like that. This?" I point to the security teams and their guns and the entities around them. "Is a bad idea." I can already imagine it. They're firing on things that aren't there or maybe are, and either way people die. Especially if they manage to blow holes through the hull of the *Aurora* in the process. Look at the damage we did to ourselves and each other without a single gun between us.

"Let us worry about that. You just focus on you," Max says, the verbal equivalent to a condescending pat on the head, if there ever was one. Then he turns around and leads on.

I shake my head. If he won't warn them, I will. I have to try.

Max stops in front of the squads, feet wide and braced in his worn leather shoes, his hands tucked behind his back, in that "I'm in charge" posture that I've never understood. "Teams Alpha, Bravo, Charlie."

"Sir, yes, sir!" they respond immediately.

"Thank you for your service," he says, and then gives a curt nod that evidently serves as a signal.

The three security teams break from their formation and head for the surrounding crates to begin loading them onto the transport. Something about this is wrong, something beyond the obvious "way too much firepower for an already unstable situation."

But the obvious problem is the one I need to handle first.

I wait and watch, as Max—and Reed tagging along after like a desperate child hoping to hang with the big kids—consults with one of the security personnel, a team leader of a different variety than I am . . . was, most likely. The rest of them move about stowing the crates and cargo, oblivious to the ghosts trailing after them.

When Max seems thoroughly occupied with his conversation, pointing at something on a projected display I can't see from here, I make my move.

Another team leader, or so I'm assuming as he's not doing any fucking work, is standing—again with his hands behind his back, what is that?—supervising his people at a distance.

I sidle up alongside of him, keeping a distance of a couple feet, so maybe it won't be immediately obvious to Max what I'm doing, if he happens to look over. "Listen. I know you don't know me. But you need to hear me. Guns aren't going to solve this."

The man—the patch on his arm reads MCCAUGHEY—doesn't respond. His mouth is a firm, determined line as he monitors the progress in front of him. He's probably been told about me, told to ignore me.

Frustrated, I continue. "It's dangerous. You won't know what's real, who you're firing on. You're going to see things—"

A woman breaks off from helping to carry a crate, sending it along with her teammates, and stomps toward me. Diaz, according to her patch. "Who are you talking to?" Diaz demands, her hand moving toward her sidearm. An unconscious protective gesture.

"McCaughey," I say with a sinking feeling, even though I know as soon as my mouth forms the syllables that it's a mistake. That I've made a big mistake.

Her head rocks back as though I've punched her, her face going pale.

Then she's up in my personal space, jabbing a finger at me. "You think they didn't tell us about you? You shut the hell up about McCaughey. You aren't getting into our heads that easily."

Next to me, McCaughey shifts, responding to Diaz's approach by stepping back and turning so he can keep an eye on her. And of course, as soon as he does, I see the front of him and I'm greeted by the gravity of my error. McCaughey is bloodied and dead, the left half of his face demolished, just meat with twisted metal shrapnel still sticking out.

An explosion during the course of a mission. Probably happened so fast, he never saw it coming. He was working then, so he continues to work now. Reliving his last moments, which are apparently tied to Diaz and possibly her teammates.

Damnit. I lost track when the security personnel started moving around. Or maybe McCaughey had blended in from the beginning, not being among the shouting, pleading ones.

I hold my hands up, tearing my gaze away from McCaughey to focus on Diaz. "I'm sorry," I say carefully. "I didn't know, but it doesn't change anything. This is still—"

"At ease, Diaz," Max says mildly next to me, startling me. I hadn't even heard him approach.

She stiffens, her spine going straight. "Yes, sir," she mumbles.

I gape at Max. What the hell does he have on them? He's just a grandpa-y guy in worn-out shoes and days or maybe weeks from retirement. A paper pusher from the QA Department.

"Go on," he says in that same gentle tone, nodding toward the shuttle. Diaz stalks away to return to her tasks, but she tosses a glare at me over her shoulder as she goes and her fists are still clenched at her sides.

I turn toward Max, mouth open to explain.

But he just sighs. "Oh, Claire."

23

The shuttle trip and transfer goes smoothly and without incident. If you don't count the thick tension in the air with me on one side of the shuttle and Diaz and her teammates on the other.

But once we—Max, Reed, the security teams—are on board the Striker-class vessel, *Ares,* he breaks the news. In typical Max fashion.

"You can understand their discomfort," he says, leading me down the corridor to my quarters. Which will apparently be secured from the outside. A private bath is attached to what is normally the cabin of a higher-ranking official on whatever business this vessel is "officially" used for, but that privilege is not quite enough to make up for the loss of freedom. Even prison cells have toilets. "Their primary objective is the successful completion of this mission. They don't want any more . . . surprises."

As it turns out, Max's version of me focusing on me—as he suggested earlier—involves "securing" me in my room. For the entire journey that it'll take us to reach the *Aurora,* meals included. I don't know if this was part of Max's plan all along. I do know I didn't help myself with Diaz.

"The *Ares* is much faster. Just three weeks to the outer edge of the commweb instead of a month. Perhaps less, as the *Aurora* is still heading toward us, and we'll be on an intercept course." His mouth flattens unhappily at this idea. "You'll hardly notice the time going by."

Five hundred hours, give or take, trapped in a ten-by-ten room. I'm pretty sure I'll notice.

I wipe my dampened palms against the jumpsuit fabric covering my legs. "Max. I don't do well locked up."

"You did just fine in the Tower, it seems." He cocks his head to the side, giving me a challenging look, as if daring me to tell the truth. "Far smaller and less luxurious accommodations there."

It's not the size of the space that matters; it's my inability to leave it when I need to. Not to mention, in the Tower, I was drugged out of my mind.

My fingers fidget with the zipper pocket hiding my pills from last night. "That's different," I say lamely.

Out of the corner of my eye, I can see Reed behind us. He smirks at me, but says nothing. The man in the old-fashioned black suit—Reed's grandfather, perhaps? It would make sense with the generation pins—hovers nearby, his stern expression focused on Reed.

Max clucks at me. "Claire, the entire ship is an enclosed space. So . . . just imagine this as a much smaller ship. With meal-delivery service."

I could argue. Or try to, at least. But being alone, rather than jammed in with the security teams, might be the better idea. If they're far enough away from me on this ship, I might not even see any of them—living or dead.

He gestures for me to step ahead of him into the room. It's a tidy space with a bed tucked against the right wall, an empty desk on the left, and shelves holding nothing but dust opposite the door. No window or even a viewscreen.

It's obviously been Claire-proofed. Nothing to do, no way to off myself, should it come to that.

I turn to face Max. "What am I supposed to do while—"

But he's already closing the door, waving away my words. "If you need anything, just let the guard know. Reed will be nearby to help."

My last view of the corridor is Max's small, smug smile, and Reed Darrow's expression of fury and disappointment at being my designated babysitter.

Up to three weeks alone with nothing but my head and the ghosts, both literal and figurative perhaps, therein.

I can't do this. My fingers go to the pocket of my jumpsuit. I could just take the pills.

No. I need my head clear when we arrive at the *Aurora*. Three weeks from now.

I cross to the far wall, twelve steps. The bookshelf is as empty as it first appeared. When I check the sleek built-in desk, the tidy compartments are equally as vacant as the shelves. Not so much as a label to read.

I pace toward the door and the bed, and then back again. The room grows smaller—and somehow warmer—with every step. There's nowhere to go. Nothing to do. I'm going to go crazy here. Crazier. And we haven't even left Earth's orbit. Why the hell would Max do this to me?

Agitation grows in me until I feel the angry fizz of it in my blood, like my skin might suddenly burst outward from the pressure of it.

Kane appears in the center of the bed, standing. His legs end abruptly at the mattress.

I freeze.

He gestures for me to come closer, with that wide-eyed look of barely restrained panic. His mouth is moving but no sound comes out, as always.

This time, though, absent the Tower's chaotic environment and mind-dulling drugs, I realize I know what he's saying. Asking, rather.

Are you okay?

Instantly, I'm transported elsewhere. The *Aurora*, in a corridor. But the gleaming wooden panels are gone. The walls here are more industrial-looking, plain smooth metal bolted into place. The hum in my bad ear is almost unbearably loud, and dizziness washes over me in waves. My head feels . . . wrong. Burning with pain, in fiery jagged lines across my skull, as if it's shattered glass barely hanging together in a frame. But I'm up, on my feet.

Are you okay? Kane asks again, this time slowing the words and enunciating the syllables carefully.

He realizes I can't hear him. But I can feel the thrum of the engines beneath my feet, and a distant, irregular high-pitched noise that takes me a long moment to identify as someone screaming. Who is screaming?

I'm good. I manage to form the words, though they are thick and slurry with pain.

Then Lourdes comes into view behind him. She is whole, intact. No bloodied hands, no missing eyes. She bites her lip in worry, then releases a stream of words that I can't catch.

To my shock, Kane turns toward her, acknowledging her presence.

She's alive?

Surprise makes my breath catch in my throat, and that is enough to break the delicate thread connecting me to the scene before me.

Kane and Lourdes vanish, and I'm once again in my locked cabin on *Ares*.

My wobbling knees start to give, and I fumble for the desk chair, sitting heavily in it before I fall.

What was *that*? A hallucination . . . or a returning memory?

I shake my head and wince at the phantom pain from an injury long healed. I don't understand this.

My hands are trembling, and I lace my fingers together in my lap to make them stop.

None of it makes any sense. The back of my head on the right side was throbbing like it was in pieces and barely holding together—it had to have been after Voller and the drill, but . . .

I don't remember anything from then. There's nothing but blackness. Not even a gap or an empty spot. Just . . . nothing.

I assumed that was because I was unconscious. I have no memory of being moved to the bridge or Lourdes hurting herself because I wasn't aware at the time.

But what if that's not right?

My heart races in my chest, a sensation mixed with queasy anticipation and outright fear.

If I'm missing a piece from that brief window in time, how can I be sure I'm not missing more than that?

I stand up again, my legs still trembling but more solid beneath me now, and cross the room to bang on the door. "Hey!"

No response, and panic zips through my veins. Are they just going to ignore me for the whole trip?

"Hello?" I pound some more, and eventually footsteps sound outside the door.

"You're not getting out, Kovalik." Reed sounds impatient. "You know if you'd just cooperated with me and—"

"I need something to write with," I interrupt. "Something to write on."

This time alone . . . maybe I can use it. Going over what I do remember, paying more attention to what I'm seeing when Kane and Lourdes and Voller appear instead of trying to avoid them.

"Isn't it a little late to be worrying about getting your story straight?" Reed asks, the sneer coming through loud and clear even through the closed door.

Officious prick. I hope whatever is on the *Aurora* gets him. Before it gets me, at least.

"Can you just get me something? Or do you need to check in with Max first?" I ask, the words dripping with faux sweetness.

He stomps off, his footsteps growing more distant, and I grimace. *Too far, Claire.* He's used to people bowing and scraping.

I settle myself on the bed, pushing my back against the wall, and trying to remember an ill-fated lesson on meditation and clearing my mind. Another Verux childhood psych expert, another technique. I was a favorite pet project for many of them over the seven years I lived in Verux's care back on Earth. An unsuccessful one, by most standards, though I learned to fake "normal" a little better by the end of it all.

But the increased throb of the engines beneath me and the momentary lurch as the dampeners kick in to compensate for our acceleration tells me we're away, making it hard to focus.

We're on our way. And Lourdes was *alive*. In a moment that I didn't recall. Which means maybe . . . she's still alive. Maybe they all are.

A deep doubting voice in me attempts to quell the too-bright spark of hope. *You know what you saw.*

Except I don't!

But you don't know what you don't know.

Frustrated, I bump my head back against the wall, as if that will somehow shake the memories loose.

A loud rattle at the door signals that the lock is being disengaged.

"Coming in," Reed announces tersely from the other side. "I got what you asked for."

I push myself off the bed and head for the door. It opens a few inches as I approach, like I might attempt to shove my way through.

With a sigh, I stay back and hold out my hands.

I'm expecting an old-fashioned tablet. Something left on board, tucked in a storage cubby somewhere, even on a highly advanced vessel like this. Occasionally, they're still needed, like on the LINA when our main processor was downloading updates off the comm-web.

Instead, Reed holds out a short cylindrical object. I recognize it only after I take it—a pen. Specifically, Max's pen, it seems, or one identical to it.

I look up at him, and he thrusts a stack of pages at me. Blank, creamy white paper, smooth to the touch. Rare, expensive.

I raise my eyebrows at Reed before taking it.

"He won't miss it, and he said to get you whatever you need," Reed says, in a way that makes me think this is less about giving me what I asked for and more about getting even with Max in some small, petty way.

Until Max sees me with it, of course.

But I'm not about to introduce that idea and have my prizes taken away.

"Thank yo—" But Reed is closing the door on my words before they're even fully out.

Fine. Whatever.

I return to the bed and scrawl my notes about what I remembered—maybe—with Kane and Lourdes. Then I hesitate. It's in the middle—after I was hurt, but before I somehow got off the ship. Maybe a timeline would be useful in sorting out what's real and what's not.

I sketch in a rough timeline, leaving most of it blank for now.

Then I put the pen down—it's strange to use one for something beyond signing my name but the drag of friction between the metal tip on the pen and the paper is oddly soothing, like I'm chiseling into rock, carving out the answers I seek—and try to focus. I need more. More of what I've somehow lost.

I try sitting up, then move to lying down. Eyes open, eyes closed. Nothing, except the soothing hum of the engines. It's as if my interest in these potential memories has caused them to skitter away into hiding.

Trying to force it isn't likely to work, and yet, I can't stop myself.

While I'm lying on the bed, determinedly staring into the darkness of my own eyelids, exhaustion eventually overtakes me. The rhythmic white noise of the ship's engines—a different pitch and resonance than the LINA's but still familiar—sounds like home, lulling me toward sleep. I hadn't realized how much I'd missed engine noise until now. The Tower was rarely silent, but it never held this particular comforting wash of sound.

Finally, just as sleep is pulling me under its dark, thick waves, I realize what was bothering me about the crates being loaded onto the shuttle and then the *Ares* besides the issue of overkill and likely ineffectiveness.

Bringing the bodies of the *Aurora* passengers and crew back home in a ship with an active environment would require some kind of preservation technique. Cold, chemicals, something. But nowhere had I seen anything marked as medical equipment.

At the very least, sealable body bags would be required, certainly.

And a hundred of those, give or take, should have taken up a noticeable amount of space. But that had not been the case, as far as I'd seen.

So . . . what exactly is Max planning to do?

24

I lose track of the days. Most of the time, I find that the fragments—
pieces of lost or buried memories—show up when I'm not seeking
them out. When I'm eating. When I'm writing out pieces of what
I already know. When I'm sporadically allowed out of my quarters
during the dead shift to run on the treadmill in the ship's gym.

My only regular company is the ghost—or whatever you want
to call it—of Reed Darrow's grandfather. He of the black suit with
wide, outdated buttons and a Verux first-gen pin. He paces in and
out through the wall closest to wherever Reed is. Likely next door.
The grandfather is a silent but steady presence that no longer un-
nerves me.

My mother has not been here once, which I don't understand.
But when I look back on it, she seems only to make herself
known when I'm panicking or in recognizable danger. Which
leads me to believe that perhaps the battalion of experts was
correct: she is in my mind. A coping mechanism for dealing with
everything else, generated out of need first on Ferris when I was
alone. Though that still doesn't explain everything, so I don't
know.

Kane and the others, though. They are here as often as ever, and
most of the time, only showing me exactly what I've seen before,
for months now.

A few times, there has been more.

A blurry Kane arguing with me, his face flushed with hectic
color, blood on the side of his head. The whole moment is washed
of detail, and the remembered pain in my head is much worse.

Lourdes, banging on the door from inside one of the suites, crying for help. I'm trying to get to her, but someone pulls me away.

A brief flash of Nysus with an elastic bandage wrapped tightly around his head.

Someone screaming in the dark, as I move through a narrow hallway, one that shows no signs of the luxury of the Platinum Level, or even one of the lower passenger decks.

That one, I think, might be part of the memory I recovered before, with Kane and Lourdes, when she was still alive.

On the bed, I lean back against the wall, dropping the pen on the page where I'm attempting to make everything fit into a coherent timeline—and scrub at my tired and burning eyes.

Here's what I know: my last memory, the one on the bridge, is not the last thing I did or said on board the *Aurora*, which isn't news. I got into that escape pod somehow.

But I'm also missing pieces from the time between when I was injured and that moment on the bridge. For example, at some point, Kane, Lourdes, and I were wandering around the ship, outside the sealed area—assuming those snippets drifting through my mind are actual memories rather than scenarios of my own invention. But why? What were we doing? What were we looking for?

That gap in my recall bothers me even more. How much am I missing? Why is it just gone from my head?

But all any of it means is I'm no closer to the truth than I was when I started. Because essentially, there are only two possibilities.

One: I left because my crew was all dead.

Two: I left even though my crew was alive and suffering. And I have no idea why.

Neither of those options is acceptable.

Shoving the paper away from me in frustration, I get up and pace the tiny room again. For the hundredth time or the thousandth, I've lost count.

Because I'm standing, I feel it instantly, the tiny, momentary lurch as the engines slow. Then the engine noise declines, just enough to be noticeable in its reduction.

My heart flaps about anxiously in my chest, but the rest of me is frozen in place. Wait, are we here? Or there, rather?

I try to count back, how many mornings have passed since that first one. The number is likely in the high teens somewhere, which means, yes, it's possible.

Closing my eyes, I try to imagine what's happening now. They're reducing speed, which means the next maneuver will likely be to come about and pull alongside . . .

I feel the shift, a small push toward portside as the ship comes about on the starboard and the gravity generator compensates.

We're here. The *Aurora* is right outside. With all the answers I've been seeking.

My mouth instantly goes dry.

I rush to the door and beat my fists against it. "Hey! Hey, let me out!" My voice is cracked and rusty, the product of speaking to no one for days.

But no one comes. There's no annoyed response from the guard on the other side of the door, no stomping of irritated footsteps.

For a moment, my imagination shows me the *Ares* abandoned, the security squads, Reed and Max, all somehow vanished. Empty seats, bowls of rehydrated food slowly turning to dust, autopilot simply following the preestablished course.

But I shove that ridiculous and paranoid thought down. I saw a member of the security team just this morning—last night?—when she brought me my food and the requisite pills, which I stored in a desk drawer with all the others. And someone has to be piloting the ship through the course change.

Which means, they've elected to—or been ordered to, by Max—leave me in here for now.

The idea of remaining in here for hours while the *Aurora* is right there, visible and on-screen with whatever clues an outside view may hold, sends a flare of fury and panic through me. I need to see it. I need to know. I don't even know which of the two options I'm hoping to be true anymore—if my crew is dead, all hope is lost, but if they're alive, then I left them—but the uncertainty is a fire burning in my gut. I cannot stand it.

I pound on the door and shout for the better part of half an hour.

I've just resorted to kicking, which is equally ineffective, when someone calls out on the other side.

"All right, all right, calm down, Kovalik." It's Reed Darrow. "Step back."

"Okay," I say without moving.

When the door opens outward, he jumps in surprise to find me so close. "Jesus!" I haven't seen him in I don't know how many days, and he looks like shit. His once-pristine suit now holds several days' or a week's worth of wrinkles. The collar on his shirt has a blotch of some kind of food. No dry cleaners in space. His chin is covered in patchy stubble and the purple circles beneath his eyes from lack of sleep are so dark they make him look like he's been headbutted. An honor I would have gladly volunteered for.

I'm guessing this is his first extended period in space. The first tour is always hard. It fucks with your circadian rhythms, the lack of sunlight and fresh air. And the jumpsuits aren't just Verux pushing protocol down our throats; they're practical.

I shove past him into the corridor, angry at him for inexplicable reasons. For suddenly seeming human and fallible, for finally getting a taste of the life he was so dismissive of in our conversations in the Tower and clearly not being able to handle it. Maybe I should find it funny, but I don't. I want to shake him instead. "Not exactly the luxury cruise you were expecting?" I call over my shoulder.

He doesn't try to stop me, but he takes long strides to catch up. Which is good because I don't know where the bridge is on this ship.

"No, but the last luxury cruise didn't work out too well, either," he points out.

Point to Mr. Darrow. "What's our status?" I ask, following him around a corner to another long corridor.

Reed doesn't respond right away, and I slow down to stare at him, fury bubbling over into words. "Are you serious right now? How the hell am I supposed to guide anyone if I don't know—"

He gives me a long-suffering sigh, as if he is the one being imposed upon. "They're attempting to make contact, but you should—"

I break into a jog, counting on him to catch up and prevent me from going the wrong way.

But as it turns out, I don't need him. Once I'm close enough to the bridge, I hear the soft murmur of restrained voices and follow the sound.

The *Aurora* hangs outside the wide windows on the bridge, centered in black space, lit up by the *Ares*'s searchlights, like a painting on display on a museum wall. Max and the others are gathered around, facing the windows, like patrons of said museum, studying some archaic and formerly lost work. *Ares* is much larger than the LINA but is still dwarfed by the luxury liner. Then again, *Ares* was built for speed and, most likely, destruction. Not fine dining and swimming in space.

I stop, my breath caught at the sight of the *Aurora* again. *We're going to be rich, baby!* Voller's voice echoes in my memory, and it's like pressing against a bone-deep bruise. I miss them, all of them. I didn't appreciate them when I had them—the makeshift family we became against my will—and now look where we are . . . where I am. I'd give anything to hear Voller's snark again. Even his snoring.

Staring out at the *Aurora* is familiar in a way I never imagined, like looking just ahead to see home. But only if your home is also the scene of a horrific crime. It is both known and unknown at the same time, foreign disguised as familiar.

Max is the only one on the bridge who acknowledges my presence. "Portside cameras," he says in greeting, turning toward me.

I nod slowly, moving closer. The gathered security personnel step back out of my way as I approach, as if I'm a disease vector for some highly contagious outbreak.

This is the view I'm familiar with. The starboard side of the *Aurora*. It's what we first saw when we found her.

But something is different.

My gaze traces the lines of the *Aurora* in front of me in a mental game of compare and contrast with the version of the *Aurora* in my head.

The pool, I realize after a moment. It's no longer a giant frozen bubble with bodies and body parts dotting the smooth, clear ice like seeds for a horrific crop to come.

"Can you zoom in on the bow?" I ask someone, anyone.

Water, murky and dark, laps against the edges of the pool. Like an invitation to come relax at the mouth of Hell.

I shudder, all too aware of what is beneath the surface. "The environmentals are on," I say faintly. That at least partially explains how I got out, if not at all why. I must have—or someone must have—repressurized the rest of the ship so the bulkhead doors on the Platinum Level could be opened. I have no memory of that, of course, but what's more bothersome is that, as far as I know, I don't even know *how* to do that. The ship's computer could have walked me through the process, I suppose.

I wait for a second, for some momentary flash of that moment, triggered by this revelation, but nothing comes. Just another blank space.

"Have you heard anything?" I ask. "Any attempt at communication from the *Aurora*?"

Max shakes his head. "Just the same message repeating on the emergency channel."

I thought that I'd inoculated myself against futile hope, until that moment, when it feels like my heart is plummeting toward my knees and I can't breathe.

If anyone was still alive, wouldn't they be waiting, hoping desperately for a response?

Max clears his throat. "Until we know what we're dealing with, Alpha team will proceed first. Full enviro suits."

"With ear protection," I say, the words tumbling out of my mouth before I even realize what I'm saying. Where did that come from? Earplugs aren't going to protect them against auditory hallucinations. But that's right. I know it is, I just don't know *how* I know. It's like that feeling when you can't think of a specific word—you can feel it, like an itch in your brain, but you just can't produce the syllables.

Max is staring at me, eyes narrowed and forehead furrowed, as if I've suddenly appeared out of nowhere in front of him.

I start to ask him what's wrong, but then he seems to recover, straightening his shoulders. "Full enviro suits, with ear protection, and—"

"And me," I say immediately. I have no idea how they're going to get over there with both ships currently moving, but they're not going without me.

Max opens his mouth to protest, but I'm ready for him.

"I'm here to do a job, to make sure everyone gets out safely, right? I'm the lone survivor. That's what you kept saying. So let me do what I came here to do." I fold my arms across my chest. If he doesn't want me to go, he's going to have to tie me up somewhere. If there's anyone from my crew left alive over there—which, I'm forced to admit, is seeming less and less likely—they've been living in a nightmarescape for two and a half months already. Oxygen and heat means decay. Forget about whatever's on the ship that's causing all of this chaos and suffering, just survival under those conditions would be torture. I can't just sit here and wait around. I need to help them, and absent that possibility, I need to know what happened.

I shift my weight from foot to foot with impatience. If I could run there, I would.

Max closes his mouth, looking resigned, and triumph spikes through me, giddy and obnoxious. It takes every bit of restraint I have not to pump my fist in victory.

"You've got to be kidding me," Reed says loudly behind me. I forgot he was even back there. "You aren't going to send her over there unsupervised."

"I'm sure Diaz, Montgomery, and Shin are more than capable of keeping an eye on Claire," Max says mildly, waving at the three security team leaders who have turned along with the rest of us to follow this exchange. None of whom look thrilled at the idea. Diaz is the same Diaz—short, pretty, with her dark hair pulled into a tight knot and a hard expression—who'd witnessed me speaking to McCaughey. She might be more than happy to dump my ass on the *Aurora* permanently or until they figure out what to do with the ship.

"Unless *you* want to go along," Max adds, seemingly almost as an afterthought, but his tone holds the air of a threat.

"Yes," Reed says, lifting his chin in challenge, as if to say, *What are you going to do about it, old man?*

Max's lips thin.

"No," I say immediately. "I can't be looking after him. He's too . . ." Pampered. Precious. Fucking annoying. "Too much work," I finish finally. Besides, Reed, as a member of a third-generation Verux family, is likely considered valuable. I do not want that responsibility hanging over my head.

"You just want a chance to make sure you covered your tracks well enough without someone looking over your shoulder," Reed taunts.

Then again, I won't need to worry about keeping Reed alive if I kill him first.

Max holds up his hand, his expression weary. "Enough. Reed, if you think you can handle it, you're in. I'm not sure what your father would say, though."

And even I, as unfamiliar as I am with corporate hierarchies and the jostling and backstabbing that must take place to ascend, recognize that as a barb.

It's also bait. Waving shit under Reed's nose and daring him not to flinch at the stink.

Reed's face flushes above his dirty collar. "He'd say that I'm doing my job. Protecting *our* company."

And bait taken. I roll my eyes.

I study Max—currently in a stare-down with Reed—trying to figure out why he bothered. He's not petty enough to push Reed into this simply because he knows he can, is he?

It dawns on me, then, for the first time, to wonder whether Reed, a symbol of the rampant nepotism in Verux, isn't just fighting to prove himself but fighting to prove himself in a specific way. Say, for example, by taking Max's job when he retires. Or, perhaps, by forcing Max out a little early to prove a point and win Daddy's—and Granddaddy's—approval.

Fuck. I do not have time for this political bullshit. Though, honestly, I feel a little for Max. He's always been kind to me, if a bit bumbling, and he deserves better than someone like Reed Darrow as the replacement on his life's work.

"So we're good," I say abruptly. "Everyone knows what they're doing. How the hell are we getting over there?"

Max and Reed continue their pissing contest of dominance until Max finally breaks it off, looking to me. "We have the codes to the engine. A built-in kill switch, a safety mechanism on all Citi-Futura vessels at the time to prevent piracy."

And people from ever truly owning their ships. If CitiFutura—and now Verux—could kill your engine at any time, then you'd be less inclined to do anything they wouldn't like. Anything that might be deemed as competition for them.

I raise my eyebrows. "And I'm sure everyone who owns those ships is aware of that particular feature?"

Max simply smiles. "Verux was not involved in CitiFutura's business decisions at that time."

Yeah, and I'm sure Verux has nothing similar in place, especially given how late they entered the shipbuilding game. Their focus on hab modules and colony living cost them, until CitiFutura imploded and Verux scooped up the pieces, likely learning all the best tricks and traps along the way.

Max turns and nods at a Verux-jumpsuited crew member at the helm. Her fingers dance across the board, and our ship slows. I face the windows and watch as the *Aurora* charges ahead without us, slipping out of sight.

My hands tighten into fists at my sides, the short edges of my nails digging into the vulnerable skin of my palms.

"Corbin?" Max asks.

Another member of the crew, this one positioned at what I'm guessing must be Communications, nods. "Packet delivered," he announces.

Nothing happens. Several more long seconds pass, and it's excruciating. Not that we couldn't catch up, but there's already been so much lost time. This feels like an exercise in patience, and patience is something I've never had an abundance of, even on a good day.

And then, slowly, on the right side of the windows, the *Aurora* reemerges as we catch up to her. My relief, once the ship is in sight again, is temporary but real.

When we are nearly even with her, the engines cut back to a low idling hum.

Max nods once, in approval. Then he looks to Diaz, Montgomery, and Shin. "You have your assignments," he says. "Thank you for your service."

That strikes an odd note in my ear. It's as though Max is already resigned to the idea that some number of them won't be returning. Which, I suppose, given my experience, seems fairly likely.

It just seems so coldly practical. Something I might once have admired, but now leaves me feeling ill. The realization is painful in its suddenness. I don't want to be who I was before, fighting attachment, keeping safe distance. There's no such thing as safe distance.

But the team leaders don't seem fazed. They're immediately in action, barking orders into their comm implants and striding for the corridor.

I follow them without waiting for the go-ahead from Max. I have no doubt Diaz and company will take any opportunity to leave me behind if they can. They haven't been on board yet. They're still confident in their ability to handle whatever this is. I envy them for that. That certainty is probably going to get them killed, but I still wish I had it.

25

The staging area, on a lower level, is a tight fit with twenty-three of us. Three security squads of seven each. Me. Reed. Our enviro suits make us even bulkier, so we're brushing shoulders just standing next to one another while we're waiting for the airlock bridge to be extended and sealed. Oversized black bags—likely with the weapons from the crates I saw being loaded—take up nearly every inch of floor space.

And none of that accounts for the dozen or more of the accompanying dead.

McCaughey, once more, stands over Diaz, who is facing me and the rest of her squad. She can't see him, obviously, but he's blocking my view of her. All I can see is her booted foot tapping against the textured metal floor, burning off excess adrenaline while she shouts at me through the cranked-up comm in my helmet. I don't have an implant, like the rest of her team. Her words are tinny and muffled, but not blocked, by the bright orange earplugs distributed to all of us. The best that Verux had to offer on board the *Ares*.

Orange earplugs. An idea is scratching at the back of my brain, but it won't emerge into fruition. What is it about those? I recommended ear protection, and Max agreed. So what? I try to chase that thought, but Diaz's voice, even dampened, is loud enough to distract.

"You don't follow orders, I boot your ass. You endanger any of our people, I boot your ass. You try any of that ghost-y bullshit, I boot your ass."

I resist the urge to point out that the "ghost-y bullshit" didn't seem so bullshit when I was talking to her former colleague.

"Is there any scenario in which you don't boot my ass?" I ask instead.

"None," she says.

Excellent. Good to know.

My temper strains to break my grip on it. I'm not an imbecile. While I don't have her training or specific skills, I've been a team leader. I know what it means to be responsible for others under my care.

Fat lot of good it did them.

I ignore that and lean slightly to the side so I can see Diaz around McCaughey's ghost. "I'm here to help. My goal is to get everyone out alive."

She sneers. "Right."

"Why the fuck are you so angry with me? I didn't give you this assignment, didn't make you volunteer." I pause, a horrible idea dawning. "You did volunteer, correct?" No one should be ordered into this situation.

Diaz jerks her chin up and opens her mouth.

"Diaz," Montgomery shouts. When she looks at him, he shakes his head, tapping his helmet, and Diaz's gaze darts to Reed, who is next to me.

Reed, however, seems oblivious. His face is sweaty and grayish in the interior lights of his helmet, which he shouldn't really have on. But whatever. He keeps running his hands down his legs, as if attempting to dry his palms even though his gloves are on, or reassure himself that the enviro suit is still in place and protecting him.

He catches me looking at him. "What?" he snaps, stilling his hands in late-breaking self-consciousness.

"First time in a suit?" I ask.

He mumbles something, but based on the movement of his lips, one of the words is "training."

"Just breathe normally, and try to focus beyond your helmet." Good advice in any situation, but particularly this one. One of the primary dangers in a suit for a first-timer is focusing on the faceplate or the way the helmet limits your vision instead of whatever is beyond, whatever you *can* see. Too easy to miss a handhold or improperly clamp a safety tether if you're not paying attention to the right thing. In this situation, being distracted by his gear is only going to make the inevitable disorientation on the *Aurora* that much worse.

Reed looks over at me sharply. "I don't need your help," he says, enunciating each word precisely to be sure I understand.

And that, of all things, severs the leash on my temper. "Yeah, you do. You all do." I raise my voice so they can all hear me, but I focus my gaze on Diaz. "I know you don't want to believe me, and that's fine. But you're going to see things over there. Living people you love, dead family you've lost. Random strangers who have died in horrific ways but are still up and walking around, even when you can see their bodies on the floor. That's how this thing—whatever it is—works. Maybe it's a living creature that feeds on fear and confusion."

Diaz rolls her eyes.

"Or maybe it's some kind of weird side effect from the off-gassing of a material they used on the ship. I don't fucking know. But it will happen. And knowing it's not real, knowing that it's a hallucination, will not save you. It *feels* real. And you'll stop being able to tell the difference." At least, if my experience serves.

"You have to keep your head," I continue. "Don't shoot at everything that moves or you'll kill any survivors—"

"Survivors." This time it's Reed openly scoffing at me.

Fucker. Maybe it's wrong, but I'm going to enjoy watching him squirm, just a little bit.

"—and blow holes in the ship that will take out the rest of us," I finish.

Diaz glares at me like she's dying to tell me where I can stow my warnings, but she keeps her mouth shut.

None of them say anything. The only sign I have that any of the rest of them even heard me is that they're all very diligently avoiding looking in my direction.

They probably think I'm crazy. I'm sure they've been warned. That's fine. They'll see for themselves soon enough.

A loud beeping sounds as the airlock opens on our end of the extendable bridge. The *Aurora*'s cargo bay doors on the other end are already open.

No one is waiting for us.

Montgomery's team is first over. I hold my breath, but when their lights sweep inside the darkened cargo bay, the LINA is still there. Holding to the floor. The sight of her shiny, familiar hull makes my stomach ache with homesickness.

I feel the brush of Kane's shoulder against mine in LINA's narrow passageways, the corresponding warmth in my chest when he smiled at me.

But I see him, standing in front of me on the *Ares*'s deck, overlapping with McCaughey, the blend of them chaotic and disorienting. Kane waves his hand at me in an urgent gesture, as always, panic etched into his expression.

I squeeze my eyes shut, waiting until the image, memory, ghost, whatever it is, fades. I need to focus.

The airlock bridge is simply an extendable portion of *Ares* that connects and seals to an entrance on another ship. Like a big seethrough tunnel. A guideline runs on either side to help you move from one ship to the other.

I've heard of airlock bridges, but never used one before. In theory, it's no more complicated than walking across a regular bridge on Earth. But on Earth, you don't look down and see the infinite emptiness beneath you. All around you.

Diaz's team is next. Most of them are already on board, opening up their crates and bags, when Reed, ahead of me on the guideline, freezes up. His panicked breathing is loud in my ears.

Shit.

I glance back. Three members from Shin's team are on the line behind me. We can't go backward.

"One hand in front of the other, focus on the cargo bay," I call to Reed, raising my voice. Max should never have let him tag along, no matter what point Max was trying to prove.

"Shut up! I know," Reed shouts. And yet, he doesn't move.

I'm not enjoying being right and Reed being miserable nearly as much as I thought I would. Then again, at the moment, he's the only thing standing between me and the *Aurora* and the answers that may lie inside. *Come on, come on!*

"Slide your back hand forward toward your front hand, and then pull yourself even," I say, working to keep my tone patient. "It's perfectly safe." As long as the seal holds. From here it looks like the temporary fixture against the *Aurora* is that same foam bullshit that Kane has . . . had to keep applying on the LINA.

I expect Reed to snarl at me again, but he says nothing. Then, after a few more excruciating seconds, he does as I said, though his hands are visibly shaking.

"You've got it. Keep going."

Slowly he inches toward the *Aurora*. The hard knot of tension in my stomach starts to ease. He's going to make it. We will make it.

I'm coming, I promise anyone who is left on the *Aurora*.

Once Reed crosses the threshold, he stumbles as stronger gravity kicks back in. One of Diaz's team members grabs him and pulls him further into the cargo bay before letting go. Reed lands on the floor in an ungainly heap, which he immediately struggles to correct by getting to his feet.

Good enough. Without Reed in front of me, I'm able to finish my crossing much faster. The second my boots touch down on the *Aurora*'s floor, though, the all-too-familiar hum of the idling engines resonates up through my feet and sends an awful chill over my skin. It is an uncomfortable but familiar sensation, a feeling of presence and pressure, almost. As though someone has a fingertip resting lightly on the center of your forehead and then gradually, almost so slowly you don't even notice it happening, the pressure increases until that fingertip is boring through your skull.

Yeah. I've been here before, and even though I still don't remember parts of it, the dread is gut-level and unforgettable.

It doesn't help that the cargo bay is dark, the only lights coming from our helmets. Frowning, I reach up to turn mine on, and Reed, watching me, mimics the movement. Clearly, the grav generator is working, and we saw the effects of the environmental systems being turned back on. So why is it dark in here? Though, now that I think about it, I don't recall any lights being visible from the outside of the *Aurora* when we pulled alongside.

"Did you cut the power when you choked the engines?" I ask anyone who is listening.

No one responds.

"Hello? What's going on with the lights?"

To my surprise, it's Max who answers me. He must be monitoring the comm channels back on the *Ares*.

"Negative," he says, the grim tone of his raised voice carrying through clearly even with my earplugs. "That wasn't us."

Hope flares in me, outrageously bright. Nysus cut the lights before, when we were trying to give the engines more power. Perhaps he is still doing that, even with the other environmental systems up and running. That sounds like something Nysus would do.

Or . . . would have done. All of this, including the ship's course, could have been set months ago. This is not proof of their survival. Just proof that they were, at one point, alive, which I already knew.

The hope in me dims at the realization. But I take a deep breath, determined to push forward.

I head toward the airlock, where the security teams have assembled. Their enviro suits, like the one I'm now wearing, are military grade and made of darker material, but theirs now bristle with weapons attached at every conceivable point. And they, presumably, have even more in the bags that several of them are carrying strapped to their backs.

This is a bad idea.

No sooner does that thought run through my head than I catch a glimpse of motion from the corner of my eye. I turn, awkwardly, trying to track it, expecting to see Reed Darrow bumbling up next to me.

Instead, my mother hovers beside me, her mouth open in a silent scream just inches from my face. She is as I last remember her, dried blood in the creases of her mouth, her eyes gone filmy and gray, sinking back into her head, and her skin beginning to sag from her cheekbones and forehead in rot.

I stagger back, colliding with someone, and setting off a chain reaction of muted protests.

But when I catch my balance and look up, she's gone.

"What is your problem?" someone demands as I turn in the ungraceful manner that the enviro suits demand, looking, checking for her. It was in this cargo bay, nearly in this exact same spot, that I saw her the last time, for the first time in years. And the last time I was here, I lost half my crew—if my memories can be trusted—and a good chunk of my mind.

Reed Darrow, finally caught up with us, watches me warily.

Seeing my mother once is fear, an anxious mind projecting. Perhaps even the much-discussed coping mechanism created long ago in a still-developing brain.

But twice. Twice feels more like an omen.

26

The cargo bay airlock is large enough for an entire team to pass through at once. Diaz forces me to wait with her people, going through after Montgomery. Shin's team is busy climbing all over the Verux equipment, the shipment designated for the Mira colony. Retrieving whatever is still usable/not outdated, I guess.

Diaz's decision adds perhaps another fifteen minutes to my wait, but the agitation in me builds with every passing second, until it feels like my teeth are vibrating with it.

Finally, on the other side of the airlock, in the corridor, I'm both relieved and disappointed to find the crew deck exactly as I remember it from my first trip through. Furniture shoved into the hall, blocking doors, keeping people in.

I wince, imagining the decay I cannot smell with my helmet and independent air supply. "There are victims here," I tell Diaz. "In the rooms. Crew and staff on this level."

Her attention focused on her team in the corridor, she gives a tight jerk of her head, a barely detectable motion. "The dead will still be dead later. Our priority is a ship-wide search."

For whatever is causing this. *And* survivors. Though she doesn't say either, and it's hard not to press her to confirm.

Montgomery's team takes point as we move down the hall, and it requires everything I have not to push past them and rush for the Platinum Level. If anyone is still alive, they would have sealed themselves back inside once I left, right? That's the most logical move for survival. So, if the bulkhead doors are down, there's a chance that someone is alive behind them.

But if they're not . . .

Ahead of me, one of Montgomery's team members jerks hard to

the right, the light on the end of his weapon illuminating a darkened doorway. It's empty, the door still firmly shut.

After a moment, his shoulders go up and down in a shrug. ". . . thought . . . saw something." His words come through patchy and faint.

One could blame it on nerves.

But I know better.

It's starting.

At the first major intersection of this corridor and one running the opposite direction, where we should be taking the stairs up, Montgomery's team abruptly splits off to the left.

"Hey, wait," I say. "It's better if we stay together." People popping up unexpectedly is only going to add to the confusion. It's not as big of a concern with Shin's team staying in the cargo bay, but if we have various personnel wandering around the passenger decks—all of them jumpy, starting to see things, and armed to the teeth—it's just going to increase the likelihood of someone getting shot.

But Montgomery and his team give no sign of having heard me or, more likely, caring about my opinion in the slightest, marching toward the opposite end of the cross-corridor.

I look to Diaz, who is waiting impatiently for me with her team at the bottom of the stairs. "It's a big ship, Kovalik. Let's go."

I watch Montgomery's team walk away, unease settling over me. What the hell are they expecting to find? But the atrium and the Platinum Level are up the stairs and ahead, and I need to be there.

The tightness in my chest increases as we ascend the stairs to the next level of cabins. Once again, all is as I remember it. Including the bloody message on the wall.

i see you

leave me alone

That causes even Diaz to pause for a second.

At the end of the corridor, one of her team members stops dead. "Do you hear that?" His voice is tinny and faint. "It's singing. Like a little kid singing." The light at the end of his weapon bobbles around as he turns, trying to find the source of the sound. ". . . all is calm, all is . . ." He sings along with it, the sound brittle and sharp.

Next to me, Reed shifts his weight. "I think . . . I think I hear it, too."

Shit. The power of suggestion? Or maybe this thing is getting stronger.

"It's not real," I say, raising my voice to be heard. "There's no one singing out here."

But as the team member's light sweeps past the staircase ahead, I catch a glimpse of white fabric with little blue flowers and small bare feet.

I suck in a breath sharply. Becca waves at me with a giggle that I hear as clearly as if she were right in front of me—no, as clearly as if she was in my fucking suit with me—and beckons me up to play.

Hallucination, ghost, or memory? I'm so done with this game and it's only going to get worse. And if it's difficult for me to handle this altered reality, experience says everyone else is going to lose their minds that much faster.

"We need to hurry the fuck up," I say grimly.

"I give the orders, Kovalik," Diaz says. But she jerks her head at her team. "Move!"

We climb the steps at a slightly faster pace, passing the level with the eerie theater, then the one with the empty and gated-off restaurant, without hesitation. But when Diaz leaves the stairs to head for the darkened atrium, I pause for just a moment to brace myself.

All the people who were once drifting overhead would not have had a gentle landing when the gravity came back on. And after almost eight weeks now, exposed to full environmental conditions, it's not going to be pretty.

Immediately, though, I see that an attempt has been made at dignity. It's cool in here, someone trying to slow decay, perhaps? Sheets, blankets, and comforters have been draped haphazardly over the fallen bodies. At least toward the front half of the room. The efforts leave off unexpectedly in the middle of the atrium, as if someone got interrupted or distracted. From that point to the back of the room, it's a chaotic jumble of limbs and flesh.

Like some kind of horrible abstract painting of a murder scene.

Diaz pauses and turns to her crew. "Go. You know what you're looking for." Then, as her team members spread out, carefully picking their way across the field of dead and setting up emergency lights on stands, she adds, "Find the ones in the best shape."

I stare at her. "What are you—"

But then my attention is caught by three bundles tightly wrapped in sheets off to one side behind Diaz, near the bottom of the beautiful spiral staircase to the Platinum Level.

Despair rises in a strangling sensation at my throat, and my legs feel jointless and loose, as if my knees might suddenly bend the opposite way without warning, as I stumble forward and then manage a run.

I stop at their feet. Three of them. One so tall and thin, it must be Voller. In the middle, Lourdes. And on the last, dried blood stains the sheet near the head . . .

A silent scream escapes me; no sound is adequate for this pain. Emptiness tunnels through the center of my body until it feels as though there's nothing left.

I failed them. I led them here. Left them to die here. They trusted *me.*

Diaz is at my side and tries to pull me back, but in that moment, I cannot, will not, be stopped.

Before she can intervene, I've pulled the coverings from each one of them. Voller. Lourdes. Nysus.

Voller's head still bears the damage of the plasma drill. Lourdes's eyes are covered by the bandages, exactly as I recall from that fragmented and tattered memory. And Nysus . . .

My hand flies up to my mouth in an instinctive gesture, but it's blocked by my helmet.

Nysus stares up at the ceiling, his skin grayish and sloughing off, but his expression is one of peace, relief. Which is belied by several inches of metal screwdriver and blue plastic handle sticking out of his left ear. I recognize it immediately. It's one of ours, a screw-driver from the LINA that we brought with us.

That makes it worse. I don't know why, but it does. I sink to my knees beside Nysus.

In my head, I see them. Voller smirking at me. Lourdes's thin, elegant fingers flying over her boards, her calm voice over the chan-nel in my helmet, telling me to come in from the cold. Nysus beaming at me as he ran a loving hand down the wood panels on the Platinum Level corridor on the *Aurora*. He thought I'd given him the best, most amazing, once-in-a-lifetime opportunity with exploring the *Aurora*.

And it was once in a lifetime. In that it killed him. My decision did that. To all of them.

Hot tears roll down my cheeks like liquid fire. All those visions, dreams, hallucinations, memories, whatever you wanted to call them were correct. I had not imagined Nysus's end with a screwdriver, but that does not change the fact that he is lying here in front of me, dead.

Maybe those psychological assessments from my childhood had been right. I was reckless with life, unfit for leadership. Because I didn't care what happened to me and they had followed me in. And I let them.

"Come on, Kovalik," Diaz says, discomfort coloring her words. "You knew it was a long shot." She edges around me and pulls the sheets back into place loosely over their faces. It looks sloppy and untidy compared to the neat work Kane had done. "We have to keep going."

I don't move.

What's the point? No, Kane isn't down here, neatly wrapped and cared for like the others, but he wouldn't be. As the last one alive, he would be left where he had fallen. And I'm not sure I can handle that sight.

For a moment, I long for the oblivion of the pills, left behind in the drawer in my cabin on *Ares*.

"I'm staying with them. With my crew," I say. Reed lingers at the edge of my vision, shifting his weight from foot to foot but wisely keeping his mouth shut.

But before Diaz can respond, a loud popping noise—short bursts in rapid succession—explodes somewhere behind me. I jump, heart pounding. It takes me a moment to identify the muted noise as a gun instead of, say, the hull splitting apart unexpectedly.

"Cease fire!" Diaz shouts, bolting past me toward her team. "What the fuck?"

"We've got movement," a thin voice says in my ear. "I saw . . . I saw movement." The team member sounds less than certain, though.

"Where?" she demands.

I turn as he points the light on the end of his weapon toward the top of the spiral staircase on the Platinum Level. It's empty.

"What did you see?" I ask.

"I don't . . . I'm not sure. A woman, maybe?" he says. "Long hair. White coat."

I cock my head to the side. That sounds like . . . which is impossible.

"You don't fucking fire without my permission," Diaz snaps at him. "We have a mission and getting us all killed before we complete it is not the plan."

Something about that sounds wrong, but I can't linger on what, not with my thoughts churning as they are.

Slowly, I push myself to my feet—my whole body aches as though I've been trampled repeatedly—and head toward the spiral staircase. I have to check, I have to see.

"Where are you going?" Diaz asks.

I ignore her and keep moving, concentrating. The staircase is a surprisingly tight and dizzying affair, easy to miss a step and fall. I've scaled the outside of it, used it as a push-off point. But I've never climbed it with the gravity on.

At the top, I'm breathless from the effort, and that condition is not improved when I get my first look at the closest Platinum suite corridor. The bulkhead door is open, retracted into the ceiling, leaving the hallway beyond dark and impenetrable.

The other one, on the starboard side, is likely open as well.

That is not a good sign, and yet, nothing less than what I was expecting.

But now, I have to see for myself.

I head down the portside corridor, the same one we used to first access the suites and the bridge. The light on my helmet barely penetrates the gloom.

Behind me, Diaz is barking orders at her team as she follows. "Just get them wrapped up!"

The doors on either side of the corridor are still closed tightly. The red *X*s on the doors marking the suites we'd checked and where Kane and I had found the dead remain in place, though it feels like centuries or another life when I was last here. It's like revisiting the scene of a bad dream.

Toward the end of the passageway, my helmet light catches on the bloody scrawled message on the wall, and this time, my brain manages to pick out a pattern in the rise and fall of the smeared letters.

i'm sorry

But who would have been apologizing, especially up here? The *Aurora* passengers and crew, at the time, were all drowning in hallucinations, paranoia, and fear.

I'm so caught by this idea that I nearly miss what's right in front of me—the edge of a towel or sheet sticking out, just a little, from underneath the door of the suite closest to the end of the hallway. Closest to the bridge.

That was not here before. That I recall, anyway. I bend down for a better look, and it becomes clear that the towel has been wedged in the gap beneath the door—like someone attempting to keep out smoke.

My heart racing, I put my hand on the doorknob and try it—the handle moves freely. Not locked, but when I attempt to push the door open, it meets resistance.

Something soft and heavy on the other side.

Like a body, some awful part of my mind suggests helpfully.

Panic lights up inside me, and I shove at the door, but it moves barely an inch. "Damnit!" My voice is shrill, breaking at the edges, and I slap at the door in futile frustration.

Diaz joins me without a word, putting her shoulder against the polished wood. I mimic her stance, and together, we push at the door until it finally gives, opening about six inches or so.

Something heavy falls on the other side of the door—I can feel the vibration through my boots on the floor, if not the sound itself.

Cautiously, I peer into the gap we've created.

At first, I can't understand what I'm seeing. The room is unrecognizable from the elegantly appointed suites I remember. The furniture is gone, nothing identifiable as such remains, in a sea of white.

And then it clicks: mattresses. I'm looking at dozens of mattresses along the walls, on the floor, stacked at least two deep.

In fact, sticking my head deeper into the gap, I see that's what we've knocked down by opening the door—mattresses. Their short ends are still pressed against the back of the door, preventing me from opening it further.

It's so dark in here, the only light coming from my helmet and . . . is that a faint glow from the far right corner? It's hard to tell with my own light interfering.

Craning my neck, I try for a better look at what might be a pale blue illumination. Like one of our emergency lights from the LINA, on the verge of dying.

Adrenaline slips into my veins, smooth and bright, like liquid fire.

"What do you see?" Diaz asks.

"Help me," I demand.

"I don't think that's a good idea," Reed says from behind me. He must have followed us up. He's trying for stern, as if he's in charge, but the words come out sounding breathless and more than a little terrified.

I ignore him. With me and Diaz pushing, the door opens enough for me to slide through, a tighter fit with my enviro suit and helmet on.

Once inside the room, it becomes clear that my initial assessment wasn't quite accurate. The room is *jammed* with mattresses, not just from this level but likely from all over the ship. I can't imagine how much work it must have been to move so many and wedge them into a single room. Towels, sheets, blankets, and clothes lie in piles and heaps all over the floor on top of the mattresses.

It's like . . . like a nest in here. The thought sends a shudder through me.

In the far corner, one of our portable work lights glows weakly where it's stuck to a mattress, the last in a long succession of portable work lights attached in much the same way. Only the ones above it are all dark. Dead.

"What do you see, Kovalik?" Diaz demands again as I step onto the mattresses and attempt to make my way toward that corner. My balance is awkward and wobbly on the plush surface, reminding me suddenly of my clumsy and panicked attempt to escape the woman under the bed. The dead woman who'd reached out to grab my ankle. It had not been real, not in the way we currently define reality, but it had *felt* as real as anything I've ever experienced.

"I don't know," I say finally. "I'm trying to get closer and—"

A pile of clothing at the edge of the fading work light, mostly in shadow, shifts abruptly. My breath catches in my throat, and I stumble back a step. My foot catches in the gap between a pair of mattresses, twisting my ankle sharply to the right.

I fall before I can catch myself, landing flat on my back, and the bundle of rags expands, unfolding, to tower above me.

27

In the dim light, it takes me longer than it should to pick out familiar features from the looming figure. The tangled and matted hair, normally golden skin turned ashen and smudged and dirty, and . . . bright blue eyes staring down at me.

Kane.

As I struggle to sit up, his hand flies up to block the brightness of my light—now aimed toward him. When I manage to push myself to my feet—my right ankle now throbbing—he recoils, scurrying away from me.

He's thin, diminished. Starving.

But alive.

After so many weeks alone. I left them here alone.

I push that thought away to focus on Kane.

I stand slowly, gritting my teeth against the corresponding throb in my ankle. I hold my hands up, showing that I intend no harm. "Kane, it's me. It's Claire."

But he gives no sign of recognizing the name or my voice. He shrinks into the corner of the room, sinking to the mattress-covered floor and curling up into a ball. "No, no, no."

I can see his mouth moving even if I can't hear him.

"Kovalik!" Diaz shouts. "What is going on?"

"Just stay back," I say. "Give me a second." More people in here might confuse Kane further, if there's anything left of his mind capable of discerning reality. And that might not be the case. He—and Nysus—have been alone since I apparently left them here. Then Nysus died—or was killed, oh God—and Kane was on his own. Of all people, I know what that kind of isolation can do to a mind.

And that was without whatever is on the *Aurora* and causing this madness to begin with.

Shame heats my blood.

I flip the release latch on my helmet, and the hiss of the pressure seal jerks Kane's attention toward me. He watches as if I'm a snake about to strike. Moving slowly, I remove my helmet and set it to the side.

The air is stale and smells of old sweat, fresh panic, and unwashed skin. And beneath that, the pungent stench of rot—it hits the back of my throat with a punch and I gag involuntarily.

All of it immediately transports me back twenty-plus years and for a moment, I'm lost in a darkened corridor, the only living person on the planet for thousands of kilometers and listening for the impossible whisper of my mother's voice.

Then Kane lunges at me, his teeth bared. "Get out!" His gaze seems sharper now, focused on me instead of my vague direction.

I jump, startled, but manage to overrule the reflex to step back. "Kane, it's Claire. Kovalik."

This time, though, he seems to have no problem recognizing me. "Get out!" he bellows.

A spike of fear mixed with despair stabs straight through my heart. *He knows what I did, he doesn't want me here.* Even if it's as part of a rescue. A much-too-late rescue.

"Kane," I begin, stricken. "I'm sorry, I—"

"I'm coming in," Diaz calls, and I make the mistake of glancing toward the door.

"No," I say. "Just give me another—"

Kane launches himself at me, and I catch the blur of motion a split second before his body collides with mine, hard.

We hit the mattresses at an awkward angle, my arm caught beneath me, making it impossible to adequately defend myself or even hold him back. Though, do I have the right to even attempt it? Isn't this what I deserve for what I did?

But he doesn't lock his fingers around my throat or slam a fist into my face.

Instead, he's staring down at me, his hands planted on either side of me, his head cocked to one side and forehead furrowed with confusion as if he can't quite figure out what he's seeing. Beneath the tangles of his hair, a flash of familiar orange. Earplugs. Like the ones in our ears right now.

Like the first officer of the *Aurora* when we found his body. He was still wearing them. And we found those other pairs in the trunk in the emergency crew bunk room.

"Why did you—" I begin.

"Back off!" Diaz shouts, pushing her way into the room, her weapon aimed at him. Reed squeezes in after her.

"Don't!" I say. "It's fine, I'm fine." I don't want Kane to panic, and Diaz to shoot him if he moves in her direction.

But Kane, after a quick glance up at Diaz and Reed, dismisses them entirely. "I told you, it *is* her," he says instead, addressing an empty spot three feet to his left.

The hope that was filling my chest drains out with a gurgle.

He turns his attention back to me, but his expression is like that of someone caught in a fever dream. Alert but still distant. Here, but not. "I knew you'd come back."

Guilt pummels me, but before I can even formulate a response, he continues the conversation. "No, no, that's not what I said." He glares at another invisible person, this one on his right. "I will. I will tell her."

Diaz makes a noise somewhere between disgust and pity and lowers her weapon. Off to the side, Reed stands stiffly—as stiffly as one can on a mattress—looking both annoyed and disappointed. That Kane is alive and he, Reed, was wrong.

Guess that apology for calling me a murderer is not going to be forthcoming. Though, just because I didn't kill my crew for a larger prize, as Reed accused, doesn't mean I didn't just as surely get them killed.

Kane backs off me, and then offers me a hand in an absurdly

normal gesture. After a moment of hesitation, I take it and he pulls me up.

Pain zings through my ankle, and I wince. Kane holds on to my arm until I have my balance.

"The mattresses make it better. Softer," he says in a conspiratorial voice, leaning closer.

Uh-huh.

"Nysus diverted power to increase the noise dampeners, too, beyond the specs," he continues. "We have to go slower than before, but it helps."

I gape at him. That sounded almost like a coherent thought. And it might be true, given the status of the lights.

"We can't find it," Kane says to me, his expression suddenly bleak. "We looked everywhere." His gaze flicks to the side, and he nods in response to someone I can't see or hear. "It has to be tied to the engines somehow." He pauses. "But it lives up here." He jabs at his temple with his finger. "Eating and chewing and devouring."

What are you talking about? I bite back the question. Any response I might get would only be a mix of gibberish and something that sounded almost like sense, sending me on a scavenger hunt of meaning. Trying to pick out just enough to give me hope that he's trying to truly communicate.

A deep sadness wells up in me, rising until it feels like I might drown in it. Kane Behrens, the physical person, is still alive, lungs still pumping, heart still beating. But the man himself—who he was—is gone.

"We can't root it out," Kane says sadly, letting his hand fall to his side. "Nysus tried."

I flinch, remembering the screwdriver.

"We need to get him out of here," I say to Diaz. "Now. He'll be better as soon as he's away from this place." Which is, at best, an optimistic overstatement of my deepest hope rather than anything I have proof of, but I'm not going to let Kane sit here for a second longer. That sure as hell won't help him.

Diaz starts to turns away, and McCaughey is back, looming over her. She jolts slightly, the tremor barely visible in her posture, but I notice. She saw him. Or saw *something*.

Diaz is not immune to what's happening here, though she somehow seems to be able to ignore it better than the others.

"Sir, we have a confirmed survivor," she says, as she finishes turning away from me.

The ghost of her former commander watches her carefully, despite the missing half of his face.

I can't hear Max's response, my helmet on the mattress on the floor where I left it. I fumble for my earplugs, pulling them free.

"Yes, sir. Right, sir," Diaz says.

Kane tugs gently at my arm. "Maybe they can find it," he says.

"Yeah, maybe," I say. But I'm keeping my eye on Diaz. This shouldn't be a difficult moment. You found a survivor. Step one, get him off the fucking ship and back to safety.

But Diaz is still talking. "It seems so, sir."

"Nysus tried to search using the specs, like we talked about, but . . ." Kane pauses to shake his head violently, like a dog trying to free water from its ears. Then he glares at someone who isn't there. "Shut up! That's not right! I told you, no! She didn't betray us, she's right here!"

Self-loathing burns in my chest. "It's okay," I tell Kane soothingly. "It's okay."

Kane blinks, returning his attention to me. "The ship is just too large," he says, as if the interruption never happened. "Even the engine room is too big when you don't know exactly what you're looking for." He gives a despairing laugh. "You were right."

A vague echo of a memory bounces through my mind, faint but present. The voices on the bridge, when I woke up next to Lourdes. The last memory I have, lying in the dark, staring at the two versions of Lourdes in horror, whispers in the distance. Was there more? More of that moment taken from me?

"Understood," Diaz says.

I glance over in her direction, only to find that she's already in motion. But instead of coming back toward us, she's heading away.

Toward the door.

That amorphous sense of dread and suspicion that has been swirling around in me suddenly coalesces into a razor-sharp knifepoint of confirmation. And then panic.

"Wait!" I shout, struggling to rush after her, pain sizzling up my ankle.

But I'm too late. The door slams before I can reach it, and seconds later, something scrapes across the surface. A soft hissing noise follows, and a thick white liquid pours through the keyhole—damn old-fashioned locks—rolling down the smooth wooden surface on our side before solidifying in place.

I tug at the doorknob, trying to turn it, but the mechanism won't engage. Whatever she's put in there has thoroughly jammed up the works.

"What's happening?" Reed demands, making his way over to the door.

"She's trapped us in here." I try to scrape at the substance on the door, but it's oddly abrasive and tears at my gloves without so much as showing a dent from my efforts. "Damnit."

"No," Reed says flatly. "That's not—"

I step back and gesture at the door. "Please, show me I'm wrong."

Instead, he scowls at me. "Max," Reed says into his helmet comm. "Call off your dog. She's locked us in here."

I grimace at his word choice—as if being insulting will help anything, but that's just Reed's primary mode, apparently—even as the meaning, meaning he probably didn't even intend, sinks in.

Diaz is a company woman. She's not going to do anything she's not ordered to do. She was talking to Max right before she took action.

Which means . . .

Suddenly all the odd moments and behaviors I've witnessed on this mission seem to click into place. Diaz's anger about the mission in general. Montgomery hushing her when I asked if she was a volunteer. The lack of body bags. The crates marked "dangerous" and "explosive" even though the security teams were already carrying their weapons. Shin's team's fixation on the Verux-marked equipment in the cargo bay.

I'm such a fucking idiot. So consumed with my own guilt and responsibility, I completely overlooked the most obvious signs.

"Max?" Reed repeats. Fear flickers across his expression and for the first time, he looks his—very young—age. "I'm not . . . he's not responding and I don't even hear anyone else . . ."

They've cut his comm. "They're going to leave us here," I say, the words slipping out of my mouth before I can stop them.

I launch myself at my helmet and the comm channel within, as if the few extra seconds might somehow make a difference. Kane flinches away from me and my flurry of movement, huddling against the back wall again.

"They wouldn't," Reed says in disbelief as I jam my helmet back into place. "My father is—"

"Important," I say. "I know." I have to hand it to Max—it's a brilliant touch. A portion of a cover story that will make the whole thing that much more believable. And Max also gets the satisfaction of eliminating a young upstart rival on his way out the door to retirement.

"You're insane," Reed says in disgust.

"Max?" I ask. "Hello?"

Silence holds for a long moment, then I hear a sigh.

"I'm so sorry, Claire," Max says. "It wasn't supposed to happen this way."

28

"None of it was," Max says. "No one was ever supposed to find the damn ship in the first place. All of our analysts said that if it hadn't happened in the first five years, it wouldn't happen, but I guess they weren't counting on the advances in commweb tech and the fucking distress beacon holding a charge for so long."

For some reason, Max swearing is what makes this real to me. The kind, grandfatherly man who visited me as a child is gone, replaced by this icy stranger. Or maybe this is the real Max and has been all along.

"My compliments to the former CitiFutura engineers, that sustainability is impressive," Max continues with a hearty—and fake— laugh.

"What's he saying?" Reed asks, tapping at my shoulder, and I shrug him off.

"You did this," I say to Max. "You did something to the *Aurora*. Verux did." After all, that is Max's job, isn't it? To clean up Verux's messes.

"It was never supposed to be this dramatic." He gives a soft laugh. "We just wanted to make the high-profile guests a little uncomfortable. Our scientists found that intense vibrations at a specific subaudible decibel level, when generated in a closed environment, can cause headaches, paranoia, unaccountable dread, depression. Visual hallucinations in maybe two percent of the population, generally those who were already experiencing mental instability."

Vibrations. They made the ship ring like a bell. That's what he's saying. Only at a level that no one could hear.

"And that's what made everyone start killing themselves and each other?" I demand.

"No, no, no! Of course not. It's not that direct. The vibrations just make everything . . . resonate. Which can have some unpleasant side effects."

Yeah, I would call a shipful of dead passengers an "unpleasant side effect."

"That's why they were seeing things, hearing things that weren't there," I say. Not ghosts, not like me. Just whatever their "resonating" nervous systems came up with. "And you put something on the *Aurora* to do that." It wasn't a presence on the ship, just whatever this . . . device was.

No, not a device.

"A weapon," I say, the pieces finally coming together. Probably brought on board by CitiFutura crew themselves when they loaded the Verux equipment for Mira, thinking they were doing a competitor a favor. And possibly showing off a little. At that point, Verux was still struggling to build anything that could compete with a CitiFutura ship. Investors were speculating that Verux would have to hire out to CF for transportation of goods and materials and colonists for their colonies and outposts.

"The MAW 500X was a discovery, an invention," Max corrects, sounding defensive. "One that had multiple applications for crowd control, safety, and security."

And driving people insane, it seems.

I look over at Kane, curled up in a ball on the floor. I can picture Lourdes, Voller, and Nysus on the level below, quiet and still and dead beneath their tightly wrapped sheet-shrouds.

The hundreds of bodies on this ship and the escape pods that had managed to jettison successfully, spending their last moments in terror, freezing and gasping for air. Others, dying by the hand of a fellow passenger for reasons they couldn't understand. Or, tormented by visions of the living and the dead until they saw no further hope in existing and ended their own lives.

Rage bubbles under my ribs, boiling up until I can taste its bitter acid in the back of my throat.

"Once the influencers on the *Aurora* were done complaining, no one would ever want to board another CitiFutura ship again," Max says, as if that explains everything.

And it does, in a way. Without the CitiFutura threat of luxury living in space, the Verux-sponsored version of the future—habs and planet-side—would be safe.

"Verux killed to protect their profits," I say flatly. A statement, not a question. "Just like they held off on sending those air filters to Ferris Outpost." More deaths on their heads.

Max makes an impatient noise. "That was just business. Someone always has to be evaluating the bottom line. It's not personal. Ferris should have been fine for a few more weeks. You know that. They'd gone longer than that before."

"And that makes it better?" My face is growing hot inside my helmet. "I'm sure the people of Ferris don't think so. Oh, wait, they're all dead. Just like the people on this ship." Fury makes my voice shake, and I hate that it sounds like weakness.

Max tsks at me. "I told you, it wasn't supposed to happen this way. CitiFutura changed the damn specs. They used a new alloy formulation in the hull and supports. That was kept under lock and key. No one knew about it. And we had no idea that the vibrations would be intensified because of it."

"You killed them all," I say softly.

Reed moves to stand in front of me, his face gone gray and sweaty inside his helmet. "What is he saying?" he repeats.

I turn away from him.

"Look, our man on the inside, he tried to stop it," Max says. "But the captain, she took the ship off course, we don't know why."

Trying to run in the only way she knew how in her confused state of mind? Attempting to escape what turned out to be inescapable. Maybe. "Or maybe your man on the inside was following orders and hiding what you'd done when everything went to shit."

Their man. I flash to the memory of the first officer with the gunshot wound to his temple and the orange earplugs in his ears. Cage Wallace. That's why. He knew what was happening.

"We found him. He killed himself," I say to Max. Whether because of the effects of the weapon he himself activated or because of the guilt, once he saw what he'd done.

"Tell him to let us out," Reed insists loudly behind me. "Now."

"It doesn't matter anymore," Max says. "What's done is done. And trust me when I tell you this is not how I wanted to end things." He sighs. "You were my best success story. Verux victim to Verux employee. Do you know the type of spin it takes to carry that off?"

I've always known that Verux's motives for providing for me were somewhat self-protective in origin. But hearing exactly how selfish—how proud he was of what he'd done—makes my gorge rise.

It doesn't take me long to assemble the rest.

"You're going to destroy the *Aurora*," I say. "With us on board."

Reed makes a noise, something between a cough and a choked gasp.

"No," Max says. "You're going to do it. At least that's how it'll look. Engine explosion. Suffering from ill effects of your traumatic experience and secretly going off your medication . . ."

I recoil. He knew all along. I played right into his hands. And he let me. I'm sure there will be all kinds of documentation of the pill stash I left behind on the *Ares* if there hasn't been already.

"You were lost in your own delusions. You slipped your guard before we could retrieve more than a few bodies and personal effects from the dead. Who, by the way, died due to malfunctioning carbon dioxide sensors. Nothing so complicated or sinister as what you described when you were rescued. Simply not enough good air." Max sounds pleased with himself.

And he's right to. It's far more believable than the truth. Shit goes wrong all the time out here. And it's rarely, if ever, due to a deliberate act of malice.

Most of the time it's just plain old human error or equipment failure.

My story will simply be written off as the ravings of someone driven mad by trauma.

"You got away from us and tried to steal the *Aurora* in your confusion." He gives a dramatic sigh. "You tried to push old and damaged equipment too hard. The engines overloaded and . . . boom. Everyone on board is lost. A tragedy, really."

Including several security teams and the son of a prominent Verux executive, thereby dampening any potential talk of the "tragedy" being a Verux cover-up.

It is fucking cold. And absolutely brilliant. So what are they waiting for?

"I don't suppose Mr. Behrens managed to locate our property during his extended stay on the *Aurora*?" Max asks. "It would be helpful to know where they searched. Wallace hid it a little too well, and we're running out of time. The charges are set to go off, regardless of our success or failure. But I'd rather it be a success."

They want the weapon back. To use again. Or perhaps to prevent awkward questions should a thorough examination of the wreckage be performed by someone other than Verux. Even engine explosion—or the simulation of such—wouldn't destroy everything.

I take a deep breath. One of my numbered last, it seems. "Go fuck yourself, Max."

His delighted laughter follows, tinny and small, as I yank off my helmet. My heart is hammering hard in my chest, and for a moment, I can't breathe. Trapped in this one room, made even smaller by all the mattresses stuffed in here.

The mattresses.

The mattresses make it better, softer. That's what Kane had said. I'd taken it as a sign of his degraded mental condition. I thought he was talking about the floor, but he meant the sound. The mattresses must help deaden the vibrations in here, at least. Like acoustic padding. He and Nysus had figured that much out. Now, knowing what I know, I understand what I missed before when Nysus had given us what he could from the diagnostics. The maxed-out noise dampeners that shouldn't have been, the extraneous power usage. It was that damn device.

Did I know that before? That it was mechanical, man-made? I still have no idea. It also no longer matters.

I sink to the floor, next to Kane. He watches me warily.

Reed rushes over, stumbling over the corner of a mattress. He looks faintly ridiculous, still in his suit and helmet. "What's going on? What are you doing?"

"We're the cover story," I say flatly, pulling at the fasteners on my suit. "They're going to blow up the *Aurora* and blame us. Well, me."

"But he can't . . . that's not," Reed splutters. "I'm—"

"Your death is what sells it," I say. "All part of the plan. They need it to look like they suffered losses, too." I wonder how much the security teams are getting paid. Enough to make it a tempting offer for a better future for their families and loved ones, not enough to make it truly worth it once they got out here, I'm guessing.

Reed's mouth falls open and stays that way. "Wha . . . why?"

"Don't you know who you work for?" I do. In the absence of other options—a condition Verux created—I chose not to look too closely at my employer's decisions. But now, I'm reaping what I sowed.

I edge closer. "Kane. It's me." I'm careful not to touch him. I don't want to freak him out.

He blinks at me, his gaze sharpening. "Claire?"

"Still me," I affirm. For now, anyway. I shrug my suit off my shoulders, peeling it down to my waist, freeing my arms.

Kane's hand shoots out and catches my hand. His fingers intertwine gently with mine, and his grasp makes something tight in me relax.

"What are you doing?" Reed demands.

"Getting comfortable."

His eyes widen behind the glass of his faceplate. "But you can't just—"

"What the fuck do you want me to do, *Mr. Darrow*?" I ask. "We're stuck in here."

"But there has to be a way to—"

I shake my head dismissively. "Even if we could get out of this room, how do you propose we get off this ship?"

He hesitates. "The *Aurora*'s escape pods—"

"Would not get far enough away fast enough. We'd be caught in the blast. And if not, Max certainly wouldn't hesitate to order us shot down. He's in a Striker military vessel. Their gunner could sneeze wrong and eliminate us."

"Your little sniffer, then," he argues.

"We took parts from the LINA to make this ship work," I say. "And even if we could get her back together, then we've got the same problem. The LINA has no weapons, no defenses. And that's assuming we can get to her. There are three security teams on the *Aurora*. At least one of them is likely still in the cargo bay with the LINA." Searching for the device or sending over the token remains of the chosen *Aurora* passengers to back up Max's story. "I'm pretty sure they've got orders to keep us on board by any means necessary." Gunshot wounds would be easier to explain, assuming there'd be enough of our bodies to be found, than allowing our escape.

Reed opens his mouth again, but I cut him off. "I don't like this any more than you do. But the truth is: We. Are. Screwed," I say, carefully emphasizing each word. "The only way we're getting off this ship is when they blow it open."

And a small part of me—maybe that same part of me that was tempted to unhook myself from the safety tether on that last comm-web beacon—is relieved. It's over. All my choices, good, bad, or otherwise, have been taken from me.

Yes, Verux is an air-thieving, immoral, and inhumane collection of human waste. And the very thought of them getting away with this makes my blood bubble like we're in too-close orbit around the sun. But there's nothing I can do. When the odds are stacked this high against you, you take the peace you can find. Right?

Suddenly, though, the thought of space forever isn't nearly as appealing as it once was. My skin feels too tight against me, as though it's pressing for me to do something, anything, to survive. I ignore it.

Reed stands there for a long moment, staring at me.

I wonder if this is the first time that his family name hasn't rescued him. The first time in his life that something larger and outside of his control decided to take a crap on his existence.

Then he turns abruptly and bobbles his way over to the door, where he pounds on the smooth surface with his fists. "Hey!" he shouts. "Hello! If you can hear me, I will pay you to get me out! I'll pay you *more*."

So, I guess that's a yes. In spite of everything, I roll my eyes.

Kane squeezes my hand, pulling my attention back to him. "Isabelle?"

I hesitate for a second, not sure if he's talking to a vision of her or asking me. After a moment, though, it's clear he's focused on me and the present moment. For now anyway.

"I think I saw her," I say. "If it was her, she's okay." I don't tell him that the girl I saw was among the protestors—seemingly with her mother, his ex—those demanding answers for this disaster we've found ourselves in. He doesn't need to think of her that way. Unhappy, seeking a resolution that will likely never come. At least, not in the form she and her mother are probably hoping for.

Kane nods and relaxes, calmly, quietly accepting his fate. His loss. In reality, he likely accepted the fact that he would never see his daughter again weeks ago, having given up on a rescue or my return. But this, somehow, feels more final.

And his acceptance crawls beneath my skin like an itch that can't be soothed away. Kane, who gave up so much to provide for his child, has been beaten. Weeks alone, in starvation conditions, in sanity-straining conditions, and he survived. Now, when home is so close at hand, just a ship away, it's all over for him. For Isabelle.

Another child who will never see her parent again, who will have no grave to visit. Only an empty and meaningless hunk of marble with his name carved in it, sitting in a blandly pretty park on Earth somewhere.

Fury flickers, catching once again on all the dry tinder Max has provided. It's one thing for me to surrender to the inevitable, but for Kane to do it, for him to have been broken, for me to have played a role in breaking him . . . that's wrong. Just wrong.

Restless energy floods me, wiping away my bland retreat and replacing it with the need for motion. For action.

Releasing Kane's hand, I stand.

He looks up at me, hope and confusion warring in his expression.

I grit my teeth, pacing a couple of hobbling steps, back and forth. This is ridiculous. Pointless, even. It's impossible. Exactly as I laid out to Reed. Even if we can get out of this room, taking an escape pod would only grant us a few extra minutes, maybe an hour, of life. Same with the LINA.

The only ship that's safe from fucking Max is the one he's on.

I freeze, an idea dancing at the edge of my thoughts. I creep up on it slowly, afraid of chasing it away.

The ship Max is on. All by himself. With a skeleton crew. He's far less protected than the *Aurora* at the moment.

In my head, I see the bridge over the gap between the *Aurora* and the *Ares*.

Getting across, if the bridge is still in place, would be possible. And if they're sending bodies and equipment back across . . . the bridge has not been retracted yet. Theoretically. And in our suits—assuming we can find a matching one for Kane—we don't look that much different from the security teams.

If we can get back to the *Ares*, we might actually have a chance.

But that doesn't solve our problem. Problems, plural. Getting out of this room is job one. After that, it would be about getting across the bridge without being stopped by one or more of the security teams. And that's assuming we can do those things before they find the device they're searching for or Max decides to call it quits and move on to the next phase, i.e., blowing us up.

If only there were a way to distract them, slow them down . . .

I stop pacing. Or, drive them crazy.

Max said this thing causes paranoia, fear, hallucinations. Ghosts. But I've been living with most of those things my whole life. I saw my mother on this ship before the engines were even on. That was no weapon-induced hallucination.

Maybe some of what I've experienced on board is due to Verux's device—the woman under the bed, a ghost or a hallucination, I don't know—but some of it is just . . . me.

Thoughts race ahead of me, almost out of my reach.

The first time I experienced the *Aurora,* I was better able to handle it. I tried to guide Kane and the others. I was used to seeing things that no one else could see, used to having my perception of reality uncomfortably altered. Perhaps my damaged hearing—that partial deafness on my left side—also makes me less vulnerable to the vibrations. I don't know for sure.

Either way, it's an advantage. Of sorts.

What if it's one we can use? If Nysus figured out a way to crank up the noise dampeners to help cut the effects, what would happen if I could figure out how to shut the dampeners off? Maybe even increase the vibrations by revving the idling engines.

It returns in a flash, then, stealing my breath.

"It has to be mechanical. The engines go faster, the effects get worse. That's not aliens or ghosts." Nysus's whispered words reach me through the dimness of the mostly darkened bridge. I'm lying on the floor, my vision haloing around what little light there is, and my head pulsing with every heartbeat. Waves of agony cascade through my whole body. Next to me, I sense a presence, movement, but I can't quite bring myself to turn my head to look. Not just out of pain but fear of what I might see.

"Something to do with sound or vibrations. That's why the dampeners are redlining, trying to keep up with it."

The recaptured memory ends abruptly, leaving me gasping.

They were on the verge of figuring it out . . . and I left. For reasons I still don't understand.

Not that it matters now. And nothing at all will matter, including my vague outline of a plan, unless we can find a way out of this room.

I turn to Kane and move to kneel next to him. "Still me," I say. Though I wonder if his hallucinated version of me would say anything different.

He nods, but he looks as if he doesn't trust his own eyes. I let go of his hand and walk away; as far as his jumbled brain is concerned I may or may not be the same entity from a few moments ago. I understand that.

"Do you have anything in here? Supplies? Tools?" I press.

His gaze darts away from me, his attention focused on an empty corner. "She wouldn't do that," he says to no one, his breath ragged. "Just because you did!"

"Kane," I try again.

"That was different!" he argues.

With one final glare at whoever he sees there, Kane gets up and shuffles across the room. He digs under a pile of clothing and then reaches beneath two of the stacked mattresses, pulling out a dark object. A case, of some kind.

He hesitates for a second before bringing the item over to me. It's only when he holds the case out to me that I recognize it. One of our tool kits from the LINA, her designation and Verux's name printed in bright red letters across the front.

I take it, and even as I open it, I know what I'll find. A collection of small tools—screwdrivers, wrenches, utility knives, plastic ties, even a microblade saw—all arranged neatly by size and color coded.

Of course one of the pockets is empty. The largest screwdriver—the one with the blue handle—is missing. Because it's in Nysus's head, downstairs. Driven in through his ear, in an attempt to end his suffering, or at least the voices whispering to him.

I wince but manage to nod at Kane. "Thank you." Now I know

who Kane must have thought he was speaking to a moment ago: a
hallucination of Nysus warning him of what I might be planning.

   Screw that. Hell yeah, I'm going to try to use these tools to escape, but this time, we're going through the fucking door.

29

The second-largest screwdriver does nothing against the now-hardened substance Diaz poured through the door's mechanisms. I can't even get bits of the excess to chip away. All it's doing is dulling the edge of the tool.

And the microblade snaps in two without making a dent in whatever it is. What I wouldn't give for a plasma drill now.

"You're pushing too hard," Reed insists, supervising over my shoulder. "It's QuikLok. We make it for the colony habs, a way for them to secure rooms or criminals. You can't jab at it like that. I supervised the quality testing for it."

I grit my teeth and stand. Slapping the broken blade pieces in his hand, I gesture toward the door. "Be my guest."

To my surprise, he awkwardly bobbles forward—still in his suit and helmet—to kneel in front of the door. He applies the largest remaining piece of the blade to the substance, delicately scraping around the edges, microscopic shavings curling up along the blade.

I roll my eyes, fists clenched tight at my sides. We will die of old age before *that* gets us out of here.

But, of course, we won't. Because we'll be exploded into bits long before then.

Damnit. I can feel every precious second slipping away. Any moment now, we'll hear and feel the rumble of a distant blast, our only warning seconds before it tears through us. A sticky panicked sweat is making my T-shirt adhere to every inch of my skin, and it's even worse where my enviro suit still clings to my waist and legs.

It doesn't help that Becca's high-pitched giggle is echoing around the room, right at the edges of my hearing. Barely detectable and soft enough to almost be mistaken as ambient noise—a light flutter in the air filtration system or a minor squeal in the idling engines.

And I keep catching glimpses of my mother from the corner of my eye. A flash of her white coat, the flutter of her dark hair, her mouth open wide in a silent scream of warning.

If she only shows up when I'm in real trouble, then it seems about right that she's here, given our current situation.

Lourdes and Voller haven't shown up since I came back on board, I realize. Which means, what? I have no idea.

Next to me, Kane bumps up against my shoulder, startling me. He holds his hand out and for a moment, I think he's asking for my hand. Then I realize he wants the screwdriver that I'm still clutching in one fist.

I hesitate for a moment, feeling what he must have been when I asked for the tool kit in the first place.

"I won't. I promise," he says in a gravelly voice, repeating my words back to me.

I hope it's more than mimicry, like a child repeating "please" and "thank you" without really understanding the significance.

He tips his head toward the door, and I follow his gaze toward . . . the hinges. Oh shit. They're on *this* side of the door. Unlike the LINA, this is a passenger vessel, with all the accommodations and quirks of a space meant for human living. Including doors that open to the inside.

"It's worth a shot," I say with a nod, handing over the screwdriver. If you have to be trapped on a ship about to explode, best to be trapped with a brilliant and observant—if half-mad—mechanic.

"Move," I tell Reed.

He doesn't look up. "No. *I* know what I'm doing."

Running low on patience, I give his shoulder a not-so-gentle shove. He falls easily to one side, off-balance from kneeling in his suit with his top-heavy helmet.

And yes, a tiny, petty part of me enjoyed it.

Reed straightens up immediately, face flushed and mouth tight with fury. "You can't do—"

"I can, I did, and I will again if you don't shut up. I'm trying to get us out of here." More accurately, Kane is trying, but same thing.

"No wonder your crew mutinied and dumped you in that escape pod," Reed snarls at me, hauling himself laboriously to his feet, using the wall for balance.

I flip him off automatically, even as my brain is still processing his words. That's not what he was saying before. Not at all. In his version of events, I'm usually the murderer, evildoer, the greedy one who sacrifices everyone for her own improvement.

But whatever. I don't have time for his bullshit right now.

As soon as Reed is out of the way, Kane applies the screwdriver to the lower portion of the topmost door hinge.

After a quick thump to the bottom of the screwdriver, the metal pin pops free almost comically easily. The second one is a bit stiffer, and the third makes me hold my breath. But Kane eventually manages to work that one free, too.

The final pin gives with a loud pop, and the door shifts in the frame. The right side, where the hinges were, now sticks out a little toward us, as if the QuikLok had expanded inside where Diaz poured it through until the whole thing was no longer plumb.

I wedge myself in next to Kane, drop to my haunches, and carefully work my fingers into the narrow gap under the door. "Ready?" I ask.

He doesn't respond for a moment, staring blankly at the door.

"Kane," I say, raising my voice.

He looks around, his gaze sliding past me at first—like I'm completely invisible to him—before eventually returning. "You," he says finally.

"Yes, still me," I say again, battling both frustration and fear. One minute he seems fine. Well, fine-ish. Coherent enough to understand what's going on and reason through a way to assist. But the next, he's just . . . gone.

The disparity turns my insides to ice.

What must it be like in his head? Are we surrounded by people

I can't see? Is listening to me like trying to hear a whisper across a crowded room? What if I can't find a way to help him? What if he's lost in that other version of the world—that permanently crowded room—forever?

My mind immediately projects a vision of Kane in the gray Verux Peace and Harmony Tower pajamas, sitting alone in the corner of the common room, muttering to himself.

The mental picture is so real that my stomach knots with dread.

But I know, in reality, even that image is too optimistic, at this point. We would have to get off this ship first, for him to be confined at the Tower.

Which brings us back to this fucking door.

"I need your help," I say to Kane, working to keep my voice steady and calm. My thigh muscles are already twitching from holding this position. I tip my head toward the door. "I'm going to pull from the bottom. If a gap opens on the side, I need you to pull, too." I don't know how powerful that QuikLok is. It looks like I should be able to create at least a small opening.

Kane's expression shifts from bewildered to determined. "Okay."

"Okay," I repeat in relief, though I suspect this moment of clarity from him may be brief. "Here we go."

I lock my fingers around the bottom edge of the door and lean back, pushing against the floor with my feet for additional leverage and strength.

The right side of the door lurches toward us an inch or so, and Kane immediately lunges for the small opening, wedging his fingers inside. Together, we pull, me with extra determination that he should not lose his fingertips in this exercise on top of everything else.

Sweat trickles down my spine, and my feet are tingling from my cramped position. And my fingers are starting to slip.

"This is pointless," Reed says loudly from behind us.

It's hard not to want to redirect my energy toward shutting him up, but I focus.

"The QuikLok is designed to prevent this exact kind of tampering," he continues.

And maybe on a working ship, a military ship, or a hab, he'd be right. Metal doors, metal doorframes. But I'm betting, praying, even, that the wooden doorframe—part of that oh-so-luxurious environment for the Platinum Level civilian residents—is prettier than it is strong. Plus, the force of QuikLok expanding so rapidly in a contained space, that had to do some damage, right?

Just as my fingers are beginning to lose their grip, the door gives suddenly with a loud pop, flying back several inches. The unexpected release dumps me unceremoniously on my ass and sends Kane stumbling back.

I look up in relief, to find that the door is now open.

Sort of.

The top half is open about six inches, while the bottom is about half that, leaving the door leaning drunkenly inward.

I push myself up to my feet and grab the newly released edge of the door. Kane, without being asked, follows my lead. Pulling together, we manage to scrape it back another few inches.

We can make it out now. Elation is a bright spark in me, mixed with the nauseating low tones of fear over what's next.

I step back, grab my helmet and the tool kit from the LINA, just in case. I attach the tool kit through the loop at the top of its case to one of the hooks at the waist of my suit. Just like a regular workday. "Let's go," I whisper. It seems likely that if Diaz left anyone stationed nearby, they would have heard us struggling with the door, but why take the risk?

I nudge Kane through the opening first. He gets stuck for a few harrowing seconds but manages to squeeze through. Then I follow.

Or I try to.

Most of my body is out in the hall but all forward progress stops when my helmet rams into the edges of the door and frame. Unlike our bodies, it has no give. The rounded bubble shape is completely inflexible.

And the opening is simply not large enough.

"It's not going to fit," Reed hisses at me.

He's right.

And that's a problem. Multiple problems. No helmets means less protection from the MAW device, assuming part two of my plan works and I can figure out how to get the dampeners turned off. But it's worse than that, too. My hope had been to liberate a suit and helmet from a security team member for Kane. Then it would be just three anonymous suited people in the tunnel, three people who would likely be assumed to be security team members, bringing over the dead or reclaimed personal items to back up Verux's version of events. But without helmets, Reed and I will be immediately identifiable if we try to cross back over to *Ares*.

"Damnit," I mutter. I give the helmet one last desperate yank, but the clunk of metal and plastic against wood is as unforgiving as it sounds.

I have to let it go.

So I do, but the helmet falling away from my fingertips feels like surrendering. Like accepting our fate before we've even begun to fight.

I glare in at Reed, as if this development is his fault. Which, in theory, it kind of is because all of this is his fault. His and Verux's.

Behind me, Kane paces restlessly in the hallway. I don't want him to wander off. It's so dark out here, without my helmet light, but I can hear his movements, the soft whisper of his boots against the plush carpeting.

At least, I hope it's him.

I push that thought down with a shudder. It's not real. None of it. It's just a trick, feelings and sensations created by a machine.

"Come on," I say to Reed, more of a challenge than an invitation. Because if it was hard for me to give up my helmet for practical reasons, Reed will surely only go that route kicking and screaming.

He disappears from view for a moment, but before I can whisper-yell at him, he's back. Minus his helmet but carrying the dying work light from the LINA. He must have pulled it from the mattresses where Kane or Nysus stuck it.

It's not much light, but it's better than nothing.

I raise my eyebrows in reluctant respect. So, he's not completely useless then.

As if he can read my thoughts, Reed gives me a haughty sneer. Fine. Whatever.

I step back as he works to squeeze himself through. "Here, give me the light," I say.

But he refuses, locking his fingers tight around the dimming oval. Talk about a petty grasp for control.

As soon as he's free, though, I understand why.

He immediately turns away from us—away from the bridge—and starts hauling ass toward the bulkhead doors and the spiral staircase to the atrium.

I have to run to catch up to him, the empty arms of my enviro suit flapping against my legs and hips.

When I'm even with him, I push him into the wall. He stumbles over his own feet, still clumsy in the suit but not as much as he was with the helmet on.

"What the fuck are you doing?" I demand, my voice straining with the need to be quiet against the desire to shout.

Once he regains his footing, he shoves back at me. But I'm expecting it, and it does little to move me.

"This is my mission, my assignment," he snarls. "I am taking back control." He straightens up. His hand drifts up unconsciously as if to adjust the tie he's not wearing, or—I belatedly realize—his damn Verux generation pin.

I gape at him. "Did you miss the part where they're planning to kill us?"

He opens his mouth to respond, but I cut him off. "No, forget that. How about the part where *your death specifically* is meant to sell their version of events?"

"My father is an executive at the highest level of—"

"Which is exactly why Verux needs you to die here," I point out. "Besides, you're not getting out of here alive. Max will make sure of that. You're his fucking replacement."

Reed blinks rapidly, his expression going slack, as if that idea had not occurred to him.

"And these people, the security teams, they don't give a shit who your father is. They've already committed to the cause, for money, for benefits for their family, whatever. Your dad may not have signed off on your death, but I bet someone at Verux did. And if you get in the way, you're one more obstacle to them getting whatever it is they've already decided is worth dying for."

His eyes narrow at me. "You just don't want me to go to them because then they'll know you're out," he says.

He's absolutely right, of course. But how he can't see that I'm also correct about his best interests is beyond me.

God save me from stupid people. "True, but not the point I'm making," I say.

I risk a quick glance over my shoulder to where I left Kane. I can't hear him moving anymore. And, of course, without the damn light that Reed is carrying, I can't see anything, either.

My limited patience frays to the breaking point.

"Look," I say flatly. "I don't like you, but you could be useful." Well, more likely his father. Assuming we can get off the *Aurora* and in contact with the senior Mr. Darrow, a still-living Reed might prove a valuable bargaining chip if his father is as important as Reed says he is. Reed's father might be willing to take on Verux—or the faction in charge of this mission, at least—for the life of his kid, assuming we can get word to him. "My goal is to keep you alive and get you out of here. Can you say the same thing for anyone else on this fucking ship?"

Reed hesitates, and that's answer enough for me. I snatch the light out of his hand.

"Hey!" he protests.

But when I head back toward where I left Kane, Reed reluctantly trails behind me.

Kane is no longer outside the suite we escaped. The empty hall-way makes my heart thunder hard in panic.

Where is he?

I stick the upper half of my body into the suite to be sure he didn't get confused and wiggle back in. But as far as I can see with the dim light, he's not here.

Shit.

I pull myself back out. Where did he go? If he's off wandering the ship, I might never find him. At least, not before one of the security team members.

"Kane!" I call as loudly as I dare.

Reed shushes me, just to be an asshole, and I ignore him.

But then I hear something, not quite a response, or even a word. More a murmur of sound. Coming from the bridge.

I head toward that direction as fast as I can.

It's slightly brighter on the bridge, thanks to the starlight from the windows and the pale glow of the control boards.

Kane is crouched in front of an open panel beneath the navigational controls, muttering to himself as he threads through the loose wires, seemingly looking for something.

I still don't know much about the *Aurora*'s bridge layout, but I'm betting that the sound dampeners aren't located in that particular equipment bank.

I ease up closer to him. "Kane?"

He doesn't glance up from his work. "We need to go after her. It's been too long. We have to find a way."

Her. Does he mean me?

I clear my throat. "Kane. It's me. I'm here." I grab his hand, still-ing its anxious movements among the wires.

He looks up at me, but also through me. I've never felt so invis-ible and the sensation makes my heart cant weirdly in my chest. "I see her all the time, Ny," Kane says, his expression haunted. "I see her right now."

I squeeze his hand. "You did it," I remind him. "You came after me. I'm here."

"This is a touching reunion," Reed hisses. "But you promised me getting out of here alive."

Now he's nervous? Probably finally had enough time for the adrenaline to wear off and my logic to sink in.

"I need to turn off the dampeners," I tell Kane.

"Why?" Reed asks behind me. "What good will *that* do?"

I glare at him over my shoulder. "It'll do what I need it to." I could explain but if he decides to take off again, I don't want him blabbing to Max or the security teams.

I turn my attention back to Kane. "The dampeners," I say. "How do I turn them off?"

But Kane just stares at me, through me.

Shit. Okay. I can do this. It can't be that hard.

I cross the bridge to the screen where Nysus showed us the dampeners redlining and the unexplained 10 percent energy drain.

But staring at the array of options and abbreviations on the screen, I curse Verux—and not for the first time—for keeping us in our expertise silos. I can run the basics on the LINA but more from training and rote memory. Not from understanding the actual tech or engine. That was Nysus and Voller and Kane.

And I don't want to start up the wrong system, press the wrong button, and accidentally turn the lights back on or set off some kind of alarm.

Reed arrives to manage over my left shoulder. "It's that one," he says, pointing at an icon that says ENG MAN.

"You have no idea," I say, resisting the urge to simply press the button based on the confidence in his tone.

He scoffs at me. "Engine maintenance. What else could it be?"

I stare at him. "I don't know, spelled correctly?"

It takes him a second, then he gets it. "It's an abbreviation," Reed says with defensive bluster. "The point is to leave letters out."

Ignoring him, I let out a slow breath and try to hold fast to my patience, try to ignore the feeling of seconds ticking down on a timer that I cannot see.

Eventually I find a menu marked DIAG and work my way through until I find the screen with the dampener information. They are indeed operating above the upper lines of the graph, showing where Nysus worked his magic.

Then I find an indication of a menu for the dampeners themselves. And thank God, on the second submenu of that menu, is simply an option for OFF.

I press it, and the effect is instantaneous. The idling engines rumble noticeably beneath my feet, sending little waves of vibrations up through my soles.

But it's more than that, too. Dread, like a heavy, suffocating blanket, descends upon me, pressing against my chest and making it harder to breathe.

My heart flutters rapidly, as if it's trying to escape.

Movement at the corner of my eye catches my attention, and I turn abruptly toward the rear of the bridge, even though I know better.

There's nothing there.

At least, not at first.

But the longer I stare into the darkness, beyond our failing work light and the dim glow of the control panels, shapes emerge. Until they're just as bright and visible as they must have been in life.

Captain Linden Gerard staggers backward toward the hall, her expression one of shock and fury, a crimson splotch growing on her chest. She doesn't quite fall, though, bobbing in the air instead.

The gravity is shutting down. The environmentals have been turned off.

Instinctively, I reach for the edge of the control boards behind me to keep my balance. But I don't feel the gravity going slack—a sensation like someone cutting a cord between you and the other person in a continuous game of tug-of-war.

The other shape, a man with his back to me, grabs Gerard's arm and pulls her off the bridge, half walking, half pushing off the floor to glide through the air. Likely Cage Wallace, the first officer. Verux's man on the inside.

What was Gerard in here to do? To set off the distress beacon? Someone certainly had.

A moment later, a gunshot, thin and echoey, sounds. I jump, startled. "Oh God."

Blowback, blood and brain matter, sprays in a fine mist through the open doorway.

Then semidarkness returns suddenly to the bridge, and I blink several times, trying to see more.

Or unsee what I've just witnessed.

That was the end of Captain Gerard and First Officer Wallace. The murder-suicide Voller first suspected. Playing out as vividly in front of me as if it were happening right now. I shouldn't have been able to see any of it, because of the dark. Because it happened more than two decades ago. And yet . . .

Ghosts or hallucinations caused by the weapon—the MAW, Max called it? Both?

It occurs to me for the first time—and much too late—that whatever the MAW does to non-ghost-seeing people, it might do that and more to me. If that damn device made regular people see things, what would it do to someone who already does? I managed all right before, thanks to my experience with ignoring the unusual—if no one else acknowledges it, best to pretend it's not there—but that was with the dampeners on.

Now, without that protection, we might be in more trouble than I realized. We have to make our way down to the cargo bay, through a ship filled with the dead, riddled with hundreds of violent and awful deaths. Forget the MAW, there are probably plenty of real ghosts here, too.

And if that is not a recipe for losing what is left of your mind, I don't know what is.

30

The sound of screams from somewhere deeper in the ship sends a jolt through me. The distinct *rat-a-tat-tat* of automatic weapons fire follows, shattering my hesitation and waking me from my temporary paralysis.

My plan, such as it is, is working.

Even though I was expecting this result, hoping for it, the terrible noises of the stoic and resigned security team members losing their grip make me shiver. I glance around the bridge warily, anticipating the appearance of another death reenactment. But everything is dark and still. Which we should take advantage of, while we can.

"Come on," I say to Reed and Kane, forcing myself to sound more confident than I feel. "We need to go."

When I look behind me, though, Kane is where I left him, sitting near the piles of pulled-out wires at the navigation control bank. His face is newly slack, and his hands are limp at his sides. I can't tell if he heard me or not. I can't tell anything about him at all.

Dread pools in my stomach. At least before he was talking and listening. To people who weren't here, granted, but this new stillness . . . it's wrong.

Instinct screams at me to DO SOMETHING.

I push past Reed to kneel beside Kane.

"It's me," I say softly.

No response. Not even when I take his hand in mine.

Kane blinks, swallows, breathes—slowly, shallowly—but his gaze is unfocused, untethered. It's as if he's simply . . . gone.

My vision blurs with tears. Taking away the dampeners was too much for him.

"Hang in there, I'm going to get you out of here. I promise." I squeeze his hand in encouragement, but his fingers remain loose against mine.

"I just need you to get up. Please," I whisper.

But he doesn't move.

"Get up!" I beg him. I cannot, will not, leave him behind. No matter what I did before.

Desperation builds in me to a pinch point. I stand up and pull at him with all my might, leaning away from him for leverage.

"Please!" The word comes out raw and painful, closer to a shout. At this point, I'm not even sure who I'm asking. Kane. God. Fate. Whoever owes me one.

Finally, his legs move. Erratically at first, folding and unfolding as if a puppeteer is momentarily confused about which string does what. And then he stands.

It looks more like muscle memory than an actual decision. Still, it feels like a miracle in the moment, and a sob of relief escapes me. I use the back of my free hand to wipe at the tears on my face.

I'm not letting go of Kane. With my hand locked tight around his, I pull him toward the doors, and he follows.

"Darrow, let's move it," I say to Reed.

Only then do I realize that he's been too quiet. Too many opportunities for him to mock and sneer have passed by without comment.

When I look over, Reed is frozen in place, staring in terror across the bridge.

I know that stare. Too well.

"Reed." I snap my fingers. "Come on."

"Do you see him?" Reed whispers.

"I don't see any—"

"My father, he's *right there*." He pauses. "He's angry with me." Reed sounds confused, wounded.

I move to face him, but his attention remains on the specter of his father.

With my free hand, I jerk his chin down, forcing him to meet my eyes. "He's not there. It's not real. Your father is back on Earth." Exactly where we need him to be if we're going to survive this mess. "None of this is real. I need you to keep it together." I cannot drag Reed along unwillingly, screaming about his father, through this ship.

Reed rubs at his chest. "But I can feel it. I can feel how angry he is." A paranoid whine enters his voice. His gaze flicks from me back to his father.

I pinch his cheek, hard enough to leave a red mark.

He yelps, and then glares at me.

"Then you guys shouldn't have made the MAW five-hundred-whatever work so well," I say through clenched teeth.

He blinks down at me and then back across the bridge.

"He's gone," he says, stunned.

"He was never there. Remember that. Most of what you're going to see from now on is not real."

He nods but looks less than convinced.

As soon as we reach the hallway, me leading the way, pulling an unresponsive Kane at my side and Reed at the back, I realize my mistake: in my rush, I forgot the work light on the bridge.

It's so dark out here, I can't see my hand in front of my face.

Fuck.

Maybe that will make what comes next easier, if we can't see it. Maybe not.

I feel for the wall and start forward. "Stay close," I warn Reed. "If we can move fast enough, maybe we can avoid . . ."

Becca appears ahead of me, laughing and dancing in her night-gown, waving me forward.

No, apparently not.

I do my best to ignore her, keeping my hand firmly on the wall, moving it along the textured wallpaper and the smooth doors as we go. If I were to give in to distraction and simply follow her, it feels possible that we might somehow be lost in here forever. Like those fairy-tale children without their bread-crumb trail. Like when I followed Becca into the quarantined hab.

Becca vanishes unexpectedly.

And my step hitches for a second.

"What's wrong?" Reed demands, bumping into me from behind.

"Nothing. I—"

Heavy blows land against the smooth wooden door currently beneath my fingertips. From the other side. The door shakes in its frame, moved by the force.

Instinctively, I pull my hand away as if the surface is hot.

Let me out! Let me out! I won't hurt them again, I promise . . . A man's voice, but it holds such shrill notes of hysteria and unhinged laughter that it sounds barely human.

"Do you hear that?" I ask on instinct, even though I know better.

"I don't hear anything," Reed says. "I can't fucking see anything either." He sounds more annoyed than scared now, but his tone shifts, then, growing bitter. Mean. "Which is exactly the way you want it. So you can be in charge."

"Shut up, Reed." I don't have time for this.

I tighten my grip on Kane's hand and start forward again.

The voice, along with the banging, stops as soon as we move on.

But this time, dread curdles in my stomach. If the pattern holds, that only means that something else is coming.

An instant later, cool breath moves against my cheek, as if someone is standing right next to me, about to whisper in my ear.

I nearly turn, expecting to see the frightful but familiar vision of my mother, but a deeper instinct in me speaks up. *NO.*

The fear—of what I'm not seeing, what I might see—nearly stalls me out, and sweat breaks out across my forehead.

How long is this hallway? Shouldn't we be close to the end by now?

Or can I even trust my perceptions?

I grit my teeth and keep lifting my feet, one in front of the other.

The first chilly tap on my shoulder is rapidly followed by a second and a third. Like a single fingertip pressing against my skin lightly.

It's only when I feel the sensation roll down my back that I recognize it as water droplets.

The drops come faster and faster, that cool breath against my skin, as if someone soaking wet is leaning close.

He held me down. Put my face under the water. I don't know why. She sounds distraught, confused.

The female passenger frozen in the tub, the princess. I remember her. Her vulnerable form curled up in a protective, fetal posture in the tub beneath the ice.

I should have killed him first.

Those words come with a sharp tug at my cheek, followed by the sting of broken skin.

I gasp involuntarily, my hand releasing Kane's and flying to my face. Was that . . . did she *bite* me?

My fingers come away from my face damp and warm. Possibly blood. Maybe sweat. I can't tell. If the ghosts can hurt us . . .

We will never survive this.

I fumble for Kane's hand and start us moving again. "Faster," I tell Reed over my shoulder.

"You know they'll never believe you," Reed says. "Verux and my father. They know what people like you are all about. Greedy. Selfish. Always after whatever you can take that you don't deserve."

Anger flickers to life in me, hot and sharp.

"And you . . . you just want to make *me* look bad," he continues, his voice pitching lower suddenly, from indignation to fury.

A memory of my first sight of the atrium flashes in my head: all those people gliding endlessly overhead. The Dunleavy sister with the purple hair in the bathrobe with a knife strapped to her wrist. The man with the belt around his neck, the end of it still wrapped in another passenger's hands.

In the cabins, Anthony Lightfoot and Jasen Wyman, the two men who'd beaten each other to death with camera equipment.

Paranoia is one of the symptoms Max rattled off. No wonder the passengers killed each other.

"Reed, I just want to get off this fucking ship. Stay focused," I say, working to keep my voice calm. If I get agitated, that's only going to amp him up further. "You're letting it get to you."

"You want me to think that, don't you?" he demands. "But I know better. I'm seeing things more clearly than I have in a long time. *In a long time!*"

Okay, yeah. Reed is losing it. I wish to God I'd thought to put him in front of me, instead of letting him trail behind. In the fucking dark.

It's work not to hunch my shoulders protectively. It feels as if a glowing target has been painted over my back, daring Reed to charge forward.

But there's nothing to be done about that now, except to get us out. Ahead, the darkness seems a bit brighter, indicating that we might be nearing the stairway to the atrium level and the working lights that Diaz's team was in the process of setting up. I don't know that light will help anything, but it sure as hell will make it easier to see what's coming.

I think.

Soft sobbing comes from nearby, perhaps a few feet away. Brokenhearted, devastated crying, punctuated by deep gasps. It sounds . . . real, more so than anything else we've heard.

Instinct tells me to slow down, but I resist that impulse and keep walking.

It's just a device, a weapon, vibrations against the eardrum causing strange effects. That's all.

Except it's not. Device or no device, a lot of people died here in a variety of horrible, violent ways. If any place should be haunted, it's this ship. So is it any surprise there's a bunch of angry, confused spirits trying to make themselves known?

Even more than that, though, it feels as though the ship has taken on a life of her own, a conglomeration of the spirits trapped within and yet something more. An entity in and of herself. And she doesn't want to let us go.

I shake my head at myself. *Now who's letting this place get to her? Paranoia, Kovalik. It will bite you in the ass, if you don't watch it.*

"Are you crying?" Reed asks, scoffing.

"Keep moving," I say, startled. Is he hearing the same thing I am? Real or not real, then?

As we get closer, the volume of the crying increases. It sounds as if we're going to stumble over someone—her?—in a second.

Maybe . . . maybe one of the security team members fled up here from the violence and chaos below.

That thought is enough to make me hesitate, to slow for just a second as my fingers brush past the smoothness of a door.

Which is all that's needed.

A cold hand locks bruising-tight around my left ankle as I prepare to take a step, throwing me off-balance.

My arms pinwheel frantically and I lose my grip on Kane as I try to catch myself.

I can't fall. She's waiting.

The woman from under the bed. I don't dare look down, but I know it's her. Her mouth and ears stuffed with cloth, her eyes blindfolded and yet she sees . . .

Before I can restabilize, Reed crashes into my back with a grunt.

We go down hard, in a tangle of limbs.

Immediately, I scramble to free myself and stand, anticipating the icy touch of her hand again. Perhaps against my face, reaching for my eyes . . .

But before I can get very far, another hand grasps my leg— this one, though, warm and very much alive. Reed yanks me back toward him. The carpeting burns against my palms as I scrabble to stop my backward progress.

"What are you—"

"I knew it," Reed says, the words tight through his clenched teeth.

"You're trying to be the hero, and you want me to play the fool. But I'm not going to do that. Do you hear me?"

I kick out at him, but on my stomach, it's virtually impossible to connect solidly. "Listen to yourself, that doesn't make any sense. I need you to talk to your father. I need you to—"

He wrenches me from my stomach onto my back and drops his body weight down to hold me in place.

Immediately, alarm bells in my head ring.

I lash out at him with everything I've got, but I can't see a fucking thing. Electric pain ricochets up my knuckles after one particularly wild swipe; I think I caught his chin.

But other than one quick, sharp intake of breath from Reed, there's no reaction. He's too lost in his paranoid landscape.

He leans down, putting pressure on my upper arms with his elbows until it feels like the bones might shatter, and I cry out involuntarily. Tears gather at the corners of my eyes.

Kane. He's right there. But there's no sound of his approach.

"You like that?" Reed demands, leaning close enough that flecks of his saliva hit my face with his words. "Not so tough now, are you?"

Abruptly, the pressure against my arms vanishes, and a desperate exhalation of relief is building in my throat, demanding release. But I force it down, refusing to give him the satisfaction. Fucking Reed Darrow.

Then his hands close around my throat.

My body panics, reacting faster than my mind, which is still locked in disbelief that this is actually happening. My back arches up, trying to buck him off. My hands fly up to pry at his fingers, and then—finally—my brain engages. I push my feet against the floor in a half-remembered self-defense move from my Verux training days, desperate for leverage.

But Reed is so much heavier than he looks. His grip around my neck is unshaken and grows tighter. My pulse throbs frantically in my head and behind my eyes, the oxygen shortage starting to sink in.

All around me, I can feel them watching me, leaning close for a front-row seat to another death. The blinded woman from under the bed. The cackling man who wanted to be released from his room. The formerly frozen girl from the tub who bit my cheek.

They're waiting for me to join them. One more victim of the *Aurora* to join the hundreds more in this endless fucking parade of the dead.

I scratch at Reed's arms, but his environmental suit protects him. With effort, I lash out in the direction of his face and catch flesh under my nails. His hands loosen but only for a second.

Bright starbursts of color light up the darkness in front of my eyes.

You're going to die here.

My vision should be growing darker, but instead, one of those brilliant starbursts explodes into color, light, and sound.

In a flash, I can see the ship as it must have been. The smell of "new" in the freshly varnished wooden panels in the hall, the perfume of those rare flowers on display, and laughter mixed with the faint clinking of glasses and the low-level buzz of voices.

I sit up—pain gone, Reed forgotten—and watch three women come toward me. All of them are dressed in formal gowns, returning from an event. Perhaps in the ballroom or atrium on the level below. The beautiful woman with dark hair seems to float down the hall in a creation that appears to be nothing more than layers of pink netting—which seems familiar somehow, though I can't, in this moment, pinpoint why.

The youngest of the three, her hair dyed metallic silver to match her dress, carries her shoes by the straps, swinging them carelessly at her side. A bright gold chain dangles from her neck to her narrow waist and at the end, an old-fashioned key, worn as prominently as a diamond. A Dunleavy, the younger of the two. I recognize her, though she looks so different . . . alive.

These two split off first, entering their rooms, leaving only the final member of the trio, dressed in all black, her blond hair caught into an elegant upsweep. As she moves closer to me, I realize she's not in a dress, but a sleeveless tuxedo-like creation with black lapels and a flash of white at her chest, leading to a bell of split skirt.

The captain. Linden Gerard. She's heading for the bridge. Her forehead is creased in a frown, and she's pressing her fingertips at a spot between her eyebrows, her fingertips turning white with the pressure.

You're just tired. That's all. She whispers it to herself over and over again, until she's even with me.

Then she lowers her hand from her face to stare down at me.

Except she's no longer Captain Gerard, she's me.

My own face stares down at me, and I stare back, hypnotized.

Help me. Help us, we mouth. Her hands flutter at her sides for a moment before flying up to her neck, as if she's choking herself.

A flash of a white lab coat, then, and dark hair at the corner of my vision.

Claire!

My mother. When I turn to track her movement, she's gone. Everything is gone. In that moment, I'm back on the floor in the absolute darkness of the hall, Reed's grip tight around my throat.

My hands have fallen away from him to rest at my sides; I've given up.

The pressure in my head feels like it's going to spray pieces of my skull everywhere in a matter of seconds. So, it takes me longer than it should to realize that my arm is resting on something bulky and rough. I can picture it suddenly: durable canvas with the LINA's name stitched in bright red, the letters fraying a little from frequent handling.

The tool kit.

I fumble, my fingers numb and nearly unresponsive, until I manage to lock on to the textured plastic handle of a tool. A screwdriver.

With the last bit of energy I have, I haul my arm upward and toward the side of Reed's face, pointy end of the screwdriver out, aiming for his temple.

The strike doesn't have much force behind it, but I feel the metal blade scrape sideways past something soft, meeting minor resistance that gives way, until it's stopped by a solid wall of what feels like bone.

He screams, and his hands vanish from my neck. "My eye!" He half crawls, half falls off me.

Rolling over to my side, I suck in air, coughing and choking, each breath slicing through my raw throat, like inhaling shredded glass.

"I can't see! I can't . . . you bitch!" Reed sounds closer to hysteria now, never mind that he can't possibly know whether I've blinded him or not, given that it's as dark in here as it ever was. "I'm going to . . . you'll pay . . . it's just the beginning . . ."

As he continues mumble-shouting, I haul myself to my hands and knees and crawl away from him, my damaged throat pulsing like a second heartbeat but still functional.

I have to stand. I have to run. We *have to run.* In his current condition, I have no doubt that Reed will kill me if he gets another chance. Kane, too, if Reed comes across him.

Dizziness washes over me the second I'm mostly vertical, and I have a moment of swirling vertigo, intensified by the darkness. I can't see if I'm falling, which way is up or down, and my body is sending me panicked signals about the ground coming up fast.

I thrust my hand out, automatically, seeking something to hold on to.

My fingers brush over rough fabric, warmed by human skin beneath.

I jerk back before my brain clicks in. Reed is behind me, still ranting beneath his breath. And the ghosts I've encountered—so far anyway—don't hold body heat.

Kane.

I reach out again, finding his back and then his shoulder. I follow the line of his arm down to his hand, to his familiar calloused fingertips.

It is him.

My relief is so powerful it almost chokes me. A lump swells in my throat, and tears of pain roll down my cheeks.

Just as before, he won't take my hand but allows me to take his. So I do.

And we run, me pulling him along, as fast as I can, in the dark. It feels like running out in blind faith, knowing there's a drop-off into nothingness but not knowing where.

Every step feels like our last one.

I'm frantically trying to remember the gentle curve of the corridor, the exact position of those decorative tables.

I find one of them painfully with the edge of my hip; as I stumble past, the vase of dried and dead flowers wobbles on its base and falls, with a crash as loud as an explosion.

Behind us, Reed's mumbling cuts off with a snarl. Pounding footsteps ensue. And pursue.

Fuck.

Limping now, I tug at Kane to keep moving. The broken glass crunches beneath our feet, giving Reed our exact location. If he's coherent enough to listen for that and figure it out.

But the darkness ahead of me is getting lighter, I'm sure of it. Though, not as bright as it should be, given the number and intensity of the lights I saw Diaz's team setting up.

We burst past the retracted bulkhead doors onto the landing for the Platinum Level, near the spiral staircase to the atrium below. The empty pedestal that formerly held *Grace* (or *Speed*) at the top of the stairs is a welcome and familiar landmark.

And about the only one.

As we hurry toward the spiral staircase—I don't want Reed to catch up to us at all, but on that thing, with nowhere to run or hide, would be guaranteed death—I look down toward the atrium.

For a moment, my vision blurs and I see the atrium, bright and cheerily lit, dozens of passengers crisscrossing the space. Some of them are in formal dress, coming from the ballroom; others are in swimwear or robes from the spa. A small group of them sits, laughing and talking, on the as-yet-unmarred leather sofas. No signs of blood and mayhem, as they toast each other with flutes of champagne.

The *Aurora*, in one of her last moments of normal. Before First Officer Wallace turned on that device and doomed them all to hell.

I blink and the vision disappears, leaving only the dimly lit atrium full of death.

More death now.

Work lights have been turned over or smashed by bullets. A couple of them are still sizzling and sparking. And among the passengers' bodies, several new corpses dressed in familiar environmental suits.

Fresh blood, red and alarmingly bright, is smeared across the floor. And trails across the room toward the corridor in fat droplets that increase to mini-puddles before I lose sight of it.

This is where the screaming and gunfire came from earlier, then. At least some.

Good. I fight against the swell of gritty satisfaction in me, unnerved by it. I didn't *want* anyone to die.

But if it's them or us, I know whose side I'm on.

Practical, pragmatic, ugly. Maybe I'm more the child of Verux than I realized. Then again, I didn't sign on to die for the cover-up story, and I sure as fuck didn't start this.

Diaz kneels at the front of the carnage, shoulders slumped and staring blankly out at her people. What's left of them. Her helmet is tipped over on its side on the floor next to her, the light shining at an odd angle against the opposite wall. Her sidearm hangs heavily in her hand, seemingly forgotten, her arm at her side. Her chest rises and falls beneath her suit. She's still alive.

I hesitate. Is she so lost in whatever she's seeing, distracted by her loss or hallucinations or both, that we could slip past? Or . . .

Before I can do anything, even make a decision about what to do, Diaz's head jerks up sharply and she raises her weapon to aim at me.

31

I step back and throw an arm out to push Kane farther behind me. But if she pulls the trigger right now, my reaction will be too slow to save either of us.

Tensing in expectation, I wait for the loud report of the shot, the quick, powerful pressure of impact in my chest.

But there's nothing.

A trick to lure me back into view? Or something else?

She had the shot if she wanted it a moment ago. Why would she need to trick me? But then again, also, why not take the shot?

"Kovalik!" Reed bellows behind us. His stumbling footsteps are getting closer.

Fuck. I risk a glance behind me. He's not here yet, but he's coming. We have to do something or we're going to die. One way or the other. I guess if I have to choose, I'd rather it be quick with Diaz and her gun.

I edge toward the stairwell again and look over the edge into the atrium.

Diaz is still holding the gun on me, grip steadied with both hands, but she doesn't fire.

"I didn't believe you," she says.

Uncertain what's happening, but willing to engage in conversation if it keeps us alive, I nod slowly. With effort, I push the words out through my injured throat, each one sounding scraped raw. "No one did." Except Max, who was a big fucking liar.

Diaz's breath hitches loudly, and I realize she's crying.

"I saw him," she says.

Instantly, I know who she means. McCaughey.

"He was so angry at me," she says, her voice breaking. "And he was right."

Shit. "No," I say, alarm beginning to build. Holding my hands up, I take another step toward the stairs. "He wasn't. He wasn't angry at all. He was watching over you." An emotional connection between them existed, surviving even death.

"He died saving me." Her gun sags toward her lap.

"He might have done that, yes," I say quickly. "But he was not angry. I promise you that. The man . . . the ghost I saw . . ." I fight for words to explain it. "He cared, even after he was gone. Okay? What you're feeling, what you think you saw, it's the device. You *know* that. But it makes you think that everything is wrong, that—"

She moves so quickly, so unexpectedly, that I don't understand what's happening. One second, her weapon is lowered and pointing at no one and the next, it's aimed directly at her temple. Exactly where I'd been aiming on Reed.

Only she doesn't miss.

"No!" I shout, even as the gunshot echoes in the wide-open space of the atrium. Blood and brain matter spray outward, and Diaz slides sideways off her knees and onto the floor.

Damnit.

"Kovalik!" Reed shouts again, much too close. This time, I turn just in time to see him emerging from the corridor of suites. Fifteen feet away.

The left side of his face is a bloody mess. The left eyelid is torn, hanging like an uneven and damaged curtain. But the eyeball beneath is ruined, cut in two, it seems. The front part, the iris portion, is still attached, but barely. It dangles and flops, shifting with his movement.

I drag Kane down the stairs, so fast I stumble and slide down several steps at once, almost taking us both out. But we make it to the bottom.

Reed is still lurching and wheeling near the top but coming after us.

We don't have time to stop for a suit for Kane from one of the fallen in the atrium. I have to hope we can find one somewhere else once we've put some distance between us and Reed. Perhaps the cargo bay itself if Shin's team is still there in some form.

But I pause long enough to scoop up Diaz's helmet for its light and to pull the gun from her still-warm hand, dumping the gun inside the helmet for ease of carrying.

"I'm sorry," I say to her over my shoulder as we run.

The lower passenger and crew levels are the worst.

Screaming from all sides. Invisible fists banging on doors from the inside, until it sounds like gunfire. Cold whispers skating past my skin, from all sides and at such a rate I can no longer distinguish individual words. It's a dizzying, never-ending ocean of sound.

And behind us—in the distance, but still not far enough for comfort—the occasional crash and rambling shout from Reed, attempting to follow us.

Becca flits in and out of the light from Diaz's helmet, shifting from see-through to nearly solid as she moves. We're almost to the cargo bay, but we've reached the level cluttered with stacks of furniture, the makeshift barricades that now narrow our path. I zip up my suit to keep from catching on anything and put the helmet on to guide our way, a necessity even though the brightness paints a giant arrow over our location—*this way to kill them!*—for Reed.

"Diaz, do you read?" Max demands in my ear.

Over the comms, the screams from the other security teams have died off—literally, if I have my guess—but Max continues to demand updates.

I keep one hand locked around Kane's as we maneuver through the narrow spaces and one hand on the gun I took from Diaz.

I don't like it. The weight of it in my hand. The power that comes with it. The temptation.

The physical effects of the MAW are much more intense down here, perhaps because we're closer to the source. Wherever it is. The pressure in my head, what once felt like a fingertip pressing between my eyebrows, now feels like a drill bearing down, swirling and confusing my brain matter.

Voller. Maybe he'd been trying to stop this sensation. Or make it real, at least.

I flinch. Because right now, the idea of a hole in my head feels like a relief instead of an end.

And if Kane is never going to recover, wouldn't it be more of a mercy to . . .

I shake my head, as if that will make the idea vanish.

We need to go faster now. And not just because of Reed.

Finally, we reach the cargo bay airlock. Which has been left open on both sides, defeating the idea of an airlock.

Probably because a battered body is sprawled across the doorway that would open—and theoretically close—on the cargo bay side. One of Shin's team, likely. Her body is nearly severed in two, just below her rib cage. It looks like someone tried to seal the door on her as she was trying to crawl away. The horrible gaping wound across her middle exposes organs and a pink tangle of intestines and other unidentifiable bits.

I stop.

The scene has a hypnotic pull, the sheer awfulness and the illogic of it. This messy chaos was once a person. It seems too improbable.

Like a joke or a prop.

Except it's not.

Dragging my gaze away, I remove the helmet to listen as best as I can. We left Shin's team of seven in the cargo bay, examining, perhaps removing the Verux Mira colony equipment that had been their cover story to get the device on board. Can't have any evidence pointing to them left behind, even if it's in pieces post-explosion.

But now, there's nothing. No voices, no footsteps, no sounds of movement or life. Just an irregular rhythmic dripping that's somehow too loud and sets unease rippling down my spine.

After putting the helmet back on, I lead the way in, edging past the woman's body in the airlock. Kane, oblivious, isn't as careful, and I will hear the squelch of his boots in her blood for as long as I live. Even if that's only another few minutes. Especially if.

Once inside the cargo bay, though, I stumble to a halt again, my brain unable to process what I'm seeing at first in the limited view of the helmet light.

Upstairs, in the atrium, it looked more like panic combined with hallucinations and access to high-powered weapons had resulted in confusion and the accidental deaths of Diaz's team.

In here, though, it's . . . just body parts. Like Shin's team attacked one another, deliberately aiming to take each other out. But at such close range, it resulted in amputations, decapitations, and so much blood.

Red smears decorate the now-dented side of the Mach Ten's passenger door, and there's an unidentifiable piece of someone on the hood.

A headless corpse is on what's left of the shattered piano, drip, drip . . . dripping into a puddle on the floor.

Jesus.

A quiver runs through me, making the helmet light tremble and cast jittery shadows, adding the eerie appearance of movement among the dead. Or perhaps there is movement already; their ghosts rising to join the others.

I squeeze my eyes shut for a moment. *Okay, okay. Breathe.*

I am not a soldier or security professional. Ghosts or no ghosts, I'm a team leader on a commweb sniffer. Accidents happen, yes, especially in space. But we don't see this kind of deliberate personal violence, or *any* violence, except for the occasional coworker-on-coworker "Will you stop chewing so fucking loud?" attacks that have been known to happen.

My grip on Kane's unresponsive hand is tight and unpleasant, probably, for him, but concentrating on that contact grounds me. Reminds me of my purpose: getting us the hell out of here, while we still can.

And we're nearly there.

I force my eyes open and make myself focus.

A glance over at the far wall shows the retractable bridge to *Ares* is still in place. That's something, at least. A crate, several loaded black duffels, and one body bag lie in wait, as if someone was organizing a trip over to the *Ares* before sanity gave way.

The temptation to bolt for the bridge *right now* is strong. We're running out of time. I can feel it. The comms have gone silent; even Max is no longer shouting for updates. How long will he wait before giving the order to retract the bridge and retreat to safe distance? Even if all of his security forces on this ship die—or have died—before triggering the planned explosion, I'm certain he's not leaving without destroying the *Aurora*, one way or another.

I still need a suit for Kane, though. Otherwise, they'll never open the door on the other side for us.

I lead Kane over to the LINA, up the ramp to the airlock, and then once it's open, I pull him inside to the small bench where we changed into our enviro suits. The suits themselves are gone now. There might be a spare in here somewhere, but it doesn't matter. It would be an immediate giveaway that Kane is not one of the Verux security team members.

I remove my helmet and the smell of home—overheated metal, aging plastic, and Lourdes's orange tea—immediately floods over me.

My chest aches with longing, and I want nothing more than to close up the door and hide in here, pretending that nothing has changed.

I guide Kane into sitting. "Stay here, okay?" I whisper. He'll be safer in here than he would in the cargo bay where he might wander off or where Reed might find him.

Kane doesn't acknowledge my words or even my presence. His eyes blink, but it's just the mechanics, the autonomic reflexes.

He'll get better. As soon as we're out of here, he'll be better. He'll come back. It's just that damn device, I tell myself, and I try to believe it.

But when I go to release his hand, I notice the jagged tear in his skin, halfway between his wrist and elbow, still bleeding sluggishly.

I suck in a breath. It's deep. The wound needs to be glued, if not stitched.

When did that happen? When Reed was chasing us? When we were squeezing past those furniture blockades?

I raise my hand to my cheek where the possible bite is. Or perhaps something worse got ahold of Kane for a moment.

Either way, though, he never said anything. Never made a noise, even an involuntary grunt of pain.

He's not coming back. You know that.

Tears sting my eyes, and for a moment, the grief is overwhelming. I want to sink to my knees at his feet and beg him to wake up, to hear me.

I temporarily wrap his arm in a cleanish rag that I find in one of the storage bin drawers—Kane was the medic, not me, but right now infection is the lesser threat—and then I leave the LINA, closing up behind me.

It takes me longer than I thought—longer than I have—to find a mostly intact suit and peel it off its former owner. (The piano guy, as it turns out, is my best option. There's certainly no damage to his suit. Or him—below the neck anyway.)

Every second I'm anticipating the sudden rattle-clank of the extendable bridge preparing for retraction. Which would give me a few seconds, perhaps a minute at the most, before the seal is broken and the wide-open doors begin to vent the atmosphere—and everything else, including me—into space.

This is taking too long. Too long. Too long. The words are a thrumming drumbeat in my head as I rush back toward the LINA, suit in hand.

An alarm on my suit beeps, startling me. "Warning," an automated female voice says pleasantly in my ear. "Oxygen low."

Of course it is. It wouldn't surprise me if Max had ordered my supply to be shorted. Or maybe *fucking running for your life* uses up a lot of air.

"Less than twelve percent remaining," she continues. "Please proceed to a safe environment."

Yeah, I'm working on it.

But I still need to find a helmet for Kane.

For obvious reasons, Piano Guy's was not located with the rest of him.

I have a fraction of a moment's warning. The scrape of footsteps, the slightly brighter glow of a light somewhere.

I drop the enviro suit near the outer airlock door to the LINA and turn—gun pointed—toward the corridor to the rest of the ship to face off with Reed.

It's only as I make that turn that I realize my mistake. That corner of the cargo bay is as dark as ever. And would Reed have had the capacity to find a light and use it in his condition? He was, as last seen, thrashing around in the dark with no seeming plan to change any of that. His only focus was on reaching me.

Too late, I swivel back in the opposite direction toward the extendable bridge to the *Ares*, keeping my weapon aimed. I'm just in time to see Max come into view, with a powerful flashlight. At the end of his rifle.

32

Everything about Max is so familiar—rumpled suit, worn shoes, steady serious expression—that my first reaction is, nonsensically, relief. It's as if my previous experiences with him had coded him in my brain as an ally. A friend. And despite what I knew, what I'd experienced since then, that initial assessment had not yet been overwritten.

Or perhaps some part of me thinks my odds are better against Max than Reed.

Max sees me and jolts in surprise, before smiling in what appears to be genuine delight. And bringing his weapon—one of the automatic rifles that the security teams are carrying, looking comically oversized in Max's hands—to bear on me.

"I wondered," he says with a note of admiration. "I didn't think the situation would have declined so quickly without some help."

A tiny, automatic burst of pride at his praise fills me. I ignore it—hating myself in the process. It's just . . . years of habit, and a sign of the role Max once filled in my life, I suppose.

I tighten my hand on my borrowed gun, keeping it pointed at his chest.

"How did you get out?" he asks, looking around, as if expecting to see Diaz and her team backing me up, having switched sides.

The problem is that if I fire and hit him, the *Ares* will just pull the bridge back and leave us to die. I'm sure someone over there is watching.

If I fire at him and miss, I'll probably end up punching a hole in the airlock bridge—or the fucking fragile seal. Death wins again.

It feels like flipping over card after card in one of the team poker games I'd refused to join and getting nothing but jokers.

Max takes a couple steps closer, seeming unbothered by the gun I'm pointing at him, which, conversely, only makes me want to pull the trigger more.

"Stop!" I shout. My hand is trembling from the effort of holding the gun in place. And my head is throbbing so much, particularly along the line of my healed fracture, that my eyes are watering from the pain.

He's not going to stop. He's going to kill you. The whisper of paranoia in my mind is so clear, so close, it's difficult not to look around for the speaker. *He's going to turn you into nothing. Another dead meat sack in an enviro suit, like everyone else, like all the poor passengers on this ship.*

Paranoia doesn't sound like I thought it would. It's not panicky and angry. It's a calm, smooth voice, reassuringly confident.

You're going to die, unless you kill him first . . .

Max does stop, though, pausing at the edge of where the extendable connects to the *Aurora*. Maybe I should let him come in. If I kill him in the cargo bay, the crew running the *Ares* might not figure it out immediately.

But letting him approach only guarantees he'll have a better shot at me, if and when he pulls the trigger.

Actually, in that regard, I'm not sure what he's waiting for. He doesn't come any closer, nor does he seem ready to fire on me.

"Where's Mr. Behrens?" Max asks.

"Dead." The lie tears a piece from my heart. And I'm afraid it might not end up being a lie at all. Still, I'd rather Max not know the truth. To him, Kane would simply be another piece of leverage. Or another body to add to the count.

He heaves a sigh that almost sounds genuine. "I am sorry about that."

"Sure you are," I say in disgust. Motion flickers at the corner of my eye. Just out of range of what I can see without turning my head and the attached helmet light. Becca? My mother? Or Reed?

"You're taking this personally, but you shouldn't. It's just business, not a statement on who you are as a person. I've always enjoyed

our time together, admired your will to survive. And if circumstances were different, I'm sure you would have made a new life
that—"

"Shut up," I snap. "I was useful to you. That's all." My
dependence—my ignorant and willing dependence—on Verux
grates on me now. But I was a child when it started, an orphan
without family. What else was I supposed to do? Verux became my
family, in a manner of speaking, and it turns out that relationship is
every bit as dysfunctional as one created by blood, secrets, and lies.

Or, perhaps our blood, secrets, and lies are simply of a different
variety. Other people's spilled blood. Secrets that qualify as espi-
onage and sabotage. Lies as a performance for the media and the
public.

And yet, I stayed.

"Isn't that what we all want?" Max muses. "To be useful, valuable. For our contributions to matter. To leave a legacy that remains
after we're gone."

"Spare me your 'I'm an old man' bullshit," I snarl. "Your legacy is
Ferris Outpost and this." I gesture at the *Aurora* with my free hand.
"Lost lives, death, murder." Even if no one else will ever know.

His brows draw together in a furrow before smoothing out. "I
didn't create the device or decide to set it off on board. My role is
to make things better. To untangle this tragic knot that would only
bring more—"

"Make things better for who?" I demand. "You're keeping the
truth from the people who deserve to have it and protecting those
who should be punished for what they did." He is every bit as guilty
as the unknown Verux executives of twenty-some years ago who
came up with this plan.

Something crashes to the floor outside the cargo bay. One of the
lopsided furniture blockades finally collapsing? Or Reed?

It's difficult not to look over and try to track the source of the
noise.

But Max doesn't seem to notice or care. Then again, I suppose
he's planning to kill us all anyway, so what difference does it make?

Annoyance flashes across his face. "Verux does more good in the world than harm. Even you know that. Consider the work we've done in colonization and exploration. The medical advances alone in what we learned from Ferris are—"

"Tell that to the passengers and their families. Tell that to the security teams you sent to die here. Tell that to Lourdes and Voller and Nysus and Kane," I say, struggling to rein in my temper. Fury is a volcanic hot spot in my chest, aching to spew molten hate all over him.

He smiles at me so peaceably that a chill slides over my skin.

"And yet, my dear," he says, "I am not the one who led your team on board. I am not the one who encouraged them to seal themselves up in a dead ship for fame, fortune, and a better future."

His words are the equivalent of a blow to the gut, one that punches through leaving a gaping hole to the other side. I can't breathe for a moment.

"I don't believe the moral high ground will support your weight in this particular case," he says dryly.

Because he's right. I did that, all of that. No matter how good my intentions. No matter how hard I've tried to correct for that mistake after the fact. They're still dead. Because of me. Because of what I wanted.

Verux and I are more alike than I thought. Like corporate foster parent, like daughter, it seems.

My shaking hand lowers the weapon slowly. In this moment, I want to curl up in a ball on the floor of the cargo bay and just . . . stop. Everything.

The comm in my helmet rasps suddenly, making me jolt. "I've got it," an exhausted male voice says in my ear. He's wheezing, his breathing pained and uneven.

Someone is still alive? One of the security team members, it has to be. I don't recognize the voice, but I'm pretty sure all of Shin's team is in here. In pieces.

Max taps the comm implant near his ear. "Good work, Montgomery. Disconnect it and bring it to the cargo bay."

Montgomery? I wrote him and his team off as lost the second I saw Diaz and her crew. The effects of the MAW seem to be stronger in closer proximity to it.

To be fair, Montgomery doesn't sound good.

"Affirmative," he responds to Max in a raspy, clotted voice after a bout of thick, wet coughing.

But he succeeded. He found the device and he's bringing it home, like an obedient dog retrieving a stick.

My heart plummets toward my feet. Max is going to win. He's going to get the device, leave on *Ares,* and blow us up. It's all been for nothing.

A rippling sensation suddenly crawls over my skin, raising goose bumps, despite my suit. Except it's more of . . . a retraction, like the ocean pulling away from the shore. The relentless pressure in my head lessens, like a cork is in the process of being pulled, and then vanishes.

It's off. It's gone.

Max, watching me, nods. Then steps across into the bay, in anticipation of Montgomery's expected arrival.

And it clicks. *This.* This is what Max has been waiting for.

He'll go back to Verux to report his final success—he'll be the champion, the hero, one last time—and Verux will go on doing what it does. No one will know the truth. Other children will lose their parents. Isabelle Behrens, perhaps. That might be more my fault than Verux's but if I'm a product of Verux—a faulty one—then maybe they share some of that blame. Hurting individuals for the sake of greater advancement of the whole and that all-important bottom line, while pretending their conscience is clear.

I should have shot him the first second I saw him. Kane and I were never getting off this ship, anyway. Thinking otherwise was just another delusion. That delusion just happened to be one I wanted to believe in.

Tightening my sweaty grip on Diaz's gun, I bring it up again, aiming at Max as he comes toward me.

He shakes his head. "Please don't. I assure you, I have more practice at this than you do." He keeps moving, each step measured and slow.

I back up to keep distance between us. I can only imagine what a younger Max must have done on his earlier QA assignments.

"It's unlikely anyone would be able to recover enough of your body to determine your cause of death, but if you force me to fire on you, we won't be able to take that chance," he says calmly. "We'll have to create a new story. One where you attacked my team and cost innocent lives."

"So I'm either crazy or crazy violent," I say. My throat is tight, not just from Reed's attack earlier, but the lump of unshed tears. My whole life, it feels like I've been trying to avoid that classification, and in spite of those efforts, it seems that label will be *my* legacy.

Max tips his head back and forth, as if considering. "Sounds about right," he says. "Don't you think? I'd prefer to avoid that outcome, though. It raises more questions that we won't want to answer."

God forbid my death inconveniences them.

I smack into something behind me, abruptly halting my progress. Glancing up, I find the winch and safety tether for the LINA, dangling overhead. I've walked myself into the back corner of LINA. Unconsciously seeking safety, perhaps.

I put my other hand on the gun to steady the trembling. Max will shoot me before I can get into LINA, I'm sure of it. He won't take the minuscule chance of me surviving the explosion inside the LINA. And I'm not confident enough in my ability to hit him with the single shot I'll be able to get off before he fires back. So, I'm out of options and room, unless I want to turn my back on Max and try to run.

Thoughts racing, I imagine it for a moment, trying to play it out. The cargo bay is huge, and if I can get away far enough and turn off this fucking helmet light, then maybe—

"Kovalik!" The guttural shout from the darkness behind me makes me jump.

Reed. I freeze. While I feel clearer, he definitely does not sound any saner. He also sounds close. Like, right outside the cargo bay close.

Panic squeezes tight in my chest. Right now, the LINA is blocking me from sight, but that won't last if Reed comes in. And if he finds me, Max won't have to worry about a story at all. He can just step back and watch Reed kill me. I have a gun, yes, but Reed has the advantage of the dark—I'm lit up like the bright side of the moon—and I have Max to worry about, splitting my attention.

"Kovalik!" Reed bellows again, his dragging, shuffling step echoing inside the cargo bay.

Max's gaze flicks away from me and toward the entrance to the cargo bay.

So I'm not the only one with divided attention.

In that second, I have a wonderful, horrible idea.

I'm going to die; I'm not sure there's any way to avoid that now. But maybe I can do something more than give Verux a convenient story. Or even an inconvenient one.

I take a deep breath. "Over here," I shout.

Reed shuffles into the room, tripping and crashing into things. His booted feet squeak in the spilled blood.

Max looks at me as if I've lost my mind. And maybe I have. He taps his comm implant. "What's your ETA, Montgomery?"

Ah, yes, poor Max with no one left to defend him except one ailing security team leader, who is . . . somewhere in this huge ship, injured and lugging the MAW.

I take advantage of his distraction to reach up one-handed, snatch the safety tether, and snap the carabiner to one of the utility hooks on my suit. I pray that they're as strong as the reinforced ones on our LINA suits, which are made for this purpose. Well, not exactly *this* purpose.

Max stares at me, suspicious. "What are you doing?"

Reed stumbles around the LINA into view, and Max visibly recoils at his appearance. I can't look. I've got to keep my focus on Max and beyond.

"You did this to me!" he shouts, presumably at me. But almost as quickly, his attention shifts to Max. "You wanted me to die, Donovan?" he asks. He sounds more hurt than angry, but only for a second. "Just because you couldn't handle the competition," he sneers. "I'm going to show you hurt. When we get back and my father—"

Max opens fire on him before I can say or do anything.

The loud rapid pops freeze me in place; it's so much louder this close. Silence rings in my ears once the weapon stops.

Reed doesn't stagger back or stumble around clutching his wounds, as I've seen in movies. He simply folds in half at the middle and collapses. Like there's nothing left to support him, and perhaps that's the case.

I watch, horrified, a scream lodged in my throat.

But the muted thud of his body hitting the cargo bay floor snaps me out of my paralysis. Max edges closer, as if to confirm his kill. His attention is definitely elsewhere.

I suck in one painful breath, then another. Then I raise Diaz's gun away from Max's head and squeeze the trigger. The recoil makes the gun jump in my hand, once, then twice. The bullets crack into the extendable airlock.

For a heart-stopping second, nothing happens.

Max flinches automatically before he realizes that my shots have gone wide and high.

If my target were him.

He beams at me, delighted. "I told you, you don't have the—"

The seal crumbles, fracturing into chunks that drop to the joint threshold of the *Aurora* and the extendable airlock. Somewhere, a tinny alarm beeps rapidly, warning of what's to come.

Max looks back at the extendable then, his brow furrowed in confusion, but I see his realization, the moment it clicks and he turns to me. His eyes wide and mouth open in panic and fury.

But it's too late.

One more piece of the hardened foam seal hits the ground, and a line has been crossed; the integrity of the hold vanishes.

And the vacuum of space does the rest. The air in here is dying to get out there.

In a fraction of a second, the extendable airlock bends and twists away from the *Aurora,* like a giant cranky child crumpling a straw. Rapid decompression.

Max, the closest to the now open and unprotected cargo bay doors, vanishes almost in the same instant. And I catch one last glimpse of his astonished expression.

A tiny part of me mourns the loss of the man I thought he was. But that man never existed, it seems, so the mourning moment is quite short. I didn't have a choice.

I may not be able to make Verux take responsibility for their actions, twenty years ago or even now. But no one is leaving this ship with that device.

33

My feet lift off the ground, and the force of the escaping atmosphere pulls me horizontal and level with the winch holding me. But I don't go any farther. The carabiner and winch pull painfully on my suit but hold. For the moment.

The cargo bay empties rapidly. Of bodies, of crates; even portions of the piano are identifiable as they blow by.

Outside, the *Ares* moves out of the way, revealing empty space beyond. I can't imagine the alarms that are going on over there. They're lucky if they didn't hull breach when the extendable bridge tore away. But then again, maybe the ship's builders planned for that contingency. I don't know. They don't seem interested in taking a chance.

I catch a bright flash as the ship rotates and then speeds away.

But the terrible rush of air whipping past me continues. It should have stopped by now. Shouldn't it? The cargo bay is large, but not that large.

It clicks, then. *The airlock.*

On the other side of the cargo bay, the airlock is still open.

"Fuck."

This isn't going to stop until the pressure equalizes. Until *all* the air in here is out there.

That's going to take longer than I was anticipating. But as long as everything holds, I should be okay . . .

Abruptly, I feel myself lurch toward the doors. Several inches, then a few more.

The hook on my suit must be tearing, the fabric not reinforced enough.

I let go of the gun and reach frantically for the hook where the tether is attached, as if my grip might stop the final tear.

But the fabric feels whole, no disruption that I can detect.

My body lurches forward again, but this time, the squeal of metal on metal is identifiable above the roar of depressurization.

A sinking feeling floods through me.

I tip my head back to confirm my suspicion. The LINA's back end is now angled more toward the cargo bay doors than it was before.

We couldn't find, hadn't bothered with trying to find, docking clamps when we landed. There'd been no reason to; we'd expected to be leaving again shortly.

Which means, the LINA is just sitting on the cargo bay floor. Still magnetized and holding true. For the moment.

In another couple of minutes, though, she'll be pulled through the doors into space, and me with her.

If I'm lucky.

If I'm not lucky, I could end up being crushed between LINA and the wall, depending on how she's pulled and how tangled I end up being in the tether.

I fight for the release, but the carabiner is pulled so taut, with no slack in the tether, I can't get myself unhooked.

I'm fucked.

Yanking on the tether above my head, I try to pull myself closer to the winch, to give myself the room I need. But I'm just not strong enough.

The LINA scrapes forward again at an angle, her bottom hull lifting slightly but still scraping across the decking.

I squeeze my eyes shut.

Abruptly the tether in my hands goes slack, but only for a second. I open my eyes in time to see the LINA's winch unwinding madly, then I'm spinning out faster than I can see, heading straight out through the cargo bay doors.

Something must have given out. The winch is meant to lock to prevent crew from being pulled away from the LINA.

Outside, the desperate tug-of-war between the escaping air and the void beyond ceases. I'm floating. The familiar silence, weightlessness, and backdrop of pinprick stars set in black is a relief.

Home. I'm home.

The tether finally reaches its end and yanks me to a halt, which sends me spinning back in the other direction, toward the *Aurora*.

As I move that way, I catch a glimpse of the LINA being birthed through the cargo bay doors, awkwardly, partially sideways, just as I was afraid of. Her back end is much heavier, which means her front end had to swivel. Not a pretty exit.

After a moment, though, she's free, in a scattering of small debris.

Free, like me. I made it. Max is gone, the device is, too. Or will be shortly when those timed charges go and the *Aurora* explodes.

Sorry, Montgomery.

I take a deep breath. I'm exactly where I wanted to be all those months ago on our last assignment. Out here. Forever.

I probably won't even feel it, when the *Aurora* goes up. Or if so, just for a second or two.

Then nothing. Blissful nothing.

Except this time, that thought does nothing to ease the knot of tension in my gut.

I bite my lip. Why doesn't nothingness sound as appealing as it did before? The concept feels flat, empty . . . cowardly even. Like I'm hiding behind my former desires simply because that's what I used to want.

I glance over at the LINA, drifting at the other end of my tether. Kane is inside. Unaware, lost in his own world, but alive. Still breathing. Sitting on the bench just inside the airlock where I left him. Alone.

That image sparks a longing intensity in my chest. Far stronger than the pull of nothingness.

I don't want him to be alone in the end. I don't want to be alone in the end, either.

But it's more than that, too.

This close to death, with everything else gone, it's stupid to pretend.

I want to be near him. Just like I always have, even if I couldn't admit it. I want to hold his hand in mine, when the air turns to fire around us. This man who thought I was worth it when I didn't.

"I'm coming," I say, even though Kane can't hear me.

Reaching up, I pull myself along the tether, moving slowly and carefully on the line toward the LINA. Toward Kane.

I'm not even halfway when the oxygen alarm on my suit chirps again. "Three percent remaining," the female voice tells me. "At current usage, two minutes."

I pull myself along faster, as fast as I can without risking losing my grasp.

But I can already tell, there's just too much distance between me and the LINA. The tether is at its full extension, fifty meters.

"I'm not going to make it," I say, my lips going numb. My head is swirling with dizziness, and I'm having trouble focusing.

"Two percent," my suit tells me.

After all of this, I'm not going to make it. I'm going to die alone in space, after finally realizing that's not what I want. Any of it. Death, alone, space.

"Shit." I blink my eyes rapidly against the stinging in my eyes. I can't cry in zero grav. The tears won't drop. They'll cloud my vision. Or drown me.

I keep going. But my hands aren't cooperating, each movement clumsier and slower than the last.

Then the tether twitches suddenly in my hands, like a snake awakening from hibernation, and it slides forward through my slack fingers, like that same snake attempting a bid for freedom.

It takes my slowing brain a few seconds to catch up with what's happening.

The winch. It's retracting the tether, pulling it—and me, eventually—toward the LINA much faster than I ever could hope to do myself.

There's only one explanation for that. *Kane.*

He's awake and aware. At least enough to recognize that the tether is extended when it shouldn't be.

I lock my stubborn hands down tighter on the tether with effort, my heart beating too fast. The tether yanks me along, speeding me away.

"One percent," the suit woman tells me as the LINA grows larger in my view. "Situation critical."

Dizziness prevents me from screaming *no fucking kidding*.

My feet collide with the LINA first. I feel it more than see it, my vision going dark from the edges and creeping inward.

Fumbling, I reach for the airlock door and find it already open and waiting for me.

I collapse inside the airlock, and the woman on my suit isn't even bothering to speak to me. She's been replaced by an alarming and continuous beep inside my helmet that sounds disturbingly like a heart monitor flatline.

The sound of the airlock closing behind me sounds distant, far away. I have to wait until the airlock is repressurized before I can take off my helmet. But I can't . . . I can't breathe.

My hand flaps weakly near the seal for my helmet.

A muted thumping catches my attention, like a fist against a heavy surface. "No!"

Kane.

He's shouting at me. Pounding on the airlock door from the other side.

I should look up. Turn my head and see him. One last time, that would be . . .

34

"Don't move. Just stay still."

I'm floating, unaware that I'm aware until those words.

Now, now I can feel the pulsing in my temples, the ache over my whole body, the hard, unforgiving surface beneath my back.

My lungs demand a deeper breath, and I suck air in, only to lose it all in a coughing fit that makes my skull feel like it's going to explode.

I curl onto my side, dimly recognizing that my head is pillowed on something softer than the floor.

"Claire," Kane says. His hand moves over my hair gently. "Can you hear me?"

Opening my eyes takes work. It's too bright for me to see much before I have to close them again. But I recognize the interior of LINA's airlock.

I made it. Rather, Kane made it.

"Take your time," he says.

Except I can't. We don't have time to take.

I peel my eyes open again, letting them water until they adjust to the brightness, which isn't all that bright except compared, it seems, to the dimness of almost dying.

When I can look up, I find Kane leaning back against the wall of the airlock, looking as exhausted and filthy as I remember but with the bright spark of intelligence and awareness that he was missing when I last saw him. The door to the LINA stands open behind him. My head is in his lap, the helmet cast off to one side.

"What the hell happened?" he murmurs. Whether to me or himself, I don't know. "I'm sorry it took me so long to get you. I didn't know that you needed help. I didn't even know for sure that it was you on the other end of the tether. I was trying to . . . understand. It was like waking up after a dream. I was here, on the LINA, but that's not what I remember . . ." He sounds lost, confused.

I want to ask him what he remembers, but if he can be spared some of those memories, maybe he would be better off.

"When I saw you trying to pull yourself back to the LINA, I realized you needed to come back, so I started the winch up, but—"

I push against the floor with my hand to sit up. The pounding in my head makes me wish I'd died. But I'm upright, at least.

"Hey, hey, slow down," he says. "You're in no condition to—"

I start to shake my head and immediately regret it. Nausea swirls over me. "The *Aurora* is set to go up. Rigged charges. Timer."

He stares at me. "LINA's main engine is online, but I don't have helm control." He pauses. "Did we . . . no, we took it apart. I remember that." He's piecing events together.

I hate that he's going to have to relive horrible moments that I wish had never happened in the first place. But that's assuming we survive long enough for him to do so.

"I know. Do we still have maneuvering thrusters?" As far as I'm aware, our thrusters should still be operational.

Kane frowns. "Yes."

"I know it won't get us very far but—"

His expression shifts from uncertainty to determination. "The LINA is shielded more heavily underneath. If we can angle ourselves away from the blast, that'll offer a little more protection."

I nod, and he pushes to his feet to run for the bridge.

I'm slower to follow, but I get there. I pause, though, in the galley, looking at our sad collection of *Aurora* artifacts. The two Tratorelli sculptures, *Speed* and *Grace,* and the emergency beacon plucked from space at Voller's insistence with Nysus backing him up.

It wasn't worth it. None of it was worth it. Max may be gone, and the device soon to be destroyed, but that won't stop Verux from doing—or continuing to do—exactly as they have been doing for years. Chewing up lives and spitting them out.

On the bridge, Kane is strapped into Voller's seat. Likely marking the first time those safety straps have ever been used, given Voller's predilection for letting them dangle to the floor instead. The memory of Voller spinning around to say something on the verge of offensive, while grinning and daring one of us to object, makes my heart hurt.

As it is, I half expect Nysus's voice over the intercom, giving me some random fact about the flammability of the varnish on the *Aurora*'s real wood panels. And Lourdes's chair feels conspicuously empty. Her headphones still rest on the communications board, where she last left them. It's as if she's just stepped away to make her tea and will be back any second. Oh God, I *wish* that were true.

I strap in, and Kane and I watch as the thrusters adjust our position and move us away, slowly, incrementally, from the *Aurora*. Every meter feels like a hard-won step toward safety.

But when I check the cameras, we're still too close, far too close.

"Do you think—" Kane begins, but he doesn't get a chance to finish.

On-screen, the *Aurora* fills briefly with bright light, as though all the power has been restored and inside, passengers are once more dancing, talking, drinking, and living.

But it's only for a second. Then the light expands and the *Aurora* fractures and vanishes in the burst of the explosion, like a shadow in a sudden noonday sun.

There's no sound, but the force of the blast rolls out toward us and hits hard.

My body slams into the side of my chair, my upper arm pinned between my own weight and the reinforced arm of the chair.

The bone gives with a break I can *feel*, and I scream, bracing myself for the last few seconds of air and life before the LINA cracks open like an egg.

Instead, we're spinning endlessly. Alarms wail, smoke from somewhere flooding the bridge.

But we're alive. For now.

"Claire!" Kane shouts.

"I'm okay," I manage.

Through the smoke, he's a vague shadow, struggling and moving. Our spinning gradually slows. Kane must be trying to pull us out of it with the thrusters.

Then, the grav generator kicks back in, and the world of the LINA settles back around us with various thuds and crashes.

"Claire." Kane fumbles with his restraints and manages to get free to kneel next to my chair.

He sucks in a breath sharply at the sight of my arm. I can't look at it, but it must be bad if he can tell just by looking.

I hold my good hand up, my broken arm protectively against my belly. Cold sweat breaks out over my skin with the movement. "I'm fine."

A lie I promptly prove by leaning over and vomiting all over my bridge.

"No navigation. No comms. Limited life support and supplies. Maybe we should have just stayed on the *Aurora*. Dying would have been quicker."

I'm talking mainly to distract myself from Kane splinting my arm. After helping me out of the chair and moving me to the galley, where I can sort of lie down on one of the bench seats, Kane gave me an injection of something. But whatever it was, it's not enough.

He's gentle, but I'm gritting my teeth against the pain.

At least the smoke has cleared, and so far, our battered hull seems to be holding. The two Tratorelli sculptures are in heavy marble chunks on the floor where they fell, and the emergency beacon is tipped over onto its side. In any other circumstance, a damage assessment would be a top priority, but right now, I'm not sure if there's a point.

"No," Kane says to me, his brow furrowed with concentration as he wraps a stabilizing bandage around my arm. "At least here, we have a chance." He looks up at me. "You did the right thing."

His words tear a hole right through me, right through any defenses I have left.

"I'm sorry," I blurt. "I'm sorry for dragging us into this. I'm sorry for leaving. I don't even know why I did. Why didn't I bring you and Ny with me on the escape pod? Or each of us in our own, I don't . . . I just don't understand." I shake my head in frustration. "I don't remember."

His movements slow and then stop. "You didn't drag any of us into it. We all agreed, remember?" Apparently he does. That part, at least.

"Over objections," I remind him.

"When has any group of five people agreed to do anything without objections?" he points out.

"Still, I'm responsible, I shouldn't have—"

"Claire, I don't mean this in a cruel way, but you're not that good of a team leader," he says, a tired smile flickering at the corners of his mouth. "If we hadn't thought the risk was worth it, we wouldn't have gone. Period. Each of us had our reasons."

"But I left."

"You did? I don't . . . None of it seems real." He pauses, pain flashing across his face. I don't know who he's remembering, Lourdes, Voller, or Nysus. But it's someone we've lost. "It was, though?"

I nod and then clear my throat to say, "Yes. It was real."

He's quiet.

"A ship found me in one of the escape pods from the *Aurora*, a little over two months ago. The last thing I remember is waking up on the bridge next to Lourdes's . . ." I can't say it. "Next to Lourdes," I finish. "I don't even remember leaving." Shame wells in me at the confession. "I had a skull fracture, but it's healed, I should be able to remember, but I can't. That time is just . . . gone."

He resumes wrapping my arm. "And you think you left us to die. That you ran to save yourself. And you blocked the memory because of that."

A tear leaks out from one of my eyes, and I turn away so he doesn't see. "Yes."

He makes a thoughtful noise. "Has it dawned on you yet that you probably left to save us? To get help?"

I lurch upward, or try to. He puts a hand on the center of my chest to push me flat. "Why didn't I take you and Nysus with me, then?" I demand. "We all could have fit, easily."

He's silent for a long moment, and I feel a surge of gritty satisfaction. Finally, he believes who I am.

"I don't remember everything," he says finally.

And the little bit of hope left in me dies, turns to ash.

"But I know at that point it would have been hard to tell which situation was riskier," he says. "The ship with food, oxygen, water, and functioning engines, or a twenty-year-old escape pod with limited capabilities and supplies, and no maintenance for more than two decades?"

As soon as he says it, I can see his logic. I can almost hear the discussion. In my mind, I would have been the logical one to take the risk and go for help, the one without the technical or mechanical know-how needed to keep the *Aurora* (mostly) functional until help arrived. I would have argued for that.

But this is all speculation. Kane doesn't *know* anything for sure. I open my mouth to object but he beats me to it.

"I don't know what happened," Kane says. "But I know you. And no matter how hard you tried to pull away from us, to keep your distance, you would never have left us behind. You were scared of being hurt, but you're not a coward." He finishes wrapping and tapes the end in place.

"But—"

He pushes back to look at me. "If you can't trust yourself, can you trust me?" he asks, his gaze meeting mine without hesitation.

I freeze, but he doesn't back down, just watches me steadily, waiting.

"Yes," I manage, my voice creaky with the effort.

"Good. Then maybe you can put energy toward figuring out how we're going to survive this and you can tell me everything I don't remember while we're at it." He offers his hand to help me sit up.

I take it, the warmth and responsive pressure of his fingers against mine, such a contrast to hours earlier that I don't want to let go.

So I don't.

Kane glances down at our interlocked hands but says nothing. A faint smile, however, curves his mouth.

"I can tell you what I remember," I say, trying to ignore the heat in my face. "But I don't have any grand plans for escape."

"You'll think of something," he says calmly.

I roll my eyes. "This might be a little beyond me. We can't fix the engine without parts that are currently in a million little pieces somewhere back there." I gesture vaguely in the direction of the *Aurora*. "No one knows where we are. Verux assumes we're dead, which is probably a good thing. Someone may eventually come check out the explosion, but we have no way of communicating our location to ask for help. And we've got nothing to . . ." I pause, my gaze falling on the tipped-over emergency beacon.

The one Voller had insisted on pulling in and having Lourdes deactivate so no one else could track the signal to the *Aurora*'s location. The one Nysus insisted on as a keepsake. The one that's still in perfect condition amidst the hunks of marble around it.

I take a deep breath. "Okay," I say reluctantly. "I have one idea."

EPILOGUE

TWO YEARS LATER

Epicurean Space Yards, New Smyrna Beach, Florida

"Nothing like that new 'old ship' smell." Kane wrinkles his nose as he climbs the metal ramp, his footsteps clanking.

I frown at him as he passes me at the top of the ramp and then crosses the threshold into the ship.

"The T-176 model is a classic," I call after him. That's what the sales guy said, anyway. "It might be a *little* older." Point in fact, my "new" ship is a *lot* older. It's been around a decade and a half longer than I have. Not quite senior citizen status, but maybe closer than either of us would like to admit. "But it's built to last."

Thick, durable hull. Huge cargo bay. Oversized crew quarters from when trips were longer and slower. It would cost me a small fortune to charge her for a long trip, but I'm not planning any of those. Never again.

Plus, the *Charlotte* is a revamped CitiFutura product—part of their transport class—which I have considerably more faith in these days. Though making sure the remote kill switch had been deactivated was job one.

Yeah, she's got a few scrapes and dents. I reach out and rub my finger along a lengthy scratch down the side of the hull; it leaves the impression a newbie pilot might have gotten confused between port and starboard at some point in the past, to the detriment of any nearby stationary objects.

But that's all superficial. She's sturdy. Reliable. And sure, occasionally she smells of overheating metal and burning dust, but that'll work its way out eventually. Maybe. But even if it doesn't, that's okay. It reminds me of home. Which it now is. I've been living here for the last six weeks, getting *Charlotte* ready for her new life. And mine.

This ship, named for my mother, is central to my plan. It's one of the only major purchases I've made with my share of the salvage claim that Verux was forced to pay when Kane and I returned, back when Verux still thought they could buy their way out of the bad press, spin our survival as a miracle rather than an unhappy accident.

The salvagers who'd picked up our message on the emergency beacon had been more than happy to bring us aboard and let us post our story to the Forum and newsfeeds. In exchange for payment, of course. We gave them the only thing we had—the LINA. She wasn't technically ours to give, but in that situation, the salvagers weren't all that picky and neither were we.

It was, in the end, a version of the plan we'd had from the beginning. We had proof. The pieces of the Tratorelli sculptures worked nearly as well as the whole ones might have. And the blast that took out the *Aurora* also knocked out a decent portion of the commweb, backing up our story. Not to mention, Verux had made plenty of enemies who were willing to believe the worst of them. The plan just hadn't played out exactly the way we'd anticipated on that first day. And with fewer of us to reap the benefits.

In my case, those benefits included my own transport ship, my own transport business. LINA Shipping Co. LSC. It doesn't come close to making up for what we lost. Who we lost. But I'm trying to make it count.

This is my future, shaped by *me*, not Verux's greed or that of any other company. Right now, though, it's just one ship and me.

Though I'm hoping to change that.

I watch Kane prod at the hatchway, probably checking for crumbling foam seals out of habit, and my stomach lurches in a mix of anticipatory flutters and stabbing dread. *It's not too late, Kovalik. Just give Kane the tour, and let it be done. You don't have to do this.*

Except I *want* to. I think. I'm just not sure which is going to win out, the want or the fear. The possibility of success versus the very real relief from not taking the chance at all.

I follow Kane in. "Lots of available parts means cheaper repairs.

You're the one who told me that," I say, rubbing my sweaty palms against the worn legs of my jumpsuit. Wearing anything else still feels strange, even after months of dressier clothes for congressional hearings, depositions, and court dates.

Kane lowers his hand from the hatch. He looks so much healthier these days. No more gray tint to his skin, no deep purple circles beneath his eyes from stress and lack of sleep. It took months for him to make a full recovery, and he still has issues with headaches.

"I did say that," he agrees readily enough. "But it'll be a full-time job keeping her up and running. I told you that, too." He holds my gaze, bright blue eyes seeing right through me, to the core where I'm scared and he knows it.

Suddenly, we are standing too close together.

"Come on." I turn away from him, but my shoulder brushes his chest.

I shiver, heat rising in my cheeks.

Taking a deep breath, I push down unruly emotions and lead the way to the bridge, up a short flight of stairs and to the left through a narrow corridor. The overheads are higher on the *Charlotte*, so at least Kane won't have to duck.

From the corner of my eye, I catch a glimpse of Derik, drifting aimlessly down the hall away from us, his hand trailing lovingly across the wall. Derik has been dead, as near as I can tell, for at least twenty years. I haven't found his name in the *Charlotte*'s records yet, but whoever he was, he loved this ship and he seems okay here. Perfectly happy to ignore me. For now, anyway.

I've been watching for my mom, but nothing. Perhaps her absence is the best sign of all. It's safe. I think she would be pleased, though, both by the ship and its name.

The narrow corridor dead-ends into a blast door—another safety protection, given that piracy is an ever-present threat in the transport business—but the door is currently standing open, revealing the bridge. A wide, open space, compared to the LINA's. There's even a seat for my mech, assuming he—or she or whoever!—wants it. No matter what, I'll need to hire other crew.

"All the chairs have been replaced," I say to Kane, gesturing toward the bridge. "Used models, yes, but upgrades. No more worn-out padding and questionable springs." I sound defensive, and I hate it.

Kane just nods.

"The comm board has also been completely—" I begin, gesturing at the console right as it signals a new message. And because I'm the only one living here at the moment, I don't have the privacy controls on, which means the message pops right up on the main screen.

He raises his eyebrows. "A Forum subscription. To the *Aurora* threads?"

I try not to grimace. "It's proved useful in the past."

Kane stays silent, but I can feel both the questions and concern radiating from him. And it's not like that. I'm not obsessing.

"Did you see the fucking memorial?" I burst out, furious heat in my chest at just the memory of it. "Just an empty hunk of rock with their names carved in it." Just like all of Verux's other fuckups. Slap a memorial up and call it done. No. Hell no.

The civil suit—the one we're bringing against Verux with the families of the *Aurora* passengers—might help, if we win before Verux goes bankrupt. But I'm not taking any chances.

"At least this way Nysus's name will be remembered," I say, quieter. Nysus's family refused to meet or speak with me, even after I sent his share. They've never publicly acknowledged the death of their son. "All of their names will be remembered."

"What did you do?" Kane asks, eyeing me with mild suspicion.

"I made sure Voller, Lourdes, and Nysus were all officially acknowledged on the thread as the finders of the *Aurora*, along with us." Lately the media has been too focused on Kane and me, forgetting that we were once a team of five.

"And?" Kane prompts, gesturing for me to spit out the rest.

I sigh. "I might have paid the Forum to permanently rename that section. It's now the Dionysus Memorial *Aurora* Archive and Messageboard." That was my only other major purchase.

A smile spreads slowly across Kane's face. "That's a mouthful," he says after a moment.

"Yeah, but his name is on every page now, at the top," I point out.

Kane laughs. "He would have liked that."

"Yeah."

An awkward silence follows, and my fingers fidget nervously with the metal scroll hanging around my neck on a delicate chain. The scroll is warm from my skin. It's not Lourdes's necklace, but a similar one. Her mother pressed it into my hand as I was leaving after delivering Lourdes's share of the fee. It wasn't enough, not the money, not the words I had for them, to tell them how sorry I was.

But Lourdes's mother insisted I take the necklace, that Lourdes would have wanted me to have it. I hope that's true.

I don't know what the scripture inside says. I kind of like not knowing, walking around with it, a blessing from Lourdes beating close to my heart. It could just as easily be a curse, for what I did to her, but I'm somehow sure it's not. And that seems as much guidance as anything for a path forward.

Come on, TL, Lourdes would say to me now, if she were here. *Just ask him.*

I shake my head at myself, and in denial. *Not yet.*

"So you probably want to see the engine room," I say quickly, starting toward the corridor again. "Hey, did I tell you that I finally met Voller's mother? When I took her his share. She's this tall, gorgeous—"

"Claire," Kane says.

"—redhead." I stop and slowly turn to face him. My heart is beating way too hard, a thrashing animal in my chest.

"Why are you showing me around a ship that I've already seen?" Kane asks gently. "That I inspected before you even put in an offer?"

"I . . ." I hesitate.

He folds his arms and leans back against the edge of the communications console, waiting patiently. He knows. I know he knows. But he's going to make me say it, going to make me *ask.*

Part of me, furious at being cornered, wants to just walk away. Yeah, that'll show him. But more of me is relieved to have the help, the nudge I still need in the right direction when it comes to being vulnerable.

"Are you trying to hire me?" he prompts.

"No! I know you have that offer from Zenit," I say. I'd had a similar one from them, Verux's largest competitor. But that would have been the same shit, different company. No thanks.

"Are you trying to seduce me?" He's teasing, but his expression flickers with heat at the idea.

I glare at him. "No," I grit out.

Kane raises his hands in surrender. "Just asking."

I roll my eyes.

"What do you want, Claire?" he asks.

It's direct, with just enough pressure behind it that I feel compelled to answer.

"I want you to be a partner with me. In LSC." The words tumble out, sounding brazen and loud and un-take-back-able. "You don't have to, obviously. And you wouldn't have to contribute a half stake. I'm staying majority owner." Because no one is taking this away from me. "It's just short runs from here to the colonies. A couple of weeks tops, so you wouldn't be away from Isabelle very long. And we certainly have enough publicity to get us started."

"You want me to work for you," he says slowly with something that sounds like disappointment.

Frustrated, I rake my hand through my hair. "I'm not your TL. I'm not your anything."

Kane straightens up, alarmed, his arms dropping to his sides. "Claire, that's not—"

"I just want you to be with me. Us to be together. Whatever that looks like." I lift my chin defiantly, though my face feels like it's on fire. "If you don't want to work for LSC, fine. But I—"

"Yes."

I stop, mouth open mid-word. "Yes?"

"Yes." He smiles, eyes crinkling at the edges. "Though I was sort of expecting this conversation two months ago when you had me come look at the ship," he points out, moving to stand next to me.

"Yeah, well. You could have said something," I mutter.

"No," he says evenly. "I couldn't have."

He's right, as annoying as it is; I needed to get here myself.

Kane holds out his hand, and I take it.

I lock my fingers tight through his, relieved still, after all this time, to feel the firm pressure of his grip in response rather than the slackness of his fingers trapped in mine.

I still have nightmares about being on the *Aurora*. About all of it. Nothing for it but more time. And focusing on the future while still remembering the past, I guess.

"So what now?" he asks.

"I might have some champagne in the galley for a toast. Just in case." It seemed like the thing to honor Voller in this new iteration of a crew. He would have appreciated the alcohol, if not the sentiment. "A new bottle," I add quickly.

"To fame and fortune?" Kane asks, repeating Voller's words, a quick flicker of sadness accompanying his smile.

"Something like that. Maybe a little less of both, if we can manage it," I say, edging closer, my body pressed to Kane's in a firm line at his side.

Kane nods before brushing his mouth against my temple. "Sounds good to me."

ACKNOWLEDGMENTS

This book, like every book, is a tiny miracle. I'm so incredibly thankful for everyone who made it possible. Words cannot express my gratitude, but I'm going to give it a shot.

Devin Ross, thank you for being as excited about this idea as I was. I am not sure I would have ever finished the manuscript without your support and encouragement.

Suzie Townsend, Dani Segelbaum, Pouya Shahbazian, Katherine Curtis, Veronica Grijalva, Victoria Hendersen, and everyone at New Leaf Literary & Media. You always have my back and my best interests at heart. That is a rare gift in this world, and I'm so grateful to have it and all of you.

Melissa Frain, thank you for sharing my obsession with the *Titanic*. But more than that, thank you for loving this book and idea enough to want to see it come to life. Your comments on this manuscript warmed my soul, and I look back at them whenever I'm doubting myself.

Kelly Lonesome, I count myself incredibly fortunate to have you as my editor. Thank you for championing this book, for helping me make it stronger. And for just . . . getting it. Or me. The same thing, maybe!

Everyone at Nightfire, Tor, and Macmillan, thank you for taking a chance on me and this book. Writing a book is only half the battle, if that. The other (enormously intimidating) part is getting it out into the world in such a way that readers know about it and want to read it!

Timo Noack, thank you for the gorgeous and absolutely chilling artwork for the cover. It is beyond my wildest dreams!

Katie Klimowicz, thank you for the incredible and PERFECT cover! It makes me giddy every time I see it.

Kristin Temple, thank you for enthusiastically supporting this book from the beginning and every step along the way, as well as keeping me in the loop and on track throughout the publishing process.

Jessica Katz, for managing all the details from the ARC all the way to the final PDF, including my picky little notes and questions, thank you for being patient with me!

Sarah Pannenberg, Jordan Hanley, and Michael Dudding, thank you for guiding me through the frightening (to me) waters of an online presence and working so hard to spread the word about *Dead Silence* in so many fantastic venues.

Anna Merz, thank you so much for the opportunities to talk about *Dead Silence* and connect with people on horror, space horror, and my love for all things nerdy and a little weird.

I am so very grateful to the entire Nightfire *Dead Silence* team! You literally would not have heard about this book or be holding it in your hands right now without them.

Alma Katsu, T. Kingfisher, David Wellington, Melissa Landers, Rachel Vincent, Lisa Shearin, Sarah Pinsker, Kendare Blake, Mur Lafferty, and Laurie Faria Stolarz, for taking time out of your incredibly hectic schedules to read *Dead Silence* and offer such generous words about it. Linnea Sinclair, for reading multiple versions of this book, listening patiently as I bounced around ideas in the most scattered of fashions, and being my ship/sci-fi/zero grav consultant. (Any mistakes are my own.) I don't tell you enough how thankful I am that I found you and your books all those years ago and that you were willing to take me on.

Melissa Landers, for letting me email you a desperately early version of the pitch for this book and giving me feedback on what was, at that point, word salad.

Susan Barnes Oldenburg, for getting married. But also for being my sister and my best friend. And publishing/writing/life crisis consultant extraordinaire. (She listens to everything so you all don't have to.)

Matt Oldenburg, also for getting married (see above). And for making me laugh. Also, for making sure I could park inside during the winter. So glad you're officially part of this (occasionally crazy) family now.

Mark Billy, for asking the right question at the right time!

Devi Pillai, for listening patiently as I attempted to answer said question and for being the most badass person I know in real life. (The Rock holds that position in my not-real life.)

Rebecca Thompson, for Princess Margaretha's pop hit title.

Mundelein High School, especially the English Department and all my colleagues in the Media Center, thank you for giving me a work home and for being excited with me on this publishing journey.

Fox Lake District Library, for teaching me how to "library." And for always being supportive of my books and endeavors.

Amy Bland and Kimberly Damitz, for all the Georgio's nights. I miss you both and can't wait until we're together again.

My parents, Stephen and Judy Barnes, who, with two children in publishing, are champions at listening to the industry drama and navigating the ups and downs along with us. You've supported me in every way possible, and I'll never be able to thank you enough for that.

Greg Klemstein, thank you for more than twenty years of patience and support. Thank you for dragging me out of my comfort zone occasionally and letting me retreat to it when needed. And thank you for all the delicious meals! (PS Can we have the chicken thing with the rice and carrots tonight? It's my favorite!)

ABOUT THE AUTHOR

Mila Duboyski

S. A. BARNES works in a high school library by day, recommending reads, talking with students, and removing the occasional forgotten cheese stick as bookmark. Barnes has published numerous novels across different genres under the pen name Stacey Kade. She lives in Illinois with more dogs and books than is advisable and a very patient husband.

staceykade.com
Twitter: @StaceyKade
Instagram: @authorstaceykade